Dedicated to the five groups who saved the buffalo.

Fred, Mary Ann & Pete Dupree and James 'Scotty' Phillip families

Samuel Walking Coyote, Michel Pablo and Charles Allard families

James 'Tonka Jim' McKay family

Charles Goodnight family

CJ 'Buffalo' Jones family

A maternal herd in Custer State Park with many young calves still sporting their reddish-gold hair that shines bright in the sun. After three or four months the baby hair is replaced by fine, dark hair like their mothers. *A New Crop of Calves*, Badlands Reflections Photography.

Buffalo Heartbeats Across the Plains

The Last Great Hunts and Saving the Buffalo

FRANCIE M. BERG

Buffalo Heartbeats Across the Plains:
The Last Great Buffalo Hunts
and Saving the Buffalo
by Francie M. Berg

ISBN: 978-0-918532-86-2
First Printing
Copyright 2018 Francie M. Berg

Edited by Kendra Rosencrans
Production by Ronda Turbiville Fink

eBook available

Published by
Dakota Buttes Visitors Council
Hettinger ND 58639
www.hettingernd.com/buffalotrails
email: hettingerchamber@ndsupernet.com

All rights reserved.
No part of this book may be reproduced
or transmitted in any form or
by any means, electronic or mechanical,
without written permission of the
publisher, except as permitted by law.

Due to the dynamic nature of the internet,
web addresses, links or telephone numbers
may have changed since publication.

Illustration copyrights by the
photographers and sources noted.

Cover photo: *The Buffalo Hunt No 39*, 1919, Charles M Russell, (1864-1926), Oil on canvas. 1961.146

Above: South Dakota Tourism

Introduction

One spring after the snow melted, sending rushing waters to flush out dry creek beds, my younger sister Anne and I were riding the higher reaches of our range east of Miles City looking for a lost heifer when we saw something peeking out from under a sagebrush that had been partly torn loose from a sandy bank.

"What's that?" Anne circled her horse across the gravel creek bed.

"Looks like a bone—a horn."

Sliding off our horses we scrambled up the bank for a closer look.

Yes! It was not just a horn—but solidly attached to the rest of the head. As we freed it from the sagebrush tangle, out came a nearly perfect skull with matching curved horns—gleaming white in the sun. We hefted the weight of it, bigger and bulkier than any skull we had ever seen.

A relic of long ago—a buffalo skull. The black horn caps had loosened and washed away in the seventy years since wild buffalo had roamed these ranges. We'd seen the famous photos of dead buffalo, slaughtered across this very range by hide hunters, as photographed by Mr. Huffman who set up his studio in Miles City just in time for that final kill.

Later we learned this was where the last big northern herd of buffalo came in their final desperate flight from big guns in 1880. That big old sagebrush stood along their trail. We'd ridden past it dozens of times.

Buffalo don't migrate northeast in the fall. But by all accounts, these last buffalo did. Their desperate leaders relied on unwavering instincts. They weren't seeking winter warmth, but safety. Blazing guns close behind, they hit the new cowtown of Miles City, Montana, on the run.

Half plunged in and swam the Yellowstone River. They scrambled out on the other side and stampeded north—right into the raging guns of hundreds of white and Indian hide hunters. Within months all lay dead.

Some wild instinct led the other half, about 50,000—the last big herd of the once many millions—more directly east. They swept down the Yellowstone on the south side—our side—then cut across the corner of Montana into Dakota Territory. Likely they followed up Powder River Valley or O'Fallon Creek until they found sanctuary for a time in the Slim Buttes. There the Dupree hunting party found them.

Then they moved on to the Great Sioux Indian Reservation, where almost three years later they met their fate. There these last of the great northern herd made their last stand in 1883. The southern herd had been killed off several years earlier. Afterward only a few wounded survivors still hid in remote canyons here and there.

Anne and I wrapped the buffalo skull in a jacket and tied it behind my saddle. At home we nestled it beside a petrified rock near Mom's yellow rose bush at the front door. Many times our family and visitors speculated on how that big old bull had lived and died.

Years later we learned the rest of the story.

When our family came to Hettinger the summer of 1966, we didn't know we were coming to the very place where the buffalo made their last stand. As the new veterinarian my husband Bert knew he'd handle a few herds of buffalo as well as cattle, horses, sheep, dogs and cats.

He didn't know buffalo but was willing to learn, especially when old-timers told us, "The last big buffalo hunts were here."

"What? What do you mean?" we asked. "The last hunts where? In North America? In North Dakota?"

"I don't know," came the inevitable answer. "That's what they say."

Intrigued and mystified, we kept asking. Several books claimed knowledge of "last hunts." But they only turned out to be about big guns, big slaughter, rotting carcasses, somewhere in Kansas or farther south. Everyone knew the shameful history, the scar on our national wildlife story.

Then one day, browsing our library, I came across a little-known book of memoirs, *My Friend the Indian*, by James McLaughlin, Indian Agent at Ft. Yates. Flipping pages, back to front, I found myself reading a riveting tale, "The Great Buffalo Hunt."

Suddenly there it was—all laid out step by step—the Hiddenwood hunt in complete and fascinating detail by a man who was here on that hunt. He rode here, right outside our living room window, coming up Hiddenwood Creek, which runs through our town. He told of their colorful march out of Fort Yates, 2,000 Native Americans resplendent in their best hunting attire, 600 mounted riders weaving in and out, their prancing horses painted in traditional ways, bound for these ancient buffalo ranges on Hiddenwood Creek. Hmmm. Fascinating.

Soon another jewel appeared in a dusty collection. The memoirs of the Congregational missionary Thomas Riggs contained their own "Buffalo Hunt" section. Again an amazing story, told by an articulate and empathetic man who rode with the Duprees into the Slim Buttes that winter. A small band of traditional Native hunters riding into howling blizzards on a cold three-month hunting adventure.

Both hunts were traditional, conducted with religious fervor and ancient ceremony. Both fit perfectly into William Hornaday's well-documented history of 1889, *The Extermination of the American Bison*. After the wild herds were nearly gone the Smithsonian Museum sent him out west to report how this destruction could have possibly happened.

In researching his book, Hornaday really thought he was writing about the final hours of what he called "this magnificent animal." Determined to get it right, he spared no effort in contacting every possible source of buffalo know-how, from Army officers at far-flung western forts, fur traders, railroaders, hide hunters and cowboys. He knew the end for the buffalo came here, but gave few details. Except that Sitting Bull and his band killed the last 1,200.

Somehow this final triumph of the buffalo saga fell through the cracks in our national and state histories. No one seemed to know it.

From these three sources our Hettinger Dakota Buttes Visitors Council published a small 1990 book, in which we brought together for the first time the dramatic moments of the last stand of the American buffalo, *The Last Great Buffalo Hunts: Traditional Hunts in 1880 to 1883 by Teton Lakota People*.

But wait! There's more. Not just the last great hunts and near extermination, but most marvelous—the miracle of how the buffalo evaded extinction, after all. The rescue of a few calves.

And still more. Excavation of a buffalo jump reveals that primitive hunters may have used it 7,000 years ago. Stories of noble fathers, old bulls saving calves from wolves. Mystique of the white buffalo and modern dilemmas playing out in Yellowstone Park.

Best of all, buffalo coming home in great numbers to Indian reservations, to wildlife preserves, national parks and private commercial ranching in the Northern Plains, where one state, South Dakota, counts 40,000 thriving buffalo.

The places where all this happened are here at our doorstep, so to speak. Accordingly, our Visitors Council launched a series of buffalo tours and published our *Buffalo Trails in the Dakota Buttes* with its Self-Guided tour of ten historic and contemporary sites. We are engaging our schools and now, with this companion book, *Buffalo Heartbeats Across the Plains*, we bring you the rest of the story.

In this special place where the full buffalo story comes together, we hope that visitors and local people will enjoy the stories, the history and touring the sites as much as we have in arranging it for you. Also, for the complete buffalo experience, we encourage you to take some moments to contemplate a herd or two of live buffalo.

Welcome to the buffalo trails in the Dakota Buttes.

In June 1882 hunters from Fort Yates caught sight of what they thought never to see again: A herd of buffalo grazing in the distance near Hiddenwood Cliff. *Indians Sighting Buffalo*, 1896, Charles M. Russell. Amon Carter Museum.

Contents

Part I: The Last Great Hunts

1. The Great Hiddenwood Hunt 10
   "Beautiful Spot"—Hiddenwood Cliff 17

2. Winter Hunt in Slim Buttes 26

3. Sitting Bull Hunt 42
   The Final Buffalo Hunts 46

4. Scattered Survivors 56
   Theodore Roosevelt on 1883 Hunt 62

Part II: Tradition and Lore

5. The Magnificent Buffalo 76
   Plains Buffalo versus Wood Buffalo 87

6. Noble Fathers 92

7. Buffalo Lore 112

8. Way of the Hunt 128
   Traditional Uses of Buffalo 131

9. Running the Buffalo 150

Part III: Coming Home

10. Saving the Buffalo 166
    Mexican Bullfight 182

11. Buffalo Ranching Across America 186
    Low Stress Buffalo Handling 196

12. Homecoming on Tribal Lands 198
    Restoring the Buffalo 204

13. Herds in Public Places 216
    White Cloud Dynasty 226

Buffalo Timeline 234

Bibliography
Photo Credits
Hettinger, ND
Index

Stripped of their most confining clothing, and with faces and horses painted, native hunters attack the herd with a variety of weapons—guns, lance and bow and arrow. *The Buffalo Hunt* 1919, CM Russell.

Part I. The Last Great Hunts

1

The Great Hiddenwood Hunt

Pte, finding himself near to extinction
at the hands of white pot-hunters,
Sought out the reservation that he might, in the end,
fulfill his mission and die to provide walls for the tepee,
Robes for the couch, sinews for the bow and
Meat for the store of the sons of the Lakota.
—James McLaughlin, Standing Rock Agent
quoting Lakota elders, June 1882

As Running Antelope, Long Soldier and other prominent leaders rode out on a high point, just out of sight, waiting for the other hunters to come up, they saw what they thought never to see again.

An immense herd of buffalo grazed peacefully in the valley below, on both sides of Hiddenwood Creek and off into the distance, spread out over the hills. Tawny-colored calves frisked and played together.

A few hundred yards off stood the nearest buffalo. So close they could hear him grunt and snort. With the wind in their faces, they smelled his rank odor.

A wave of anticipation swept through the hunters. Since boyhood they had hunted buffalo here, near the bluff they called Hiddenwood or *Paha Can Nahma*. For hundreds—perhaps thousands—of years this place was a famed hunting ground for Plains tribes. Scattered across the wide valley were stone tepee rings. Buffalo grazed among them.

As on the previous evening, in this historic place, these men had many times been stirred by throbbing drums, hunting songs and buffalo dance ceremonials. But for fifteen years these prime Dakota grasslands had stood empty of buffalo. White hide hunters had relentlessly forced them ever farther west. Most herds were gone forever, killed off for their hides.

Then, mysteriously, this big herd of 50,000 returned.

"On the wings of the wind came the news that Pte, the buffalo, had arrived to make a Sioux holiday and provide such meat as had never been furnished even by the most conscientious and liberal of beef contractors," said James McLaughlin, Indian agent at the Standing Rock agency in Fort Yates.

The news foretold the mission of returning buffalo—to provide their starving Dakota and Lakota brothers and sisters with desperately needed food, clothing and shelter before their total extinction.

Now they grazed contentedly as if they'd never left this range. A pair of golden eagles soared on high wind currents above the hunters. A meadowlark serenaded them from the top of a small tree.

Several huge bulls stood down by the creek in the mud, drinking, pawing and splashing. Others tore into the cliff with big shaggy heads, rubbing at their itchy winter pelts and throwing up dust. Farther up the hillside in a buffalo wallow, bulls rolled and scratched their backs. Some squared off, whacking heads and horns, grunting and digging up the ground.

A good hunt seemed assured—if all went well. Excitement ran high. So did a thread of anxiety. Old men sighed and breathed prayers. Young men fought to hold their horses in check.

For nearly three years the last great buffalo herds remained on Standing Rock Reservation

Curious calf regards intruder with interest. Black on head and darkening body shows calf is over three months old. Badlands Reflections Photography.

Mothers and calves graze and doze alongside a slough. Badlands Reflections Photograaphy.

in Dakota Territory or as it was still called, the Great Sioux Reservation. They migrated here near the end of 1880 and survived until the fall of 1883. The Cheyenne River Lakota encountered them just west of the reservation in the Slim Buttes on December 24, 1880. Sitting Bull's band killed the last of them October 13, 1883.

During that time, they were set upon by numerous Native hunts large and small within the reservation, while legions of white hide hunters lurked at the borders, making illegal forays inside and killing all buffalo that ventured outside the boundries.

The southern herd was gone by then. The last of the great northern herd migrated to the Miles City area in eastern Montana, and then split. Half crossed the Yellowstone River and travelled north into the waiting rifles of hundreds of hunters, both white and Indian, and were soon annihilated. The other half came east to the relative safety of the Great Sioux Reservation.

It is amazing these last buffalo evaded bullets so long. Had they not come into these remote and rugged hills of the Indian reservation, and on that bitterly cold winter, they would certainly have met a blaze of guns and rapid slaughter, as elsewhere.

Indian elders called it a prophesy fulfilled.

In the midst of tremendous conflict, change and trauma, the return of the buffalo provided the people a sign, a momentary glimpse, that though now scattered and scarce, these mighty animals survived. A sign of hope for Native people.

Buffalo hunt ceremonial

By the time Running Antelope and Long Soldier feasted their gaze upon the massive herd at Hiddenwood, the hunting party of more than 2,000 men, women and children had travelled 100 miles across the prairie from Fort Yates, starting on June 10, 1882, moving slowly. Many walked. Some rode in horse-drawn wagons or travois pulled by horses or dogs. Six hundred hunters rode horseback.

"It would hardly be possible to make a more glittering array," wrote McLaughlin in his book *My Friend the Indian.* "The plains of Dakota had not for many years seen so resplendent a gathering of these people as that which moved out of Standing Rock just after dawn . . . And it was many hours later before the last of the straggling column disappeared from view over the buttes to the west of the agency."

Five days out the party reached the Cedar River. There they came together for a ceremonial camp, close to the crossing for the Bismarck to Black Hills trail and about fifty miles west of Fort Yates agency. They camped in a large circle of tepees facing an opening toward the west.

Here they were joined by McLaughlin, his fourteen-year-old son Harry, and four Indian policemen, who rode out that day from Fort Yates.

McLaughlin and his party were conducted through the circle of lodges, now nearly deserted. He was newly arrived in Fort Yates the fall before, on Sept. 8, 1881, in a transfer from the agency at Fort Totten reservation, Devil's Lake, and was eager to show his friendship and trust in the 6,000 Dakota and Lakota Indians under his care. Thus, he had authorized the hunt and furnished a limited amount of ammunition, normally forbidden. The chance to accompany these people (also known as Sioux) on a rare buffalo hunt and demonstrate his trust in them was an opportunity he could not let slip away.

In the Hiddenwood Hunt 2,000 men, women and children trekked here from Ft. Yates in June 1882. They slaughtered 5,000 buffalo in three days. *The Buffalo Hunt,* CM Russell.

Many of them had come to Standing Rock from a self-exile in Canada less than a year before, with the surrender of Sitting Bull's starving band.

Two thousand Native people were gathered in a great body some distance west of the camp. Seated on the grass according to rank, they formed a crescent facing west. At the south horn of the crescent were seated the important men in the hunt organization: Running Antelope, leader of the hunt and an orator of prominence. Next sat Long Soldier and beside him Red Horse, who divided with Running Antelope the direction of the hunt.

All around the crescent, with due regard for rank from the place of honor, men held the front rows, with women and children sitting behind.

A painted rock about ten inches high stood as an altar in front of Running Antelope. He gathered the eight young men selected as scouts around the altar.

These young men, chosen for their good moral character, honesty and hunting ability, were instructed to ride ahead, find the buffalo and determine the best approach. Led by Crazy Walking, they were "as fine a body of young men as could be found in the Sioux nation," according to McLaughlin. Many became men of prominence. Crazy Walking later became a judge at Standing Rock agency (his great-grandson Mike Faith serves as Standing Rock Tribal Chairman, after many years managing the tribal buffalo herd.)

Running Antelope instructed the youthful scouts at length on the importance of their mission, the need for caution, and the urgency of reporting their news accurately.

The crowd sat in breathless silence as he administered an oath to each.

Next, they smoked the pipe. The hunt leader lifted the sacred pipe and filled it, with much deliberation. Taking a spoonshaped wooden utensil used only on ceremonial occasions, he drew a coal from the fire, placed it on the tobacco. He offered the pipe to the earth in front of him, to propitiate spirits that make the ground fruitful, then to the sky invoking the blessing of the Great Spirit.

Drawing a long pull from the pipe with a peculiar hissing sound he passed it on to Crazy Walking, who placed his hand, holding the bowl of the pipe, on the painted stone and drew one puff of smoke. The young scout passed it on down the line, each repeating the performance.

Abruptly every man leaped to his feet, whooping and congratulating the scouts. The solemnities over, the pleasures of the hunt could begin.

Riding down the bushes

Hundreds of mounted riders escorted the scouts for a couple of miles. Off they went—a joyous, shouting, exuberant troop of excited hunters. They laughed, sang and careened about on their horses.

According to tradition, the first rider who returned from the escort had the privilege—and duty—of "riding down the bushes." A line of three freshly cut green bushes, set about ten yards apart, led into the horns of the crescent. Racing at top speed the first rider would attempt to knock them down. If by good fortune he knocked down all three bushes, the hunt would be a great success, with much game killed and the families rich in meat and hides. If two bushes fell, the hunt would be fairly successful. If only one, indifferent. But if the leader failed to knock down any, the hunt might as well be abandoned as hopeless.

The crowd waited.

The men dashed recklessly away touching the scouts with lucky charms, shouting out encouragement, joking and teasing them about their romantic affairs, riding with them for a couple of miles.

Suddenly a whoop rang out, echoed by hundreds of mounted men. The escort shouted farewell to the scouts and wheeled toward camp.

Riding a fast horse, the gift of Crow King, grain-fed and in top condition, McLaughlin won the race and rode down all three bushes. A great shout of joy came from the crowd. As he had hoped, he was regarded thereafter as a person who brought good fortune to the hunt and those who rode with him.

Next morning, the people moved on, traveling westward in orderly formation.

One hundred men were designated as soldiers to keep order, including young Harry McLaughlin. Their faces painted to give them authority, they enforced strict buffalo hunting codes. They held sternly in check the impatient young hunters on fast horses, eager to reach the buffalo.

Another twelve men marched at the head of the column, setting the pace. Moving slowly, with deliberation, they traveled no faster than the slowest old man who walked.

Every three miles or so, the leaders sat down for a rest and a smoke. During these rest periods men told stories of past hunts.

The main body traveled in two columns, a few hundred yards apart. To the south were the Hunkpapa and Blackfeet bands of Teton Sioux. On the north, the Yanktonais. James McLaughlin rode first with the Hunkpapas and later with the Yanktonais, when they demanded the benefit of his good medicine. The party covered about ten miles and then made camp.

That evening brought feasting, dancing and storytelling. Great orators and warriors were in the camp and recounted stories of courage and skill: Gall, a great orator and natural leader, Running Antelope, Red Horse, John Grass, Crow King, RainintheFace, Spotted Horn Bull, Long Soldier and Shave Head.

The march lasted four more days, during which the leaders continually scanned the western hills for signals from the scouts. Majestic rockcrested buttes and ridges rimmed the horizon on all sides—silhouetted by magnificent sunrises and sunsets. The June

Indians killing buffalo. Library of Congress

"Beautiful spot"—Hiddenwood Cliff

Hiddenwood Cliff marks the famous buffalo hunting campground used by nomadic Plains Indians for hundreds, perhaps thousands, of years. This wide valley, located 12 miles east of Hettinger, ND, on US Hwy 12 just north of the state line, was filled with stone tepee rings when the first settlers came.

Burial platforms were in the trees at Hiddenwood. Mont Monroe, an early rancher, found a beaded child's dress in the branches, a solid mat of beads with the cloth rotted away. Others have found arrowheads, tools, stone and bone artifacts and military buttons.

The stone tepee rings hark back to an earlier time before the horse, when dog travois carried all the hunters' worldly goods. By the 1750s horses carried wood tent stakes to hold down the tepees, replacing stones.

Settlers called this favorite picnic spot Brushy Banks, and later, Bushy Banks.

It is believed the "Great Buffalo Hunt," described by Indian Agent James McLaughlin, in which 5,000 buffalo were slaughtered, began here on about June 20, 1882, and continued up Hiddenwood Creek for two days.

On July 8, 1874 General George Custer and the 7th Cavalry camped here on Hiddenwood Creek during their expedition to the Black Hills to explore for gold. They travelled with 2,000 men, 1,000 cavalry horses, 300 beef cattle and 150 wagons, each drawn by six mules. Illingworth photo. SD State Historical Society.

Hiddenwood is the camping place where the Sioux army scout Goose brought General (Lt. Col) George A. Custer and the 7th Cavalry July 8, 1874, on their expedition from Bismarck to the Black Hills to explore for gold, two years before the disastrous Battle of the Little Big Horn.

A news reporter on that expedition wrote, "We have suffered and panted through a march of 20 miles to enjoy this balmy evening and beautiful spot—the most beautiful of any we have yet seen. This place is called HiddenWood, by the Indians, because the hills so cluster around it that the trees cannot be seen two miles away. One of the few shady oases in this desert of prairie land and very grateful after a week's marching."

He described their camp at Hiddenwood Cliff that evening, "For a background a sunset as gorgeously beautiful as any that ever glowed ... and a high, jagged bluff, covered with clusters of trees, with a clear stream of water running at its base; in the foreground a smooth grassy plain covered with tents, hooded wagons, and grazing horses; a band in the center playing familiar airs, and an atmosphere cool, fresh, and bracing—and you have a picture of our camp tonight."

grass grew long, lush and green that spring, right up and over the rocky ridges. They travelled up broad green valleys and plateaus.

Within striking distance

A spring-fed creek, still high with run-off from spring rains, wound along the base of the bluffs against the ridge, with a broad open flat stretching away to the west. This was Hiddenwood Creek, named by Plains Indians for Hiddenwood, the cliff or bluff where "the hills so cluster around that the trees cannot be seen two miles away."

Farther up the creek, on the south side, the cliff itself rose steeply. The broad open plain before it was a traditional camp site for Plains Indians hunting buffalo, used for hundreds, likely thousands of years. Scores of tepee rings could be seen clustered in the grass through the entire valley. This was where the Sioux Army Scout Goose had brought Lt. Col. George Custer and the 7th Cavalry on their gold-seeking expedition from Bismarck to the Black Hills only a few years earlier when they camped beneath Hiddenwood Cliff July 8, 1874.

Fresh clean air on a light breeze touched the faces of the buffalo hunters.

This was the finest buffalo grazing country on the continent, declared McLaughlin. He breathed deeply, surveying the lush and nutritious green grasses that extended out over the prairie.

On the fourth morning a tiny flash of light glinted from the far horizon ten miles off.

"Ah," one of the leaders grunted softly, pulled up his horse and pointed.

Each scout carried a small circular mirror. No horse was visible, but even at that distance the leaders read the message through mirror flashes: "A huge herd of buffalo is grazing within sight of the scouts!"

The advance guard halted and returned the signal.

In hushed voices the message rippled through the long lines of travelers. Their faces lit with great joy and excitement.

Another flash. Before long they saw the scouts and horses cut against the skyline.

The hunting party made camp that night on Hiddenwood Creek within striking distance. Everyone was tense with anticipation, voices hushed, with none of their former boisterous behavior or exuberant laughter. Even small children in Indian families knew how to keep quiet. With a hand over the mouth, babies learned not to cry.

The grazing buffalo must not be alerted to the hunters' approach.

Next morning the camp was the scene of great excitement and activity.

The hunters sharpened their knives on the day of the hunt. Skipping this important step could, by tradition, interfere with its good medicine. Half a dozen grindstones were set up and dozens of men hovered over each, awaiting their turn.

Certain rocks jutted from the ground; cut with ancient knife slashings, they revealed centuries of use as natural whetstones.

While the men sharpened their knives Shave Head, an Indian policeman, remarked that "the Father"—McLaughlin—wanted a live buffalo calf.

No longer were the hunters agency Indians, dressed in shirts and trousers. Every man simply wore a breech-cloth. Some tied colorful handkerchiefs around their heads. Their faces glowed with red and yellow paint and black streaks. Horses too wore feathers and paint.

Six hundred mounted hunters rode out in two broad columns, led by Running Antelope and Red

The medicine man or shaman was important to the success of buffalo hunts. *The Medicine Man*, 1908 painting by CM Russell.

Horse. Hunkpapas and Blackfeet rode west along Hiddenwood Creek. The Yanktonais circled farther north to approach the herd from northeast.

The men rode silently, in a state of tense excitement, keeping low in the draws and ravines, sheltered from sight, to avoid alerting the buffalo.

The hunt begins

Now, up on the high point, Running Antelope and the others gestured and whispered, planning their approach, as they waited for others to arrive.

All gasped as they rode up and glimpsed the broad valley filled with buffalo. Silently, feverishly, they spread out along the flanks. These were people with buffalo hunting running in their veins and in their hearts. Since early childhood they had listened to stories of courage in the hunt, deeds of strength and endurance against great bulls, of buffalo mystique and legend. They lived in buffalo hide tepees, slept under soft buffalo robes, ran lightly through cactus in tough hide moccasins, and delighted in eating dried buffalo meat and pemmican.

For too long they had tasted only bland beef as issued in rations from the Fort Yates agency. It never satisfied, elders complained. They longed for the 'ping' of fresh buffalo meat and the thrill of buffalo hunting.

The horses felt the excitement too, lifted their heads, snorted, pranced and reared.

Crow's Ghost raced back to where McLaughlin waited at the rear, held up his hand and whispered, "Stay here. Let the first ones go ahead. Don't get in their way!"

Then he dashed off and joined the leaders.

At McLaughlin's elbow rode John Eagle Man, the agency policeman. He held back, sporting only a breech-clout with a red handkerchief tied about his temples, having shed his usual citizen's dress.

"There are plenty of buffalo here for all of us," Eagle Man said in a low voice. He looked anxiously ahead as if eager to start hunting, but stayed at McLaughlin's side.

Running Antelope glanced back at the hunters lined up just

below the crest of the bluffs and across the creek on the far slope. Every eye was on him, ready to go.

In that moment he lifted his arm high and drove it forward in a forceful gesture.

They were off! The hunters swooped down at full speed, attacking the buffalo from the hills on both sides of Hiddenwood Creek.

Five or six gray wolves slashing viciously at the throat of an old lone bull up a draw, streaked out of range, looking back as they ran, and disappeared over the ridge. A few antelope, grazing on the flat, leapt up a side hill and turned to stare curiously, their sharp eyes alert.

Rifles cracked and buffalo fell. Some began to run. Riders with fast horses raced ahead, cut in close to the leaders and dispatched them with a bullet or two.

The buffalo turned in confusion, confronting their attackers with furious thrusts and slashes of massive heads and horns. They grunted, roared and flung their short, stubby tails over their backs.

Each hunter rode close alongside his buffalo and shot it in the heart or lungs. Usually the animal fell with one shot. No bullets wasted. He made sure it was dead and raced ahead for another shot.

On distant slopes buffalo merely looked up and returned to grazing.

Most of the men carried repeating rifles, breechloaders that fed bullets from the rear rather

Two bulls take a break at mid-day. Badlands Reflections Photography.

In early summer, new calves shine red-gold in the morning sun. South Dakota Tourism.

than the front of the barrel, making for faster reloading.

Not all could afford guns. Some older men and boys, in their poverty, used only bow and arrows. A few had no guns because McLaughlin did not trust them enough to allow weapons. Many of them had fought against General Custer and the 7th Cavalry at the Battle of the Little Big Horn only six years before.

Wolf Necklace, an older man of about sixty, was one hunter without fire power. He carried only a bow and arrows, rode an old gray pony and followed a wounded buffalo with four or five arrows protruding from its side. As his pony walked slowly alongside, he now and then shot another arrow into it, but without the muscle power needed to bury it deeply.

A friend rode up with a pistol and offered to help.

"No. Don't shoot!" Wolf Necklace cried. "The arrows will work in and he will die."

He was right. After a few minutes the big animal fell dead.

The estimated 50,000 buffalo ranged over this part of Standing Rock Reservation, widely scattered into smaller herds, according to McLaughlin.

The hunters were riding their best horses, swift runners. Older seasoned "buffalo horses" if they could get them. Men with younger, inexperienced horses worried that, though fast, they might fail to perform in close quarters alongside these strange, pungent-smelling beasts that they had never encountered before.

Indeed, from the first charge, plunging, rearing horses could be seen through the valley with their riders struggling to gain control.

Fortunately the shooting did not alarm the larger herd and they did not stampede or run. Buffalo have a keen sense of smell and when spooked can outrun a horse and move the herd many miles out of range. The tactic of circling in front and killing leaders confused them. Cows defended their calves, and when the mothers fell the calves stayed close, nosing the carcass.

One man died of a heart attack. Friends found him crouched behind a rock, his horse grazing nearby, its rope trailing. His gun was cocked and braced against the rock, his finger on the trigger, in the very act of shooting.

Another man lay unconscious. His horse had fallen with him.

One bloody hunter lost three fingers, blown off when his gun burst.

An enraged buffalo attacked another man. The belly of his plunging horse was ripped open by a bull's sharp horns, its entrails dragging on the ground. The man's leg was gashed and bleeding from ankle to knee.

McLaughlin and the Indian police riding with him stopped to care for the injured, bound up their wounds, stopped the bleeding, and carried them to some kind of shade. None of these men was attended by friends or relatives, as usually happened in such a crisis. In their feverish

excitement, hunters raced by the injured without pausing. Some lay bleeding in the sun for hours.

As they rode over the crest of a small hill, McLaughlin and Eagle Man pulled up to watch the turmoil below.

A lean hunter, Peter Skunk, had wounded a big bull with his revolver. The bull charged and his terrified horse threw him. The horse ran off as the bull charged again.

Luckily, Skunk landed near a large boulder. He darted behind it, the bull close behind. The furious animal charged. Skunk dodged around the rock, first to one side, then the other. He waved his singleshot pistol, but had emptied it into the bull. With no time to stop and reload, he kept dodging around the rock with the enraged bull close behind, grunting and snorting.

McLaughlin called out an offer to help, but Skunk waved them off.

"No!" he shrieked. Game belonged first to the man who killed it. Sharing came later.

For another five minutes they watched as the hunter dodged the bull, back and forth around the outcropping boulder. Finally, exhausted, the wounded bull paused in its furious charge.

Skunk reloaded, leaned over the rock and planted a close shot

Buffalo graze a ridge, silhouetted against a South Dakota sunset near Wind Cave. National Park Service.

behind its ear. The bull dropped.

McLaughlin reported his own good luck, guided by the advice of Crow King and his Indian policeman John Eagle Man. Holding back from the first charge they were rewarded when a small group of buffalo cut off to the side, directly in front of them.

"I picked out a fine three-year-old cow and fired into her flank at close quarters. I aimed a little high, the cow turned, and my pony, knowing more about buffalo hunting than I did, wheeled to keep out of her way. The sudden swerve of the pony almost unseated me and sent my Winchester flying twenty feet away. The cow turned at once to follow the herd, and I picked up my rifle and followed her, but before I could get another shot the animal again charged. I shot her between the eyes as she rushed at my mount, which only made her shake her head and wheel to follow the herd. But a well-directed shot behind the right fore-shoulder settled the cow, and I had my first buffalo."

McLaughlin shot five cows, then stopped, knowing he had no means of caring for more meat.

It was a long and successful day, with no rest. The hunters kept up the slaughter until they lost their horses or were exhausted. The leaders took an informal count of what each man had harvested that day—and reached a total of 2,000 buffalo killed.

No attempt at butchering was made that first day.

Women cooked humps and other tender morsels and fed the hunters who returned to camp long after dark, too tired for celebrating or storytelling.

Moving camp

Early next morning the women broke camp and moved closer to the kill farther up Hiddenwood

Creek.

McLaughlin slept late. When he opened the tent flap, to his surprise he found the entire camp gone. The people and their tents had vanished.

Even more amazing was what they left behind. His tent stood alone. But ranged about it, tied to stakes, were twenty-two buffalo calves.

"The Indian response to my request for a single calf!"

That second day the people butchered and cared for the meat.

All knew their jobs. They attacked them enthusiastically in the pleasure of working together, laughing and calling to each other. The men skinned, quartered the animals, and hauled the meat in to the new camp at Hiddenwood by travois, pack horse and wagon. Women began the formidable task of slicing large chunks of meat into thin sheets for drying. Deftly they rolled each chunk of buffalo beef over and over with one hand while slicing thinly with the other. These sheets they hung on willow racks to dry in the sun. When cured, they'd make and store the meat as pemmican and jerky.

The big hides they stretched out and staked on the ground to

Babies tied on their backs, Indian women move their hunting camp. *Indian Women Moving Camp,* 1898, CM Russell.

dry. As summer hides, they would remove the hair for rawhide and tan the leather for tepees, moccasins and other needs.

That afternoon the horse herd was grazing not far away when suddenly a herd of four or five hundred buffalo stampeded through camp and carried off five horses. McLaughlin and four others lost their horses and were unable to turn them back. McLaughlin's horse ran with the buffalo until fall, when another hunting party captured it by "creasing" the neck. This technique for catching a wild horse meant knocking it down with a bullet shot through the skin at the top of the neck, hitting a nerve just forward of the shoulder—and getting a rope on its neck before it jumped up.

That evening the people feasted as described by McLaughlin. Everyone ate their fill. It was a joyous feast such as had not been held at Standing Rock for many years. Mighty hunters ate with mighty appetites. They danced. They sang. Famed orators and chiefs recounted tales of courage, fortitude and tragedy in hunting and battle.

"The head men of the Sioux Nation were on that hunt and at peace on the banks of Hiddenwood Creek that night," McLaughlin wrote. "Years later, in the trying times of the ghost dancing, there was bitterness, enmity and death, but that night Hunkpapas, Blackfeet, Upper and Lower Yanktonais and whites were friends in feasting as they are friends today. And I never visit my old home at Standing Rock but that some of them gather at my door and go over the story of the great buffalo hunt of 1882."

On the third day the hunters ran buffalo again. The herd had moved only a few miles farther west up Hiddenwood Creek. That day they killed 3,000, for a total of 5,000 buffalo killed during two days of slaughter.

Four men—Crazy Walking, Standing Soldier, Henry Agard and Frank Gates—killed twenty-six buffalo each. Other heroes of the hunt were Bull Head, who was killed eight years later in carrying out McLaughlin's order for the arrest of Sitting Bull, Shave Head, who died with Bull Head, and Black Bull who lived to an old age.

After the third day they slaughtered no more, but remained camped near the kill site where they finished the butchering and drying the meat and hides.

McLaughlin said the hunting party had killed many and yet showed restraint. "I never have known an Indian to kill a game animal that he did not require for his needs. And I have known few white hunters to stop while there was game to kill. The hunt stopped when 5,000 buffalo had been slain."

2

Winter Hunt in Slim Buttes

Good things I am bringing,
something holy to your nation.
A message I carry for your people
from the Buffalo Nation.
　　　　—White Buffalo Woman,
　　　　　upon appearing to the Lakota

The winter of 1880-81 was a season of big snow, deep, with bitter and lasting cold. Hardly a winter to spend living in tepees in the rugged Slim Buttes—where cold winds swirl and howl through the pine trees and snow packs deep into rocky canyons.

But when the Cheyenne River Lakota heard the news that a sizeable buffalo herd was sighted near the Slim Buttes they could wait no longer. Their elders prophesized that the big herds—long gone from the area— were coming back to help feed and clothe their Native brothers and sisters before they disappeared forever.

Excited by the prophecy, the Dupree families alerted their relatives and friends, and set out as soon as they could. They were overjoyed at the

High protein grasses cure on the stem in the Great Plains, nourishing buffalo throughout the winter. Badlands Reflections Photography.

Buffalo bull lunges up shadowy bank. NPS.

chance to harvest buffalo in winter, make fine warm robes from prime hides with long, heavy winter hair, and most of all, to satisfy their longing for food from the old days, for buffalo meat that has "a ping to it—the meat that satisfies." They stuck it out for three months even though they had prepared for only three weeks.

The story of the rise, disappearance and return of the buffalo on the Great Plains is a story woven through a time of massive change, contention and challenge after the Civil War, as the U.S. government turned its attention to settling the vast lands between the Mississippi River and the Rocky Mountains. Following the history of the buffalo is one way of seeing into the multiple events that transformed this region and resulted in Native people being confined to reservations and reducing the numbers of buffalo, once numbering in the millions, to only a few hundred.

The buffalo had all but disappeared from the prairies. In those uneasy days after the 1876 Battle of the Little Big Horn, the Lakota were not allowed to leave their homes to hunt buffalo without permission from the Indian Agent. Many of them had fought against General Custer and the 7th Cavalry in that fateful battle.

The last big buffalo herds remained for nearly three years on the Great Sioux Reservation. The Cheyenne River Lakota were first to encounter them, on December 24, 1880, just west of the reservation, apparently as they migrated in from Montana.

That first hunting party in the winter of 1880-1881 gathered at the ranch of Fred and Mary Ann Dupris at the mouth of Cherry Creek where it emptied into the Cheyenne River, thirty-five miles west of the Missouri River. They picked up others at the Moreau River. The group consisted of fifty-six men, about forty women and a few small children—101 in all.

Thomas Riggs, a young Congregational missionary serving Lakota at the Oahe Mission near Pierre, was invited by Mary Ann to share their family tent. She was the mother-in-law of Clarence Ward, his assistant at the Mission. Riggs and Ward—known as Roan Bear in his tribe—crossed the Missouri River on the ice the day before Thanksgiving with a buckboard, two-horse team and Rigg's famed buffalo horse Sam.

A French-Canadian fur trader, Fred Dupris (also spelled Dupree) had built a log trading post and also ranched, building up a herd of 200 cattle using his wife's reservation grazing rights. He and Mary Ann Good Elk Woman, a Minnicoujou, had eleven children as the center of their own active community. As each son and daughter married, they moved into a growing row of cabins built of cottonwood logs on a beautiful wooded flat.

"The Dupuis home was known as a place for sharing good times and food in the true Indian way. . . It was said that some fifty people ate supper there each evening," wrote Calvin Dupree in the *Eagle Butte News*, Jan. 29, 1981.

An older man in his mid-seventies, Fred declined to go with his family on that strenuous winter hunt. The Dupree brothers took a wagon. Some other families packed their supplies in travois of tepee poles dragged by horses or dogs.

On the Moreau River, in a heavy snowstorm, they met the rest of their party. Among them was Chief Big Foot who was killed with his band ten years later in the Wounded Knee massacre. A sympathizer of Sitting Bull, he had led his people in a daring escape down the Wall, through what became known as *Big Foot's Pass.*

Snow fell almost continuously. Crusted snow and blizzard conditions added to the difficulties. They followed the Moreau valley west, some days making only three or four miles in deep snow that grew deeper day by day.

Riggs felt impatient at this slow pace, but his friends emphasized the importance of not tiring the horses. Each man's best horse—his buffalo-running horse—ran loose all the way and was fed at every opportunity with strength-giving shavings of inner bark and twigs of young cottonwood trees.

"My own Sam was an old hand and knew all that a horse could know about running buffalo, besides being very fast. Every man in camp knew him, for he was the horse that Canptaye (Wood Pile) had on the Little Big Horn against Custer in '76. He was a professional and deserved the honor the Indians gave him." Riggs carried a sack of oats to feed his horses.

The snow deepened. Finally after many days, they saw in the distance toward the northwest the pine-covered Slim Buttes *(Paha-zibze-pila)*—a higher elevation of pine hills where the snow settled deep into canyons, wash-out holes and dry creek beds.

Everyone grew excited and talked of how tired they were of eating porcupine, skunk, venison and badger meat—during the journey they had killed and eaten 148 porcupines and 200 deer.

"It was said we had 300 horses and 500 dogs," Riggs noted. "When I asked why so many dogs, the reply was to fatten them up. On the hunt they got good and fat, so could be used for food. The process of preparing them was swift. The dog was killed, the hair singed off and he was ready for the pot."

Scouts sworn to service

The older hunters began planning how to send out scouts to find the buffalo, as they set up temporary camp at the foot of the Slim Buttes.

Plans were made in the *soldier lodge* or council tent, the heart of the camp, a place of much religious ceremony, feasting and smoking of the pipe. This was a tepee somewhat larger than the others, which no woman was allowed to enter. Women came only to bring food and set it outside the entrance. All general matters and plans were discussed within and decisions made that were announced later throughout the camp by the *eyanpaha* or crier.

Two men were selected as scouts, given detailed instructions and sworn into service. They made silent pledges, each with hands placed palm down flat on the earth.

"Many others joined in this vow and prayer," said Riggs. "I sat next to Touch-the-Cloud (*Mahpiyaiyapato*) and noticed that he rubbed away the grass and leaves at his side and sat with one hand flat on the earth. Seeing that I was noticing this, he said, 'I am offering prayer with one hand and I now do so with both.' I did the same. The earth is the mother of all and prayer is offered in this way as the oath is administered, lest the all-mother give alarm to the buffalo and carry to their ears knowledge of the presence and purpose of men."

The two scouts left camp early next morning on their second best horses, reserving their best for the hunt to come.

Just before sunset they signaled from a ridge about a mile from camp. In signaling, their horses first appeared some distance apart, high on the skyline. They rode toward each other, came together, rode back and repeated this several times.

"That is good," reported a man named Charger, reading the message.

Yellow Owl added, "We'll have plenty of meat by this time tomorrow."

Riggs smiled. He had great respect for the Indian telegraph system of mirrors, smoke and distance runners. He'd been informed of the death of General George Custer on June 26, the next day after the Battle of the Little Big Horn when friends brought the message to Oahe: "Yesterday the Long Hair (Custer) and the soldiers with him were all killed—some of the other soldiers were killed but most got away."

Thus, hundreds of miles away Riggs knew of Custer's death the very next day. When he inquired of his usual sources, he was told it was not true. It was a full two weeks later when the Far West steamboat docked in Bismarck with the wounded, the modern world found out it was true.

The two scouts repeated their riding maneuver on a nearer hill. Then they galloped into camp and delivered their message with proper ceremony.

The crowd responded with shrill cries of "Hai-ee! Hai-ee!"

The party broke camp early next morning. They set up their tents and tepees more permanently in a protected place, an amphitheater on the southwest corner of the Slim Buttes with wood and water available. There they turned the horses loose to graze. Two or three feet of snow covered the rich, cured grasses, but the savvy Indian horses pawed away the snow to eat their fill.

A welcome sight—buffalo!

The day of the first hunt, the men set out before daybreak

Indian on Horseback, 1907, CM Russell.

Buffalo returned to Dakota Territory in late 1880. It was a winter of deep snow and bitter cold on the Great Sioux Reservation where they migrated. NPS.

toward the place the scouts directed. They led their buffalo horses and extra pack horses. Many men and horses would fall that day, older men predicted. Others laughed, saying the deep snow would make a soft landing.

Soldiers, appointed to keep order, painted their faces black to enforce authority. Their duties were to keep the party together and stop any impatient hunter from charging ahead and alarming the buffalo. A fair and equal start for everyone was considered critical.

The two scouts, riding ahead and off to the side, hastily waved the hunters out of sight and farther east. They intended to come on the buffalo against the wind, swinging wide through a long winding valley. Now, ahead some distance, the lead hunters glimpsed their first buffalo. Five or six of the big shaggy animals plowed their way through deep snow in the pines and disappeared over a rocky slope.

A welcome sight—their first buffalo in many years. Swiftly they changed to their buffalo-running horses. Most used a lightly-stuffed running pad; others rode bareback.

The excitement grew intense, affecting the horses as well as the fifty-six edgy hunters. Buffalo may have poor eyesight, but a keen sense of smell and hearing. Had they already caught the scent of Native hunters? Were they even now galloping out of sight over the next ridge?

Fearing the game would escape while they circled, the men hurried their horses through the deep snow. No one could see out of the ravine. All rode silently. Some slashed their horses into a frenzy, recklessly using heel and quirt to ready them for the rush ahead.

One impatient hunter grew angry with the scouts, grumbling that they were directing them too far off course.

He whipped up his horse to cut across the snow covered draw. Suddenly a cloud of snow shot up, and both man and horse disappeared into a deep, snow-filled washout hole.

The man struggled to crawl out past plunging, kicking legs. No one came to help him. After much effort he dragged his horse out and they both shook off the snow. He came back quietly, cleaning the snow from his gun.

"He is cooled off now," Roan Bear whispered loudly to Riggs, riding beside him.

It was the day before Christmas, early on a gray and chilly December 24th morning. The only white man on the hunt, Riggs—himself the son of missionaries to the Sioux—spoke their language and was eager to learn Lakota customs and religious traditions in hunting big game. Some men rode stoically, making

Buffalo cows graze a ridge. *Easy Winter*. Badlands Reflections Photography.

no show of their eagerness. Others rode like demons, wrote Riggs in his memoirs, *Sunrise to Sunset*.

The head of the valley brought them to level country. There, hardly eighty rods away, a buffalo herd of about fifty stood bunched together, facing them, startled and ready to run. As the hunters came up out of the ravine, the huge animals snorted and broke into a lumbering gallop, flinging up their stumpy tails as they charged off.

Then suddenly they vanished over a cutbank as if swallowed by the earth.

In a flash the first riders were after them—and dropped out of sight just as unexpectedly.

Swept along by a mad rush of hard-whipping riders, Riggs reached the edge of the bluff and saw chaos below.

At the bottom was a wide sheet of ice. Over twenty horses were down, their riders scrambling to recover and hang onto their mounts. To avoid losing their horses in just such an emergency, and adding to the confusion each man had a small looped rope about twenty feet long tied to the bridle bit, with the other end tied to his belt.

There was no stopping the wildly-riding hunters. Riggs tried to pull up at the edge of the cliff. But it was too late.

"It was a most impossible sort of drop-off and I would have given all I had to be able to pull up on the brink. My horse would not have it, and with my heart well up in my throat we went over and were across with the fortunate ones before I had time to think of the next thing to be scared at." His horse Sam leaped clear, landed

Native hunters shortened their bows to shoot from horseback and used a variety of weapons—pistols, trade guns, spears, bow and arrows, and sometimes knives. *Buffalo Hunt*, 1896. CM Russell.

clean and half-skidded off the other side of the ice sheet without injury.

"What a horse I had!" he marveled. "Indeed, I had now drunk deep of the wine of the mad chase and would not stop at anything!"

Across the creek, other horses raced after the fleeing buffalo, now galloping headlong up the next slope.

The hunters rode their best horses, of known speed and staying power, saved for just this moment. Only a few were experienced buffalo horses from former hunts.

Smelling the rank buffalo odors, they snorted and plunged through the snow, mad with the chase like their riders, whipped into a sweating froth.

The buffalo had a head start and their lumbering gallop was deceiving. They covered the ground fast.

The hunters dashed after them in hot pursuit as the last ones disappeared over the ridge.

At one point, Riggs, holding his heavy rifle, lost the loops of the light coiled rope that attached him to Sam's bridle.

"My hands were very full . . . I was as excited as any and it was all I could do to control my horse who would first carom against the horse on one side and then against one on the other, much to my discomfort and deep anguish of soul, for in the midst of this my line slipped from my belt and dropped behind, a most tempting loop for someone to step into and I'd be jerked off and covered with snow!" To pull in, recoil and tuck away his line was "nerve-splitting work."

The lead hunters began to shoot. So did reckless hunters behind them, much to the disgust of those in the front. They turned and shouted angrily as bullets whined past their ears.

In moments the frenzied hunters were among their prey, attacking buffalo from all sides, shooting from horseback. Two or three men circled ahead and dropped lead buffalo that started to run. This confused the others and they slowed their flight.

Every man cut out his buffalo and rode close for a fatal shot. Wounded buffalo charged at their assailants.

Nearly all the hunters carried guns. Most fired single shot and magazine rifles. A few had pistols. Riggs carried a .50 caliber bolt-action single shot rifle. As an extra he had brought along a lever-action single shot .45 caliber Sharpes rifle, which he loaned to Big Foot (*Si tanka*) for one of his men to use.

One buffalo was killed by Little Bear in the old way with his bow and a single arrow. He rode a famous pinto horse, a seasoned hunter, who knew how to get in close. The arrow entered the right flank and drove entirely through

Buffalo double up at creek crossing, then trail single file through the snow. NPS.

the tough hide and body. Its steel point came out low through the stomach on the opposite side.

"In former days this was often done," said Riggs. "But it requires great strength of both bow and arm."

Usually several arrows were necessary, he was told, and often a buffalo ran for miles even after being hit in a vital spot.

Riggs could discern no method to the madness of the hunt. It seemed every man for himself. Still he knew that long established buffalo hunting rules held. Even in the excitement of the moment no one dared flaunt them.

In a short time all the buffalo lay dead. The black humps of fifty carcasses littered the smooth white snow on the slope among the pines. Only one had escaped over the hills and out of sight.

Men riding slower horses, especially relatives of the lead hunters, were already skinning and cutting up their animals. The hunters jumped down and claimed their prey. Two men immediately began to argue over a buffalo that lay between them.

Disputes often erupted over who had killed a buffalo, Riggs reported. In fact, "there was more or less stealing of game. The relatives of a prominent man were quite likely to claim the kill as his. And the rightful owner would lose it unless the size of the bullet or some special marking gave conclusive evidence."

The Lakota recognized this problem with jokes such as, "Lucky is the man who has many relatives," and, "The slow horses get all the buffalo."

Another saying was "A shot buffalo has no tongue!" If a hunter left his carcass—perhaps to care for another—when he returned the tongue was likely gone. This was not considered theft, and it was common for the one who took it to give a feast after the hunt, by way of making amends.

By long established custom the division of the meat was clear. The hide, one side and one hind quarter belonged to the man who had killed the animal. His first assistant in skinning had the other side and hind quarter, while a second assistant received the two front quarters and brisket.

Riggs observed that as the hunters cut up the meat they often selected

Buffalo disappeared from their rich Dakota ranges for fifteen years, because of hunting pressure from the east. Badlands Reflections Photography.

Buffalo Hunt, 1907. CM Russell.

dainty morsels of liver or belly fat for quick lunch as they worked.

The hunters finished skinning and loaded the hides and meat onto their pack horses. Little of the bone was taken, but the pack animals carried some astonishingly heavy loads, said Riggs.

Many praised their horses for speed and fearlessness in the hunt, for courage in bringing their riders up close alongside their prey for the fatal shot.

Three months of the hunt

After that first day, hunters usually went out in smaller groups finding scattered herds of buffalo in and around the Slim Buttes. The men made their way back to camp loaded with an abundance of meat and robes, which the women helped unload and cared for over the next days. Fires crackled, pots boiled. People ate with great relish the tasty buffalo meat. All were smiling and happy.

The dogs got their share too, snarling at each other over the innards.

When blizzards blew at their worst, weary hunters likely sat by their fires through the day—talking, joking, eating, sleeping and trying to keep warm. Laughter and joyful voices often rippled through the camp, diffused by the thin walls of tents and tepees.

Women worked continually with skill and efficiency to care for the enormous amounts of meat and hides. Yet spirits ran high. Girls giggled as they worked; grandmas smiled their secret pleasure. Young men teased each other.

Evenings the Lakota sat around campfires in tents, telling heroic stories of hunting and battle. Likely they also talked of what they all knew was coming—the day when wild buffalo herds would disappear forever.

Yet it was tough going for everyone. The high, rough lands of the Slim Buttes were cut by deep washouts along canyons and dry creek beds. Steep cuts were often hid by snow drifts and such brilliant whiteness on sunny days that some hunters went temporarily snow-blind.

Since the hunt lasted so long, about four times as long as expected, the hunting party ran short of food, except for meat. Coffee, flour and tobacco disappeared in a few weeks. Then they ran out of salt. Corn was parched and used for coffee until it too was gone. While the sugar lasted, they brewed rosebush tea from the berries, roots or wood of wild roses.

"We have been eating meat alone for over four weeks," Riggs wrote in his journal. Then it became six straight weeks of meat.

One evening a group of six hunters ran into an immense herd of buffalo stampeding into the hills from the southwest. This was perhaps a part of the big migration heading into the Great Sioux Reservation. It was a night "so dark that even the stars had gone to sleep." The men were returning through deep snow to a temporary camp after dark, their pack horses loaded with meat, nearly exhausted.

However, one of the hunters, named Cokantanka, immediately called out, "I make a night run—come!"

No one offered to join him,

Jerked meat dries on racks in a Cheyenne hunting camp, while women stretch and stake out hides on ground. *Curing buffalo hides*, 1880. ACM.

and he charged alone into the herd

Cokantanka had fought in the Battle of the Little Big Horn as one of Sitting Bull's top lieutenants. His agency name was *Lazy White Bull* but it was more properly translated, Riggs explained, as *White Buffalo Cow Leader*.

His first shot missed, and he suddenly found himself in the middle of a tight, stampeding herd.

This was one of the most reckless acts he saw during the hunt, Riggs recalled later.

"They were running on all sides of him, bumping against his legs," reported Riggs. "In his excitement he threw the lever of his gun so quickly and so hard that the hammer jarred down and the shot went off in the air. This didn't steady his nerves any . . . and he did the same thing again!

"That exhausted all the shells in the magazine and he started to hunt in his belt for cartridges. He found he had only three left, and as his belt had slipped around they were in the middle of his back. He had to throw off his blanket to reach them. When he finally got out one cartridge, he very carefully pushed it into the chamber and although the buffalo were still bumping against him, he kept his wits about him and finally managed to work out of the running herd and get his buffalo."

With his buffalo down, Cokantanka called and his friends rode to help him.

On another day Roan Bear shot a buffalo that fell as if dead. He dropped off his horse to bleed it, but just as he was about to cut its throat, the buffalo leaped to its feet.

"He jumped on his horse which began to pitch with him. It was not until the buffalo was almost horning into the pony's tail that the pony woke up and moved."

As the horse began running away, chased by the buffalo, Roan Bear turned and fired. Luckily, his buffalo dropped dead.

That night when he brought the hide into camp, he hung it inside the tent and challenged his friends to find the hole where the fatal ball had entered. But no one could find a hole in the hide. Some said the bullet entered through the eye. Others maintained that Roan Bear scared the buffalo to death.

Riggs enjoyed the good humor of his fellow hunters. One night he camped with forty men about twenty-five miles north of the Slim Buttes. They had no food and only one tent. Someone went out and shot an old bull and they stretched two pieces of canvas wagon sheet for the eight men who couldn't get into the tent. Riggs slept in the partial tent, which was no more than eight feet long. One man had a three-quart pail and some ground coffee tied in a rag, so they made coffee and roasted their share of the meat. Despite the crowding, Riggs said it was a pleasant evening filled with much joking and laughter.

One day Riggs was alone on a branch of the South Grand River when he shot a large buffalo in blizzard-gale winds. When he tried to skin it he could not turn it over. Sam was no help so he turned him loose, hanging onto his pack horse. At last he cut the hide in half down the back and got it loaded. Climbing on the pack horse on top of the half-hide, he struggled through the storm and snow drifts till nearly daybreak before reaching camp.

That evening the hunters were telling stories of their difficulties during the blizzard, each more

Buffalo crosses frozen river and scrambles up the snowy bank. NPS

hilarious than the one before.

Riggs had his own story to tell.

"After skinning the enormous buffalo," he said. "I threw the green hide over the horse and sat on it. The hide froze stiff as marble and in passing through a deep drift, I was lifted clear off my horse, which passed out from under me and left me straddling the frozen hide on top of nothing."

This brought shouts of laughter and he was dubbed the unluckiest hunter of the day.

"To this day my story is told over and over by hundreds of Indians," he wrote years later. "And I am joked for riding a frozen hide as a saddle with no horse under it."

Homeward bound

Finally the hunt ended. The homeward trek went slowly with fully loaded travois, pack animals and wagons. Snow lay two feet deep in many places and so crusted over that horses' legs were badly cut as they broke through the icy crust.

To avoid the slow travel Riggs and Roan Bear left the wagons and rode a four-day shortcut to the Dupree ranch across several high ridges in bitter cold. The second night they camped on Fox Ridge, sleeping on a couple of blankets on two feet of frozen snow. "The coldest camp I can remember," wrote Riggs. They reached the ranch in four days.

There the elderly French fur trader Fred Dupris, Roan Bear's father-in-law, welcomed them warmly "in true early-day manner with tears, laughter, curses and prayers curiously intermingled."

They warmed at his stove and gratefully ate a meal that—after weeks of straight buffalo meat—happily included "real coffee with sugar, white bread and potatoes."

For the Cheyenne River Lakota, this was their last winter buffalo hunt. Riggs reflected that he was much impressed with the way his companions prepared for and carried out the hunt throughout with religious feeling and fervor.

"Much that is good of their ancient religion shows in every detail," the missionary wrote.

Everyone judged it a successful hunt. No one was injured. The party killed around

Tracks in the snow. CM Russell

The Cheyenne River Lakota spent much of the winter of 1880-1881 hunting buffalo in the Slim Buttes. The cold wind blew and snow piled deep in the pines. *Lost in a Snowstorm*, 1888, CM Russell.

2,000 buffalo. They took home more meat than the ponies could pack and 500 buffalo hides. The prime hides, cured with the hair on, made the finest of robes.

The future of the buffalo and the future of the Native people was impacted by this winter hunt, not just because it was the first in fifteen years. Fred Dupris is said to have "sent out his sons for buffalo calves." However, they were grown men and he an elderly man.

Descendants say it was their Lakota mother Mary Ann who suggested it. Was the next step decided right there in the hunting tent? On those long, cold winter nights by the campfire did Mary Ann Good Elk Woman and her sons and daughters talk over how they could rescue and raise buffalo calves? Did she suggest that some of those range cows grazing her reservation allotment surely could be persuaded to raise buffalo calves—and thus save some of these magnificent animals from extinction?

Likely it was the next summer—or perhaps the following, in 1881 or 1882—when Pete Dupree and some of his brothers set out for the South Grand River with team and buckboard wagon. They brought home five buffalo calves—and changed history.

A small herd of buffalo finds rich grasses on a high plains plateau. SD Tourism.

3

Sitting Bull Hunt

I could see our country was changing fast,
And that these changes were causing us to live very differently.
Anybody could now see that soon there would be no buffalo
on the plains, and everybody was wondering how we could live
after they were gone.
—Plenty Coups, Chief of the Crows
from his autobiography *Plenty Coup*

The years following 1876 were especially traumatic and painful for the Standing Rock Sioux tribes.

After the Battle of the Little Bighorn they drifted back to their assigned reservations. Many had fought and won that battle on June 25, 1876, along with their allies the Northern Cheyenne. But the buffalo had gone farther west. That day brought tragedy for both sides: death for General George A. Custer and 225 of his soldiers of the 7th Cavalry; short-lived victory and severe reprisals for Native Americans assigned to Dakota reservations.

Buffalo's heavy bodies sink low in the water when swimming rivers. Sometimes a mother lets her calf scramble onto her back for a rough crossing. Badlands Reflections Photography.

They paid a heavy price for their victory at "Custer's Last Stand." Almost immediately their large reservation was reduced in size. They lost their much-cherished Black Hills and another western strip of land equal to the width of one county—from 104 to 103 degrees of latitude.

These were hunters who had to surrender their guns, ammunition and horses. If they wanted to eat they accepted the frugal provisions doled out to them. Hunters were still expected to provide deer and small game for their families.

The agency at Fort Yates alone held 6,000 Dakota and Lakota people, according to the new Indian Agent James McLaughlin, who arrived in the fall of 1881. Similar agencies were established farther south on the same reservation. McLaughlin called his charges "destitute" in a letter to Washington. He mentions that the people were "principally huddled about the agency" in Fort Yates, at the eastern edge of their reservation. They were "Hunkpapas, Yank-tonais, Blackfeet (Lakota), Minniconjous, Sans Arcs, Oglalas, Brules and some minor bands [all Sioux]." When there, his Indian police could keep an eye on them.

Worse, these once independent people were forced to live under a policy that required them to give up their culture and traditions. Federal policy decreed they accept the lifestyle and values of mainstream America. On orders from Washington, the local Indian Agents insisted they build log cabins, take up farming and replace their spiritual traditions, cultural values, religion, language and life ways with those of the non-Indian population. Beloved children were shipped off to boarding schools—sometimes across the continent, to far-off New Hampshire, Hampton Institute in Virginia and Carlisle Indian School in Pennsylvania, even for years. Unfamiliar diseases hit, and some proved deadly. Food rations often came up short. Dishonest agents sold food and blankets intended for Native Americans; thieves stole what they could.

Their great horse herds and guns were gone. Indian Agents held the Native hunters in check with what must have seemed an iron hand. Their hunting permits allotted specific days for each hunt, after which they expired. If caught hunting without a permit or with an expired permit they risked severe punishment including: imprisonment, confiscation of a horse or farm wagon or having family food rations cut. Sometimes they were furnished guns and ammunition for the allotted days of a hunt.

People accustomed to caring for themselves through tribal law and custom were suddenly dependent on the government. They could no longer care for their families or travel freely even within the reservation.

Losing their horses was a tragic blow. In late August 1876, after the Battle of the Little Bighorn, the military began rounding up and taking horses from both friendly and hostile Indians, leaving perhaps one or two for farm work. Whatever minimal compensation Native families received for their horses was woefully inadequate. McLaughlin noted that the Sans Arcs at Rosebud agency alone "turned over 777 ponies, 97 guns, 53 robes," and received only $2,248.95 in return.

Josephine Waggoner, born in 1872, known as the historian of the Standing Rock Sioux people, shared sad memories of those years in her book *Witness: A Hunkpapha Historian's Strong-Heart Song of the Lakotas*. She described the devastation:

"So great was the pride in owning a herd that the owners fairly lived with them. . . grooming, pampering, even painting ornaments on their pet horses. I have seen Indians talk to their horses as though they were human."

One hot day as a little girl, Waggoner watched big clouds of dust as great herds of horses were brought in.

"The hillsides were a black mass of moving horses, thousands of them being driven in from every direction. They were held west of Fort Yates. Mother, my sister and I climbed the hill near Yates where many others had gone to view the raiding of horses. In a few days the horses were taken toward Bismarck. There were many fine horses among the herd."

Native people had spent years breeding up their horses to the quality of Kentucky race horses, Waggoner said. Their horses were so unique that many owners imprinted them at birth by rubbing with human scent. They believed that a dedicated rider became one with his horse, says Dave Archambault, 2015 Standing Rock Sioux Tribal Chairman and owner of several of the Nakota horses said to originate with Sitting Bull.

"The life, the hope, the pride of the Indian was gone with them. It was like losing your father and mother," wrote Waggoner. "No one in this machine age could ever understand the love between master and horse. The love of a man toward a spirited,

Visions of Yesteryear, by William R. Leigh. Woolaroc Museum, Bartlesville, OK.

The Final Buffalo Hunts

It's not clear how many buffalo hunts took place during these final years of buffalo hunting that harvested the last 50,000 during the thirty-four months between December 24, 1880 and October 13, 1883. All were Native American hunts on the Great Sioux Reservation except as noted. Doubtless a number of unauthorized hunts took place. By the fall of 1883 the vast herds of wild buffalo were all gone, but for a few stragglers here and there.

In 1880-1881
- The Slim Buttes winter hunt began Dec 24, 1880; killed 2000 buffalo
- 17th Infantry under Col Gilbert claimed right to hunt illegally on the reservation
- October 12 hunt authorized by new agent James McLaughlin

1882
- Hiddenwood hunt began about June 20; 5,000 buffalo slaughtered
- Herd of 5,000 that left reservation at north border killed during 150-180 mile run
- White hide hunters found on reservation with 1,000 illegal hides
- Five hide hunters arrested with 1,000 buffalo hides twenty miles inside western border
- Native hunt harvested 2,000 buffalo that fall, as reported in *Bismarck Tribune*
- McLaughlin issued a hunting permit to begin Oct. 12, on the Cannonball River; 2,000 robes taken

1883
- 200 Native hunters killed 1,480 buffalo, reported in mid-January
- Large hunting parties reported as coming from agencies farther south; likely killed thousands
- Herd of 10,000 grazing near the reservation border; all killed by Native and white hunters
- Sitting Bull and his band killed the last 1,200 wild buffalo October 12 and 13

Note: These last great buffalo hunts and the last stand of the American buffalo in their free-ranging state mainly took place in what is now Adams County in southwestern North Dakota and Perkins County in northwestern South Dakota. Additionally, the hunt in the Slim Buttes, which had recently been removed from the Great Sioux Reservation, took place just ouside the reservation boundary in what is now Harding County, SD. The area of last hunts thus includes the towns of Hettinger, Haynes, Bucyrus and Reeder, ND, and Bison, Buffalo, Lodgepole, Ralph, Reva, Prairie City, Meadow, and Lemmon, SD.

Watchers of the Plains, CM Russell

courageous horse was wonderful. It was like the love of a beloved child, only a man is dependent on a horse."

Three years of hunts

The first hunt after the buffalo's return was apparently the extremely cold, deep-snow winter hunt in the Slim Buttes that lasted from December 1880 into February 1881.

Later in 1881, Col. C.C. Gilbert who was stationed at Ft. Yates with the 17th Infantry wrote McLaughlin's predecessor, Indian Agent Joseph A. Stephan, demanding that his soldiers be allowed to go hunt buffalo.

When Stephan attempted to discourage this illegal invasion of the reservation by non-Indians, the Colonel wrote again more forcefully. "I do not intend that the soldiers shall miss their opportunity . . . It would be a just cause of dissatisfaction if their opportunity is to be lost." Later he added bluntly, "2nd Lieutenant R.W. Dowdy will conduct a hunting party in the direction of the North Fork of Grand River, Dakota Territory [with] Scouts Butcher and Left Hand."

McLaughlin wrote several letters to Washington requesting permission to allow the Native people to go on a buffalo hunt. Finally he wrote, "I do not think advisable to deprive these Indians of their chance of the hides." And later, "I have granted permission of this agency" for a hunting party to leave on a hunt on October 12. He assured the Commissioner that they'd be under the immediate charge of a white man employee of the agency, in whom he had "every confidence." McLaughlin addressed his official letters to "Hon. H. Price, Commissioner of Indian Affairs, Washington, D.C., and signed off, "Very respectfully, Your obedient servant, James McLaughlin, U.S. Indian Agent."

Doubtless unauthorized hunts occurred over the three years. McLaughlin came at a difficult time and apparently tried to hold to

Losing their horses was a tragic blow for Native Americans. "The hillsides were a black mass of moving horses, thousands of them. . . The life, the hope, the pride of the Indian was gone with them.," wrote Josephine Waggoner, Sioux historian. SD Game, Fish & Parks.

unreasonable standards laid down in Washington by men who knew little about the realities of the west and even less about Indian people.

McLaughlin's correspondence with the Washington office hints at the turmoil of those years.

"A few hours after my arrival, Sitting Bull with his 146 immediate followers was taken down the Missouri River to Ft. Randall. I was left to deal with nearly 6,000 Indians who had been out in active hostility for several years," he wrote in his memoirs.

Sitting Bull and his band fled to Canada after the Custer battle, then spent two years in prison in Ft. Randall, Nebraska. Later he joined Buffalo Bill Cody's Wild West Show and went on a tour of Europe. In 1890 Sitting Bull was killed when McLaughlin ordered his arrest over fears of his leadership during the Ghost dancing.

At least one other buffalo hunt was launched that fall after the Hiddenwood hunt. One or more Native American hunts took place in October 1882. An item in the *Bismarck Tribune* on Oct 6, 1882, noted that "not long ago another hunt got over 2,000." McLaughlin issued a hunting permit to begin Oct 12 and on Nov 1 wrote Washington, "The Indians have returned from a successful buffalo hunt, bringing back over 2,000 robes and a large number of other peltries."

In one of these hunts, the men captured and returned McLaughlin's horse, which had escaped in a buffalo herd that swept through camp at Hiddenwood.

With several years' experience as the Indian Agent at Devils Lake and a Lakota wife, McLaughlin seemed to have the Native interests at heart. Yet he ran a tight ship. Soon after his arrival, under federal orders, he sent his Indian police through the reservation and confiscated horses, guns and ammunition.

Women scrape fat and muscle from the hides before curing them in the hunting camp, while a child plays close by. *The Silk Robe,* 1890. CM Russell.

Hunting offenses

Federal law forbade non-Indians from hunting buffalo on the reservation, stating: "Every person, other than an Indian, who . . . hunts or traps, or takes and destroys any peltries or game, except for subsistence in the Indian country, shall forfeit all the traps, guns and ammunition in his possession and all peltries so taken; and shall be liable in addition to a penalty of $500."

Waggoner tells of numerous offenses from non-Indian hunters. She said Gall's band had trouble with them, probably in the fall of 1882. "The white hide hunters had come into the reservation and killed thousands of the buffalo in their last retreat . . . Gall and his band, with Crow King and his men, followed the Cedar River. They ran into a camp of white men where Ed Hotchkinson's ranch was afterwards on the Cedar. There was no one at home when the Indians got there. They could count 1,000 hides drying on the ground and a wagonload of dry beaver hides."

McLaughlin was determined that whites hunting illegally on the reservation be held accountable for their offenses. In a July 11, 1882 letter to Washington, he reported his Indian police had discovered the camp of white hunters twenty miles within the western boundary of the reservation. They were able to capture only one of the hunters and he escaped. However, the police brought in the confiscated camp equipment and teams of horses.

Another group of five white hide hunters was arrested by his Indian police on Standing Rock with about 1,000 buffalo hides in their camp. The five men were brought into the Ft. Yates agency Nov. 1, 1882, along with their six wagons, eleven horses, four rifles, a "large lot of ammunition" and their camp supplies. Only the hides were left behind for want of transportation. The prisoners remained there in custody for two weeks until the Deputy U.S. Marshal arrived and took them to Bismarck.

But white hunters were almost impossible to convict, as McLaughlin found.

Frustrated at being compelled to feed hay to ten of the offender's horses in the corral for several months, McLaughlin wrote to the Marshal in Yankton requesting he take charge of the horses. The Marshal refused.

Outraged when the hunters were acquitted by the U.S. Commissioner in Bismarck because the "witnesses did not see them shoot or kill any buffalo," McLaughlin campaigned for a second trial. He sent five Indian policemen to testify at the second trial. They reported seeing one of the hunters "busily engaged in picking up hides," while all about lay the skinned carcasses in two permanent camps.

Again the court found insufficient evidence and the hunters were acquitted. To his chagrin, McLaughlin was ordered to return all their property, including the six wagons, two camping outfits and the ten horses he had cared for so long.

The U.S. government apparently intended to compensate horse owners or to exchange the horses for cows. The agents tried to keep track of their value and origins, but that proved impossible. Among McLaughlin's letters, much discussion concerned who had owned the horses, particularly those surrendered in 1880 and 1881 at Fort Keogh, near Miles City.

Distrusting the government and military, many Native people hid what guns they could. Waggoner said her family and others hid dozens of good guns under their cabin floor. Nevertheless, great wagonloads of guns and ammunition came in to the military warehouses. It was said the military used the ammunition. No one was allowed to sell guns to Indian people.

Hunting along the border

During the summer of 1882 several buffalo herds left the reservation at various points, despite efforts of the Lakota to hold them by burning grass along the border and other techniques. Small herds escaped from time to time, and were immediately set upon by white hide hunters. Most often that slaughter was swift.

One large herd crossed the northern border and stampeded west up the Cannonball River, with scores of hunters in hot pursuit. The buffalo then crossed the Little Missouri River and the Yellowstone River near Glendive, Montana, traveling a distance of perhaps 150 to 180 miles before being totally annihilated.*

By the time they reached the Montana border there were about 400 to 500 buffalo in the herd, pursued by "a yelling, swearing crowd of white men and Indians on foam-covered horses," reported a Grand Rapids, Wisconsin, newspaper of the day.

"From the hunters it was learned that the hunt began in Dakota, on the Cannon Ball River where not less than 5,000 of the animals were found grazing. A few of the men had followed them the entire distance, but although the party that passed here numbered only thirty, its members estimated that from first to last, 300 or 400 men had taken part in the slaughter.

"The wanton destruction of this herd has caused great indignation throughout the entire section traversed," concluded the news story. "But as it seems to be the policy to exterminate the bison, nothing will be done about it. . . It is regarded as a great pity there was not a law enforced ten years ago making it a penal offense for a white man to slaughter buffalo so recklessly."

Another report from the Amidon area, northwest of the reservation, told of a big herd of 19,000 buffalo seen near the Rainy Buttes in eastern Slope County. The year of this sighting was likely the summer of 1883, since the historian adds the herd was cut to 1,200 head during that summer.

The *Dickinson Press* reported that fall that Indian people were firing grass outside the reservation border. "The Sioux are burning all the country over outside, and driving the buffalo onto the reservation. The stockmen are complaining that they have been so bold as to ride up and fire the prairie right in front of their men who were at work trying to put the fire out." The intention in burning grass was to form a buffer of scorched earth to discourage buffalo from leaving the reservation. Setting a fire outside the borders also could turn escaped buffalo back onto the reservation.

Hunts in 1883

In mid-January 1883 one report said that in a recent hunt "200 Sioux killed 1,480 buffalo." This hunt occurred in early January or perhaps toward the end of the previous year.

The last hunts during summer 1883 probably involved many Lakota and Dakota bands from other agencies farther south on the same Great Sioux Reservation. Early that summer McLaughlin learned that large parties were preparing

---

*This running hunt apparently began in what is now North Dakota, near present day New Leipzig or Elgin, and continued up the Cannonball River through Mott, New England and its headwaters near Amidon and a few miles into Montana.

Breaking up the Great Sioux Reservation

The Great Sioux Reservation was created by the Laramie Treaty of 1868 to include all South Dakota land west of the Missouri River to the Montana line.

The western boundaries of what are now the Standing Rock and Cheyenne River Reservations were moved twice, from 104 degrees of longitude, along the Montana border, to 103 degrees and then to 102 degrees where they remain currently.

In 1876 the Black Hills Agreement reduced the reservation by a 50-mile strip on the west and added lands north to the Cannonball and Cedar Rivers in what is now North Dakota. In 1889 the border was moved east another 50 miles and the land divided into six separate reservations including Standing Rock and Cheyenne River Reservations.

It was in this region between the last two boundaries that the American buffalo made their last stand in 1880 to 1883 (between 103 and 102 degrees longitude). Then part of the Great Sioux Reservation, this is now Adams County, ND and Perkins County, SD.

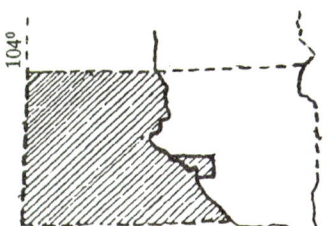

LARAMIE TREATY—1869
Created the Great Sioux Reservation from all South Dakota lands west of the Missouri River.

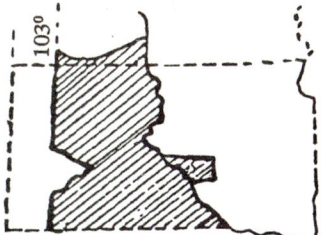

BLACK HILLS AGREEMENT—1876
Removed Black Hills and 50-mile strip from reservation.

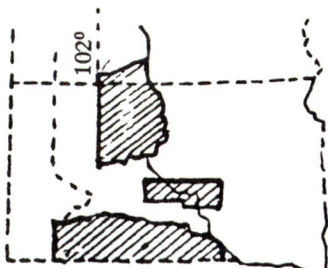

DIVISION INTO 6 RESERVATIONS—1889
'Surplus' lands between these reservations opened to homestead settlement.

Indian Frontier of the American West, 1846-1890. Robert Utley.

to come to hunt buffalo from the agencies at "Cheyenne River, Crow Ronge Creek and Lower Brule, Yankton, Rosebud and Pine Ridge Agencies."

He urged the Commissioner of Indian Affairs in Washington to instruct the separate Indian Agents to withhold permission until fall when hides would be prime and crops harvested. He complained that it was hard to keep his people farming when others were out hunting buffalo.

The Great Sioux Reservation was still very large during this window of time. It extended approximately 230 miles north and south by 130 miles wide. All the Indian agencies there were still connected. However, the Native people were divided among their assigned agencies and had to obtain a permit to travel between them.

Defined in 1868, the reservation assigned to the Sioux originally included the entire western half of South Dakota plus the Cannonball and Cedar rivers of North Dakota. Then with the Treaty of 1876, the Black Hills were removed and the border moved 50 miles farther east, from 104 degrees to 103 degrees west longitude.

This painting captures the excitement that greets a small party of Blood hunters as they return to camp at dusk, bringing the buffalo meat and hides that mean survival for their families. *Indian Hunters Return,* 1900, CM Russell. Montana Historical Society

The final breakup of the Great Sioux Reservation came in 1889 when the various bands were forced to give up more land, due to the clamour for more homestead lands. At that time, despite Indian opposition, the western border was moved another fifty miles farther east and separated into six reservations.

Likely the buffalo hunts by various Lakota and Dakota bands went on through summer and early fall. McLaughlin informed Washington in a May 28, 1883, letter that "Buffalo are reported in large numbers on this reservation." Most of the big herds, he said, still ranged in the rugged northwestern area, between the Moreau and Grand rivers, "about half way between the Black Hills and Bismarck."

Non-Sioux Indian tribes from other reservations petitioned to hunt in Dakota Territory, but almost certainly McLaughlin disapproved and tried to keep them out. In the spring of 1883, a poignant letter appeared in the *Bismarck Tribune* (May 29, 1883), signed by ten Mandan and Gros Ventre Chiefs living at Fort Berthold Indian Reservation, farther north at the big bend in the Missouri River. They expressed their deep longing to hunt the buffalo "so near."

Dear Sir:

I want to tell you the news in this agency. All the Indians working good we think, and all whites tell us we doing well. We are working hard here. We have agent here, but he do not help us. He helps his folks—that's all help we get from him. When he talk to us people here he talk like he was very kind to think of us Indians here.

We want go out hunt buffaloes, is 60 miles from Ft. Berthold which so near. We want go out so bad get some to eat and agent tells us we cannot go. He says if we go out guns and ponys, wagons be taking away from us—this is what he tells us.

We often ask him to more eat and he tells us he is going to get plenty eat for us but we get tired waiting. Been three years ago. He is trying to make people to live half sick hungry. They got to get some to eat—they cannot. This what agent J. Kauffman tells us. We are poor but we do not steal potatoes and oats. He told us Chiefs we steal, we are Bad people. We do not. We are friend with all whites. We trying to learn ways of Whites.

This from your Friends

Crows Breast, Gros. Ventree Chief.
Hawk   "   "
Bad Gun   "   "
Man Bull   "   "
Toe   "   "
Black Horn   "   "
Sun of the Stars, Mandan Chief
Crows Breast   "   "
Little Bull   "   "
Wolf Chief

By fall of 1883, remnants of the big northern herd grazed in the same region. But numbers dwindled swiftly as the buffalo were killed off by Indian hunters and the ever-present white hide hunters who scouted the reservation perimeters and hunted illegally.

Likely some of the buffalo also stampeded across the border under the extreme hunting pressures. A big herd of some 10,000 reportedly was grazing on or near the reservation border, when set upon by both white and Indian hunters. Vic Smith, the well-known hide hunter, told William Hornaday, "A host of white hunters took part in the killing of this last 10,000."

On Sept. 15, 1883, McLaughlin authorized what may have been the Sitting Bull hunt. Likely he also issued ammunition. He wrote this letter to Philip Wells, Head Farmer and Chief of Indian Police of the Standing Rock Agency:

Sir:

You are hereby directed to accompany the Indians of this Agency on a Buffalo hunt on the Sioux Indian Reservation. You will remove all trespassers found hunting or trapping on the reservation and prevent the Indians from interfering with any person off the reservation, also prevent them molesting any person found on the reservation as that will be attended to by the Indian Police and yourself.

The time allowed is 40 days from the 14th and you will see that the Indians are all back at this agency on or before the 23rd of October, and if any parties wish to leave for home at any time before the main party you will see that they are permitted by the Indian Soldiers to do so. You will use your best judgment in all matters and questions that may arise and if necessary communicate with me by courier.

Very Respectfully,
James McLaughlin,
S.R. Indian Agent

N.B. You will not interfere with the Indians as to their rules of hunting but you must see that no disorderly act is committed and you will use the police force in the enforcement of order. Running Antelope is appointed Indian leader of the hunt and he will aid you in all matters of this hunt.

One large buffalo herd still remained. Hornaday wrote, "The herd which at the beginning of the hunting season ranged in western Dakota, was speedily reduced. Vic Smith, claimed to be 'in at the death.'

"Just at this juncture, October 1883, Sitting Bull and his whole band of nearly 1,000 braves arrived from the Standing Rock Agency and in two days' time slaughtered the entire herd."

The Sitting Bull hunting party was reportedly well equipped with ammunition, guns and bows and arrows. Their final hunt began Oct 12, 1883, about eighty miles west of Ft. Yates Agency and killed 1,200 buffalo in two days.

Thus, officially it was the Sitting Bull band from the Cheyenne River Reservation that took down that final free-ranging herd of 1,200 buffalo and was well documented as "The Last Great Buffalo Hunt" of all.

In summing up, Hornaday again quoted Vic Smith, "There was not a hoof left. That wound up the buffalo in the Far West, only a stray bull being seen here and there afterwards."

Long shadows in the snowscape mark the short days of winter for buffalo in the north. NPS.

4

Scattered Survivors

I can remember when the bison were so many
That they could not be counted,
But more and more Wasichus came to kill them
Until there were only heaps of bones scattered where they used to be.
The Wasichus did not kill them to eat;
They killed them for the metal that makes them crazy.
When we hunted bison, we killed only what we needed.
 —Black Elk, Hehaka Sapa, Sioux chief
 Black Elk Speaks, John G. Neihardt

After that last great buffalo hunt in October 1883 by Sitting Bull's band, only bleached bones and a few scattered survivors marked the vast grasslands where once so many millions of the great animals had grazed.

Across buffalo country in the spring of 1884, hunters waited for the buffalo to arrive.

None came.

Yet few believed the end had come, William Hornaday reported with some astonishment in his 1889 book *The Extermination of the American*

A herd of buffalo takes a break on water in their summer pasture in the pines. Badlands Reflections Photography.

Bison. "Curiously enough, not even the buffalo hunters themselves were at the time aware of the fact that the end of the hunting season of 1882-83 was also the end of the buffalo, at least as an inhabitant of the plains and a source of revenue," he wrote.

"In the autumn of 1883 they nearly all outfitted as usual, often at an expense of many hundreds of dollars, and blithely sought the range that had up to that time been so prolific in robes. The end was in nearly every case the same—total failure and bankruptcy. It was indeed hard to believe that not only the millions—but also the thousands—had actually gone, and forever."

For many years, rumors persisted that the big herds had migrated north into Canada or hid out in some remote badlands or mountains, and would someday return to repopulate the great buffalo plains and prairies.

"Many think the whole great body went north into British territory. . . Nothing could be more illusory than this belief. In the first place, the herd never reached the British line and if it had would have been promptly annihilated by the hungry Blackfeet and Cree Indians, declared to be in a half-starved condition," wrote Hornaday. The great herd that went north was utterly extinguished by the white hunters along the Missouri River and the Indians living north of it.

"The only vestige of it that remained was a band of about 200 individuals that took refuge in the labyrinth of ravines and creek bottoms that lie west of the Musselshell between Flat Willow and Box Elder Creeks, and another band of about seventy-five which settled in the badlands between the head of the Big Dry and Big Porcupine Creeks, where a few survivors were found by the writer in 1886," in central Montana.

Even native hunters returned empty-handed. October 1883 marked the last season for wild buffalo herds. Few believed that the end had come. *Indian Scouting Party,* 1900, CM Russell.

Tales of 'last great buffalo hunts," here and there, turned out to be pure rumor or the slaughter of small wild bands of survivors.

Rumors circulated as to where the buffalo had gone. But Hornaday—from his exhaustive research of all possible sources—makes it plain: "The hunting season which began in October 1882, and ended in 1883 finished the annihilation of the great northern herd, and left but a few small bands of stragglers."

He gave an example of three experienced hunters who "went out from Miles City on October 23, 1882, due east to the badlands between the Powder River and O'Fallon Creek, and were on the range all winter. They found comparatively few buffalo," and saw many Indian hunters returning empty-handed.

Theodore Roosevelt came west to hunt buffalo in the fall of 1883, at age twenty-five, and saw a few of these survivors in the badlands east of the Little Missouri. They were wild and gun-shy. He and his hunting guide rode ten days before they could get close enough for him to shoot and kill one old lone bull. He lamented that this was the end of the great herds, "a veritable tragedy of the animal world."

In the still hunt a hunter made a stand from a point above the herd, bracing his rifle. The secret was to shoot leaders that tried to escape, while others milled around in confusion. *The Still Hunt* by JH Moser from William Hornaday's *The Extermination of the American Bison*.

Wanton slaughter destroys southern herd

In 1869 the Union Pacific, first transcontinental railway, crossed the nation and permanently divided the buffalo into two great herds. The southern and northern herds soon were separated by 100 miles on both sides, as sporting men and hide hunters rode the rails and branched out from small towns along the way to slaughter all nearby herds.

Railroad expansion enabled hunters to reach great areas of the plains previously inaccessible.

In the next few years two more railroads cut across the heart of the southern plains. Farther north, the whole process delayed until 1882, when the railroad bridge crossed the Missouri River at Bismarck.

The southern herd contained twice as many buffalo, but less land than the northern herd, according to William Hornaday.

The rush to slaughter the estimated 3.5 million head of buffalo on the southern ranges began in 1871 and reached its height in 1873.

The "still hunt" or "stand" developed in the south as the systematic way to kill enormous numbers of buffalo. It finished off the biggest share of the southern herd in just three years.

"Of all the methods that were unsportsmanlike, unfair, ignoble and utterly reprehensible, this was in every respect the lowest and the worst," raged Hornaday.

Anyone could do it. Thousands joined the rush. The people who turned out to hunt buffalo, he said, included railroaders, teamsters, fortune-seekers, professional hunters, trappers, guides "and everyone out of a job." During the years 1871 to 1874, "but little else was done in that country except buffalo killing."

Ideally it took four men and a wagon—a shooter, two skinners, and a camp tender to cook, stretch hides and care for the horses. They might be hired by a merchant on the frontier, or go out on their own. A tent, blankets, barrel of water, sack of flour, dry beans, a side of bacon, coffee, sugar, molasses, a little salt, guns, skinning knives, a big supply of ammunition and the outfit was ready to go.

What these men had that no hunter ever had before were powerful, long-range guns. The Remington and Sharps 40-90 and 45-120 were favorites.

All knew how to "make a stand." The secrets were simple: Lie on a ridge above a herd of fifty or so buffalo, brace the rifle on a rock and fire away. Kill any leaders that start to run. Others likely only sniffed at them and milled in confusion, waiting for another leader until all lay dead.

Hornaday explained the buffalo reaction.

"When he heard the loud report and saw a little cloud of white smoke rising from a clump of sage brush or the top of a ridge, 200 yards away, he wondered what it meant and held himself in readiness to follow his leader in case she should run away. But when the leader of the herd fell bleeding and no other buffalo assumed the leadership, instead of fleeing, he merely did as he saw the others do and waited his turn to be shot. They cluster around the fallen ones, sniff at the warm blood, bawl aloud in wonderment, and do everything but run away.

"The policy is not to fire too rapidly, but every time a buffalo attempts to make off, shoot it down. One shot per minute was a moder-

The last great wild buffalo herd migrated north through the Miles City area the fall of 1880. There half crossed the Yellowstone River and met blazing guns of white and Indian hunters. Photographer L.A. Huffman had just set up shop in Miles City and filmed the carnage. Huffman photo.

ate rate of firing... With the most accurate hunting rifle ever made, a dead rest and a large mark practically motionless, it was no wonder that nearly every shot meant a dead buffalo. Success in getting a stand meant the slaughter of a good-sized herd."

Then the formidable task of skinning began. The men stretched each robe on the ground while still warm and cut the owner's initials in the muscle on the inside. The next day, they did it all over again.

Railroads hired these hunters full time to furnish meat for workers laying track. One of these was Buffalo Bill (William F.) Cody, who killed 4,280 buffalo in eighteen months for the Kansas Pacific Railway. Later Buffalo Bill took his Wild West show on the road and across Europe.

The slaughter was tremendous. In the southern plains some hide hunters claimed they harvested as many as 2,500 to 3,000 buffalo during a single season—November to February. One man reported he killed 91 buffalo in one stand, and another, that he shot 112 head within a radius of 200 yards in less than three-quarters of an hour.

One September day in Dodge City, Kansas, a hunter named Thomas Nixon boasted he would set a record "for all time." Taking his friends along to witness, he located a buffalo herd and moved into position. Signaling his start, he began firing. As buffalo dropped, others pawed the ground, sniffed from one fallen animal to another, sometimes butting heads or prodding them with their horns. The survivors did not run until Nixon stopped shooting and walked toward them. In forty minutes he had killed 120 buffalo.

Much of the harvest from such slaughter lay wasted, with no meat taken. Often even the hides rotted due to the inexperience and carelessness of hunters. At the height of waste, in 1871, every hide shipped to market represented no less than five dead buffalo, according to Hornaday's careful estimates, gathered through extensive interviews and correspondence with military men, fur traders, hunters and frontiersmen.

From spring 1872 to the fall of 1875, the southern herd disappeared. Only a few scattered survivors had fled farther southwest to "wild, desolate and inhospitable" country—inhabited only by desperate Indian bands.

Buffalo Bill Cody took Sitting Bull along with his Wild West Show across Europe. Their photo taken in Montreal, Canada in 1885.

Theodore Roosevelt on an 1883 Hunt

Theodore Roosevelt came west to hunt buffalo in September 1883, at age 25, just as the last of the big wild herds vanished forever. On a ten day hunting trip, riding from the Medora area toward the Standing Rock Reservation, he and a local guide four times sighted lone bulls and small bands of buffalo. Below are excerpts from his account.

We came across the fresh track of a bull buffalo (and) rode up the ravine, carefully examining the soil for nearly half an hour. Buffalo wander a great distance, for, though they do not go fast, yet they keep travelling as they graze, all day long; and though this one had evidently passed but a few hours before, we were not sure we would see him . . . Finally, as we passed the mouth of a little side coulee, there was a plunge and crackle though the bushes, and a shabby looking old bull bison galloped out and, without an instant's hesitation, plunged over a steep bank into a patch of broken ground around the base of a high butte.

So quickly did he disappear that we had not time to dismount and fire. Spurring our horses we galloped up to the brink of the cliff; it was remarkable that he should have gone down it unhurt. Getting our horses over the broken ground as fast as possible, we rode round the butte only to see the buffalo come out and climb up the side of another butte over a quarter of a mile off. In spite of his great weight and cumbersome, heavy gait, he climbed up the steep bluff with ease and even agility, and when he had reached the ridge stood and looked back at us for a moment.

In another second he made off; and being evidently accustomed to being harassed by hunters, must have traveled a long distance before stopping, for we followed his trail for some miles, yet did not again catch so much as a glimpse of him . . .

Late in the afternoon we made out in the middle of a large plain three black specks, which proved to be buffalo—old bulls. We left the ponies in a hollow half a mile from the game, and started off on our hands and knees. After taking advantage of every hollow, hillock or sagebrush, we got within about 125 yards of where the three bulls were feeding, and as all between was bare ground I drew up and fired (at the nearest). The bullet told on his body with a loud crack, the dust flying up from his hide; but it did not in the least hinder him, and away went all three with their tails up. For seven or eight miles we loped our jaded horses, occasionally seeing the buffalo far ahead.

When the sun had just set, we saw all three had come to a stand in a gentle hollow. They faced us and then made off, while the ponies put on a burst that enabled us to close in with the wounded one. Within 20 feet I fired my rifle, but the darkness and violent labored motion of my pony, made me miss. I tried to get in closer, when suddenly up went the bull's tail and, wheeling, he charged with lowered horns. My pony spun round and tossed his head. My companion jumped off and took a couple of shots, missed in the dim moonlight, and to our unutterable chagrin the wounded bull vanished in the darkness. . .

As we rose over a low divide we saw several black objects, and a glance satisfied us they were buffalo. We began to stalk them, creeping forward on our hands and knees up wind. We got within less than a hundred yards of the nearest, a large cow. The rain was beating in my eyes, and the drops stood out in the sights of the rifle so that I could hardly draw a bead; and I either overshot or else at the last moment must have given a nervous jerk and pulled the rifle clear off the mark. At any rate, I missed clean, and the whole band plunged down into a hollow and were off before I could get another shot ...

While passing near the mouth of (a) ravine, both ponies threw up their heads and snuffed the air, turning their muzzles toward the head of the gully. I slipped off my pony and ran quickly but cautiously up along the valley. Before I had gone a hundred yards, I noticed in the soft soil at the bottom the round prints of a bison's hooves; and immediately afterward got a glimpse of the animal himself—a great bison bull—as he fed slowly up the ravine, not fifty yards off. As I rose above the crest of the hill, he held up his head and cocked his tail in the air. Before he could go off, I put the bullet in behind his shoulder.

The wound was an almost immediately fatal one, yet with surprising agility for so large and heavy an animal, he bounded up the opposite side of the ravine, heedless of two more balls, both of which went into his flank and ranged forward, and disappeared over the ridge at a lumbering gallop, the blood pouring from his mouth and nostrils. In the next gully we found him stark dead, lying almost on his back, having pitched over the side when he tried to go down it. He was a splendid old bull, still in his full vigor, with large, sharp horns, and heavy mane and glossy coat, and I felt the most exulting pride as I handled and examined him. . .

That evening . . . we sat before some embers raked apart, and grilled and ate our buffalo meat with the utmost relish.

—*The Works of Theodore Roosevelt*, 1923

Roosevelt said he shot his "splendid old bull" on the Little Missouri River, fifty miles south of his ranch near Medora, ND. Badlands Reflections Photography.

Wars of revenge and retaliation

Angered at the ruthless buffalo slaughter, with carcasses rotting across the plains, their livelihood rapidly disappearing and settlers encroaching on their lands, Indian tribes struck back. They attacked wagons of immigrants and buffalo hunters and raided settlements.

The fierce and bloody Plains Wars flared between 1862 and 1890, reaching their height in the ten years between 1869 and 1878, when it was said that more than 200 battles, raids and skirmishes were fought.

Following the Civil War thousands of restless people flowed onto the western plains. Hide hunters, ranchers, homesteaders, gold miners and speculators invaded Indian hunting lands on every frontier, destroyed buffalo herds and threatened Native ways of life. Railroads crisscrossed formerly remote areas, planting new towns and settlements all along their routes. Wealthy and titled noblemen from Europe and the east had long brought their entourages on safari to hunt buffalo and other wildlife in the western plains. Now more had the means to ride the rails and shoot buffalo from train windows.

Tensions ran high in Indian country. Some tribes signed

Herd of buffalo moves up a grassy sagebrush hill, snatching a few bites as they go. Badlands Reflections Photography.

treaties selling or giving away land and pledging peace in exchange for reservation living. But the promise of food rations, clothing, blankets, health care and schools, often came up short. Some were forcibly relocated into the "Indian Territory" of western Oklahoma and Nebraska. Still others resisted and fought fiercely for their culture and hunting rights.

Tragically, this violent and bloody warfare included the killing of innocents and regrettable attacks of revenge and retaliation on both sides. Amid a trail of broken treaties and short rations at the agencies, the U.S. Army sent detachments of cavalry and infantry into Indian lands to crush resistance. General Sheridan, a Civil War general, launched devastating winter campaigns beginning in 1868 as a way to find and attack elusive Indian bands in their winter camps.

Repeatedly Indian tribes sent delegations to Washington to protest the waste of their traditional food supply and plead for a stop to the wanton buffalo slaughter. Western states took up the issue of protecting buffalo, and weak bills were passed in Idaho, Wyoming, Montana and Colorado by 1872. But without enforcement the destruction went on as before.

An 1868 treaty granted good hunting grounds to the Sioux "as long as grass grows and water runs" on any lands north of the Platte River. But within five years two chiefs complained that the white settlers were denying them those hunting rights.

In Congress the buffalo slaughter was often debated and generally condemned. Determined efforts were made between 1871 and 1876 to stop non-Indian hunting and preserve the buffalo. These were peak years of slaughter of the southern herd as well as fierce Indian resistance.

In 1874, Rep. Greenburg L. Fort of Illinois introduced a bill making it illegal for any person not an Indian to kill a female buffalo in any of the territories of the U.S. and allowing no more buffalo killed than needed for food or preserving meat for market—on penalty of $100 for each buffalo unlawfully killed.

With much favorable support in Congress Fort's bill passed both the House and Senate, but President Ulysses Grant did not sign it into law, giving it a "pocket veto."

As the former Commander of the Union Army in the Civil War, Grant supported his Army generals. It was common knowledge in Washington that his chief military leaders, William T. Sherman, the new Commanding General of the Army, and Philip H. Sheridan, both Civil War generals, took a hard line on the buffalo question.

They "held the position that the only way to force the Indians to comply with military orders was to clear the plains and prairies of buffalo," according to buffalo historian David Dary. "President Grant himself privately supported his old comrades, but publicly said as little as possible on the subject."

General Sheridan was said to have testified before the Texas Legislature at a joint meeting of the Senate and House in 1875 praising buffalo hunters. Dary said he could find no official record of this meeting but that, according to the story, Sheridan told the Texas legislators that the hide hunters "have done in the last two years more to settle the vexed Indian question, than the entire regular army has done in the last thirty years. They are destroying the Indian's commissary, and it is a well-known fact that an army losing its base of supplies is placed at a great disadvantage."

Not all Army officers agreed with Sheridan. A number advised Congress the only way to assure

Two calves, their coats bright in the morning sunshine, follow their mothers along the pine trees. NPS.

peace was to honor the treaties.

Col. W.B. Hazen, stationed at Fort Hays, Kansas, wrote Congress in 1874 urging a stop to slaughter by white hide hunters. "The buffalo is a noble and harmless animal, timid and . . . valuable as food for man … The theory that the buffalo should be killed to deprive the Indians of food is a fallacy, as these people are becoming harmless under a rule of justice. I earnestly request that you bring this subject before Congress with the intention of having such steps taken as will prevent this wicked and wanton waste, both in the lives of God's creatures and of the valuable food they furnish."

An angry letter supporting legislation came from Lt. Col. A.G. Brackett of the U.S. Second Cavalry. "The wholesale butchery of buffaloes upon the plains is as needless as it is cruel. It would be equally good sport, and equally dangerous, to ride into a herd of tame cattle and butcher them indiscriminately," he wrote.

Col. E.W. Wynkoop, an officer and former Indian agent, advised Congress, "There is another strong reason, apart from cruelty which should compel Congress to take action. [The buffalo slaughter] is one of the greatest grievances the Indians have and, to my personal knowledge, frequently has been their strongest incentive to declare war."

In early 1876, Fort reintroduced his bill in the U.S. Congress with even stronger words, preserving the buffalo "for the use of the Indians, whose homes are upon the public domain, and the frontiersmen who may properly use them as food."

Fort pointed out that the large sums of money the government spent to buy cattle to feed Native Americans could be saved if Congress would preserve the buffalo herds and allow them to kill what they needed for meat.

The House again passed his bill, with a resounding "yes" vote of 104 to 36 "no's." However, it went to the Senate and stalled in committee without action. Another bill Fort introduced to tax buffalo hides disappeared in committee.

Native resistance continued until all the buffalo had vanished. Then, with their means of livelihood gone, there was little choice but to give up, band by band, and settle near the reservation agencies.

A scattering of sightings

Small bands of buffalo that escaped the final hunts survived here and there for a time. Stories persisted of small remnant herds in sheltered valleys, or an old bull living alone in the badlands. Ranch families tried to keep the survivors' existance quiet. But inevitably it seemed, their presence became too widely known and a "last buffalo hunt" brought them down.

In 1884 a Wisconsin newspaper reported a few buffalo remained on the upper Moreau River in the area south of Buffalo, Reva and Bison, S.D. It described a buffalo bull that bonded with range cattle and came in with them to the sale barn. "An old bull was recently driven into Fort Meade with a lot of domestic cattle by the cowboys. He looked as the last of the race. It is regarded as a pity that there was not a law enforced ten years ago making it a penal offense for a white man to slaughter buffalo so recklessly."

As late as October 1891, two wild buffalo—a bull and cow—came nearly into the town of Ashley, in southeastern North Dakota. A number of residents from Ashley and the surrounding area took chase with "pitchforks, whips and small-bore guns," much to the anguish of others who wanted to leave the animals unmolested.

Only the sheriff was armed for shooting big game, but he refused to fire, saying he had come out with his wife and son to see a buffalo in its natural state. It grew dark and the chase ended with both buffalo still at large. The *McIntosh County Republican* reported that this pair was probably the last remnant of the North Dakota buffalo herds.

Sporting men rode the rails and shot buffalo from the trains. Library of Congress.

Hide hunter expertly strips a hide from the carcass in northern Montana, 1878. Huffman Collection.

Causes of annihilation

Hornaday argued that the millions of buffalo could have been harvested by the U.S. government for great national benefit, instead of allowing their total destruction by wasteful white hide hunters. The buffalo were "the most economically valuable wild animal that ever inhabited the American continent." He contended that at the very least, a large herd should have been maintained to feed the Indian people living on reservations, rather than buying great quantities of beef for them.

Furthermore, he maintained, buffalo were all too easy to kill and needed protection. He gave six reasons why their destruction was so easy:

1. The destructiveness of civilization was the primary and over-all cause, the other reasons being secondary.

2. Mankind's reckless greed and improvidence in not caring for natural resources.

3. The utterly inexcusable absence of protection from government at all levels.

4. The fatal preference of hunters for killing cows over bulls.

5. Development of breech-loading rifles and other high-powered sporting firearms.

6. The phenomenal stupidity of the animals themselves and their indifference to man. (He explained this as, having lived safely in big herds without large predators, the buffalo never developed a real fear of humans).

Together these six factors acted against the buffalo with full force, Hornaday said. He left out two other reasons, although he made a case for them: the increasingly high prices paid for hides, and the permissiveness of Army generals in allowing buffalo slaughter under their noses.

Nevertheless, Hornaday regarded buffalo extinction as inevitable.

A disease theory

Some writers have refused to believe hunters could kill so many millions in such a short time. They insisted that disease was a major contributor in the extermination of the great wild buffalo herds.

Support for that notion came from R.M. Bunn, a homesteader in eastern South Dakota. He found a great many whitened bones on his claim, including "the skeletons of fifty animals of all ages under the shelter of the highest hill in the neighborhood." He could find no bullet holes in the skulls, and declared an epidemic must have been responsible.

Theodore Roosevelt soundly refuted this theory. He wrote to Bunn, "I am very sorry not to agree with your reasoning. I was an eye-witness to the extermination of the bison. They were killed by hunters—partly by the red men but chiefly by the whites. Nothing else was any real factor. Occasional great snow storms such as you describe caused local extermination during certain years. … [But] the extermination of the American Bison in the fifteen years culminating in 1883 had nothing whatever to do with climatic conditions. It was due to the number of hunters. The man with the rifle was the sole, appreciable, active factor."

However, Bunn's theory circulated widely. Maria Sandoz repeated it in a 1954 book. And as late as 1983, Rudolph Koucky, MD, a physician, published his own disease theory based on a cluster of buffalo skeletons he had found in 1926, while hunting on a former northern buffalo range.

The bones were "arranged much like a herd of cows lying on a meadow. I examined the skeletons and with my training as a pathologist, could find no suggestion the animals had been killed. They had simply laid down and died. Obviously, the entire herd had been sick." He diagnosed tick fever brought in from Texas with cattle herds as a probable cause.

But President Roosevelt was doubtless correct in demolishing the disease theory. There was no suggestion of disease from the many articulate writers and careful observers who travelled throughout the west during the last half of the 19th century. They did not mention sick buffalo. On the contrary, they praised the animal's hardiness. Further, the bones found were very old, forty to fifty years or more— and bones deteriorate greatly with a few decades of lying out in the hot sun of the plains. Also, buffalo hunters learned to aim for heart or lungs, soft targets, not the huge hard head. So no bullet holes. Lastly, bones clustered together suggest some hunter made a stand there, not that sick wild animals came together to die—which is unlikely.

The robe and hide trade

William Hornaday sought to gather statistics on the hide and robe trade in the hope of shocking Americans into realizing the value of their wildlife and how rapidly it could be destroyed forever.

At the hands of the white buffalo hunter, it was a wasteful harvest. The hide hunter took only the skins leaving the meat of thousands of carcasses to rot on the prairie. The meat hunter took only meat, sometimes only prime cuts, leaving the hides. And those trading in tongues, most wasteful of all, simply cut them out, shipped them downriver in barrels of brine, leaving the rest of the animal behind.

Hornaday pointed out that it took fifteen to twenty-five Native hunters to kill 1,000 buffalo in an annual or semi-annual hunt by running buffalo on horseback, while a single hunter with a long-range breech-loader, making a "sneak" and getting "a stand on a bunch," could kill 1,000 to 3,000 in one season alone.

To collect hide records, he contacted railroads, shippers and leading fur houses in New York City and St. Louis. The total value paid out to hide hunters, he reckoned, was at least $15 million and most likely $20 million. This added greatly to "the wealth of the people of the United States."

In the south alone, this represented the killing of all the 3.5 million buffalo reportedly ranging there in the early 1870s. Two fur houses alone purchased nearly 250,000 buffalo hides and robes over a period of eight years for one company and four years for the other. For these they paid $1.2 million "to sell again at a good profit."

By this time one fur buyer was paying $8.50 for robes and $3.50

for hides. Robes included the preferred cow skins taken in winter, to be cured with the hair on. Large robes became sleigh blankets, bedding and overcoats.

Hornaday declared a buffalo robe made an overcoat "the warmest and most cumbersome that ever enveloped a human being." Made into overshoes "with the woolly hair inside—absurdly large and uncouth, but very warm." He confessed to being torn, when he wore them, between "mortification at the ridiculous size of my foot gear, big boots inside huge overshoes—and supreme comfort derived from feet that were always warm."

Montana buyers recognized several qualities of robe according to color and texture above the ordinary: a rare "beaver robe," of exceedingly fine, wavy fur, the dark, rich color of beaver; "black-and-tan," jet black with tan markings; the very rare "buckskin robe" from a white buffalo; and the "blue robe," with a decidedly bluish cast and long, fine fur. The best were Indian cured and brought specialty prices.

The skins of bulls over age three and cows killed in summer sold as hides for leather. Demand increased rapidly when a newly discovered tanning process enabled a Pennsylvania tannery to convert the toughest hides to more useful leather. Buffalo could then be hunted year around.

Steamboats carried huge loads

A buffalo coat. Hornaday declared it "the warmest and most cumbersome that ever enveloped a human being."

of buffalo hides down the rivers. One small steamboat brought a load of 10,000 hides so large that it hid every part of the boat except for the pilot house and smokestacks when it arrived in Sioux City, Iowa, from the Yellowstone River.

In its biggest year, 1882, the Northern Pacific railway hauled 200,000 buffalo hides out of Montana and the Dakotas. The next year, it carried just 40,000 hides—the end of the harvest.

Buffalo furnished Native Americans of the plains and prairies with nearly everything needed in food, shelter and clothing. They wasted nothing in earlier times, not ruthlessly slaughtering more buffalo than needed.

Indian tribes engaged in commerce too, of course, from the time they saw their first French trader. It's what the trading posts were all about. First, fine furs—beaver and mink until they were trapped out. Then buffalo robes. Traders encouraged a brisk exchange with their tempting array of trade goods—knives, axes, guns and ammunition, calico, beads, mirrors, bells, woolen goods and blankets, sugar, flour, coffee, tobacco and liquor.

However, not until the Métis began their large communal hunts did Native Americans engage in large scale commerce. With their family connections to Hudson Bay and other fur companies, the Métis had ready markets for hides, dried meat and pemmican. About half of their buffalo harvest was kept for their own winter provisions and the other half traded and sold.

The peak year for the Hudson's Bay Company may have been 1844, when it traded for 75,000 buffalo robes in Canada. Many of these likely came from the Métis settled around Winnipeg. Other Métis hauled their hides to St Paul, which by 1850 was the headquarters for outfitting traders.

"It was no uncommon sight to see from 1,000 to 1,500 [Red River] carts. . .loaded with buffalo robes, furs of all descriptions, dressed skins, moccasins, buffalo tongues and pemmican," said Charles Larpenteur, a fur trader on the upper Missouri from 1833 to 1872.

Meat commerce

Despite the waste, it should be recognized that much buffalo beef was eaten on the spot by the hunters themselves, both Indian and white, and by the Métis families during their large, extended hunts. Some hide hunters cut off the hams and hindquarters of fat cows and sold fresh meat to towns along the railroads. Western hotels, restaurants and rooming houses regularly served tasty buffalo steak, roast and stew. In addition, railroad companies hired hunters to supply their track-laying crews, and Army forts, to feed their troops. Even the explorers Lewis and Clark designated hunters to supply their camps.

The Métis women specialized in making pemmican, a nourishing and durable food much in demand on the frontier. After a kill they brought up carts to help skin and cut up the buffalo. They sliced the

In 1878, Charles Rath sat on 40,000 buffalo hides in the hide yard of the store he owned with Robert M. Wright in Dodge City, Kansas. Wright said of Rath, "He bought and sold more than a million of buffalo hides, and tens of thousands of buffalo robes, and hundreds of cars of buffalo meat, both dried and fresh, besides several car loads of buffalo tongues."

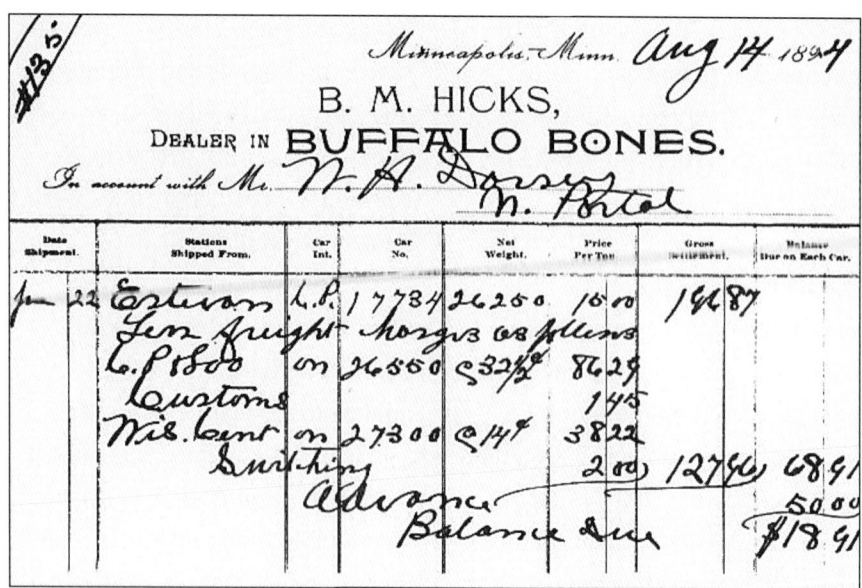

An August 1894 receipt from B. M. Hicks, Dealer in Buffalo Bones, for a shipment of buffalo bones filling three railroad cars. Saskatchewan Archives Board.

meat into thin strips and hung it on poles to dry in the sun or over a fire and rendered buffalo fat in kettles.

Then, as described by Rev. Belcourt, a Catholic priest who went along on Métis hunts, the dried meat was placed on a buffalo hide and pounded into small particles and the melted fat or tallow poured onto it.

"The whole mass is worked together with shovels until well amalgamated, when it is pressed, while still warm, into bags made of buffalo skin, which are strongly sewed up, and the mixture gradually cools and becomes almost as hard as a rock. If the fat used is taken from the parts containing the udder, the meat is called fine pemmican.

In some cases, dried fruits, such as the prairie pear and [chokecherry] are intermixed, which forms what is called seed pemmican. The lovers of good eating judge the first described to be very palatable; the second, better; the third, excellent." Each bag weighed 100 to 110 pounds, he said. It required one whole

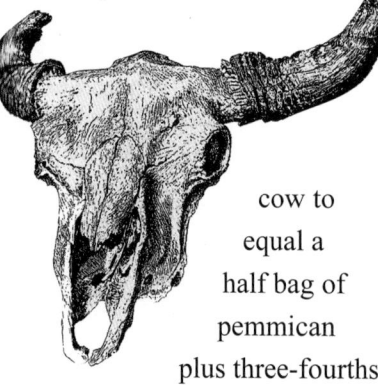

cow to equal a half bag of pemmican plus three-fourths of a bundle of dried meat. Eight to ten buffalo cows filled one cart.

The jerked meat, or jerky, they cut into long strips about a quarter of an inch thick and hung on a trellis to dry. When dry they bent it into lengths and tied bundles of 60 and 70 pounds each.

The men broke the bones, and boiled them in water to extract the marrow used for frying. The oil was poured into bladders, weighing about twelve pounds, the yield of the marrow-bones of two buffalo. The demand for all this in the fur trade was generally greater than the supply, reported Belcourt.

Bone pickers

Even after the buffalo were gone, they played a role in settlement. Hide hunters turned to bone picking, and many homesteaders sold a wagon load of buffalo bones as their first crop.

Stacks of bones lined the railroad tracks. Again, ships played their part, leaving from Texas ports laden with bones. On the northern plains bones were shipped down the Yellowstone and Missouri rivers on boats to the railhead at Bismarck, where they were loaded on railroad cars and shipped to eastern markets.

One traveler going west on the Canadian Pacific in 1888 said he and a friend at first began to see white bones sprinkled across the grasslands.

"Soon we met great trains—each of many box cars—laden with nothing but these weather-whitened relics. Presently we came to stations where, beside the tracks, mounds of these bones were heaped up and rude men were swelling the heaps with wagon loads gathered far from the railroads. A great business had grown up in collecting these trophies."

The bone trade was lucrative, but short-lived. Refineries paid $2.50 to $3 a ton for bones and later up to $18 and even $27 as they grew scarce. Based on an average price of $8 per ton they brought $2.5 million into Kansas alone between 1868 and 1881.

One St. Louis firm was estimated to have paid out more than $28 million for buffalo bones. Hoofs and horns brought $12 to $15 a ton. It took about 100 buffalo skeletons to make a ton of bones, according to estimates. Bones were refined for sugar and explosives, fertilizer and fine bone china. Horns and hooves were fashioned into buttons, combs and knife handles and used to make glue.

The *Topeka Mail and Breeze* in Kansas claimed that the quantity of buffalo carcasses involved in the bone trade "would make a string of boxcars 7,575 miles long—enough to fill two tracks from New York to San Francisco."

Twenty-five years after the last great buffalo hunts, bones still lay heavy on the land his father homesteaded northeast of Reeder, ND, near the headwaters of Hiddenwood Creek, says Harold Hanson, who farmed the land for many years.

"The buffalo bones were so thick on that south quarter, that my father could not break the land without first picking up bones. He stacked the bones in big piles in the field, like rock piles."

When the buffalo vanished, hide hunters turned to bone picking and many homesteaders sold buffalo bones as their first crop.

A pile of bison skulls in 1880 towers more than fifty feet in the air above a worker at the Michigan Carbon Works in Detroit where the bones were to be processed for industrial use. *Buffalo Nation* by Valerius Geist.

In Moose Jaw, Saskatchewan, a pile of bison bones await shipment to munition plants during World War II to make gunpowder and explosives.

The bones stayed piled there until World War I when they were hauled into Bucyrus, sold and shipped by train to munitions factories.

Buffalo chips

One last gift of the buffalo still dotted the western plains.

When trees were scarce, Native Americans burned buffalo chips. Pioneers saw the value and burned them too for a quick, hot fire with little smoke. The chips were conveniently-sized, about a foot in diameter and two or three inches thick. But for some eastern-bred women it was difficult to adapt to bringing dried manure patties into the kitchen for cooking a meal over that flame.

A Dakota cowboy told the story of one day meeting a homestead woman out on the prairie. She was collecting buffalo chips, holding each one out in front of her with two sticks as she dropped it into her wooden wheelbarrow. He stopped to chat a bit.

"Newcomer," he chuckled to himself as he rode on.

A year later he rode that range and saw the same woman. This time she handled the buffalo chips with expertise. Gripping her scooped apron with one hand, she loaded in chips with the other, tucking a last chip under her chin.

In another community the new teacher asked her school board parent for some kindling to start the fire. Looking embarrassed, he said he'd already delivered it against the woodshed. She went back and looked, but saw no wood. Puzzled, she walked once more around the woodshed.

"What was that pile of dried manure?" The light dawned. Gingerly she put a dried buffalo chip into her stove and found it burned well.

Buffalo chips—one last gift from the buffalo—burned with a quick, hot fire for fuel where trees were scarce.

Old bulls often spend time alone, grazing at some distance from the herd, or off in tandem with another old bull. This bull's horns bear the scars of past battles. Badlands Reflections Photography.

Part II. Tradition and Lore

5

The Magnificent Buffalo

The magnificent dark brown frontlet and beard of the bison,
the shaggy coat of hair upon the neck, hump, and shoulders,
the dense coat of finer fur on the hindquarters,
Give the bison a grandeur and nobility of presence
which are beyond all comparison amongst ruminants.
— William T. Hornaday
The Extermination of the American Bison 1889

The buffalo with his great size and stature, confrontational eye, beautifully-shaped black horns and semi-tragic history, has long captured the imagination of people everywhere.

William Hornaday, in his exhaustive 19th century Smithsonian study of the species, compared the American buffalo to other large cud-chewing ruminants throughout the world. Some, such as the tall gaur of India, may be larger, he said, yet none presents as striking an appearance or is as impressive as the male buffalo.

He speculated on which aspect was most commanding of the large bull he shot for the Smithsonian exhibit, "the massive, magnificent head, with its shaggy frontlet and luxuriant black beard, or the lofty hump, with its showy covering of straw-yellow hair in thickly-growing locks four inches long." The magnificent head, he decided, was the bull's most outstanding feature.

"The hair on the top of the head lies in a dense, matted mass, forming a perfect crown of rich brown (burnt sienna) locks, sixteen inches in length, hanging over the eyes, almost enveloping both horns, and spreading back in rich, dark masses upon the light-colored neck and shoulders. On the cheeks the hair is of the same blackish brown color, but comparatively short, and lies in beautiful waves. On the bridge of the nose the hair is about six inches in length and stands out in a thick, uniform, very curly mass, which always looks as if it had just been carefully combed.

"Immediately around the nose and mouth the hair is very short, straight and stiff, and lies close to the skin, which leaves the nostrils and lips fully exposed. The hair of the chin-beard is coarse, perfectly straight, jet black, and 11½ inches in length on our old bull. The end of the muzzle is very massive, measuring two-feet-two inches in circumference just back of the nostrils."

Both bull and cow are intimidating figures, Hornaday wrote, but the bull is larger and his gaze more challenging. He is tall and massive, strangely narrow in profile, with shoulders broader than hips—all this accented by the large shoulder hump. His hair hangs long and heavy over the front quarters, a "thick mass of

Bull and cow. Their horns turn upward in matched curves; her horns are slimmer than his, especially at the base. Badlands Reflections Photography.

Tribal herd grazes through a prairie dog town across a green valley in the Porcupine Breaks near Ft. Yates, ND. Courtesy LaDonna Allard.

Rock Sioux Tribal herd refers to a distinctly dark herd of thirty or so in one area of the north buffalo pasture.

On the chaps, color shades gradually from the shoulder down into a dark brown, then black at the knee. The upper front legs are lost in a thick mass of long, coarse, straight hair nearly a foot long. This growth stops at the knee, but hangs down to within six inches of the hoof.

luxuriant black locks," with even longer hair over forehead, beard, mane and chaps of the forelegs, but short and sleek over the rear and tail.

Hornaday summed it up by declaring the buffalo bull has "a grandeur and nobility of presence which are beyond all comparison amongst ruminants." Indeed, he is "the grandest of them all."

Author Tom McHugh marks their dimensions in his book *The Time of the Buffalo*:

"A full-grown male Plains Buffalo weighs between 1,400 and 2,200 pounds, stands between 5 and 6½ feet high at the shoulder and measures from 9½ to 11½ feet in total length including tail. The horns may be as much as three feet apart at their widest spread.

"The cow is smaller, weighing from 750 to 1,100 pounds, standing 4½ to 5½ feet in shoulder height and measuring less than 10 feet in length. Less shaggy on head and chin, she has a smaller hump." He rates the buffalo bull—largest land mammal in the New World—as "half a ton more than his closest rivals, the moose and the big Kodiak bears."

Color varies through and between buffalo herds, from rich burnt-sienna brown to nearly black.

"The last buffalo we got from Theodore Roosevelt Park are very dark—almost black, They like to stay together." Mike Faith, tribal chairman and former manager of the Standing

Young bull's spike horns show his age as around two years old. Badlands Reflections Photography.

Seasonal differences appear too. The buffalo that in winter sports a dark brown coat with a bronze glow lighting the woolly hair across his shoulders and hump has, by spring, become faded and bleached, even rusty, the cape a dull golden flap ready to be flung aside.

New growth of hair on the beard and front reaches amazing lengths. From Hornaday's own hunt he reported:

"I have in my possession a tuft of hair . . . which measures 22½ inches in length, from the frontlet of a rather small bull bison. The beard on [this] specimen was correspondingly long, and the entire pelage was of wonderful length and density."

Newborn buffalo calves glow red-gold with a thick growth of long woolly hair, which soon darkens, especially on the crown of their heads. They are born without a hump—but that doesn't take long either. By three months the hump emerges and so do inch-long stubs of horns. Calves shed their baby coat after three or four months, to be replaced by a growth of fine, new, dark hair. The first signs of change appear about a month earlier, in the darkening of the mane under the throat and the top of the neck. By October the transformation is complete, and not even a patch of the old red hair streaks the new suit of brown. As yearlings, their horns grow into straight, conical spikes, four to six inches long and perfectly black.

Bulls and cows both have stout black curved horns with a relatively sharp tip, the female horns being more slender. Horns grow larger each year on bony cores and are not shed.

Their black cloven hooves leave rounded hoof prints. Like other ruminants such as cattle, sheep and deer, buffalo have multiple stomachs. They chew their cud and thus, do not have top front teeth.

Both hearing and smell are acute. Buffalo can pick up weak and distant sounds, as well as strange odors on a stray breeze.

Eyes are positioned on opposite sides of the buffalo's head. This makes it difficult for them to see and focus ahead without turning. Many have concluded that buffalo have poor eyesight. However, Steven Rinella, who studied all aspects of buffalo alertness in

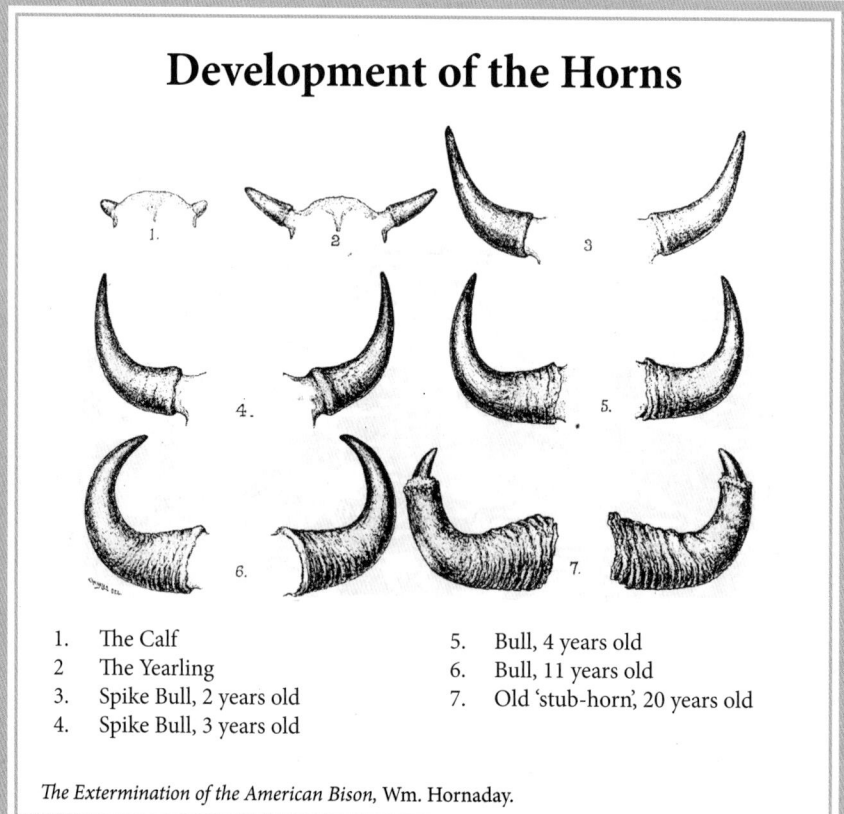

Development of the Horns

1. The Calf
2. The Yearling
3. Spike Bull, 2 years old
4. Spike Bull, 3 years old
5. Bull, 4 years old
6. Bull, 11 years old
7. Old 'stub-horn', 20 years old

The Extermination of the American Bison, Wm. Hornaday.

With fresh cord still clinging to his navel, a newborn calf finds the mother's nourishment he needs. Badlands Reflections Photography.

preparation for his lonely Alaskan buffalo hunt, after his tag was drawn in lottery, says this eye location allows for panoramic vision.

"A buffalo can see almost ninety percent of its surroundings without turning its head. If he catches sight of any movement in this wide range to the sides and rear, such as lurking wolves or hunters, he keeps watch on it—while at the same time relying on his excellent smell and sound to identify possible threats." This compares with less than a fifty percent range of view for humans, he writes in *American Buffalo: In search of a lost icon*.

Rinella explains that in contrast, the eyes of predators such as wolves and mountain lions (and humans) are located in front for narrow focused vision. This gives them great depth perception that allows them to strike targets quickly and effectively, but lacks the watchful panoramic view of the buffalo.

Natural vigor and stamina

Buffalo are known for their great natural vigor, stamina and strength.

A freak blizzard in October 2013 killed tens of thousands of cattle in western South Dakota, as well as sheep and horses, when four feet of heavy wet snow with powerful winds drove them over banks, into creeks and waterholes and piled up against fences in deep snowdrifts. Some ranchers lost fifty to seventy-five percent of their livestock and faced financial ruin. Following that deadly storm, the National Bison Association checked with local buffalo breeders; none reported buffalo loss.

In another deadly storm the winter of 1997-1998, with heavy financial losses to livestock, the toll was apparently only one buf-

When snow lies deep on the prairie, buffalo swing their heads back and forth, clear a place of snow, and find nourishment in the grass below. NPS.

falo death. He was run off an icy bridge by an eighteen-wheeler.

The worst blizzard in North Dakota history was March 2nd to the 5th in 1966, taking the lives of 19,000 cattle. Nationwide, 175,000 cattle died.

His whole herd went hungry during that storm, said one Kidder County cattle rancher. "You couldn't do anything, you couldn't see nothing."

When finally able to get to his Herefords, they were in tough shape. "All the cattle had ice and snow on their eyes and they couldn't see," he said.

That blizzard prompted a South Dakota rancher who raised both cattle and buffalo to totally convert his herd to the species that survived the blizzard unscathed, according to author Douglas Ramsey in *One to Remember: The Relentless Blizzard of March 1966.*

A record 15.5 inches of snow fell in Bismarck on the second day, and 35 inches piled up during the epic event, with relentless winds of 70 to 80 mph. Snow drifts measured at least six feet deep in downtown Dickinson, and in some areas topped thirty feet, choking roads all across the state. A Northern Pacific passenger train carrying 500 people was stopped and buried

With heads almost buried in snow, buffalo find grass or browse and thrive even in deep-snow winters while other animals starve. NPS.

by the storm near New Salem.

"The buffalo, being native to the plains, form a 'V' shape with the bulls facing into the wind and the cows and calves inside. During the blizzard they moved three times. They move till the snow gets too deep, then they move again," said Ramsey.

Those who raise buffalo testify to their hardy endurance in cold weather. The animals have dense hair growth, so dense—coarse guard hairs with soft wool underneath—that every square inch has ten times as many hairs growing from it as does an inch of cow hide, reports Dale F. Lott, University of California Wildlife, Fish and Conservation biologist. In extreme cold when fat stores are low, he says this means "the difference between life and death."

Buffalo face into the harsh blizzards that sometimes hit the northern plains, protected by their massive heads and shoulders. With forequarters well insulated by their heaviest hair growth, they stand or move slowly into the wind until the storm blows over. Unfortunately, cattle and sheep do just the opposite—a sometimes deadly choice—turning their backs to a fierce blizzard. They drift with the wind into water holes and rivers or over high banks, where they may drown or die in pileups.

When snow lies on the prairie, buffalo plow down to find grass.

Their humps contain muscles supported by vertebrae that allow them to swing their massive, low-hanging heads side to side, sweeping away snow to reach plants and grass. When water is frozen, they eat snow.

Ernest Thompson Seton declared their hardiness during the hard winter of 1885-86. Reporting on a Manitoba herd in Canada, he wrote, "These Buffalo receive no care beyond what is necessary to prevent their wandering away... They live on the open prairie summer and winter, subsisting on the wild grass, even when they have to dig for it through one or more feet of snow. Nor is it a bare existence that they so maintain. For when I saw them late in January, they were finding grass enough not merely to feed, but to fatten them. When a blizzard comes on, they lie down close together with their backs to the wind and allow the snow to drift over them, so that under the combined protection of the snow and their own woolly coats they are perfectly comfortable.

"In January 1884 one of the cows calved on the open prairie and though at the time the thermometer registered 38 degrees below zero, neither cow nor calf appeared to suffer the slightest inconvenience."

"Buffalo face the storm and lower their heart rates and metabolism so their strength is maintained," notes Mike Faith. He says Native people see this hardiness as an affirmation of their own ability to survive adversity.

Even rattlesnake bites don't seem to bother buffalo much. If bitten, they may swell a little at the site—but are not affected as cattle can be, say buffalo ranchers.

Amazing agility

Along with the buffalos' great size, strength and stamina, they show an amazing agility and speed. They can bound six feet straight up when cornered. In a standing long jump they can clear fourteen feet, according to Rinella.

In the days of wild buffalo, it was often remarked that although they seemed docile and even sluggish, chewing their cuds, they could come alert in an instant, "spin on a dime" and gallop headlong over country impossible for a horse to follow. Known as extremely nimble in the rugged badlands of the Plains, buffalo scrambled quickly up steep banks and plunged down precipices. When alarmed they threw themselves down nearly vertical canyons and leaped up the opposite wall with the agility of wild goats. Yet, such is their strength and resilience, that

In fierce blizzards bulls form a "V" shape around the herd, facing into the wind, with cows and calves protected inside. NPS.

rarely were they seriously injured by tumbles which would kill any other animal.

When Theodore Roosevelt came west to hunt in September 1883 he discovered this for himself—though he nearly missed finding buffalo altogether. His local guide found a couple of lone bulls and a few distant stragglers just outside Standing Rock reservation boundaries. All were extremely wild.

Of the first bull Roosevelt wrote, "As we passed the mouth of a little side coulee, there was a plunge and crackle through the bushes, and a shabby-looking old bull bison galloped out and without an instant's hesitation plunged over a steep bank into a patch of broken ground. So quickly did he disappear that we had not time to dismount and fire. Spurring our horses we galloped up to the brink of the cliff down which he had plunged. It was remarkable that he should have gone down it unhurt.

If buffalo had shown this same wariness during the 1870s as these few survivors did, Hornaday wrote, regretfully, "There would now be 100,000 head alive instead of only about 300 in a wild and unprotected state."

A herd of buffalo may appear docile and sluggish, but when alarmed they can come alert in a panic and plunge down precipices and up steep banks. NPS.

Their ability to recover fully from life-threatening injuries amazed his party.

Nearly every bull his crew shot on their last hunt for Smithsonian specimens carried old bullets in their bodies. The largest bull held four bullets of various sizes fired at different times. Amazingly, several had healed from previously broken legs.

Still, even in their chosen habitat and despite their natural hardiness, hazards lay in wait, especially for the very young and very old. Winter starvation took its toll, as did disease and parasites. Packs of wolves killed lone bulls and often devastated the calf crop. Many buffalo drowned while crossing rivers when the ice was breaking up. In the summer of 1867, over 2,000 buffalo out of a herd of some 4,000 lost their lives in the quicksand of the Platte River while attempting to cross, said Hornaday.

Ice Ages

Scientists say the first buffalo arrived in North America from Asia, crossing on the Bering Land Bridge in Alaska, which at that time was a wide strip of land perhaps hundreds of miles wide. A glacial age had lowered the seas by freezing more ice in the north.

This occurred between 43,000 and 9,000 years ago, a period known as Rancholabrean (named for fossils found in the Los Angeles La Brea tar pits), according to Llewellyn Manske, PhD, Research Professor of Range Science, NDSU Research Extension Center in Dickinson, North Dakota. Recent evidence suggests there may have been an earlier wave of bison that came 195,000 to 135,000 years ago and then died out, according to research by Earth and Atmospheric Sciences Professor Duane Froese of the University of Alberta, Canada, and colleagues, reported by the 2017 National Academy of Sciences.

During the Rancholabrean period several large species of bison and other mammals made multiple crossings back and forth—mammoths, mastodons, the wooly rhinoceros, and beavers large as black bears. They joined a parade of horses and camels, native to America. Preying on them were large, savage meat-eaters—saber-toothed cats, short-faced bears, cheetahs, lions and dire wolves, says Manske.

Most of these huge mammals vanished around 9,000 years ago—a mass extinction that is still a mystery of debate. Fortunately, the horse—much beloved of buffalo hunters—found a new home in Eurasia before dying out in America. Horses returned later with Columbus and the Spanish Conquistadors.

The giant *Bison latifrons* stood much taller than modern buffalo, weighed one-third more and grew horns with a ten-foot spread. Geared for running, they must have faced severe pressure from predators. Other buffalo species came, too. But only one survived and likely crossed with similar types to become the smaller *Bison antiques* that was hunted by early Clovis Indians near the end of the Rancholabrean period. From this developed our even smaller modern buffalo.

With less competition for food and fewer predators, the buffalo dispersed throughout central North America and multiplied into great herds, writes Valerius Geist, zoology professor at the University of Calgary in Alberta and author of *Buffalo Nation*.

Plains buffalo vs wood buffalo

Modern American buffalo developed into two subspecies well suited to their respective environments—the prolific plains buffalo of the open country and the shy wood buffalo of the forests. Under scientific classification, the American plains buffalo is listed as genus *Bison*, species *Bison bison,* and subspecies *Bison bison bison.* The wood buffalo is *Bison bison athabascae.*

The abundant plains buffalo lived in great herds throughout the open grasslands and spilled into the forest fringes of North America, while the less prolific wood buffalo lived in forests and mountains and ranged farther into northern Canada and Alaska.

Differences between the two subspecies show up in bone structure and *pelage,* or pelts and hair cover. Plains buffalo have more rounded humps compared with the wood buffalo, which have higher, often sharply-angled humps located farther forward. The plains buffalo have more predominant hair character—large chaps, a full beard and neck mane and a clearly-defined cape, while wood buffalo have no chaps, sport only a thin pointy beard and skimpy neck mane. Their less-defined cape blends smoothly back to the loins. Wood buffalo also tend to be a darker color.

Statistics from Canadian public herds show differences in weight and size as well, with the wood buffalo generally larger and heavier. Parks Canada has maintained a database of their buffalo since 1956, including weights. In all those years only one plains bull weighed more than 2,000 pounds (one ton), while over one-third of the wood buffalo bulls weighed a ton or more.

Interestingly, early scientists of the 19th century marked these differences and gave the two subspecies their scientific names. Then came a time of debate. Many argued the differences were not genetic, but simply a function of the environment where they live.

However, a large-scale study in the early 1990s analyzed Canadian data and found the two subspecies maintain their respective traits regardless of where they live and what they eat. More recent research at the University of Alberta reveals genetic differences, thus proving the early scientists correct.

Crossbreeding

Some early buffalo breeders experimented with crossing buffalo and cattle, hoping to improve the hardiness of cattle and increase beef production for buffalo. This was generally considered unsuccessful. The offspring—called "cattalo" and later, "beefalo"—were highly infertile and generally performed poorly. The experiment failed to improve quality for either buffalo or domestic cattle, failed to show hybrid vigor and were soon

The first buffalo apparently crossed the Bering Land Bridge from Asia between 43,000 and 9,000 years ago. Several species crossed back and forth with other large mamals. The longhorn *Bison priscus* (at left) was found preserved in Alaskan permafrost; the giant *Bison latifrons* (center) lived here for some 300,000 years then died out; today's much smaller *Bison bison* (right) appeared after the Ice Age. Drawing by Valerius Geist.

Plains buffalo versus wood buffalo

The differences between plains and wood bison can be separated into pelage and structural characteristics. Plains bison tend to have hair characters which are larger and more obvious. Whereas plains bison have large chaps, a full beard and neck mane and a well-demarcated cape, wood bison have no chaps, a thin pointy beard, a rudimentary neck mane and a cape that grades smoothly back to the loins. Structurally the highest point of the hump on a plains bison is directly over the front legs while in wood bison it is well forward of the front legs. The wood bison is also considerably larger. Parks Canada maintains a bison weight database going back to 1956 and during all that time there is only one record of a plains bison bull weighing more than 2000 pounds (one ton, or 909 kg) while over one-third of the wood bison bulls exceed this weight.

There has been some discussion as to whether the subspecies are simply ecotypes—that if a wood bison was placed in plains bison habitat, or vice versa, it would assume the traits of the host bison, simply due to the environmental pressures. Recent research at the University of Alberta has conclusively proven a genetic difference between the two subspecies.

Plains bison bull. © Parks Canada

PLAINS BISON

- Highest point of hump is directly over the front legs
- Large thick chaps on front legs
- Thick pendulous beard
- Full neck mane extends below the chest
- Sharply demarcated cape line behind the shoulder
- Thick bonnet of hair between the horns
- Cape usually lighter in color
- About one-third smaller than a wood bison

Wood bison bull. © Parks Canada

WOOD BISON

- Highest point of hump well forward of front legs
- Virtually no chaps on front legs
- A thin scraggly beard
- Neck mane short, does not extend much below chest
- Cape grades smoothly back towards the loins with little if any demarcation
- Forelock lies forward in long strands over forehead
- Hair usually darker, especially on head

Used with permission from Parks Canada

dropped. At other times, when running with cattle, buffalo have accidentally produced cross-bred calves.

In the process some cattle genetics were introduced into some buffalo. Although it is slight, today this is considered unfortunate. Research at Texas A&M University tested DNA on more than 30,000 buffalo in both private and public herds across North America and found that a very small number, about six percent, showed evidence of cattle DNA. That level averaged less than 1.5 percent of their genetic make-up.

It isn't much, but many buffalo ranchers and tribal herd managers are testing their herds and culling any animals with remnants of cattle genetics. The code of ethics adopted by the National Bison Association prohibits members from intentionally crossbreeding. Most breeders today are dedicated to protecting the integrity of the species. They are concerned with maintaining historic buffalo traits that produce nutritious meat, help buffalo survive harsh weather and require little management.

Huge herds

Wild buffalo herds could be huge, especially during breeding season when the herds came together. Early explorers tried to estimate how many buffalo they viewed at one time when the hills grew black with grazing animals as far as they could see.

During their journey Captains Lewis and Clark described their astonishment at the huge buffalo herds seen through the Dakotas and west to the Rocky Mountains. On their return in August 1806, they saw a vast herd near South Dakota's White River "more than we had ever seen before at one time . . . we are convinced that 20,000 would be no exaggerated number."

A North Dakota railroad surveyor stood on a high point from which he reported, "For a great distance ahead every square mile seemed to have a herd of buffalo upon it. Their number was variously estimated by members of the party, some as high as half a million. I do not think it any exaggeration to set it down at 200,000."

On viewing a large herd of cattle one day, Canadian John McDougall was startled to learn there were 23,000 head in the herd. He said that cattle herd in a single valley appeared to be far smaller than the many immense buffalo herds he had seen spread out over a dozen hills and plateaus in the plains. Comparing them to that smaller cattle herd, he concluded, "Many times from hills and range summits, I had seen more than half a million buffalo at one time."

One traveler, Thomas J. Farnham, crossed Kansas for three days on the Santa Fe Trail in 1839, driving a team all the way through what appeared to be one large migrating herd. He wrote, "We travelled at the rate of 15 miles a day—15 times three equals 45. Take 45 times 30 [miles across] and you get 1,350 square miles . . . so thickly covered with these noble animals, that when viewed from a height it scarce afforded a sight of a square league of its surface."

Colonel Dodge reported he drove twenty-five miles through a herd migrating north along the Arkansas River. He estimated it was at least two miles wide, averaging fifteen to twenty buffalo per acre. Hornaday concluded Dodge had seen 480,000 buffalo. When he added those Dodge saw earlier that day from the top of Pawnee Rock, the day's total reached 500,000—half a million.

Hornaday speculates that if Dodge's herd had been fifty miles long by twenty-five miles wide

Wild buffalo gathered in huge herds during breeding season and migrations. One North Dakota surveyor climbed a high point and estimated he saw 200,000 head; another traveler estimated he had seen 500,000 buffalo in one day's travel. SD Game, Fish & Parks.

"as it was known to have been in some places," it would have contained 12 million head. Deducting two-thirds of this—in figuring a probable wedge shape in the front of the herd—he came up with over four million in the herd, "Which I believe is more likely below the truth than above it."

Thirty million buffalo

Many have asked the question: How many buffalo were here when the first Europeans arrived?

With the huge herd totals found in single herds, it was formerly believed that 60 million or even 75 million buffalo grazed North American grasslands. But that's too many, say today's wildlife and range experts. More than double a reasonable total.

Those large numbers were based on information put together for his 1909 book *Life Histories of Northern Animals* by Seton. The famed naturalist multiplied the estimated square miles of buffalo range by their carrying capacity to come up with those figures. However, he estimated the heavily-used buffalo range at about three million square miles. This is more than double today's figures, which are based on 1.5 million square miles of plains, 0.5 million of prairie and 1.0 million of forests.

The California scientist, Professor Dale F. Lott, who grew up on the National Bison Refuge in Montana, objected in his 2002 book *American Bison: A Natural History*. He charged that Seton drew a line around every reported location of bison in North America including most of the Rocky Mountains and all of Idaho, where bison were rare to nonexistent. Lott said Seton then calculated the entire region at close to full carrying capacity, even though buffalo were likely rare on the broad fringes of that range.

In fact, the known buffalo ranges did not contain three million square miles, reports Llewellyn Manske; they contained only about 1.2 million square miles. This includes an area from the foot of the Rocky Mountains to the Appalachian Mountains and from southern Texas to the Canadian Shield in Manitoba, Saskatchewan and Alberta—all of the tall grass, mixed grass and short grass prairies and parts of the eastern deciduous forest and aspen parkland, for a total of 575,000 square miles in the Great Plains and 650,000 in the Central Lowlands.

Manske also says a more conservative estimate in stocking rate than Seton's would allow about 24 acres per animal (26.7 bison to the square mile of 640 acres). This brings the estimated peak population closer to 30 million, plus about 4 million additional animal unit equivalents allowed for elk, deer and pronghorn antelope living there. It sets a more realistic upper limit of what was likely possible.

Naturally, it's impossible to accurately estimate the buffalo numbers in pre-history. With many unknown variables, no techniques can be completely precise. Since it is all speculation, experts say it shouldn't really matter. However, Lott suggests the larger number has made "a better story" in the environmental narrative blaming humans for the destruction of their natural resources.

"Everywhere you look you get the same story: 60 million bison in primitive North America and as few as a thousand twenty years after the end of the Civil War. . . Our faith in its reality is an important part of our view of our environmental and social history and has been used to quantify our ancestors' stewardship of the land they colonized."

Lott concludes, "About all we can confidently say is that primitive America's bison population was probably less than thirty million—perhaps on average three to six million less."

Scientists today believe the buffalo ranges contained about 1.2 million square miles, east from the foot of the Rocky Mountains to the Appalachian Mountains, and north from southern Texas to the Canadian Shield in Manitoba, Saskatchewan and Alberta. Allowing about 24 acres per animal this brings the estimated peak population at the time of European contact to around 30 million. Badlands Reflections Photography.

6

Noble Fathers

Bison social behavior is too marvelous a tale to go untold . . .
The most complex relationships play out during
the intense though brief breeding season.
Attraction, rejection, acceptance, competition and
cooperation create vital, compelling, generally
short-lived and shifting relationships.
The simpler, more durable but equally important relationships
cows develop with one another. . . the social
relationships of calves, especially with their mother.
—Dale F. Lott
American Bison: A Natural History 2002

In the wild, buffalo bulls often displayed a strong sense of responsibility for protecting the herd. *The noble fathers*, they've been called.

In deadly storms, it was said, the big bulls formed a triangle and stood with heads into the wind, shielding cows and calves from the storm. When threatened by wolves or hunters the herd set up a strong defense, coming together in a tight group with bulls on the outside.

Native hunters knew they needed to get past the bulls to shoot the

Buffalo bulls felt a strong sense of responsibility for protecting the herd. They've been called "noble fathers" for protecting small calves from the ravages of wolves. In fierce storms, too, they shielded cows and calves from the wintery blasts. Badlands Reflections Photography.

A magnificent monarch of the plains stretches forth to survey his kingdom, and perhaps, his competition. Badlands Reflections Photography.

more tender cows and younger animals they preferred. A white man who joined the annual Miami hunt of 400 Native hunters in Kansas in August 1854 explained how the Miami reached the animals they wanted.

"They shoot down several bulls. As a gap in the line is thus made, they dash their ponies through the breach, conforming speed and direction to that of the herd. Gradually working toward the center, they find the cows, calves and two-year-olds, thus securing the finest robes and choicest meats. When their revolvers are empty, for only revolvers and bows and arrows can safely be used in this mode of killing, they gradually worm their way out of the herd in the same manner as they entered."

A novice buffalo hunter, Charles B Matthews, explained in a letter to the *New York Times* why he, his wife and friends did not shoot the younger,

---

* It was this writer's privilege to watch the bulls' protective nature displayed one morning when we rode horseback in the North Unit of Theodore Roosevelt Park with family and friends. We came over a hill to see grazing below a scattered herd of some sixty buffalo. Alarmed by the sudden appearance of fifteen riders coming over the hill, the buffalo snorted and ran. But they didn't run far. As we paused to watch, they bunched up and took a tight defensive position in the broad valley below. The bulls circled to the outside, facing us with their massive heads. They pawed up chunks of dirt and roared a challenge. Cows and calves moved to the inside. We were fascinated that after more than a century of living inside park boundaries, safe from hunters and wolves, today's 'noble fathers' still protected the cows and the calves and advanced head on to face our supposed threat. No hungry wolves would have feasted on tender calves that day! Their challenge was exactly as described by Col. Dodge in the 1870s. He said, "The bulls with heads erect, tails cocked in air, nostrils expanded and eyes that seem to flash fire, walk uneasily to and fro, menacing the intruder by pawing the earth and tossing their huge heads."

more tender buffalo. "I think we killed none but males, as they take the outside of the herd. You do not see the cows and calves until you get pretty well into the herd."

Buffalo in the wild were regularly preyed upon by packs of wolves. Captains Lewis and Clark wrote in their journals of the large buffalo herds and "their shepherds, the wolves."

Healthy, mature buffalo were rarely killed by wolves and they typically ignored wolves not displaying hunting behavior. But a lone bull, especially when old, injured or sick, often fell victim. So did young calves struggling to keep up, although old bulls many times ran to the rescue and chased the wolves away, as reported by Lt. Col. Richard I. Dodge, an Army officer stationed at Ft. Dodge in Kansas. He had often seen evidence of this protective nature of the bulls, he said.*

Dodge told of a "most remarkable instance related to me by an army surgeon." The surgeon was returning to camp one evening after a day's hunt, when he saw a curious knot of six or eight buffalo bulls acting strangely. A dozen large gray wolves danced about them, keeping just out of range and "licking their chops in impatient expectancy." Riding closer he saw the reason the wolves dared not attack was because all the bulls faced out from a tight circle,

When a pack of wolves found an old bull too weak to defend himself they closed in. They slashed at legs and throat as they darted in and out, wary of the vicious thrusts of massive head and horns. Note the buffalo's tail in the air denoting extreme stress. *Buffalo Nation*, V Geist.

shaking their massive heads and horns fiercely.

After a few moments the little knot of bulls started off for the main herd, a half mile away, still keeping close together.

Then to his very great astonishment, the Army surgeon saw what was being protected inside the circle—a newborn calf, scarcely able to walk. After tottering fifty steps or so the calf fell down. Immediately, the bulls stopped and again formed a protective circle around it, while the wolves sat down and licked their chops. He watched as the drama repeated itself again and again before riding off.

He told Dodge he had no doubt that "The noble fathers did their whole duty by their offspring and carried it safely to the herd."

In another rescue, George Bird Grinnell reported that a Blackfoot Indian told him of watching a bull charge a grizzly bear that had attacked a heifer. The grizzly was lying hidden by a trail near a creek, waiting for a small bunch of buffalo to come down to water. Led by a young heifer, they came in single file. When the heifer passed under the clay shelf where the grizzly hid, he reached down with both paws, caught her around the neck and leaped upon her. She struggled to escape as the others ran off.

Suddenly a "splendid young buffalo bull" came rushing down the trail and charged the bear, knocking him down. They fought fiercely. The bear tried to catch and hold the bull by the head or shoulders, but could not. The bull slashed viciously with his horns. When the grizzly had enough he tried to escape, but the bull would not let him go. He kept up the attack until he killed the bear, and even then continued to gore and toss the carcass off the ground. He seemed insane with rage and the Blackfoot hunter was much afraid he'd be discovered and attacked too. He felt greatly relieved when the bull finally left the carcass and went off to join his band.

Ernest Thompson Seton writes that a cow when calving will fight off one or two wolves, but if more, she calls for help. "Her loud angry snort will quickly bring the bulls to her aid."

Thus it seems that buffalo fathers and uncles are ready to do their duty in protecting the young, said Seton. When the herd lies down at night, they may be scattered, but the appearance of a wolf is enough to bring them together "the bulls, as a matter of course, now taking the outside."

Living in maternal herds

Buffalo are social animals. They like grazing along together in herds, most often in relatively small herds of less than a hundred, often within sight of a loose larger herd.

In most seasons the cows and bulls sort themselves into separate male and female groups.

Early explorers mentioned their amazement at these groupings. A Spanish explorer travelling with Francisco Vásquez de Coronado in Mexico, wrote of the buffalo they encountered in Texas in 1543: "We were much surprised at sometimes meeting innumerable herds of bulls without a single cow and other herds of cows without bulls."

Tom McHugh, author of the 1972 book *The Time of the Buffalo* calls them 'cow groups' and 'bull groups.' At first glance, he says, "the term 'cow group' may seem a misnomer, for [it] often includes a few bulls. But cows make up a

majority of the membership and are in almost complete control . . . even during rutting season, when its ranks are swelled by numbers of bulls."

Young bulls hang around with their mothers until two or three years old, when they leave to join other males in small bachelor herds. Lone bulls are often found at quite some distance from the herds. These are usually old bulls that got kicked out or wanted to quit the herd, say their owners. Maybe they lost too many fights. Sometimes two or three will stay in the same vicinity, moving together or travelling in tandem, at some distance from each other.

During non-breeding seasons in the Plains wildlife refuges, cow groups average about twenty, occasionally as many as seventy, McHugh says, but "with the approach of the rut it increases into the hundreds as several groups merge and are joined by numbers of mature bulls."

The matriarch of each herd is an older cow—a grandmother. She is the leader and decides when they'll go for water. When it's time, she starts off down the trail, followed single file in a line that can extend for half a mile (though sometimes an aggressive bull will lead.) Deep narrow trails cut a foot or more into the clay banks of nearly-dry creek beds where buffalo drink.

The cow herds are related groups that stick together clannishly, claimed C.J. "Buffalo" Jones, from observations of his buffalo in Kansas and many purchases over the years, as well as those in Yellowstone Park where he was an early game warden.

"There is no animal in the world more clannish than the buffalo. Each small group is of the same strain of blood," said Jones. "The male calf follows the mother until two years old. The female calf is permitted to stay with her mother for life. The resemblance of each individual of a family is very striking, while the difference between families is apparent to the practiced eye. The several animals know each other by scent and sound. They grunt similarly to a hog, but in a much stronger tone, and are quickly recognized by every member of the family. When

Buffalo cows and calves make up maternal herds with small bachelor herds and single bulls off to the side, except during mating season when large herds come together. Young bulls hang around their mothers until two or three years old. Badlands Reflections Photography.

Buffalo calves are playful creatures: they play Tag and King of the Mountain; they run and jump, bucking and kicking, around the herd. Badlands Reflections Photography.

separated by a stampede or other cause, they never rest until they are all together again."

Cows are generally affectionate and attentive, fiercely protective of their calves. Buffalo Jones said when he roped a calf and attempted to lead it, the mother often would "quickly place herself in front of her baby and thrust a horn under the loop of the rope and hold the horse and rider perfectly solid, while if the rope is slackened, she in some instances will free the calf entirely."

To communicate with her young, the buffalo mother utters a muttering, grunting or snorting sound—and the calf answers in much the same way. When hungry or thirsty, the calf's cry has been described as "a low-pitched, pig-like grunt through the nose."

In crossing rivers observers said cows often allowed calves or yearlings to climb on their backs. Thus the mothers conveyed their young safely across deep rushing rivers, even in large herds.

The birth of calves

When the time comes to give birth a buffalo cow goes to a secluded spot such as a well-screened ravine to bring forth her young, nourish and defend it until it is strong enough to join the herd.

But she doesn't necessarily go alone, observes Mike Faith, of Standing Rock. He says the mother has her own network of four or five animals—females she's close to, perhaps including her own offspring. They stay around, not so close as to interfere, but instinctively watching out for predators. Somehow, he says, they sense it is important the mother bonds with her newborn calf, licking, nuzzling, grunting, urging him to suck.

"The others are watching so there's no interruption of this process," reports Faith. "If she gets up and moves away before she's ready they might not bond. If she gets spooked, she might abandon her newborn and not come back. The calf might die of starvation."

When threatened, the buffalo mother usually defends her calf. Although historically during the acute stress of a hunt it was noted that some cows ran off and left their calves, other accounts testify to their protective nature and their return to look for lost calves.

"When a cow and her very young calf are attacked by wolves, the cow bellows and sometimes runs at the enemy and not

infrequently frightens him away," John James Audubon wrote in *The Quadrupeds of North America*.

Reddish-gold calves are born in April to June. They can keep up with the herd two or three hours after birth and are well protected by their mothers and other members of the herd.

Buffalo cows are known for ease of calving, with relatively small newborns weighing only thirty to fifty pounds. The calves grow fast and within a year have gained ten times their birth weight. Naturally hardy, they usually get up and walk within a couple hours of birth, according to the National

Mothers keep close watch of their playful calves. Buffalo cows are known for easy calving with small reddish-gold calves born in April through June. At three months or so, their heads turn dark and humps and black horns begin to appear. NPS.

Bison Association. One new calf was reported as following its mother almost immediately. It "ran bucking around its mother when it was only a little more than a half hour old."

Young calves often play together. McHugh describes a group of seven exuberant calves he watched one afternoon:

"All of a sudden they perked up their tails, kicked their hind legs in the air and bolted across the meadow to engage in what looked like a game of tag. As they milled chaotically, one calf bounded out of the little band, inviting another to follow. A companion came forth and the leader broke into a rapid gallop, challenging him to a race around the herd. Before long all seven were tearing about in a frenzy of activity, butting, kicking and bounding to and fro in carefree frolic."

One observer reported the calves as "very playful little animals."

Adult buffalo were not known as playful. However, Seton says that a New Mexican cowboy described to him a playful band of adult buffalo he watched one day at their watering place. "After drinking very heavily they played about like calves, and a number amused themselves by jumping off a steep bank into the water four feet below, running round to climb the bank at a low place and repeating the performance many times.

Dominance issues

Buffalo are social animals with a great understanding of where they stand in the herd's ranking. Larger bulls and cows tend to dominate in the pecking order. Size makes a difference, but other traits matter as well, including strength, fighting skill, endurance, maturity and aggressiveness.

Tom McHugh spent three months studying the hierarchy ranking through patterns of dominance and submission in a Jackson Hole Wildlife Park herd of sixteen buffalo. He identified and named each individual and recorded its rank through interactions with each of the others.

Buffalo calves are naturally hardy. They are born small, get up and walk soon after birth, nuzzle for milk and grow rapidly. Badlands Reflections Photography.

Most often a dominant buffalo walked over and displaced subordinates just by his presence, without force or threat. Most of their interactions were peaceable, as all knew and understood their rank order compared to each of the others. The lower-ranking animals simply moved away while wending their way carefully through the herd to avoid other superiors, while indicating submissiveness. McHugh noted all this was subtle and almost imperceptible, but universally recognized and respected by the animals.

The dominant bull might shift from one pile of hay to another, nudging away a cow feeding there. That cow moved to another pile, displacing a lower status cow, who moved on in a chain reaction that could shuffle most of the herd.

While this tended to be peaceable, about one-fourth of the interactions involved warnings and threats or actual use of force. Threats might involve a steady stare, swinging horns menacingly, or placing a chin on the rump of a subordinate to force it to move away. When threats failed, a battle might follow.

McHugh said disruptions occur when new individuals enter the herd, calves are born, or young bulls begin to assert their increasing strength over formerly superior cows. Once a new hierarchy is established, combat dies down as each individual recognizes and accepts its new status. When subordinates submit peacefully, group life is reinforced, not disrupted.

In August and September during rut, or breeding season, big bulls stage fights as they battle for dominance. Usually the younger and weaker bulls give up quickly and wander away. Older, larger bulls breed the most cows. NPS.

Rutting season

During historic breeding seasons—also called the *rut* or *running season*—great fights were staged between big bulls as they moved between herds and fought for dominance. This was the time when males and females came together in huge herds. It began in late summer when calves were two to four months old.

George Catlin, artist and observer on the upper Missouri during the 1830s, once saw several thousand buffalo in rut raising huge clouds of dust. They pawed the earth, "in mass, eddying and wheeling about… plunging and butting at each other in the most furious manner.

"The males are continually following the females and the whole mass in constant motion. All [roaring] in deep and hollow sounds; which, mingled together like the sound of distant thunder at the distance of a mile or two," wrote Catlin.

"The actual combats, which were always of short duration and over in a few seconds after the collision took place, were preceded by the usual threatening demonstrations, in which the bull lowers his head until his nose almost touches the ground, roars like a foghorn until the earth seems to fairly tremble with the vibration, glares madly upon his adversary with half-white eyeballs and with his forefeet paws up the dry earth and throws it upward in a great cloud of dust high above his back."

Bulls display their dominance by grunting, wallowing and fighting, their stout, sharp horns aiding in self-defense. A challenging bull might grunt, snort, blow or growl to get a female's attention and the defending bull roars back in an impressive bellow that is described as closely resembling the roar of a lion.

This dominant bull (at right, larger and with larger horns than the cow) "tends" his cow. He stays with her, chasing away rivals. Badlands Reflections Photography.

"I have been assured by old plainsmen that under favorable atmospheric conditions such sounds have been heard five miles," wrote Hornaday.

One day an enormous buffalo herd crossed the Missouri River in front of Catlin's canoe.

"It was in the midst of the 'running season,' and we had heard the roaring of the herd when we were several miles from them. When we came in sight, we were actually terrified at the immense numbers that were streaming down the green hills on one side of the river, and galloping up and over the bluffs on the other. The river was filled and in parts blackened with their heads and horns as they were swimming about, following up their objects, and making desperate battle whilst they were swimming . . . furiously hooking and climbing on each other," wrote Catlin. His party ran their canoe ashore and waited several hours for the herd to cross.

The older males, over age seven when they reach their full growth, do most of the breeding. Dominant bulls will bring together a small harem of females, chasing away rivals. Once a bull has found a female close to estrus, he will stay by her side and 'tend her,' keeping others away until she is ready to mate.

Since an equal number of bulls and females populated the old wild herds, this caused much fighting in breeding season. Most often the younger bulls gave up quickly by wandering off. So did old bulls getting the worst of a fight. But occasionally some fought to the death.

Sometimes lesser bulls ganged up on an old bull, preventing him from running away.

In one report, eighteen to twenty bulls engaged in a ferocious fight, butting and goring each other, but directing their efforts specifically at one huge, gaunt old bull. Repeatedly attacked and badly hurt, he fell down, but kept rising to his feet to fight back. Finally he fell, bleeding profusely and unable to rise again. The others wandered off leaving him to die.

In pastures today there are fewer bulls, but escape for a defeated bull is limited by fences.

"When pastures get too small, with too many bulls, there's more fighting and more cows don't get bred," says Mike Faith.

In most tribal herds, he explains, bulls are thinned out from time to time. Choice young bulls are most often selected for ceremonial feeds. They symbolize strength, vigor and good health for young men and provide honor for guests. Old bulls, too, even though too tough for many cuts, furnish abundant meat for hamburger and stew. In addition, occasional buffalo hunts may be staged for paying guests, who often prefer a big old bull with an impressive head for mounting.

At the close of breeding season the large wild herds resolved into their usual smaller herds and scattered in search of grass. Eventually the large assemblies of herds again covered many square miles of open country.

By the end of the rutting season, the bulls are thin and subdued in spirit, wrote Seton.

"But the rich pasturage begins to improve their condition. By October the good fare shows in all. Their new growing coats are sleek, their bodies reinvigorated, their tempers more sociable." They are ready for winter and, in some cases, for migration.

In Yellowstone Park, where buffalo live in an environment very like the wild, some 4,600 buffalo live in two breeding herds. These two large herds join in their two separate locations for breeding—one in central Yellowstone and the other to the north.

Cows normally breed in August or September and calve from April through June, with a gestation period of nine months to

Bulls that put up a fight get thin and battered during the rut. Afterward their bodies hasten to replenish the lost fat for winter. NPS.

somewhat longer.

Under favorable ranching conditions today buffalo cows live twenty to twenty-five years, producing a calf each year. But in Yellowstone Park, in the wild, they rarely live past age fifteen and may produce a calf only every other year.

Shedding and wallowing

Shedding their heavy winter coats engages buffalo bulls for much of spring and summer.

Hornaday described this process in detail in his 1889 Smithsonian study. "Promptly with the coming of spring, if not even the last week of February, the buffalo begins the shedding of his winter coat. It is a long and difficult task, and with commendable energy he sets about it at the earliest possible moment. It lasts him more than half the year, and is attended with many discomforts."

Shedding occurs in two distinct processes as described by Hornaday. One for the heavy, woolly forequarters, head, shoulders and cape. The other for the lighter hair on hind quarters. For the rear parts and hips, the old hair simply loosens and drops off in "great woolly flakes a foot square, more or less." But even this can take months during which "great ragged streamers of loose hair . . . flutter in the wind like signals of distress."

More dramatically, the heavier hair on neck, forequarters, and hump alternately sheds and gets

All through spring and summer the bull wallows in dirt and water-soaked wallows to rub off patches of hair and insects. According to Hornaday, shedding is a long and difficult task, "They stretch out at full length, rub their heads violently to and fro on the ground. The old and new hair cling together with provoking tenacity long after the old coat should fall." Badlands Reflections Photography.

The bull's one redeeming feature in all this rag-tag display is "the handsome head, black with new hair as early as the first of May, preserving the bull's majestic appearance throughout this long shedding effort," wrote Hornaday. SD Game Fish & Park, Chris Hull.

rubbed off. By then the rich brown winter coat is faded to light brown or dull golden tan.

"The new hair grows so rapidly and at the same time so densely, that it forces itself into the old, becomes hopelessly entangled with it, and in time actually lifts the old hair clear of the skin. The old and the new hair cling together with provoking tenacity long after the old coat should fall, and on several of the bulls we killed in October there were patches of it still sticking tightly to the shoulders. Under all such patches the new hair was of a different color from that around them," he wrote.

The bull's one redeeming feature in all this rag-tag display is "the handsome head, black with new hair as early as the first of May, preserving the bull's majestic appearance throughout this long shedding effort," said Hornaday.

The bull attacks clay banks. He rubs on trees and rocks. He fights. He wallows.

Hornaday explained how horns get worn down on the outside:

"Bulls are much more given to rolling than the cows, especially after they have reached maturity. They stretch out at full length, rub their heads violently to and fro on the ground, in which the horn serves as the chief point of contact and slides over the ground like a sled-runner. After thoroughly scratching one side on mother earth they roll over and treat the other in like manner. Notwithstanding his sharp and lofty hump, a buffalo bull can roll completely over with as much ease as any horse.

"The vast amount of rolling and side-scratching on the earth indulged in by bull buffaloes is shown in the worn condition of the horns of every old specimen. Often a thickness of half an inch is gone from the upper half of each horn on its outside curve, at which point the horn is worn quite flat."

George Catlin expressed his amazement at how vigorously bulls attacked buffalo wallows, the shallow pools they carved into the soil.

"In the heat of summer, these huge animals no doubt suffer very much with the great profusion of their long and shaggy hair . . . The enormous bull, lowered down upon one knee, will plunge his horns, and at last his head, driving up the earth, and soon making an excavation in the ground into which the water filters from amongst the grass, forming for him in a few moments a cool and comfortable bath . . . He throws himself flat upon his side, and forcing himself violently around,

This young bull emulates the older bulls in scraping the faded hair from his cape. He rubs on rocks and trees, attacks clay banks, fights and wallows. By fall he emerges with a luxriant coat of rich brown, "fine, clean sleek and bright in color, not a speck of dirt or a lock awry anywhere." Badlands Reflections Photography.

with his horns and his huge hump on his shoulders presented to the sides, he ploughs up the ground by his rotary motion, sinking himself deeper and deeper in the ground, continually enlarging his pool, in which he at length becomes nearly immersed, and the water and mud about him mixed into a complete mortar, which drips in streams from every part of him as he rises up upon his feet, a hideous monster of mud and ugliness.

"The leader, having cooled his sides, stands in the pool until inclination induces him to step out and give place to the next in command who stands ready, and another, and another, who advance forward in their turns to enjoy the luxury of the wallow, until the whole band (sometimes 100 or more) will pass through it in turn, each one throwing his body around in a similar manner and each one adding a little to the dimensions of the pool . . . Perhaps in the space of half an hour, a circular excavation of fifteen or twenty feet in diameter and two feet in depth is completed and left for the water to run into, which soon fills it to the level of the ground."

Long after the wild herds disappeared, buffalo wallows could be seen as hollows with muddy bottoms and distinctive grass growth.

Wallowing benefits the bull in a number of ways, besides scratching his itch. It eases the biting of insects—flies, ticks and lice. It marks the wallow with his personal scent, thus establishing dominance. During breeding season, bulls wallow to display their strength and vigor. It has also been linked to social behavior and play that enhances group cohesion.

"When he emerges from his wallow, plastered with mud from head to tail, his degradation is complete," wrote Hornaday. "He is then simply not fit to be seen, even by his best friends."

Cows shed their lighter hair somewhat more easily.

By fall a wondrous transformation takes place and the rich brown coat is luxuriant and fully grown. "The buffalo stands forth clothed in a complete new suit of hair—fine, clean, sleek and bright in color, not a speck of dirt or a lock awry anywhere."

Reading such descriptions, it becomes abundantly clear why Native Americans launched their big semi-annual hunts in the fall—that's when buffalo robes are prime. Without this new thick hair growth, hides taken in summer

A group of cows and half-grown calves graze a rocky hillside. Badlands Reflections Photography.

Wolves usually hung out with the buffalo herds, picking off the ill and injured. Lewis and Clark wrote about the buffalo with "their shepherds, the wolves." The buffalo paid little attention to them, seeming not to care except when a pack of wolves attacked a lone calf. NPS.

produced only rawhide or leather tanned without hair.

Risk of attack on humans

Although they often seem quite docile, bulls and cows fight fiercely in defense of calves or when agitated. Threatened or cornered, they can be dangerous.

Around the turn of the last century Ernest Thompson Seton published several books on game animals of North America. His writings testified to the "fierce, combative nature of buffalo cows with calves and the bulls at all times."

While in wildlife lectures he often assured audiences that often-feared creatures such as the wolf, cougar and bear were absolutely harmless to humans if left alone, this does not apply to buffalo, Seton said.

"I must now frankly admit a notable exception—the Buffalo. At all times and places the Buffalo, male and female, old and young, are savage, treacherous animals; always a menace to man and beast; never to be trusted. . . . One never knows when this may break out. A number of men have been killed by tame Buffalo—and those who know them best, trust them least. . . . The Buffalo is a dangerous animal, the only really dangerous one in America. If we had exact figures to show, I believe we should find more human beings killed by Buffalo than by any other of our wild creatures."

A wounded buffalo often made battle with the Native hunters in "the utmost fury," said Catlin. "In their desperate resistance the finest horses are often destroyed. But the Indian, with his superior sagacity and dexterity, generally finds some effective mode of escape."

Buffalo can easily outrun humans—they've been clocked at forty miles an hour. While a good horse can run faster, it cannot outlast them, Native hunters explained. Buffalo could run at top speed for ten miles, they said. Their horses could not.

Even today, buffalo are considered wild animals, in the sense that lions and tigers born in zoos are wild. They may be tamed but are not domesticated—which means to breed in certain traits considered desirable and breed out undesirable traits. This would alter the traits passed on to offspring, which buffalo breeders avoid.

Thus each animal has its own unpredictable personality. As wild animals they may appear gentle and quiet, but experts warn this can change in an instant.

In the twenty years between 1980 and 1999, more than three times as many people in Yellowstone National Park were injured by buffalo as by bears. Peaceful-seeming buffalo charged and injured seventy-nine people, while bears injured twenty-four. One died of buffalo injuries, two from bear attacks.

In a seminar for tribal buffalo managers, Dr. Trudy Ecoffey, InterTribal Buffalo Council Wildlife Biologist, cautioned the managers about getting up close.

Her advice was *"Don't!* It is difficult for people who are around buffalo often to tell when an attack will occur, and for the person who is never around them almost impossible."

The lumbering walk of the buffalo is deceiving, she said. They can turn, accelerate and charge in a heartbeat.

A clue to their agitation is the stubby tail. When it hangs down and switches naturally, the buffalo is usually calm. But if the tail flips up and over the back he may be ready to charge.

Other signs of anxiety are grunting or shaking the head, warns Ecoffey. These actions should prompt people to give the buffalo plenty of room and preferably, to place something huge between them and the buffalo.

Migrating herds

Fall migrations often took buffalo herds south a few hundred miles. There they wintered under more favorable conditions than each band would have experienced farther north. In this scenario, some buffalo still occupied the whole of the Great Plains south of the Saskatchewan River in Canada most of the time.

Buffalo can easily outrun humans, and horses over the long run. They've been clocked at 40 miles per hour. Badlands ReflectionsPhotography.

However, it seems that migrations were unpredictable. Large areas to the south that for many years were completely empty of buffalo suddenly became overrun with them. Some bands apparently did not migrate much, but remained in the same general area throughout the whole year.

Apparently their movements depended on such factors as food availability, hunting pressure and—perhaps most important—their premonitions of the severity of the winter to come.

George Catlin was one who argued against the likelihood of buffalo migrations. From his 1840s observations and what he gathered from Plains tribes, he declared: "These animals are not migratory. They graze in immense and almost incredible numbers at times and roam about and over vast tracts of country, from East to West and from West to East as often as from North to South."

He said there was no need for seasonal migrations as buffalo get along regardless of the weather and seem "to flourish and get their living without the necessity of evading the rigor of the climate."

Buffalo probably did not migrate in the manner of birds—long distances every year to known destinations.

A buffalo bull wades into a small river in mid-summer and drinks long of water filled with silt. Badlands Reflections Photography.

However, stories of their large migrations are well documented.

As Seton put it, "When in late November frosts send forth the word to move, it is usual to find the clan reunited, moving as before with the old great-grandmother in advance, the young ones scattered through it, the father and grandfather behind, and the dethroned great-great-great-grandfather roaming alone in the offing."

Col. Dodge carefully observed movements of the southern herd over several years. He wrote: "Early in spring, as soon as the dry and apparently desert prairie had begun to change its coat of dingy brown to one of palest green, the horizon would begin to be dotted with buffalo, single or in groups of two or three, forerunners of the coming herd.

"Thicker and thicker and in larger groups they come, until by the time the grass is well up the whole vast landscape appears a mass of buffalo, some individuals feeding, others standing, others lying down, but the herd moving slowly, moving constantly to the northward.

"Some years, as in 1871, the buffalo appeared to move north in one immense column oftentimes twenty to fifty miles in width, and of unknown depth from front to rear. Other years the northward journey was made in several parallel columns, moving at the same rate, and with their numerous flankers covering a width of 100 or more miles."

"Rivers . . . if frozen, are unnoticed. If open, they are swum," noted Seton. "If covered with rotten ice, the ice is broken eventually by the weight of the herd and many are drowned, but the rest swim through and continue their march. An onset of hunters may swerve them for a time, but it does not change their main trend."

Sometimes herds moved quietly, without excitement. At others in a rush, rapidly covering great distances. If a railroad lay across their route—as did the newly built Atchison, Topeka and Santa Fé in the spring of 1872—the herds were so single-mindedly bent on crossing the tracks that they threw off trains, reported Dodge.

"If a herd was on the north side of the track, it would stand stupidly gazing, without a symptom of alarm, although the locomotive passed within a hundred yards. [But if] on the south side, even though at a distance of one or two miles, the passage of a train set the whole herd in the wildest commotion. At full speed, and utterly regardless of the consequences, it would make for the track. If the train happened not to be in its path, it crossed the track and stopped satisfied. [But] if the train was in its way, each individual buffalo went at it with the desperation of despair, plunging against or between locomotive and cars.

"Numbers were killed, but numbers still pressed on. After having trains thrown off the track twice in one week, conductors learned to have a very decided respect for the idiosyncrasies of the buffalo, and when there was a possibility of striking a herd 'on the rampage' for the north side of the track, the train slowed up and sometimes stopped entirely."

The whole country looked like one mass of buffalo moving slowly north, Dodge said. But in fact the mass was made up of many separate herds of 50 to 200 animals. These broke off as they moved north, scattering left and right to summer feeding grounds.

Migration routes tended to follow river valleys. The James River valley in Dakota Territory was a well-known north-south route. Native hunters often camped there to intercept buffalo herds.

Only during migrations and breeding season did the buffalo join in massive herds, wrote Seton. Bands of a few thousand were found at all seasons, but the millions came together only on some great general impulse.

Most buffalo today do not migrate, being limited by pasture and receiving supplemental feed in winter when needed.

However, the two big herds in Yellowstone Park, where ranges are large and mountainous, do migrate down from high summer ranges to lower grasslands as the snowpack increases at higher altitudes. The central herd moves down toward park boundaries in the northwest and may remain there well into calving season. The northern herd too moves to lower elevations within the park. In severe winters with deep snow this can become a problem when buffalo migrate beyond the park boundaries into cattle ranching country.

A buffalo herd spreads out and feeds on the hills and valleys near the Shadehill Lake and Buffalo Jump. Courtesy of Jim Strand.

For thousands of years buffalo were honored by Native Americans of the plains in story, song, dance and ceremonials. They lived together in harmony, interconnected physically and spiritually. Badlands Reflections Photography.

7

Buffalo Lore

*The Buffalo was part of us,
his flesh and blood being absorbed by us
until it became our own flesh and blood.
Our clothing, our tipis, everything we needed for life
came from the buffalo's body. It was hard to say
where the animals ended and the human began.*
—John (Fire) Lame Deer, Oglala
Lame Deer Seeker of Visions,
with Richard Erdoes, 1972

The buffalo is honored as sacred by the Plains Indians in stories, songs, dances, artwork and religious symbols and ceremonials. For thousands of years buffalo were interconnected with the Indian culture, both physically and spiritually. They were considered as relatives who protect the Indian people and deserve protection and gratitude in return. As brothers and sisters, they lived together in harmony. In traditional Plains belief, buffalo gave themselves up willingly as food for Native people, and furnished many other gifts as well. Daily the people thanked the buffalo and prayed for them to continue helping them survive.

Cave of Origin

The creation of humans and buffalo as emerging from a cave or hole in the ground is a traditional belief held by many Plains tribes. For many Lakota that cave is Wind Cave in the southern Black Hills, one of the world's longest. The pine-covered hills there are coursed throughout with large caves, interconnected through tight honeycombed passages.

A Pawnee traditional belief tells of the beginning of the world from such a cave or hole.

Long ago all living things waited far underground. Great herds of buffalo lay there, all the people, antelope, wolves, deer, rabbits, and even the little bird that sang 'tear-tear.' They waited as if asleep.

One day Buffalo Woman awoke, stretched and began to walk slowly among the others touching them lightly. As she did they began to stir and stretch. She headed toward an opening where she saw a great shining light and felt warmth streaming into the cave. A young cow rose and followed her. Then came another buffalo and another and soon a great line was moving out of the opening into the bright, warm, grassy place that was the earth. Next the people woke up and streamed out one by one, followed by all the other animals and even the small tear-tear bird flying toward the warming sun. They spread out in all four directions toward the circling horizon. And the people knew they were in the right place, the place where they would live together with their relatives, the buffalo.

A traditional Cheyenne belief brought knowledge of how the sacred buffalo arrived on the Plains. Long ago, a tribe of Cheyenne hunters camped near a spring at the head of a small rushing stream. Farther downstream the creek disappeared into a deep hole.

The people were starving and could find no food, not even a rabbit or a grouse.

One day the Chief called a council meeting. "We must explore the hole," he said. "It may be dangerous, but we have brave hunters. Who will go?"

No one responded. Finally, one young brave painted himself for hunting and stepped up. "I will go and sacrifice myself for our people."

He arrived at the hole, and to his surprise, he found two other Cheyenne hunters near the opening, where the stream rushed underground.

"Are you here to taunt me," the young hunter asked. "Will you

Hikers investigate hole in a gumbo butte. Perhaps long ago an aged grandmother told a creation story near this very cave to small children gathered around. Photo by Nicole Strand Haase

only pretend to jump when I do?"

But the other two braves assured him they were going with him. They joined hands and together jumped into the opening, falling into deep darkness. Finally their eyes began to adjust, and they discovered a door.

The first hunter knocked, but there was no response. He knocked again, louder.

"Who are you and what do you want, my brave ones?" asked an old Indian grandmother as she opened her door.

"Grandmother, we are searching for food for our hungry tribe," the young man replied. "Our people never seem to have enough."

"Are you hungry now?" she asked.

"Oh, yes, kind Grandmother, we are very hungry," all three braves answered.

She opened her door wide, inviting them in. "Look out there!" she pointed out her window. A beautiful wide prairie stretched before their eyes. To their surprise they saw great herds of buffalo grazing contentedly. The young hunters could hardly believe what they saw!

She seated the hunters and brought each of them a stone bowl full of buffalo stew. It was deli-

In traditional belief the buffalo were put on earth to feed the native people. They gave themselves up willingly as food and brought many other gifts as well—hide for tepees, blankets and clothing, medicine, and bones for tools, sleds, ornaments and toys. SD Game, Fish & Parks.

cious. They ate their fill and still more meat remained.

"Take these special bowls of buffalo meat back to your hungry people," the grandmother said. "Tell them I will send buffalo."

"Thank you, thank you, thank you, kind Grandmother," said the three young Cheyenne braves. They helped each other climb back up the hole without spilling any of the buffalo meat from the bowls.

The people were delighted to see them safe and bringing food. Everyone in the camp ate heartily and rejoiced over the tasty new food. And even more meat filled the old grandmother's three magic bowls.

When the Cheyenne waked at dawn the next day, they looked out of their tepees and saw that vast herds of buffalo had mysteriously appeared, surrounding their village and covering the hills and prairies far into the distance. They knew this would be a good supply of food, shelter and clothing for their people. Gratefully they gave thanks to the spirit grandmother and to the buffalo for their generosity.

White Buffalo Woman

White Buffalo Woman is a holy being who figures powerfully into Plains lore. Although she first appeared in human form, she was also a buffalo, one of the brothers and sisters who gave their flesh so the people could live. In some cultures she is known as the one who brought the sacred pipe, along with herds of buffalo. After she presented the people with the pipe, the holy woman walked away toward the setting sun. As she went she rolled over four times. The first time she changed into a black buffalo calf, the next time a brown calf, then a red calf. The fourth time she changed into a white buffalo calf and disappeared from sight over a nearby hill.

As she did, great numbers of buffalo came running down the hill. From that day on the buffalo provided the people with all the food they needed, plus skins for their tepees, warm clothing, bones for tools and sacred items for religious ceremonies.

Another tradition tells of the release of buffalo before they ran freely over the earth. A powerful being named Humpback owned all the buffalo. He kept them locked in a stone corral in the mountains where he lived with his young son. He shared them with no one else and refused to give any meat to his neighbors, even though they were starving. People sought help from the wily Coyote.

Coyote called them to council. "Let's go over to Humpback's

White Buffalo Woman figures powerfully into plains lore. Sometimes she appeared as a white buffalo; at others as a woman, bearing gifts and teaching the people. Below is White Cloud, symbol of hope and good times to come for many who came to Jamestown, to honor her. ND Tourism.

corral and make a plan to release the buffalo."

After dark they inspected the corral. The thick stone walls rose too high to climb and there was no gate—only an entrance that led through the back door of Humpback's house. For four days they watched the father, his son and the buffalo.

Then Coyote had an idea. "Have you noticed that the boy has no pet to play with? I'll change myself into a puppy for the boy. Once I'm in the house I can open the door and stampede the buffalo out of the corral."

The next morning when the boy went to the spring to get water he found a small dog there drinking. He picked up the dog, laughed, snuggled and played with it, and carried it back home.

"See my nice puppy!" he said. "I want to keep him for my pet."

"Take him back! A dog is good for nothing," scolded his father. "Besides he's probably not a real dog—some schemer has done this to get our buffalo. Look—we'll test him."

He held a hot coal from the fire close to the puppy's eyes. It barked three times.

"All right. It is a real dog," decided Humpback. "You can keep

Indian man talks to Beaver and Coyote and gets directions, in legend of 'How the buffalo lost his crown.' *Indian Talking to Beaver and Coyote*, CM Russell, Montana Historical Society.

it. But only if it stays away from the buffalo."

That night when father and son went to sleep, Coyote opened the back door and ran to the buffalo, barking and nipping at their heels. The terrified buffalo were never chased by a dog before and they stampeded through the house, smashing down the front door. Humpback awoke and tried to stop them, but could not. Every buffalo escaped and ran over the green hills, scattering throughout the earth. Coyote ran after them and the people danced with joy.

After the last one had galloped away, Humpback's son looked for his small dog. "Where is my puppy?" he cried. "I want my pet puppy dog."

"That was not a dog!" Humpback shouted angrily. "It was Coyote the Trickster. He fooled us. See him out there dancing with the people. He turned loose all our buffalo and we can never get them back again."

Storytelling

Telling stories was an art and an important way of passing down religious beliefs, history and tribal culture. The same traditions in several variations might be told by storytellers from different tribes, especially if they shared kinship or traded with each other.

Restrictions and taboos applied to storytelling. Certain stories were passed down to a specific medicine man, and he alone was allowed to tell them. Traditional beliefs were taught at a grandmother's knee—or by grandfathers.

There were stories of the origin of buffalo, the flood that covered the earth, the close connections of the people with the spirit world of their relatives—buffalo and other wildlife and birds. Other stories modeled good behavior such as kindness to the less fortunate and the generosity of every good hunter in sharing his game. Stories and legends of Native people are told for different reasons—to teach, to entertain, to ridicule, to cause fear or laughter—but all bring the knowledge of elders to younger generations.

Traditional storytellers believe the old stories are best told in the native language and to listeners who understand their culture. They say an amusing story is "not as funny" in English. Much of the spirit, humor and excitement get lost in translation.

Often the venerable grandmother, with a twinkle in her eye, entertained with hilarious tales about coyote tricksters and other mischief.

The following story may have been told just for fun with its twists, turns and surprises for a giggling circle of attentive children.

At one time all animals lived together in peace—no one ate anyone else. They ate only grass and fruit and leafy plants. But Buffalo wanted to be chief and draw strength by eating the others. This he deserved, he said, as the largest and strongest of all.

Inside the lodge, a mother tells a story and teaches her son about hunting while she prepares a meal. *Inside the Lodge,* CM Russell, MHS.

The Human People objected, so Buffalo challenged them to a race to decide who would be chief. The People agreed, but since they had only two legs to Buffalo's four, they claimed the right to choose Bird People to race for them—with their two legs and two wings. They chose Hummingbird, Meadowlark, Hawk and Magpie.

All the birds and animals painted for the race in colors that turned out to be permanent. Skunk painted a white strip on his back. Raccoon painted black circles around his eyes. Meadowlark painted herself a golden breastplate.

The race started at Buffalo Gap on the edge of the Black Hills, according to some storytellers. Hummingbird took the lead, but his tiny wings soon tired and the fastest buffalo, Runs Slender took over. Meadowlark caught up with him at the turn-around stick, but flew wide at the turn and again fell behind. She cheered as Hawk flew past her. But Runs Slender kept his lead. Then Magpie passed Hawk and swept up right behind the fast buffalo. At the finish line Raccoon stood holding out her hand to touch the winner. Magpie pulled ahead by just the length of her bill and her wing brushed Raccoon's little hand just before Runs Slender Buffalo thundered past.

Thus the Human People won the race and became great hunters and feasted on buffalo meat, while buffalo wandered the great Plains, eating grass and chewing their cud. The People never ate the magpie, hawk, meadowlark or hummingbird, who had befriended them.

Stories are important among the Crees and Métis in Saskatchewan where a wealth of oral history interviews and stories are collected at the Gabriel Dumont Institute of Native Studies Virtual Museum.

Some Cree elders consider traditional stories as the backbone of their culture, saying, "When our stories disappear, our people will disappear."

It is said to be rare in the Cree culture to tell others how to behave. Instead, advice or criticism may be conveyed by telling a story. Nevertheless, there is always a great deal of laughter. Jokes are told at all meetings and often on oneself. Often a joke begins seriously as if telling a real event, and only at the end is revealed to be an invented story.

A noted Cree-Métis mischief-maker is "Wisakecahk," who in corruption of his name is sometimes called "Whiskey Jack." Hundreds of stories, in endless variations, tell of the jokes Whiskey Jack plays on his brothers and sisters, the animals, plants and rocks. A shape-changer, he speaks the languages of animals and plants. Some traditional stories about him have a moral—giving children a lesson on behavior. Often they are told for the sheer fun of it.

Stories about Wisakecahk often begin with him walking around feeling hungry. Too lazy to work, he enjoys tricking other animals into giving him their dinner—or in becoming his dinner. In various twists and turns, the joke is often on Whisky Jack himself.

Other tricksters are the Little People—or Mannegishi. Known by the Cree, Ojibwa and Métis, they are small, without noses, and with big heads relative to their small bodies. They live between the rocks in the fast-flowing rivers of the north woods ready to tease and torment voyagers who come past in canoes loaded high with buffalo hides. They especially delight in spinning the canoers out into treacherous currents and tipping them over the edge of sudden waterfalls, down into deep rocky pools below.

Ojibwe elders explain how the buffalo got his hump. Long ago Buffalo had no hump. One summer a naughty young buffalo raced across the prairies chasing small animals and trampling the nests of little birds. The foxes ran with him and scrambled after the eggs of injured birds. The mother birds cried about their broken nests.

Wenebojo was watching. He hit Buffalo on the shoulders with a stick. "You should be ashamed. Now you will always have a hump on your shoulder, and always carry your head low because of your shame." The foxes ran to dig holes in the ground and hide. Wenebojo told them, "Because you hurt the birds, you will always live in the cold ground."

Traditional stories often strengthen the bond between buffalo and humans. The elders taught, "Buffalo are our brothers." Some traditions suggest that buffalo could shift back and forth into human form. Humans, too, could sometimes shift between forms.

One day a young hunter who followed the sacred traditions, bringing food to his people and always thanking the buffalo for their gifts, saw a buffalo cow walking near a stream. She turned into a beautiful young woman and he immediately fell in love. Her hair smelled of sage and prairie flowers.

They married, had a son named Calfboy and lived happily in the Indian village for a time. But people there did not like the buffalo woman much. Her hair fell in

Beaded moccasins and belts and hatbands from Standing Rock. L Allard.

wild tangles. They said she smelled strange and didn't understand their ways. One day when her husband was gone hunting, they told her to go back home. She picked up Calfboy and ran away. Frantic when he returned, the brave young hunter went in search, following their moccasin trail all day.

That evening he found them. His wife said, "I need to go home to live with my people. But they will kill you if you follow."

"I don't care," he said. "I love you both and I'm going with you."

In the morning when he awoke they were gone. He followed their moccasin tracks and again found them at evening camp. For three days the same thing happened. Then came the morning when the tracks leading away were of a buffalo and a small calf, instead of moccasin prints. He followed them and from the top of a ridge he saw a big herd of grazing buffalo.

Calfboy came galloping up on all fours, crying, "Papa! Go back! They're going to kill you."

The brave hunter said, "No, son. I came to stay. I belong here with you and your mother."

A huge old buffalo charged at him, but he stood his ground and showed no fear. He survived every test and finally the chief said because he loved his family so much he could stay. They covered him with a buffalo hide and rolled him over and over, squeezing out his breath and rubbing off the human smell. He tried to stand upright, but could not. Finally he went down on all fours.

That day the buffalo became fast friends with humans. Because the brave young hunter loved his wife and child so much, the buffalo agreed to give humans their meat, their hides and all so that they and their children could survive. The people thanked the buffalo and made a solemn promise to treat them always with respect and gratitude.

Dancing brings buffalo

Because buffalo were seen as all-important spiritual beings, and their absence brought great hardship, Plains Indians appealed to them with songs, dances, rituals and prayers to bring them back.

In the story of Calfboy, a huge old buffalo came charging up but the father stood his ground and showed no fear. From that day the Indians and buffalo were friends and respected each other. Badlands Reflections Photography.

The well-known painting "Buffalo Dance," of the Mandan Indians on the upper Missouri is one of several versions the artist George Catlin painted and sketched of this kind of dance during his visits in the 1830s. Dancers wore buffalo headdresses and imitated the animals' movements to honor the buffalo. In effect, the dancers became buffalo.

Here's how Catlin describes the buffalo dance:

"About ten or fifteen Mandans at a time join in the dance, each with the skin of the buffalo's head (or mask) with the horns on, placed over his head, and in his hand his favorite bow or lance, with which he is used to slay the buffalo. The mask is put over the head, and generally has a strip of skin hanging to it, of the whole length of the animal, with the tail attached to it, which, passing down over the back of the dancer, is dragging on the ground.

"When one becomes fatigued, he signifies it by bending forward, sinking his body toward the ground. Another draws a bow upon him and hits him with a blunt arrow, and he falls like a buffalo—is seized by the by-standers, who drag him out of the ring by the heels, brandishing their knives about him. And having gone through the motions of skinning and cutting him up, they let him

Plains Indians engaged in buffalo dances and religious ceremonies to bring herds of buffalo closer. They relied on buffalo for food, shelter and many other needs. *Buffalo Dance,* George Catlin.

off, and his place is at once supplied by another, who dances into the ring with his mask on. And by this taking of places, the scene is easily kept up night and day, until the desired effect has been produced, that of 'making buffalo come.'"

During the dancing, older men beat on a large drum.

"Drums beat and rattles shake, songs and yells are shouted and lookers-on stand ready with masks on their heads and weapons in hand to take the place of each dancer as he becomes fatigued and jumps out of the ring," wrote Catlin.

He testified that buffalo always appeared because the dance lasted until they did, "sometimes two or three weeks without stopping an instant, until the joyful moment when buffaloes made their appearance."

Sure enough, scouts on the hills brought first news by throwing their robes in the air. "At this joyful intelligence there is a shout of thanks to the Great Spirit, and more especially to the mystery man and the dancers, who have been the immediate cause of their success! So they *never fail.*"

The men with the Lewis and Clark expedition in the winter of 1804-1805 also attended a Mandan buffalo dance and agreed that within days a herd of buffalo showed up.

A similar buffalo dance was held in Bull Head, SD, as 4th of July entertainment in 1913, after the wild herds were gone—although Scotty Philip's herd still ran on public lands near the reservation. The Lakota dancers wore headdresses adorned with buffalo horns, and bent over as they circled to imitate the actions of buffalo.

The dances were performed by men of the Buffalo Society and, among the Santee, by men who had had visions of the buffalo, as described by Robert H. Lowie. For example, Lowie explained "One man might dream that he . . . had been shot by an arrow so that he could barely get home. (He) painted himself vermilion to represent the trickling down of the blood. Another man dreamed of being shot with a gun. Such a one would act out his dream during a Buffalo dance.

Songs to bring the buffalo

The medicine man's song and actions to bring back buffalo in time of food scarcity is reported by Frances Densmore in her 1918 book *Teton Sioux Music*.

The medicine man painted red and blue stripes on a buffalo skull and laid a filled pipe on a bed of fresh sage beside it. As he sang this song in the dark, the skull turned into a real buffalo and called others, in Nakota-Lakota belief. The buffalo is singing as he offers the pipe, the red earth and the blue earth.

A pipe they mentioned as they walked,
I have offered this as I walked.
A red earth they mentioned as they walked,
it has been placed upon me as I walked.
A blue earth they mentioned as they walked,
it has been placed upon me as I walked.

In the old days, this song brought herds of buffalo close to the Native camp, writes Densmore. Many were slaughtered and saved the people from starvation. Densmore interviewed and recorded many older people singing songs and telling their stories, using interpreters when needed. Then she carefully followed up by reading her manuscript back to them and revising with their suggestions. Often she provided the musical score as well as both English and Native tongue.

Northward they are walking is another song Densmore recorded, used to bring buffalo during the Teton Sioux buffalo dance.

Northward	wazi'yata ki'ya
they are walking	ma'nipi
a sacred stone	tun,kan
they touch	i'ca litag ya
they are walking	ma'nipi

Another buffalo song, *Against the Wind,* is to be sung with the drumming: "I drove the tribe against the wind, which struck their faces like a lance" *(Ite' tate' iya'pe waye' wahu'keza owan'ca waye').*

Dreams— believed to be messages from the spirit world—held great meaning for Native people. Brave Buffalo, a Nakota, heard the following song in a dream when he was only ten years old. He dreamed a buffalo came to him while sleeping in the mountains and took him to a tent above the earth, filled with buffalo. The chief told the youth he was selected to represent the buffalo in life, and gave him a wooden cane to remind him, according to Densmore. At the same time he received his name and power to become a medicine man.

For the rest of his life Brave Buffalo is said to have carried that cane. He became known for his bravery and his power to deflect attacks from arrows and bullets, says his great granddaughter, LaDonna Brave Bull Allard, of Ft. Yates.

I will appear	wahínawápiȟ kte
behold me	waȟmáyaȟka yo
a buffalo	tataȟka waȟ
said to me	hemákiya

Religious artifacts and medicine bags

Medicine men of the Sioux, Assiniboine, Pawnee and other tribes used buffalo skulls and other sacred parts in rituals and ceremonies to bring in the herds. Mandans presented a bowl of food to a buffalo head after meals to attract living animals, according to Wayne Gard, in *The Great Buffalo Hunt.* Afterward they sometimes addressed the diety of the herds: "Great Bull of the Prairie, be here with your cow."

The buffalo was revered by the Cheyenne in the sweat lodge, as described by George Bird Grinnell. Before the entrance of a sweat lodge, they propped an ancient buffalo skull on a pile of stones, mound of earth or against a sagebrush.

Long ago, it is said, a medicine man's dream told him to do this, then go in and take a sweat. When he came out he filled the pipe and asked the Creator to bring plenty of buffalo on earth for the people to eat. He smoked, presented the pipe to the skull and asked it to rise and come to life so that the people might have its meat to eat and its skin to make lodges. When they followed this practice, sometimes the buffalo talked to them, although not everyone could understand.

Medicine men used special spiritual powers, rattles made from gourds, and mysterious medicine bags that mingled herbs, charms and tufts of buffalo wool. Medicine bundles are still sacred and only entrusted to revered bundle keepers. Bundles are handled reverently and opened according to definite rules. The opening of the Cheyenne sacred arrow bundle, focuses on an elaborate tribal rite extending over four days.

Other items with great spiritual power include war shields, war shirts, and ceremonial pipes, many of which have been cared for by tribes for centuries. The sacred bundles figure prominently in rituals. In some cases the bundle is a personal one, the contents suggested by a guardian spirit, while in others it becomes a tribal property with a long tradition.

The Northern Cheyennes cherish their "buffalo hat," a buffalo hide cap with painted horns attached. It was preserved by an honored medicine man along with four sacred arrows—two for good buffalo hunting, two for war. Used in important ceremonies, these are known to protect the people, give them health, long life and plenty, along with strength and courage to conquer their enemies. The Blackfeet kept a "buffalo stone."

During buffalo hunts, religious ceremonies attended every aspect, such as those described by the missionary Thomas Riggs and Fort Yates Agent James McLaughlin in the beginning chapters of this book. The people followed tradition in planning the hunt, sending out scouts, offering prayers for safety of hunters and giving thanks for success. Riggs told of following the native tradition of placing one or both hands flat on the ground and petitioning Mother Earth for help in the hunt.

After the long winter hunt in the Slim Buttes with the Duprees and their band of Cheyenne River Sioux, Riggs wrote that he was impressed with how they carried out the hunts throughout with religious feeling and fervor.

"Much that is good of their ancient religion shows in every detail," he declared.

Other beings were sometimes called on to help find buffalo. People watched a cawing raven that circled their camp and then flew away showing the way to the herds. Comanches sought the aid of a horned toad, which was known to scamper off in the direction of the nearest buffalo.

Artistry and holy places

Buffalo also figure in Native artwork in significant ways. Early Indian people used paintings, sculpture, beaded items and buffalo images shaped into effigies to reinforce cultural connections to the buffalo. Buffalo designs were painted on tanned or raw hides to embellish tepee covers and liners, shields, bags, clothing and drums.

One kind of historical record common among Indians of the Plains

Buffalo skulls and bones were used in ceremonials; so were medicine bags and bundles holding sacred objects, rattles, herbs and tufts of buffalo wool. NPS.

was the annual *winter count.* Painted on a buffalo hide, the winter count was a pictograph calendar that highlighted a single major event for each year in the tribe's history—such as a successful buffalo hunt. A single pictogram was selected to define the entire year and these were arranged in rows, a spiral or serpentine pattern. They were called winter counts because they counted the year from first snow to first snow.

Special ceremony applied to the care of a robe from a rare white buffalo. In some tribes, if a white buffalo was killed in a hunt, the fatal arrow was purified in the smoke of burning sweet grass. A knife was similarly purified before the animal was skinned. Only women noted for purity of life could tan a white hide, and after the tanning a medicine-man purified it. The tanned robe was always kept in a rawhide case and usually buried with its owner. If willing to sell it, he also gained honor. A small piece was worth a horse.

A man called Charlie Jaw said that he killed a white buffalo at age thirteen when his band was in Canada. He kept the hide all winter and sold it next spring to a man named Bone Club for two horses, a big buffalo-hide tent, and many other articles, he said.

Special places were revered. Rock carvings and petroglyphs can be found on cliffs throughout the west. Traditionally this art holds mystical power.

Rock art is an ancient tradition, dating perhaps to the earliest humans in the area, according to Marcel Kornfeld, George C. Frision and Mary Lou Larson in their book on prehistoric hunters. They describe important advances in dating techniques along with having a better understanding today of the cultural context as a key in analyzing their meaning. Thus, sites known for decades are being revisited, thoroughly mapped and recorded. Wyoming rock art has been at the forefront of much of their research. Their teams also investigate Montana sites found nearby in the Tongue River and Powder River Basin. Many of these include buffalo images along with their rounded hoof prints.

The Medicine Rocks, petroglyphs on the rocky crown of a hill on the Cannonball River north of Standing Rock Sioux Reservation, is one of six such sites in North Dakota. Known to early European travelers, including Lewis and Clark in 1804 and Prince Alexander Philipp Maximilian in the 1830s, the Medicine Rocks feature buffalo effigies and the deeply carved tracks of buffalo travelling across a high rocky point, capturing the view of a wide area. The little-known site, not far from where the last buffalo were hunted at

A buffalo skull painted and adorned with feathers from Fort Yates. L Allard.

Hiddenwood on Standing Rock, is still visited as a sacred site with ceremony and gifts of tobacco and cloths by Native people. Visitors are asked to be respectful and refrain from climbing on the rocks or disturbing offerings left at the site.

The Black Hills are perhaps most revered of all, with their crown jewel, Bear Butte—a volcanic eruption on the northeast corner. Bear Butte rises from the flat plain in the shape of a large slumbering bear. With its sweat baths and private vision-seeking trails, it is a sacred place for many Plains tribes and personal pilgrimages.

Farewell to the Buffalo

Their close relationship with the buffalo is expressed by John Fire Lame Deer, "*his flesh and blood being absorbed by us until it became our own flesh and blood. . . It was hard to say where the animals ended and the human began.*"

Buffalo provided everything the Kiowas needed, as told by a grandmother called Spear Woman. They stitched their tepees of buffalo hides, as well as their clothes and moccasins. They ate buffalo meat all through the year. They made containers of hide, bladders and stomachs. Even more important, buffalo sustained their culture, their spiritually and religion. They were the life blood of tribal life.

But war raged between buffalo and the white men, who shot them mercilessly up and down the Plains by the hundreds and thousands. At last the buffalo saw they could no longer protect the Native people.

One day a band of Kiowa camped on the north side of Mount Scott, Oklahoma. Next morning a young woman rose very early.

Artist paints animal figures on the hide side of buffalo robe in the tepee, while his wife looks on. *The Picture Robe*, 1899, CM Russell.

A mist rose over Medicine Creek. As she peered through the haze, she saw the last buffalo herd like a spirit dream moving toward the base of the mountain. The face of the mountain opened and in walked the big herd bull, followed by cows, calves and young males.

Before the mountain closed up she saw fresh, green grass inside, clear streams and flowers blooming up the slopes. The buffalo walked into this beautiful world and were never seen again.

8

Way of the Hunt

I go to kill the buffalo
The Great Spirit sent the buffalo
On hills, in plains and woods
So give me my bow, give me my bow
I go to kill the buffalo.

—Sioux song
   from *Teton Sioux Music*, 1918, Frances Densmore

For thousands of years Native Americans hunted buffalo on foot with homemade weapons—spears, clubs, bows and arrows. It took a powerful arm to shoot a fatal arrow through tough buffalo hides and was not easy to get close enough for the kill.

Buffalo hunting was a spiritual experience for hunters. They sought divine intervention before and during hunts. Religious rites, prayers and gratitude played an important part in every hunt, as they did in daily life.

"Before the buffalo run, a ceremony took place, with prayers to the Great Spirit that all would go well, for success in the hunt with no injury or accidents," wrote Josephine Waggoner, a Hunkpapa historian.

For Plains tribes, buffalo were the source of life itself. A prosperous

Stampeding buffalo over a cliff without horses or guns took careful planning and a sizeable herd for success. Photo courtesy of Head-Smashed-In Buffalo Jump World Heritage Site.

fall hunt saved them from winter starvation and provided warm robes against the cold.

They ate buffalo meat—fresh and preserved—steak, stew, jerky, pemmican, tallow, organ meats, bone marrow and tongues. The skin dressed as robes or leather, cured for tepee covers, clothing, moccasins, bedding, blankets, bridles, saddles, ropes, bull boats stretched over round willow frames, shields, bags for storing and carrying, as well as sinews for bow strings and thread and hair made into belts and ornaments. Bones, hooves, horns and skulls were used in religious ceremonies and fashioned into spoons, drinking vessels, weapons, hoes, toys and made into glue. Even buffalo chips became valuable fuel for heating and cooking—often the only fuel available.

Buffalo gave the Plains people everything they needed to live—food, shelter, clothing and much more. They wasted nothing and every part was honored.

As tribes grew larger, they invented a spectacular way to obtain large quantities of meat all at once. Long before they saw their first horse, ancient Indian hunters of the plains discovered the secrets of the buffalo jump—the natural curiosity of the buffalo, their unique eyesight with broad field of vision, their tendency to stampede when panicked—that made it possible to trap and slaughter huge numbers.

"Nowhere else on earth, at any point in time, did people obtain more food in a single moment than

For a successful jump, archaeologists believe it was important to gather a rather large herd and rush the buffalo into a stampede as they near the cliff, so leaders were forced over the edge by horned masses pressing from behind. Otherwise agile leaders would dodge aside. Photo courtesy of Head-Smashed-In Buffalo Jump World Heritage Site.

Traditional Uses of the Buffalo

Skull
Altar
Dehairing Tool
Sun Dance

Brains
Food
Hide Preparation

Horns
Arrow Points
Cups
Fire Carrier
Headdresses
Ladles
Medication
Ornaments
Powderhorn
Signals
Spoons
Toys

Blood
Paints
Puddings
Soups

Beard
Ornaments

Bones
Arrowheads
Awls
Eating utensils
Fleshing Tools
Game Dice
Jewelry
Knives
Painting tools
Pipes
Quirts
Saddle Trees
Scrapers
Shovels
Sleds
Splints
Toys
War Clubs

Tongue
Choice Meat
Comb (Rough Side)

Teeth
Ornaments

Fat
Soaps
Tallow
Tanning
Hair Grease
Filled Pipe Sealer
Cosmetic Aids

Liver
Food
Tanning Agent

Gall
Yellow Paint

Tendons & Muscles
Arrow Ties
Bowstrings
Cinches
Sinew

Foot Bones
Teething Toys
Toy Buffalo or Horse

Rawhide
Horse-water Trough
Moccasin Soles
Containers
Quivers
Ropes
Shields
Splints
Lariats
Buckets
Caps
Drums
Rafts
Saddles
Shrouds
Straps

"Par fleche"
Masks
Cinches
Ornaments
Rattles
Sheaths
Snowshoes
Trunks

Stomach Liner
Cooking Vessels
Water Container

Scrotum
Containers
Rattles

Bladder
Food Pouches
Medicine Bags
Water Container

Meat
Immediate use
Dried
Meat/Jerky
Pemmican
Sausages

Tail
Decorations
Fly Swatter
Knife Sheaths
Medicine
Switch
Whips

Dung
Diaper Powder
Fuel

Hoof Sheath
Containers
Glue
Rattles
Spoons
Wind Chimes

Stomach Contents
Medicines
Paints

Dew Claws
Glue
Rattles
Wind Chimes

Tanned Hide
Backrests
Bags
Beds
Belts
Blankets
Bridles
Caps
Cradles
Doll Mittens
Dresses
Leggings
Moccasin Tops
Pillows
Pouches
Ropes
Shirts
Sweat lodge Cover
Tapestries
Tipi Liners
Tipi Covers
Winter Robes

Hair
Bracelets
Braided Ropes
Doll Stuffing
Hair Pieces
Headdresses
Horse Halters
Medicine Balls
Moccasin Lining
Ornaments
Pad Fillers
Pillow Fillers

Courtesy of Intertribal Buffalo Council

The drop off these cliffs at First Peoples Buffalo Jump State Park, west of Great Falls, MT, averages twenty-one feet, but may have been double that before the filling from bones, earth and artifacts that stretched below for over 1,000 feet along the cliffs, scientists say. During World War II, 328 tons of bones were shipped from this jump site to munitions plants on the west coast for making explosives. FM Berg.

they did at a communal bison kill," said Archaeologist Jack W. Brink, of the Royal Alberta Museum, who works with Head-Smashed-In Buffalo Jump.

The buffalo jump

The rough, broken terrain and badlands of the Great Plains were well suited to the buffalo jump. Steep, high cliffs border rivers and creeks. Sudden, fierce storms send raging waters against the cliffs, breaking off banks, forging new waterways and scouring out drop-offs and rock formations.

Large herds of buffalo frequently grazed the broad rich grasslands on the plateaus above these cliffs. It took a careful plan, expertly executed, and a well-directed stampede to drive them over. And then sharp spears, clubs and stone knives to finish off any crippled animals on the rocks below.

No one knew their prey better than did these ancient hunters of the prairies and plains. Skilled hunters sensed the best way to direct each hunt, whether to drive or entice willing buffalo and when to send them into stampede.

"Prehistoric hunters were capable of killing the animals under their own terms and not those of the animals," write Marcel Kornfeld, George C. Frison and Mary Lou Larson, in their authoritative 2010 book, *Prehistoric Hunters-Gatherers of the High Plains and Rockies*, now in its third edition.

Today we have much data on early hunting techniques in the Plains, thanks largely to the senior author of that book, George Frison, who wrote the first two editions in 1978 and 1991, did much of the research, and revolutionized **theories on early hunting cultures.**

Called, "Dean of the great people in the research and study of buffalo jumps," George Frison, former head of the anthropology department at the University of Wyoming, visited more buffalo jumps than any other person on earth, according to Jack Brink.

Frison became a scientist in what may have been, for him, the best possible way—by starting at home. It took him nearly four decades of ranching to realize that to have the career he wanted, he needed an education in archaeology. Born in Wyoming in 1924 and raised on the family ranch at Ten Sleeps, Frison spent his early years working cattle, while at the same time collecting artifacts and hanging around a nearby dinosaur dig. He joined volunteer archaeology teams, and as a hunter himself, his passion became the early hunters of big game in the area—the ways they hunted buffalo and mammoths, working with the natural traits of the animals they knew well.

Dissatisfied with theories he encountered, Frison enrolled in the University of Wyoming in 1962 at age 37 and received his PhD five years later. He returned to that university as head of the new Department of Anthropology. Soon he was organizing field work at numerous Wyoming sites, and began publishing articles and books on the findings and how they fit his theories. Frison believed archaeologists of the day failed to consider the behavior of wild animals and often portrayed buffalo hunters using unrealistic and illogical methods.

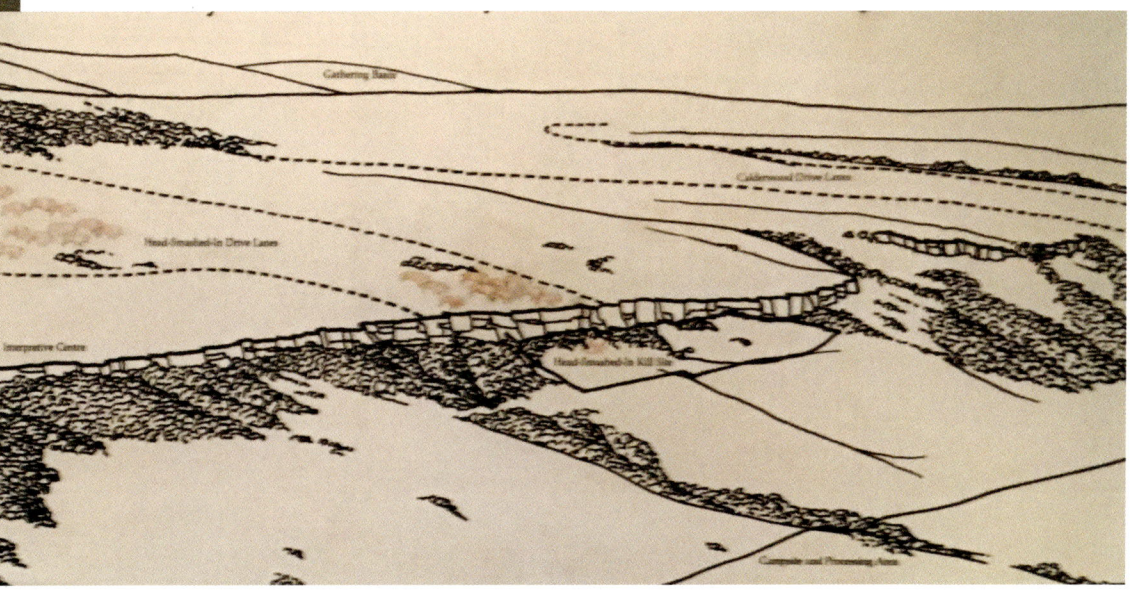

Drive lanes above the jump may have looked something like this, as mapped from rock placements at Head-Smashed-In and the Calderwood jump. FM Berg.

Head-Smashed-In and First Peoples

Buffalo jumps are found throughout the Great Plains. Two of the most amazing and spectacular are Head-Smashed-In Buffalo Jump near Fort Macloed in southern Alberta, Canada, and First Peoples Buffalo Jump, only a few hundred miles south, near Great Falls, Montana.

Head-Smashed-In is ideally located for buffalo in hilly, broken country close to a river, with excellent grazing of the massive basin area and plateaus behind the jump. It was first used about 5,700 years ago.

Originally the drop off the rocky cliff was around sixty-five feet, but bone and other deposits

The rocks located for cairn lines are clustered together, spaced about fifteen feet apart. Current thinking is that rather than being piled into cairns, these may have denoted platforms for building living barriers. FM Berg.

have piled halfway up over the thousands of years, leaving only a thirty-three foot drop. On the prairies above, a massive drive lane and rock cairn complex involves thousands of cairns extending more than six miles back from the cliff.

The hunting party quick-butchered the carcasses at the jump site, then finished processing meat and hides farther below at a camping site near water, both rich in artifacts. Several other jumps are known in the area, as well as additional camp and processing sites, a vision-quest site, a historic burial site, eagle-trapping pits, bedrock quarries and a series of petroglyphs.

The *Head-Smashed-In* name comes from a Blackfoot oral tradition of a young boy who wanted to watch the buffalo fall from the cliff. He found a protective overhang and hid as they came thundering over. The hunt was unusually good that day. As the buffalo bodies piled up, he became trapped between them and the cliff. When his people came for the butchering, they found him with his skull crushed by the heavy buffalo carcasses.

Named as a UNESCO World Heritage Site in 1981, the Canadian Head-Smashed-In Buffalo Jump

Ancient people may have propped tree branches with brush, rocks, clumps of sod, buffalo chips and grasses at each location to wave in the breeze, conveying a sense of motion, as if people were waving hides along the drive lines. Courtesy of Head-Smashed-In Buffalo Jump World Heritage Site.

has a magnificent interpretive center with outstanding exhibits and is being operated with the advice and assistance of Native Blackfoot people from the area. The guides are Native people and they tell stories of their own tribe. Research began there in the early 1960s.

First Peoples Buffalo Jump State Park, west of Great Falls, formerly known as the Ulm jump, is located on a rocky escarpment so long that it is being called possibly "the world's largest buffalo jump." First Peoples has a spectacular location in the Missouri River valley where the Rocky Mountains rise rapidly to the Continental Divide on the west and south, and nearby Highwood and Little Belt Mountains stand out as dramatic uplifts in the surrounding plains.

The rocky crest has an average drop of twenty-one feet on the nearly mile-long butte. Below the drop, concentrated cultural materials of bones and artifacts stretch for over 1,000 feet, and less dense remains extend nearly 10,000 feet. The earliest of three carbon datings is 1,000 years ago, with many areas as yet undated. Artifacts found there include tools, arrowheads and lance points, scrapers, cutting tools, broken pottery and a maul for pounding dried meat and berries into pemmican. The Interpretive center opened in 1999 and is permanently staffed, amid concerns over looting, being close to a large population area. During World War II, 328 tons of bones were shipped out from below the First People jumps and butchering sites.

Known buffalo jumps number in the hundreds across the Plains, and it seems likely that represents only a small percent of what's out there.

Other well-known Canadian sites include the Old Women's Buffalo Jump, and Dry Island Buffalo Jump Provincial Park. Montana reportedly has the highest concentrations of Buffalo Jumps, but only three with interpretive centers: in addition to First Peoples, these are Madison Buffalo Jump State Park, west of Logan

When ready, the drive lines may have looked like this, with the aim of keeping buffalo in the low area funneling them toward the drop-off. Sometimes the drive lines stretched for miles. Courtesy of Shayne Tolman, *Imagining Head-Smashed-In*.

and the Little River site west of Havre. Other jumps are known in southeastern Montana, Big Horn County, Montana, where HooDoo Creek runs into Dry Head Creek, used by the Crow Indians. The complex of drive lanes and jump cliffs is known to the Crow Tribe as "Where They Get Their Meat," says Joseph Medicine Crow of the Crow Indians. Stories of these are learned from tribal storytellers. Others include the Yonkee complex near Broadus, and nearby, the Vore site in that corner of Wyoming.

Many jumps that have been investigated in the past are really begging for some reworking and reinterpretation, given the knowledge and methods now available, says Frison. Other likely sites, doubtless well used in their day, are located but have not been excavated or verified.

Local folks wondered for years about a bone site in the area of the last great buffalo hunts south of Lemmon, SD. A steep cliff, rich with two layers of buffalo bones—the top layer twelve feet thick under twenty-five feet of earth, and beneath that four feet of earth and another four feet of bones overlooked the North Grand River, now dammed into Shadehill Reservoir at that point. Bones, horns, teeth and large masses of almost indestructible stomach contents were well preserved, although not fossilized. People speculated as to whether this was a buffalo jump used by native hunters during at least two different periods, or perhaps a natural trap where lightening or fires drove large buffalo herds over the edge.

More recently Shadehill has been declared a buffalo jump by the South Dakota Game, Fish and Parks department that administers the recreation park around Shadehill Lake. Other archaeologists who have researched prehistoric activity in the area include a team from the University of North Dakota archaeology department

Shadehill Buffalo Jump from north side of the lake. SD Game, Fish and Parks sign describes jump and about 115 possible prehistoric sites and artifacts found in area. Photo by Vince Gunn.

The optical illusion at the edge of First Peoples Buffalo Jump makes the drop nearly invisible. One day a worker nearly drove his pickup off the rocky edge. FM Berg.

in 1990 and another that more recently excavated a Wind Farm project just north of Hettinger. They suggest Shadehill Buffalo Jump was used to hunt buffalo by prehistoric people during the Early Plains Archaic tradition, 5,000 to 7,500 years ago, likely using atl-atl weaponry—dart points with a throwing stick. An informative Game, Fish and Parks sign points out that some 115 prehistoric sites with artifacts have been discovered in the area, extending back thousands of years.

The Shadehill buffalo jump, like many others, was mined for bones during World War II. "Much of the natural phosphorus extracted from the bones went for the manufacture of munitions," says a Canadian source.

Jumps had many variations, depending on the terrain, herd location and wind direction.

The Vore Buffalo Jump, not far from Devil's Tower in northeast Wyoming, does not involve a typical cliff, but rather, a trap. Vore, named for the rancher who found it and donated the land, is a large natural sink hole at the base of a long sloping ravine that opens out into a broad, flat valley, conveniently just off highway I-90. It was discovered in the building of that interstate highway. The Native hunters drove their stampeding buffalo like a herd of cattle down that ravine, pointing them tightly toward a deep hidden hole in the grass. Analysis of bones and artifacts reveal the sink hole opened up around 1550 and was used by many tribes through 1800.

Drive lines and cairns

A key to success in buffalo jumps lay with skilled use of the "gathering basin" and the cairn lines on either side of the drive lane. Snaking over the hills, some cairn lines stretch for miles behind a jump, wings spread wide across the plain, then funneling in tighter toward the cliff.

Such drives were not necessarily the work of a single day. These hunters knew when to press and when to hold back.

Even today in corralling their buffalo, herd manager Robbie Magnon, of Fort Peck Sioux and Assiniboine Reservation in northeastern Montana, explains the best

In deep-snow winters buffalo could be trapped in snowdrifts by men on snowshoes. Sketch by George Caitlin.

way to avoid upsetting buffalo is by spending a couple of days bringing them in to the corrals.

Between their large pasture and the working corral are two or three successively smaller pastures. The first day, driving several pickup trucks, the Fort Peck crew might not bring the buffalo through the first gate, but by exerting gradual pressure from a distance, patiently haze them closer. That night the herd might walk through the open gate on its own. The handlers close it and proceed in the same way toward the next gate.

The drive lanes outlined shallow valleys that the buffalo naturally followed as they approached the cliff. The valley directed the animals forward while hunters and cairns held the high ground on both sides, pressuring them to stay low. Other hunters fell in behind to keep them from turning back.

The buffalo were sometimes teased into the drive lanes by a medicine man acting as a decoy, who traditionally held special power over them. Dressed fancifully or perhaps in a buffalo or wolf skin, the shaman attracted their attention and excited their curiosity by prancing and bowing, alternately appearing and disappearing. Several of the closer buffalo began to watch and to approach, then eventually to chase the medicine man as he sped away.

George Bird Grinnell wrote that the medicine man zig-zagged this way and that, never attempting to drive them, but always to lead.

"The driving began only after the herd had passed the outer rock piles, and the people had begun to rise up and frighten them."

The cairns show up as five or ten inconspicuous rocks clustered together, spaced perhaps fifteen feet apart. At one time it was believed the hunters built them into solid rock piles. But current thinking is that they were more like platforms to show the locations to build a livelier barrier, which might have some resemblance to the hunters themselves.

We can imagine the lively effect of tree branches propped up with brush, clumps of sod and buffalo chips and topped by long waving grasses. They likely conveyed a sense of motion, similar to a person waving a buffalo hide, as the archaeologists suggest. White interviewers of tribal elders have sometimes called them *deadmen*.

With their wide peripheral vision the buffalo would see hunters everywhere but straight ahead.

Those who placed the thousands of rocks in the cairn lines detected every nuance in the roll and sway of the land, as if they could view it from above. As if figuring out where each effigy would need to go to control the animals.

Sometimes a line of smoke and flames held the secret to the jump's success.

When using fire, the hunters gradually formed a semicircle behind the herd. At a signal from the hunt leader, each fired the dry prairie grass in front of him, creating a wave of crackling flames. Panicked, the buffalo ran faster and faster in a final stampede toward the opening.

The stampede needed to come at the very end, within the last quarter or half mile so the herd did not string out, with slower animals falling behind, according to Frison and his co-authors Kornfeld and Larson. In their 2010 book they refined the theory of how that worked.

First, the hunters needed a sizeable buffalo herd to stampede successfully, so they would crowd together. Then if the leaders balked or tried to escape off to the side, this was prevented by the mass of large, heavy animals pressing from behind with sharp horns. Too late, this carried them over the precipice.

In a small or scattered herd the agile leaders could detect trouble in time to stop, dodge sideways or make a complete 180 turn. And if one escaped, likely all would follow.

The cliff scene is summed up: "The final moments of a great buffalo drive were without parallel in the events of world prehistory.

"For sheer raw power, unbridled danger, nail-biting suspense and rampant drama, there may be nothing in the archaeological record that can match the final few seconds of a herd of stampeding buffalo arriving at the edge of a steep cliff," writes Brink.

After the buffalo plunged over, the hunters rushed to finish off injured animals that survived the fall, killing with clubs, bows and arrows and lances shaped with stone tools, and tipped with stone, bone or shells. They completed the butchering process at a nearby camp using stone scrapers and knives, fleshers of shoulder blade bones, and punches from elk antlers. They pounded dried meat into pemmican with grooved mauls

Rushing waters of small rivers break out new gulches, box canyons and steep cliffs in flood stage. Pete Dupris may have come to this very spot on the South Grand River with team and wagon to save buffalo calves *(Site 5 on the Buffalo Trails Tour.)* FM Berg.

made from smooth river stones.

Thousands of years later many such artifacts are dug out of the bone beds.

The box canyon or arroyo trap

In rugged areas of the plains, prone to erosion, sometimes the sudden rushing waters and waterfalls form box canyons with steep vertical walls on three sides—the perfect trap for a small bunch of buffalo pursued by determined hunters.

Traps have claimed less attention than buffalo jumps—with their great heaps of bones and arrow points. But Kornfeld, Frision and Larson say that likely more buffalo died in various kinds of traps than were killed in buffalo jumps.

A classic example of what archaeologists call a "box canyon" or "arroyo bison trap" is the Hawkin site just south of Sundance, Wyoming. Bones and artifacts show that at least 80 animals had been driven from the bottom up to the headcut where they were killed. Dating analysis shows the Hawkin site was used as early as 6,600 years ago.

The Agate Basin arroyo site has been researched in northeastern Wyoming, as well as to some extent in the surrounding area in Montana and the Dakotas. Others are along the Cheyenne River south of the Black Hills, where arroyo traps have been identified.

Wyoming archeologists twice excavated the Wardell Buffalo Trap northeast of Big Piney. Used 800 to 1,600 years ago, hunters drove their herds as far as a mile, with sagebrush and grease-wood wings extending a fourth to a half mile toward the river to help funnel buffalo into the arroyo trap. The two field seasons—the original dig in 1970 and a three-month Bureau of Land Management

This dry gulch with steep walls and hidden turns could have served as a natural trap for buffalo hunting along the South Grand River. Archaeologists say more buffalo probably died in such traps than in large communal buffalo jumps. FM Berg.

dig in 2005—yielded over three tons of bones and more than 400 projectile points. This large quantity of bones and artifacts led to a huge leap in knowledge of late prehistory occupation of the Green River Valley. The difficulty in researching arroyo traps and the reason they've been neglected, the Wyoming experts tell us, is that the evidence tends to wash far downstream and scatter in many directions, in contrast to buffalo jumps, where big piles of bones, arrowheads and butchering tools are preserved at the site, usually protected by layers of earth.

With traps, the bones and artifacts lie in the bottom of draws and canyons washed by every flood. Heavy runoff carries most of the remains downstream, while some collect with mud and trash and form a barrier—even changing the course of the stream. This might be exposed at a later time with more runoff.

In this sketch a narrow ravine with steep sides formed a trap for buffalo, along with careful planning and placement of hunters. Courtesy of Head-Smashed-In Buffalo Jump World Heritage Site.

They note that many events of cut and fill have occurred over hundreds and thousands of years of hunting —making it both positive and negative for discoveries. Times of fill covered and preserved the evidence of ancient hunting, while the down cutting swept away the evidence and scattered it far and wide.

Naturally, rivers and headcuts migrate over time and may not continue to form steep-sided box canyons in places they once did.

A gulch that could have been used as an arroyo or dry gulch trap can be seen on the *Buffalo Trails in the Dakota Buttes* tour of the last buffalo hunts *(Site 5)* on the South Grand River. To investigate the terrain at this point, hikers follow the fence southeast and at the end take the steep sandy trail down toward the water. About halfway down the trail, off to the right, is a dry gulch with steep sides and a headcut that could act as a trap, or box canyon.

Like other plains rivers, the Grand River repeatedly cuts into the buttes lining its banks, washing away the face of steep cliffs and breaking out new gulches and draws. Some gulches lead to an abrupt "headcut" where floodwaters have dropped in waterfalls—forming a steep wall at the upper end.

Let's imagine a family group of prehistoric hunters looking down on a band of ten or twenty buffalo in the low grassy area along the South Grand River (pictured on page 139 and 140). From the plateau above, the hunters plan their approach. Scanning the area for drive lines used in previous hunts perhaps reveals two or three possibilities. They'll want the breeze from the buffalo in their faces to avoid sending early warnings.

The hunters decide to bring the buffalo into the gulch along the near side of the river on the narrow strip of land that runs below the bank. For this they will need to drive the buffalo up on the west side of the river, past the point where it turns abruptly against the bank. The leaders recognize the weak links in their plan and determine where to station persons to step out of hiding at just the right moment.

If all goes well, three or four hunters haze the entire herd from a careful distance along the trail under the bank. As the buffalo reach the opening a woman and dog step out ahead. Seeing her, they turn smoothly into the gulch as if relieved to find an escape. Twists and turns in the brushy gulch disguise what lies ahead—a box canyon with high straight sides. The hunters rush forward to slaughter as many buffalo as possible, piling up large bodies across the narrow entrance. Up above wait women with children and dogs, ready to jump out of hiding when needed, to guard any weak points and keep the panicked animals down in the gulch.

Off to the left of the sandy trail is another long draw with sides too gradual for trapping buffalo. It's a nice draw for climbing, following one of the many deer trails going up both sides through shady cottonwoods—an ideal route for hikers to return to the flat above.

Note: Just a few miles downstream the Shadehill Buffalo Jump *(Site 6)* rises from the lake, dammed during the 1950's. The same prehistoric hunters who hunted box canyons up the river likely used that jump for large communal hunts.

Although this dry gulch trap has not been excavated, others in this area have been, several nearby in northeastern Wyoming.

Trapping buffalo in a dry gulch or box canyon is a method that archaeologists are paying closer attention to today, due to the diligence of Wyoming researchers.

The Surround

The first successful method for large hunts may have been the "surround," speculates David A. Dary. It required less preparation, but considerable good luck.

In the surround, a band of Native people, both men and women, cautiously encircled a band of buffalo of manageable size. Then running circles around the animals and shouting, they slowly closed the circle.

If all went according to plan, the confused buffalo began milling around in a defensive circle, instead of running away. The bulls tend to circle protectively around the outside, with cows and calves in the middle.

The hunters fired their lances and arrows, killing the bulls in front of them. As they fell, they piled up a barrier around the circle, trapping the others inside until all were killed. Logs or trees were often incorporated to form a fence on one side.

In *The Blackfeet: Raiders on the Northwestern Plains*, Weasel Tail, an aged Blood Indian described a surround by his ancestors from the days before horses:

"After swift-running men located a herd of buffalo, the chief told all the women to get their dog travois. Men and women went out together, approaching the herd from downwind so the animals wouldn't get their scent and run off.

"The women were told to place their travois upright in the earth, small end up. The travois were so spaced that they could be tied together to form a semicircular fence. Women and dogs hid behind them.

"Two fast-running men circled the buffalo herd, approached the animals from upwind, and drove them toward the travois fence. Other men took positions along

Buffalo Hunt Surround. Hunters quietly encircled the buffalo, then attacked from all sides, trying to mill them into a circle of confusion. Painting by G. Caitlin.

the sides of the route and closed in as the buffalo neared the travois. Barking dogs and shouting women kept the buffalo back. The men rushed in and killed the buffalo with arrows and lances.

"After the buffalo were killed the chief went into the center of the enclosure, counted the dead animals and divided the meat equally among the participating families. He also distributed hides to the families for making lodge covers. The women hauled the meat and hides to camp on their dog travois. This was called a surround of the buffalo."

Grinnell described a surround making use of a decoy from early interviews he did with tribal elders.

"The people would go out on the prairie and conceal themselves in a great circle, open on one side. Then some man would approach the buffalo and decoy them into the circle.

"Men would now show themselves at different points and start the buffalo running in a circle, yelling and waving robes to keep them from approaching or trying to break through the ring of men. Of necessity this required great judgment and care, for once the herd started through in one direction it was impossible to turn. It would rush through the ring and be gone."

When large herds of buffalo grazed in the vicinity, it was a rule that no one go off to hunt alone or in small groups, which could stampede them many miles away. The rule was strict and any offender suffered severe consequences.

"Depending on the severity of the offence . . . the offender was punished by being whipped, his horse or dog killed, bow and arrows or gun stock broken. Sometimes they even cut up his tent and broke the poles," says Louis Garcia, Researcher and Historian for the Spirit Lake Dakota.

Native people were taught to refrain from the greed of taking more meat than entitled, thus leaving others to go without their share. Meat was divided by long tradition, according to Waggoner. In the early days, she said, when an animal was killed, the principal men examined the animal to see what arrow hit the fatal spot. "The mark of the arrow showed what band could butcher the beef. . . Sick, poor or aged, the head of every family received their share in equal amount. Most desirable cuts were issued in rotation within each band so as to avoid dissatisfaction."

Impounding

It is amazing that people with only stone tools could build pens strong enough to hold a herd of wild buffalo and drive them into it. But it is said that impounding was common among the Plains Crees in the south Saskatchewan country, as well as with the Assiniboine, Blackfeet and Gros Ventres and other tribes of the northwest, according to William Hornaday.

Basically a round corral, these were sometimes built by making an opening at the upper edge of a twelve-foot bank. The buffalo could easily jump down, but not leap up so high as to get back out.

Impounding is viewed as more difficult than the surround, since it required building a buffalo-proof enclosure and finding buffalo nearby. In rocky or wooded country, the hunters built strong enclosures of rocks and trees. These were used over and over in areas frequented by buffalo, successfully when the animals cooperated.

Old Weasel Tail, a Blood Indian, described the impound method: "Near the edge of timber and toward the bottom of a downhill slope the Indians built a corral of wooden posts set upright in the ground to a height of about seven feet. They connected the posts by crosspoles tied in place with rawhide ropes.

"Around three sides of the corral they laid stakes over the lowest crosspoles. Their butt ends were firmly braced in the ground outside the corral. These stakes projected about three feet inside the corral at an angle, so their sharpened ends were about the height of a buffalo's body. If the buffalo tried to break through the corral they would be impaled on these stakes.

"From the open side of the corral the fence of poles extended into two wings outward and up the hill. These lines were further extended by piles of cut willows in the shape of conical lodges about half the height of a man, tied together at their tops. These brush piles were spaced at intervals of several feet.

"On the hill just above the corral opening a number of poles were placed on the ground crosswise of the slope and parallel to each other. The buffalo had to cross these poles to enter the corral. The poles were covered with manure and water, which froze and became slippery so that once the buffalo were in the corral they couldn't escape by climbing back up the hill.

"Before the drive began a beaver bundle owner removed the sacred buffalo stones from his bundle and prayed.

"He sang a song, 'Give me one buffalo or more. Help me to fall the buffalo.'"

Hunters then went out to drive the herd of buffalo toward the

In an impoundment hunters built a strong enclosure of rocks, wood, trees or sharpened stakes near the bottom of a slope. The buffalo jumped down over poles at the entrance, making it difficult to get back out. Wm Hornaday, *The Extermination of the American Bison.*

corral. As the animals passed them going down the slope, women and children flew out of their hiding places. Once inside the corral, men and boys killed the buffalo from outside the stout fence.

"Then the camp chief went into the corral to take charge of the butchering and the division of the meat. While butchering, the people ate buffalo liver, kidneys and slices of brisket raw. Each man who killed a buffalo was given its hide and ribs. The slaughtered animals were cut into quarters which were divided among the families in the camp. Each family, whether large or small, received an equal share. Two young men took choice pieces of liver, kidneys, brisket, tripe and manifold to the beaver bundle owner who had remained in his lodge during the slaughter, but whose power had brought success in the hunt."

A man that William Hornaday cited as Professor Hind described a plains Cree pen he saw on the headwaters of the Qu'Appelle River in Canada in 1858. About 120 feet in diameter, it was built of tree trunks laced together and braced from the outside. Two rows of bushes, the Indians called "deadmen," guided the buffalo into the pound. The deadmen extended about four miles into the prairie, placed 50 feet apart at the entrance to perhaps two miles apart at the other end.

"When the skilled hunters are about to bring in a herd of buffalo from the prairie, they direct the course of the gallop of the alarmed animals by confederates stationed in hollows or small depressions who, when the buffalo appear inclined to take a direction leading from the space marked out by the deadmen, show themselves for a moment and wave their robes, immediately hiding again," he told Hornaday.

"This serves to turn the buffalo slightly in another direction and when the animals, having arrived between the rows of deadmen, endeavor to pass through them, Indians stationed here and there go through the same operation, and thus keep the animals within the narrowing limits of the converging lines.

"At the entrance to the pound there is a strong trunk of a tree placed about a foot from the ground and on the inner side an excavation sufficiently deep to prevent the buffalo from leaping back when once in the pound.

"As soon as the animals have taken the fatal spring, they begin to gallop round and round the ring fence, looking for a chance to escape, but with the utmost silence women and children on the outside hold their ropes before every orifice until the whole herd is brought in. Then they climb to the top of the fence and, with the hunters who have followed closely in the rear of the buffalo, spear or shoot with bows and arrows or firearms at the bewildered animals—rapidly becoming frantic with rage and terror within the narrow limits of the pound.

"A dreadful scene of confusion and slaughter then begins. The oldest and strongest animals crush and toss the weaker. The shouts of the excited Indians rise above the roaring of the bulls, the bellowing of the cows and the piteous moaning of the calves."

Travelling in Montana with the Yellowstone Expedition as late as 1873, J.A. Allen, said he several times saw the remains of pounds and their converging fences above the mouth of the Big Horn River, according to Hornaday. Thomas Simpson, reported that in 1840 three camps of Assiniboine Indians were in the vicinity of Carlton House in Montana. Each had a buffalo pound into which they drove forty or fifty buffalo every day. A pound was discovered about ten miles from Ft. Union in eastern Montana, along with thousands of buffalo bones. Another is near the junction of the Elbow and Bow Rivers near Calgary in Alberta.

Obviously, much could go wrong with even the best plans. Driving buffalo into a corral was no easy task. Sometimes none were found within miles of the trap. Other times shifting winds brought the scent of hunters, or some unusual sound or movement at the wrong time spooked the buffalo away from the funnel-like chute. Or perhaps the corral couldn't hold them.

Professor Hind reported ten days before the impound he described, 200 buffalo were driven into the same pen. But a wary old bull spotted a weak spot in the fence, charged it at full speed and burst through to freedom, followed by the herd. On foot, there was no way the hunters could recapture a buffalo herd galloping off into the distance, tails flung in the air.

Hunting success was of critical importance in the days of the dog—as that time was called. Sad stories passed down through generations tell of hunting failures resulting in near starvation for the tribe. Many of the buffalo impound sites survived and were used from time to time even after horses arrived.

Dogs in deep snow

Hunters made use of patches of deep snow and sand as traps.

In winters of deep snow Cheyenne hunters led trained dogs

No one knew their prey better than native hunters of the plains. Leaders followed traditional ritual, studied the buffalo herd, conferred together, then dashed into the hunt. *Watching for the Smoke Signal*, 1907, CM Russell.

on the hunt, according to Grinnell. They chased the buffalo into the deepest drifts in draws, set free the dogs to worry them and then ran up and killed them with lances. Buffalo floundering in pockets of deep snow, fighting off dogs, were easy prey even for hunters on foot.

After killing and cleaning buffalo, the ancient owners fed the dogs, then loaded packs on the dogs or harnessed them into dog travois to carry the meat back to camp. After the packs were taken off, the dogs circled back to the kill to eat their fill. Females with young pups returned to camp to disgorge food for their young—and then raced back for more.

Another hunt in deep snow is described by Paul Kane, the Canadian artist.

"Upon ascending the bank, we found ourselves in the close vicinity of an enormous band of buffaloes, probably numbering nearly 10,000. The snow was so deep that the buffaloes were either unable or unwilling to run far and at last came to a dead stand. We therefore secured our horses and advanced towards them on foot to within forty or fifty yards when we commenced firing, which we continued to do until we were tired of a sport so little exciting. For, strange to say, they never tried either to escape or to attack us."

Some tribes fashioned snow shoes for deep-snow winters. Buffalo could also be trapped on ice in wintertime.

When food was scarce good hunters went out often, alone or with a few friends.

In oral histories gathered by A.B. Welch is a story told of an outstanding hunter named John Grass from the Mandan, Arikara and Hidatsa tribes in northern Dakota.

One extremely cold day Grass took a small hunting party out from camp on foot.

"John Grass was carrying his bow. He carried his arrow carrier in front that time. His left hand froze tight about the bow. They could not open his fingers. They found a buffalo then. They cut it open along the belly and shoved his arm and bow inside. His hand was melted then. That was a very bad thing that time."

Single hunters could pick off old bulls separated from the herd and wounded by wolves, provided they could hold off the pack of wolves.

It was said that Flathead hunters were skilled at killing buffalo by rock throwing, choking or knifing them. A South Dakota report tells of Native hunters digging hiding places or caves in soft banks near trails leading down to water. Then they hid in the cave and killed buffalo as they went to drink.

Making a calf

Sometimes hunters disguised themselves with animal skins.

"We fell in with a small band of buffaloes and Francois initiated me into the mysteries of 'making a calf,'" explained Kane, hunting in Canada. This ruse was performed by two men, one covering himself with a wolf pelt, the other with a buffalo robe.

"They then crawl on all fours within sight of the buffaloes and as soon as they have engaged their attention, the pretend wolf jumps on the pretend calf, which bellows in imitation of a real one. The buffaloes seem to be easily deceived in this way. As the bellowing is generally perfect, the herd rush to the protection of their supposed young with such impetuosity that they do not perceive the cheat until they are quite close enough to be shot.

"Indeed, Francois' bellowing was so perfect that we were nearly run down. As soon, however, as we jumped up, they turned and fled.

"We shortly afterwards fell in with a solitary bull and cow and again 'made a calf.' The cow attempted to spring toward us, but the bull seeming to understand the trick, tried to stop her by running between us. The cow dodged and got round him and ran within ten or fifteen yards of us, with the bull close at her heels, when we both fired and brought her down. The bull instantly stopped short and, bending over her, tried to raise her up with his nose, evincing the most persevering affection for her. Nor could we get rid of him so as to cut up the cow without shooting him also, although bull flesh is not desirable at this season of the year."

In using disguises, Native people took on not just the appearance of the animal they had become, but they moved as it did.

"Having thousands of years to observe the behavior of all the game of the Plains, these fellow residents of the land would have an intimate knowledge of how each species walks, runs, sways, pauses, sniffs the air, lowers its head and paws the earth . . . They transformed themselves," said Jack Brink in *Imagining Head-Smashed-In: Aboriginal Buffalo Hunting on the Northern Plains*.

Another ruse of the two Canadians was *Making a snake*, "Which we often practiced with great success at Edmonton. It consisted in crawling on our bellies and dragging ourselves along by our hands, being first fully certain that we were to the leeward of the herd, however light the wind, lest they should scent us. Should there be twenty hunters engaged in the sport, each man follows exactly in the track of his leader, keeping his head close to the heels of his predecessor. The buffaloes seem not to take the slightest notice of the moving line, which the Indians account for by saying that the buffalo supposes it to be a big snake winding through the snow or grass."

Then came the horse, and soon after, trade guns.

Hunters often disguised themselves to get close enough for a fatal shot. The skins of wolves, familiar to every herd, caused little fear among buffalo. *Buffalo Hunt, Under the White Wolf Skin,* 1875-1878, G Caitlin.

Horses arrived on the plains by the mid-1700s and many tribes changed to buffalo-hunting nomads. Native Americans became perhaps the best horsemen the world has ever known. SD Fish, Game & Parks.

9

Running the Buffalo

Each [Métis] hunter then filled his mouth with balls
which he drops into the gun without wadding.
We now put our horses to the full gallop...
The scene became one of intense excitement;
The huge bulls thundering over the plains in headlong confusion,
Whilst the fearless hunters rode recklessly in their midst.
—Paul Kane
Wandering of an Artist among the Indians
of North America, 1859

The glorious days of "running buffalo" and "the chase" arrived with the horse in the 1700s. For most of two centuries, Native Americans of the Plains knew the exhilaration of hunting buffalo on horseback.

From childhood, Native boys and girls lived on horseback. They grew up with horses, trained horses and helped their fathers bring a favored horse into the tepee in bitterly cold weather when blizzards raged, feeding them tender twigs and dried cottonwood leaves. In battle, a warrior could hang off the opposite side of his horse to pick up a fallen comrade and both of them gallop off safely, hanging down on the off side, out of sight.

The first horses arrived in America with Columbus and the Conquistadors on his second voyage in 1493. It took several generations of Spaniards breeding horses, building missions and extending settlements across the southwest among the Pueblo, all the while doing their best to prevent Indians from learning to ride—before horses found their natural home in the west.

By the early 1700s the Comanche and Apaches owned sizeable horse herds and during the next forty years—through escape, raiding and trade—a new horse culture grew up across the west from south of the Rio Grande to the northern plains and prairies of Canada.

Horses brought mobility to the Plains Indians, with their enormous distances to travel. Many tribes became buffalo-hunting nomads. Having horses meant they traveled faster and farther in search of buffalo, while carrying with them all their worldly goods.

Once they had the horse, hunting became much easier, more successful—and more exciting.

Native Americans became excellent riders, perhaps the best horsemen the world has ever known.

The Chase

They called it "the chase" or "running buffalo"—the new hunting method was more efficient and far more exciting than before horses.

Even William Hornaday in his sober assessment called running buffalo, "A superior sport—manly, exhilarating and well spiced with danger. Even the horses shared the excitement and eagerness of their riders. It …demanded a good horse, a bold rider, a firm seat and perfect familiarity with weapons. The excitement of it was intense, the dangers not to be despised and, above all, the buffalo had a fair show for his life, or partially so, at least."

The hunts described in the first two chapters of this book are both examples of traditional *buffalo running,* although they differed greatly from each other. Leaders of the hunts laid careful plans. Throughout, the people integrated devout religious fervor, ceremony and ancient tradition in their preparations and in the daily events of the hunt.

In the Hiddenwood hunt, appointed police or *aki'cita* kept order. The chosen scouts rode out, located the enormous herd of buffalo, signaled their discovery from ten miles off and advised the approach. Divided into two columns, the 600 mounted hunters stealthily approached the herd from both sides. Then, following strict orders to start at the same moment—on threat of severe punishment—the hunters swept down on their game. In two days of slaughter they killed 5,000 buffalo. After this the shooting stopped and they cared for the meat and hides.

The winter hunt by the Cheyenne River Lakota in the Slim Buttes was structured more loosely, more family-oriented and the hunting lasted a long three months, counting travel time. As in the Hiddenwood hunt, religious ceremony and tradition were integrated throughout, and the police and scouts were selected in similar ways. But the method of hunt differed in that the buffalo were scattered into smaller bands through rough country and in deep snow. So at times all the hunters went out together, and other days they hunted in small groups in different directions. They killed 2,000 buffalo and took about 500 robes over the many weeks, while the women cared for meat and hides.

Running buffalo is described this way by an oral historian:

"Whenever the hunters discovered a herd of buffalo, they usually got to leeward of it and quietly rode forward in a body, or stretched out in a regular skirmish line, behind the shelter of a knoll, perhaps, until they had approached the herd as closely as could be done without alarming it. Usually the unsuspecting animals, with a confidence due more to their great numbers than anything else, would allow a party of horsemen to approach within from 200 to 400 yards of their flankers and then they would start off on a slow trot.

"The hunters then . . . dashed forward to overtake the herd as quickly as possible. Once up with it, each hunter chooses the best animal within his reach, chases him until his flying steed carries him close alongside, and then the arrow or the bullet is sent into his vitals. The fatal spot is from twelve to eighteen inches in circumference, and lies immediately back of the foreleg, with its lowest point on a line with the elbow."

George Grinnell, described an Indian hunt before they were armed with guns.

"The most exciting, and by far the most interesting, hunts in which I ever took part were those with the Indians of the plains. They were conducted almost noiselessly, and no ring of rifle-shot broke the stillness of the air, nor puff of smoke rose toward the still, gray autumn sky. The consummate grace and skill of the [half-] naked

The Scouting Party, 1897. The selected scouts surveyed the area thoroughly, then reported back the location of any buffalo, as well as any signs of hostile tribes. CM Russell.

Indians, and the speed and quickness of their splendid ponies, were well displayed in such chases as these."

Grinnell wrote poetically of the pleasure in watching the graceful Indian horsemen, "They swing and yield to every motion of their steeds with the grace of perfect horsemanship. The ponies as quick and skillful as the men, race up beside the fattest of the herd, swing off to avoid the charge of a maddened cow and, returning, dart close to the victim, whirling hither and yon, like swallows on the wing. And their riders, with the unconscious skill, grace and power of matchless archery, are drawing their bows to the arrow's head and driving the feathered shaft deep through the bodies of the buffalo. Returning on their tracks, they skin the dead, then load the meat and robes on their horses and with laughter and jest ride away."

The Plains Indians shortened their long bows to three feet for better shooting from horseback. With the short-range weapons available to them, Native hunters had to kill at close range. In running buffalo they rode close alongside the animal before they let fly their arrows and spears. Even the early trade guns were of such small caliber and with such light charges as to require close quarters.

The new, easier ways of hunting with horses did not totally end the old practices of buffalo jumps and traps. When the opportunity arose for using buffalo jumps or ancient impoundment structures, the mounted hunters took it, as some historical accounts testify. But it was on their terms, rather than a last desperate measure.

Before the hunt, Indian hunters removed saddles and adorned their horses with paint and feathers. They tore off their shirts and pants, and stripped down to breechcloths, as explained in oral histories.

"Every man had his arrows ready, with the special mark so he could claim the animals he killed. It was like a horse race. Those who had fast horses tried to get the fattest buffalo. Each tried to

The graceful native riders with their skillful ponies, wrote George Grinnell, "race up beside the fattest of the herd, swing off to avoid the charge of a maddened cow and returning, dart close to the victim, whirling hither and yon, like swallows on the wing." Badlands Reflections Photography.

get the best possible animals as his trophies of the hunt."

When running buffalo, every hunter appreciated the talents of his partner—an experienced, well-trained buffalo horse. A good horse for the chase was naturally fast and long-winded. When trained, it responded instantly to the rider's commands—to a shift of weight or a knee pressed against its ribs—yet could act quickly on its own initiative. With the courage to run close to buffalo, a good buffalo horse knew how to avoid contact with the shaggy beast at close range and keep clear of the vicious slash of horns. Moreover, it was sure of foot. It could run swiftly over uneven ground and across prairie dog towns without stumbling.

Their fastest horses could outrun the buffalo when fresh, but buffalo outran them over distance. Buffalo could stampede at top speed for ten miles or more, even in rough country. So it was important to get ahead quickly and bring down the leaders.

Great horses

According to all accounts the Indian horses were better trained than those of their white rivals, reported Hornaday. He credited this to the fact that shooting a bow required free use of both hands. This was only possible when the horse took the right course of his own free will or could be guided by knee pressure alone, holding close to the buffalo during a charge. Indeed, he said, "in running buffalo with only the bow and arrow, nothing but the willing cooperation of the horse could have possibly made this mode of hunting successful."

Indian horses seemed to take special pleasure in running buffalo. "But for the willingness and even genuine eagerness with which the buffalo horses entered into the chase, hunting on horseback would have been attended with almost insurmountable difficulties," he wrote.

The Hon. H. H. Sibley told of the dedication of one horse that had lost its rider on a Red River Métis hunt.

"One of the hunters fell from his saddle and was unable to overtake his horse, which continued the chase as if he of himself could accomplish great things, so much do these animals become imbued with a passion for this sport!"

Another hunter left his favorite buffalo horse in camp for a day's rest. He asked his wife to tie the horse. But the horse pulled loose and galloped off to join the hunt.

"He continued to keep pace with the hunters in their pursuit of the buffalo, seeming to await with impatience the fall of some of them to earth. The chase ended. He came neighing to his master, whom he soon singled out, although the men were dispersed here and there

Mounted Warrior, 1898, CM Russell.

for a distance of miles," wrote Sibley.

The explorers, Captains Meriwether Lewis and William Clark, too, were impressed with the passion for buffalo hunting of the Indian horses they purchased in trade. In returning by boat through the rich buffalo country along the Yellowstone River, Clark reported that Sergeant Pryor, who was in charge of bringing the forty-nine horses by land, found it almost impossible to drive them with the help of only two men.

"In passing every gangue of buffalow, the loos horses as soon as they saw the buffalow would imediately pursue them and run around them. All those that speed suffient would head the buffalow and those of less speed would pursue on as fast as they could. He found the only practicable method would be for one of [the riders] to proceed on and whenever they saw a gang of buffalow to scear them off before the horses got up."

Accidents and endurance

Running buffalo at close range was extremely dangerous. Often the hunter found himself hemmed in by the stampeding herd, in clouds of dust, so that neither he nor his horse could see the terrain beneath them. Fatal accidents to both men and horses were numerous.

Sometimes a wounded buffalo fell in front of a hunter riding at full speed. The only way to save himself was to leap his horse over the huge shaggy animal. A hunter had to keep his wits about him and be ready for any emergency, reported George Bird Grinnell, who spent time with several Plains tribes.

"Though he might run buffalo a thousand times without accident, the moment might come when only instant action would save his life." A noted naturalist, Grinnell joined the Pawnee in their last great hunt in 1872.

A man named Fool Bear told of an accident during his first buffalo hunt. Colonel A.B. Welch recorded his story among oral histories given by older men of the Mandan, Arikara, Hidatsa and Sioux tribes along the Missouri River in Dakota Territory during

Daring hunters swept in close, fired at point-blank range and stayed alert for any mishap. Wounded buffalo often charged their assailants. *Buffalo Hunt,* 1896, CM Russell.

the later 1800s.

"I was 17 years old when I took my first buffalo hunt with a regular party," said Fool Bear. "We went out to the west along the upper waters of the Cannonball River. I was with the right wing of the party and my friend was riding close by me. We were on the edge of the herd. It was moving rapidly. There were great clouds of dust. Many animals rushed out of the dust cloud.

"My horse stepped into a badger hole and broke his leg. I was on foot. A cow gored my horse. They were all around me. They snorted and plunged. I ran fast, but could not get out of the press. My friend could not reach me with his horse.

"I ran between two animals, a young bull and an old cow. I grabbed them both by the hair of their shoulders and held them together. I drew out my knife and watched the work of their fore shoulders. When the place was open I killed the cow with my knife in her heart. I did the same with the ten-year-old bull. I jumped on the backs of the herd and ran to the outside then. My friend was there. I got up behind him. We worked our way to the outside of the press. I gave him the right to paint this upon his tipi. I was young then and active—and brave."

Bears Arm, second chief of the Hidatsa, told how he, too, got caught on foot in the midst of a buffalo herd.

"A buffalo hunt had been arranged by our head men. The scouts told us of a great herd across by Washburn. We were living at that time at Fish Hook Village. We found the herd. We arranged the way to run them. I had a good trained buffalo horse. I was not hungry just then. I did not want to kill cows. I rode along [and] saw a splendid big fellow.

"I rode along his side, on the right side. Always kill buffalo bulls from that side. You can shoot arrows better. I picked out the spot to sink my arrow. I shot. I made the hit I wanted, but the arrow did not reach his heart.

"The buffalo made a very quick turn. He caught my horse and threw him into the air. While he was tearing his guts out, I got away afoot. I was among the animals. They were scared and running fast. The dust was thick. The roar of the feet was terrible. No one could reach me now. I grabbed a cow by the hair of her neck. I ran along by her side. She was afraid of me and soon was outside the main herd.

"I got away then. I did not kill her because she had been good to me. The old bull did not run far. He was shot in the lungs and was bleeding bad from his nose and mouth now. He stood apart alone and died standing up. I lost my horse [but] got the biggest hide there."

The painter George Catlin described joining a hunt in the 1820s:

"I dashed along through the thundering mass as they swept away over the plain, scarcely able to tell whether I was on a buffalo's back or my horse, hit and hooked and jostled about, till at length I found myself alongside my game, when I gave him a shot as I passed him."

Also fortunate was a Native companion who shot a big bull. His horse was gored by heavy horns as the dying buffalo lashed out, his hooves beating the air. As the horse fell across the buffalo, his friend flew over its back and landed hard. Picking himself up and feeling for his gun, his eyes and mouth full of dirt, he pulled at the reins. His horse opened its eyes and sprang to its feet, the dead buffalo lying between them.

Hunters said the big bulls took the outside of a herd when running, trying to protect the cows and younger bulls that stayed in the middle. A wounded bull could suddenly turn on his pursuer and gore horse or rider to death. Still, most hunting fatalities came from falls of horse or man.

"The danger is not so much from the buffalo . . . as from the fact that neither man nor horse can see the ground, which may be rough and broken or perforated with prairie dog or gopher holes," said one observer. "I have never known a man hurt by a buffalo in such a chase. I have known of at least six killed, and a very great many more or less injured, some very severely, by their horses falling with them."

Hornaday described his "mortal dread" of riding across a prairie dog town during a chase.

"The mouth of a prairie dog's burrow is amply large to receive the hoof of a horse, and the angle at which the hole descends into the earth makes it just right for the leg of a running horse to plunge into up to the knee and bring down both horse and rider instantly. The former with a broken leg, to say the least.

"If a rider sits loosely and promptly resigns his seat, he will go flying forward as if thrown from a catapult, for twenty feet or so, perhaps to escape with a few broken bones, and perhaps to have his neck broken or his skull fractured on the hard earth. If he sticks tightly to his saddle, his horse is almost certain to fall upon him and perhaps kill him."

Alexander Ross described a hunt by 400 Métis hunters from the Red River settlement. "The surface was rocky and full of badger holes. Twenty-three horses and riders were at one moment all sprawling on the ground. One horse, gored by a bull, was killed on the spot. Two more were disabled by the fall. One rider broke his shoulder blade. Another burst his gun and

Hunters said the bulls took the outside of a herd, trying to protect cows and calves. Most hunters tried to get inside the herd where they shot the more tender cows and young bulls. *Early Day White Buffalo Hunters,* 1922, CM Russell.

Stories of amazing hunting exploits and daring deeds were told and retold around evening campfires. *Theres Only One Hold Shorter,* CM Russell

lost three fingers. And a third was struck on the knee by an exhausted ball."

But the rewards were perhaps worth it, he wrote. "These accidents will not be thought over-numerous, considering the result. For in the evening no less than 1,375 tongues were brought into camp."

Amazing feats

Stories of amazing exploits by hunters were told and retold around evening campfires.

Among the Cheyenne, Grinnell recorded more than one instance when a hunter shot an arrow entirely through the bodies of two buffalo. And if an arrow did not sink deep enough, the hunter often jerked it out of the running buffalo and shot it again.

Tales of daring that unless seen seemed scarcely credible, Grinnell said. In one of these, the Cheyenne hunter Big Ribs rode his horse close up to the side of a huge bull and, leaping on his back, rode the buffalo for some distance and then with his knife gave him the deathstroke.

Strong Left Hand, a Cheyenne with special power and accuracy in stone-throwing, said he once killed a buffalo with only a stone, and in the same way, he had also killed an eagle and an antelope.

"We had been shooting at buffalo," he said. "They started to run and as the last one was going by I ran ahead of it and as I did so, picked up a stone from the ground. As I got in the buffalo's way it charged me, and raised its tail showing that it was angry. Just before it reached me, I threw the stone and hit it in the forehead, and it fell over, dead."

In another story, a hunter called the Trader was thrown from his horse onto the horns of a bull. One horn hooked under his belt and held him there while the galloping bull tossed him furiously back and forth. Unable to jump off, the Trader bounced along on the buffalo's head for a considerable distance. Finally the belt broke and he fell to the ground unhurt, while the bull ran off.

Métis hunts

The Métis (pronounced *Mah tee'* or *Mah tees'*) made a wholesale commercial business of hunting buffalo. They developed a market and used horses and guns from the first, yet ran buffalo in traditional ways, according to historic accounts.

They launched two big buffalo hunts a year, a two-month summer hunt in mid-June after planting crops, and a fall hunt when buffalo were fat and their hides prime. During these hunts they swept westward into Alberta and Saskatchewan and southwest into the great plains of Montana and the Dakotas. About half their produce of food, hides and robes was sold to the fur companies of the Northwest, the other half kept for their own use.

The Métis' roots went back to Indian mothers—mostly Cree, Ojibwe, Chippewa, and Assiniboin. Their fathers or grandfathers were French, Scotch or English, explorers and fur traders who paddled their canoes up the western rivers in the 1700s and settled with their families along the Red River of the north on both sides of the Canadian-US border. The fathers brought horses and guns; mothers contributed traditional hunting culture.

By 1820, Métis settlements included several generations of mixed-blood people living in the fertile Red River valley of Manitoba and Dakota Territory. By 1850 more than half the 5,000 to 6,000 people in the Canadian settlement in and around Fort Garry (now Winnipeg) were Métis, while south of the border the census counted 1,116 at Pembina, ND. An estimated 4,000 Métis lived in the Pembina Hills.

In French style they farmed small plots of land fronting on the Red River, which flows north into Lake Winnepeg and Hudson Bay. On these fertile lands they grew Indian corn, wheat, barley, potatoes and vegetables, as well as engaging in hunting and trapping.

When hunting they travelled in large groups for protection against plains tribes—especially the Sioux, who claimed hunting rights to the same territory and resented their wholesale slaughter.

As early as 1823 William H. Keating described a colorful group of Métis buffalo hunters who came from Fort Garry to rendezvous at Pembina, south of the border, waiting for others to arrive. Three hundred people came together to hunt in the Dakota plains and prairies, with at least 200 horses and 115 Red River carts. A fun-loving people, they filled their evenings with dancing and fiddle playing.

The Métis hunts were known by their long caravans of Red Riv-

Built like French peasant carts, Red River carts of the Métis, had two large wheels to smooth out the ride on rough prairies. The loud screeching noise of the ungreased wheels could be heard for miles. Long lines of carts, pulled by an ox or horse, crossed the west carrying pemmican, furs, trade goods and children. State Historical Society of North Dakota 00087-00074.

er carts crossing the prairies bound for the buffalo ranges and then, loaded with hides and pemmican, travelling to markets in Ft. Garry or St. Paul, Minn. Red River carts were built in the style of French peasant carts with two over-size wooden wheels, large enough to smooth out the ride over rough terrain and bound with leather straps. Each family filled several carts with hides. Small children rode on top. The loud screeching noise of the ungreased wheels could be heard for miles.

Devout Catholics, the Métis brought their priests along. They held Sunday services and did not hunt or travel on that day. At the same time they carried on traditional Indian hunting practices, as noted in their rules for the 1840 hunt.

In cool weather, Métis men wore woolen pants and a Hudson Bay coat with hood attached, often tied at the waist with a red sash, and slung their powder horn and shot bag over one shoulder. Women wore calico dresses with long, full skirts. Both men and women wore brightly-decorated moccasins, skillfully beaded in distinctive floral French patterns.

Women played an important role in every buffalo hunt. From the first, European fur traders needed Native women to cook for them, to prepare food supplies for winter, make and repair clothing, moccasins and snowshoes, and heal them when sick or wounded. Women packed extensive provisions for buffalo hunts, cooked, cared for babies and drove oxcarts. Often they left younger children to be cared for by others at home. After every buffalo kill, the women butchered, dried meat and made pemmican—the chief food product used in the far flung fur trade.

Victoria Belcourt Callihoo, a beloved and well-known Métis elder from northern Alberta, said she went on her first buffalo hunt at age thirteen. She went to help her mother, who was a medicine woman and a much needed healer during the hunts.

Paul Kane a Canadian artist, described his first Métis hunt on the prairies of Dakota Territory in June 1846. About 200 hunters and a number of women and children took part. Several of Kane's paintings depict scenes from that hunt.

At last "our scouts brought in word of an immense herd of buffalo bulls about two miles in advance of us. They are known in the distance [as bulls] by their feeding singly and being scattered wider over the plain, whereas the cows keep together for the protection of the calves, which are always kept in the centre of the herd."

As they prepared for the charge, older men strongly cautioned the less experienced not to shoot each other. Kane noted this was a "caution by no means unnecessary, as such accidents frequently occur."

The Métis men wore Hudson Bay coats with hood attached, tied at the waist with a colorful sash. Women wore calico dresses with long skirts and beautiful beaded moccasins. *Canadian Cree Trapper,* 1905, Edgar S Paxson.

Each hunter then filled his mouth with balls, "which he drops into the gun without wadding; by this means loading much quicker, and . . . whilst his horse is at full speed. It is true that the gun is more liable to burst . . . nor does the gun carry so far, or so true. But they always fire quite close to the animal."

The hunters charged at full gallop, all at once.

"There could not have been less than 4,000 or 5,000 [buffalo] in our immediate vicinity. All bulls, not a single cow amongst them. The scene now became one of intense excitement. The huge bulls thundering over the plains in headlong confusion, whilst the fearless hunters rode recklessly in their midst, keeping up an incessant fire at but a few yards distance from their victims. Upon the fall of each buffalo the successful hunter merely threw some article of his apparel—often carried by him solely for that purpose—to denote his own prey, and then rushed on to another. These marks are scarcely ever disputed, but should a doubt arise as to the ownership, the carcase is equally divided among the claimants," recounted Kane.

"In the meantime my horse, which had started at a good run, was suddenly confronted by a large bull that made his appearance from behind a knoll within a few yards of him, and being thus taken by surprise, he sprung to one side and getting his foot into one of the innumerable badger holes with which the plains abound, he fell at once, and I was thrown over his head with such violence that I was completely stunned, but I soon recovered. Some of the men caught my horse, and I was speedily remounted."

Kane counted himself lucky when he saw an unconscious man nearby being carried back to camp.

"I again joined in the pursuit and, coming up with a large bull, I had the satisfaction of bringing him down at the first fire. Excited by my success I threw down my cap, and galloping on, soon put a bullet through another enormous

Rules for the Métis hunt

The following rules were made for the 1840 hunt.

1. No buffalo to be run on the Sabbath Day.
2. No party to fork off, lag behind, or go before, without permission.
3. No person or party to run buffalo before the general order.
4. Every captain with his men, in turn, to patrol the camp, and keep guard.
5. For the first trespass against these laws, the offender to have his saddle and bridle cut up.
6. For the second offense, the coat to be taken off the offender's back, and be cut up.
7. For the third offense, the offender to be flogged.
8. Any person convicted of theft, even to the value of a sinew, to be brought to the middle of the camp, and the crier to call out his or her name three times, adding the word "Thief," at each time.

An estimate claimed that the Métis from the Red River of Canada and northeastern Dakota killed 30,000 buffalo in 1850. They kept about half their production and sold the other half to Hudson Bay and other fur companies. Red River camp and carts. MHS.

animal. He did not however fall, but stopped and faced me, pawing the earth, bellowing and glaring savagely at me. The blood was streaming profusely from his mouth, and I thought he would soon drop. He suddenly made a dash at me."

Kane fired again, a fatal shot.

The chase continued about an hour and extended over five or six square miles. Five hundred dead and dying buffalo littered the area. Returning to camp the hunters found a confused bull had charged among the tents and tepees, and finally entered one, scattering the women and children. Unable to chase him out, they shot him from the opening in the top of the tepee.

Next day the hunters again pursued a large herd of bulls "with good success."

The plain, he said, now resembled "One vast shambles. The women being all busily employed in cutting the flesh into slices and hanging them in the sun, on racks made of poles tied together."

Kane does not explain why they opted to shoot bulls instead of scouting farther for cow herds. Most Native hunters expressed a strong preference for cows, since their meat was more tender and tasty and the hides more pliable that that of old bulls. Perhaps it was because the Métis's primary products were pemmican and dried meat, for which tenderness was less important. Further, of course, the bulls produced larger quantities of meat.

The women made pemmican by pounding the dried meat into pieces, placing it into an oblong bag of buffalo hide, and then pouring in an equal amount of hot buffalo fat. They mixed the contents thoroughly and sewed the bags shut.

Each bag weighed ninety to 100 pounds and held on average the carcass of one buffalo. One cart carried ten of these bags or about 900 to 1,000 pounds of buffalo

Buffalo leg bones broken in ancient manner to remove bone marrow, from Hettinger, ND area. FM Berg

meat—the product of eight or ten cows. One pound of pemmican was considered equal to four pounds of ordinary meat.

The Métis kept about half of what they produced for their own use and sold the rest to fur companies.

All the pemmican they could spare was eagerly purchased by the Hudson Bay Company to send out to trading posts where food was scarce, especially after they absorbed the North West Company. They also hauled pemmican and hides to the American Fur Company at Fort Snelling and St. Paul in long squeaking caravans of Red River carts to exchange for cloth, blankets, sugar, coffee, tea and ammunition.

The summer hunts increased in size—from 540 Red River carts in 1820, to 820 in 1830 and 1,210 carts in 1840—as the demand for pemmican grew.

That summer, in 1840, the Métis hunting party returned from the hunt with about 1,089,000 pounds in all, equal to the dried meat of 10,000 to 10,500 buffalo. This was the work of 620 hunters, 1,010 women and children, 403 buffalo-running horses, 655 cart horses and 586 work oxen. Accompanying the hunting expedition were also 542 dogs, reported Kane.

Hudson Bay and other fur companies depended on the products of their buffalo hunts well into the 1870s.

The large Métis hunts did not go unnoticed. Many Plains tribes, as well as the U.S. government, protested the Canadian Métis's sweep through their traditional hunting lands as buffalo declined throughout the western Plains of Dakota and Montana.

In 1852, Chief Green Setting Feather of the Turtle Mountain Chippewa complained of the Métis hunter: "The manner of his hunt is such as not only to kill, but also to drive away the few he leaves, and waste even those he kills."

At all times, day and night, the Métis kept watch and guarded their camp from occasional Sioux attacks. Kane said they had a great "fear of the Sioux, in whose territory we then were, and whom they dreaded . . . as we were on their hunting grounds and in the territory of the United States, being still a few miles south of the boundary line."

At night, the carts were set in a wide circle with forks facing out to form a solid defense. Tents lined up in rows on one side within the circle, and on the other side, loose horses and oxen grazed. The animals were kept outside the circle when deemed safe.

Isaac Stevens, surveying for a railroad in July 1853 reported meeting a large party of Red River hunters camped near Devils Lake in July 1853. From fear of attack the horses and oxen were held within the circle of carts and thirty-six men stood guard that night. The camp included 1,300 people, sleeping in 104 tepees and some in carts, covered with skins.

"At night we were annoyed by the incessant howling and fighting of wolves and the innumerable dogs that had followed us to the hunt," said Kane.

It was estimated that the Métis alone killed 30,000 buffalo annually in 1850. Every year more carts went out, and every year they brought back more meat and hides until the herds could no longer be found.

By 1879 the Métis hunters found only a few Plains buffalo left in Canada. Blackfeet tribes in western Montana and Canada were reportedly starving.

Buffalo Hunt, 1838-1842, Alfred Jacob Miller

PART III. COMING HOME

10

Saving the Buffalo

*It is a melancholy contemplation for one
who has traveled through these realms, and
seen this noble animal in all its pride and glory,
to contemplate it so rapidly wasting,
Drawing the irresistible conclusion that its species
is soon to be extinguished,
And with it the peace and happiness of the tribes
who are joint tenants with them in these vast plains.*

—George Catlin, *Letters and Notes on
the Manners, Customs, and Condition
of North American Indians,* 1841

After the last big hunts in 1883 nearly all the estimated thirty million buffalo that once ranged the face of North America were gone. Buffalo had made their last stand in the badlands and buttes of Dakota Territory on the Great Sioux Reservation. The vast buffalo ranges stood empty.

A maternal herd of mostly cows with young calves grazes next to a pine forest. Badlands Reflections Photography.

Buffalo were nearly extinct. The "bottleneck"—as it's been called—tightened. The low point came in the 1890's, or perhaps a bit later, around the turn of the century when the "safe and protected" Yellowstone Park herd was decimated by poachers.

The tight bottleneck nearly choked off the species completely then. It could have happened. The American buffalo could have died out forever.

In 1887, the Smithsonian Museum sent William Hornaday out west to count what remained of the buffalo and to record what had happened to the millions. Hornaday looked, listened to knowledgeable people and, devastated, wrote his report:

"There is no reason to hope that a single wild and unprotected individual will remain alive ten years hence. The nearer the species approaches complete extermination, the more eagerly are the wretched fugitives pursued to the death whenever found."

His official count of the surviving buffalo totaled only 1,091 head for all of North America, including 256 in captivity. Half the total he credited to "very old rumors" of 550 wood buffalo in northern Canada. That was likely an exaggeration, he admitted. But, "We will gladly accept it."

However, even this low number was destined to drop. The lowest official number fell to 800 in 1895 according to the count of Canadian historian Ernest

A public herd grazes in pasture of heavy sagebrush. NPS.

Thompson Seton, as referenced by David Dary. By 1902 the largest herd Hornaday found, 200 in Yellowstone Park, had dropped to a low of only two dozen, as the herd was nearly annihilated by hide hunters lurking at its borders and poachers within, according to the National Park Service. The Lacey Yellowstone Protection Act, passed by Congress in 1894, called for stronger punishment for poachers. But it was poorly enforced and local game wardens hardly existed.

These few still alive had learned to survive in remote areas and canyons distant from any roads, wary of hunters. Many carried old bullets in their flesh. Toward the end of the century, mounted buffalo heads became popular and taxidermists near the Park paid twenty-five to fifty dollars each for fresh heads.

By the summer of 1912, Hornaday recorded the actual count in Yellowstone as forty-nine, including ten calves. He fumed over an outrage in Colorado. In Lost Park a pair of "rascally taxidermists" had prompted the killing of the state's very last buffalo.

Hornaday voiced his despair over their probable extinction in his 1889 book *The Extermination of the American Bison*:

"The wild buffalo is practically gone forever, and in a few more years, when the whitened bones of the last bleaching skeleton shall have been picked up and shipped East for commercial uses, nothing will remain of him save his old, well-worn trails along the watercourses, a few museum specimens, and regret for his fate."

Rescuing a few calves

Samuel Walking Coyote of the Pend d'Oreille tribe had no intention of raising buffalo. He lived with his Flathead wife on her reservation in western Montana.

Two calves play together and explore buttes on their own. Badlands Reflections Photography.

Then in the fall of 1872 he traveled east across the Rocky Mountains and spent the winter hunting buffalo with the Blackfeet. There he fell in love and married a Blackfeet woman, conveniently forgetting his Flathead wife, according to David Dary in *The Buffalo Book*.

Next spring he wanted to return and knowing the Fathers at St. Ignatius Mission disapproved of having more than one wife, he thought a nice gift might put him right with them. Eight orphan buffalo calves that had wandered into his hunting camp and attached themselves to his horses seemed likely to gain their favor. So he and his new wife set out on the long, rough trail back across the Rocky Mountains. Finally, they reached the Flathead mission with six buffalo calves, two having died along the way.

But his gift was rejected. Punished and banished from the tribe, Walking Coyote and his Blackfeet wife left the Mission and moved farther up the Flathead Valley. The six calves thrived there on rich grasses even though mountains on the west side of the Continental Divide were not the natural home of plains buffalo. The Native community grew committed to the little herd's survival, writes Ken Zontak in *Buffalo Nation: American Indian Efforts to Restore the Bison*. "Every Indian in the valley, believing these to be the last ones, aided in their protection. Always there was an Indian rider in their vicinity."

Meanwhile, James McKay, a Scotch-Métis living near Winnipeg, Canada, known as "Tonka Jim," became alarmed at the scarcity of buffalo. Frequently he joined the large twice-yearly Red River Métis hunts and with each hunt it seemed they had to

Herd of cows and calves moves out of pines and brush into the open for better grazing. NPS.

go farther west and south into Montana to find buffalo. On an 1873 Métis hunt McKay captured three calves with the help of friends and the next year, another three, bonding them with nurse cows on his Deer Lodge ranch some twenty-eight miles west of Winnipeg. Later he purchased a few more calves from Native hunters who went west to hunt and returned through Winnipeg.

In the Texas Panhandle, Charles Goodnight caught three calves not far from his ranch. He found if he chased a herd of buffalo, the calves soon tired and fell behind. Then if he changed course and turned aside, they followed his horse all the way to his ranch. where he coaxed them onto range cows and turned them with his cattle. Another day two calves followed him home.

By 1887 he had built a buffalo herd of thirteen, bringing together calves he caught and raised with others donated by friends and neighbors.

C.J. "Buffalo" Jones started out as a commercial hide hunter from Kansas, but set aside his big rifle, gathered some of the last wild buffalo calves and purchased a few grown buffalo from ranchers in Kansas and Nebraska. He said he had killed "thousands" in his hunting days and felt remorseful.

"I am positive it was the wickedness committed in killing so many that impelled me to take measures for perpetuating the race which I had helped almost destroy."

When in 1888 he had the chance to purchase eighty-six Canadian buffalo originating from the herd of Tonka Jim McKay, Jones took it. Shipping them home to his ranch at Garden City, Kansas, proved a challenge, but once there, they increased rapidly. He began selling a few buffalo to zoos, parks and private individuals.

In Dakota Territory, where the last wild buffalo herds still grazed on reservation badlands, Pete Dupree and some of his brothers, sons of Mary Ann Good Elk Woman and Fred Dupris, and perhaps sisters as well, went out with a buckboard wagon and brought home five buffalo calves. They found them, apparently on the South Grand River, likely the spring of 1881 or 1882. Mary Ann was the woman who invited the missionary Thomas Riggs to join them and share their family tent on their last winter buffalo hunt in the Slim Buttes that began in December 1880. *(See Chapter 2.)*

Historians often credit their father Fred Dupris for "sending out his sons" to capture buffalo calves. But Dupris was an older man in his mid-70s by then and stayed home while his family went out on their last long, cold winter hunt in the Slim Buttes. His sons were grown men. A likely scenario may be that Mary Ann Dupree and her sons and daughters hatched the plan to rescue buffalo calves during that long three-month buffalo hunt in the Slim Buttes. They would have spent much time together in the tent that long cold winter and were familiar with concerns of the buffalo disappearing forever. Several stories of their buffalo rescue exist, even that they found the calves much farther west on the Yellowstone. But the version that they rescued them on the South Grand River makes most sense as it was close to their home on the Cheyenne River, as well as the place where the last buffalo grazed.

After fifteen long years of heartbreak over their earlier disappearance, the buffalo had returned to them. Here they were in the Duprees' own backyard, so to speak. If they failed to save them now, who would?

Those who suggest they brought the five calves home with

them in February at the end of their winter hunt, however, appear to be in error. Their wagons carried full loads of hides and meat and the trip home through deep crusted snow was extremely difficult. Any buffalo calves, nearly a year old by that time, would have been too aggressive to handle. Also the missionary Thomas Riggs in summing up the details of their hunt successes made no mention of capturing calves.

At home Pete Dupree found range cows to mother his buffalo calves and thus avoided the typically high death loss of such calves. "Mothering up" could not have been easy—coaxing range cows to accept the strange-smelling calves and the lanky youngsters to nurse low-slung cows. But once bonded, they grazed together on lush reservation lands.

Smithsonian buffalo hunt

By this time the buffalo were nearly wiped out as a species.

Almost certain of their impending extinction, William Hornaday, chief taxidermist at the Smithsonian Museum in Washington, DC, took stock of the museum's inventory. In the entire national collection he found only a few old and dilapidated buffalo skins, one mounted female, a couple of heads and a skeleton.

Alarmed Smithsonian officials agreed to send Hornaday at once to find wild buffalo, if any were still living, and bring back specimens. In the event of extermination, which seemed all too likely, at least there'd be mounted buffalo to view in the nation's most important museum. And since other large museums would doubtless want relics of the soon-to-be-extinct mammal, they called for twenty to thirty skins, plus skeletons and heads. Hornaday hoped to bring back sixty to eighty specimens. As it turned out that proved impossible.

On May 6, 1886, William Hornaday and two or three assistants set forth by train to Miles City, Montana, to launch their own last buffalo hunt. They wanted dead buffalo, so their skins could be preserved for museums. In Miles City they picked up horses, provisions and an Army escort from Fort Keogh. Nearly everyone they met declared all the buffalo were gone from central and eastern Montana. But they kept going, chasing rumors from distant cow hands. Hornaday's party finally found its way into the rugged badlands near the head of the Little Dry and the Missouri River Breaks.

There they discovered and captured a lone, lost buffalo calf. Ten days later they found a couple of bulls. They shot one and realized he was shedding his winter coat, leaving the hide so tattered and seedy looking it could not be mounted. They decided to wait till fall for hides in prime winter condition. After beseeching local ranchers to spare their intended targets, they took the live calf and returned to Washington.

In late September they returned to the same remote badlands, some 135 miles northwest of Miles City.

"Wild and rugged butte country, its sides scored by intricate systems of great yawning ravines and hollows, steep-sided and very deep, and bad lands of the worst description. Such as persecuted game loves to seek shelter in," wrote Hornaday.

In two months of hard riding they found a few small bands of extremely wild stragglers—a lone buffalo bull here, two or three cows with calves there. Seven in one bunch. By this time they had ten saddle horses and the help of a few soldiers from Ft. Keogh.

At left, Hornaday's famous six-buffalo masterpiece in huge glass case set a new standard for Smithsonian Museum taxidermy in 1888. Seventy years later the pieces were shipped to Montana and separated. Refurbished, all six came together again in 1990 and now stand on a pedestal in the Montana Agricultural Center and Museum in Fort Benton. A shrine to the buffalo's loss and rebirth and the group's dispersion and reunion.

Splitting up, they rode twenty-five miles or more each day in different directions.

Searching out "the heads of those great ravines around the High Divide . . . [where] the buffalo were in the habit of hiding," they eventually killed twenty-two buffalo—bulls, cows and calves. Not the number Hornaday hoped for, but a raging November blizzard with bitter cold cut short their hunt.

Hornaday felt pleased with the big bull he shot himself.

"A prize! A truly magnificent specimen. A 'stub-horn' bull, about eleven years old. His hair in remarkably fine condition, being long, fine, thick and well colored—sixteen inches in length in his frontlet."

His bull stood a full six feet tall when they added the four-inch hair on the hump, two inches taller than their next largest bull. In length, he was nine-feet-two-inches, head to tail. In circumference, eight-feet-four around the chest just behind the foreleg. The bull had been shot several times before. Within the carcass he carried four old bullets of various sizes, as did nearly every bull they killed in those hidden canyons.

Returning to Washington, Hornaday and his assistant taxidermists set to work. After a full year they unveiled their masterpiece. There, in a huge glass case, visitors to the Smithsonian Museum viewed an enchanting scene. The grouping of six buffalo in an authentic Montana setting, included Hornaday's prize stub-horn bull. The *Washington Star* described the exhibit on March 10, 1888:

A little bit of Montana—a small square patch from the wildest part of the wild West—has been transferred to the National Museum. . . The hummocky prairie, the buffalo-grass, the sagebrush, and the buffalo. It is as though a little group of buffalo that have come to drink at a pool had been suddenly struck motionless by some magic spell, each in a natural attitude, and then the section of prairie, pool, buffalo, and all had been carefully cut out and brought to the National Museum. A triumph of the taxidermist's art.

It was a sight Hornaday feared no one would ever be able to see alive again. He hid a message voicing his despair in a small sealed metal box in the Montana dirt of the Smithsonian display. Discovered nearly three-quarters of a century later when the exhibit was moved to Montana, curators read Hornaday's heartfelt plea:

My Illustrious Successor

Enclosed please find a brief and truthful account of the capture of the specimens which compose this group. When I am dust and ashes I beg you to protect these specimens from deterioration and destruction.

—W.T. Hornaday
Chief Taxidermist, March 7, 1888

Passing the torch

By 1884, Sam Walking Coyote owned thirteen tame buffalo. But they were becoming a problem. Hard to control, they broke down his neighbors' fences and destroyed crops. He finally sold them for $2,000 in gold—he insisted on gold coin—to Charles Allard and Michel Pablo, ranchers in the valley.

Mothers of both these new partners were Native American and Pablo's wife was Salish. They purchased twenty-six additional buffalo and eighteen cattalo from Buffalo Jones of Kansas. By 1895 their herd numbered 300.

That year Allard died at age forty-three. His half of the herd, 150 head, dispersed to several buyers. Some went to Kalispell and others to Yellowstone Park.

In 1906 Pablo learned the Flathead reservation was opening to homesteaders—he'd lose his free range. He offered to sell his buffalo, now doubled again to 300, to the U.S. government for $200 each to replenish the Yellowstone Park herd.

President Roosevelt favored the idea, but Congress balked at the price. With Canada long bereft of nearly all its plains buffalo, Canadian officials proved eager buyers. Pablo agreed to sell them his entire herd, but as it turned out, shipping them to Canada proved a challenge.

The next year the Michel Pablo herd from western Montana began shipping. This was a grand genetic mix of buffalo that originated from calves captured in both Canada and the United States, as far distant as Saskatchewan, Montana, Kansas and Texas. All had multiplied greatly. By the time Pablo and his cowboys rounded them up, loaded and delivered by train to Canada, which took six years, his herd had doubled and he unloaded a total of 716 buffalo at Elk Island National Park and Buffalo National Park, according to Canadian zoologist Valerius Geist, in *Buffalo Nation: History and Legend of the North American Bison*.

Hornaday's Buffalo Count

Running wild and unprotected	
Texas Panhandle	25
Colorado	20
Wyoming (southern)	26
Montana, Musselshell area	10
Dakota (western)	4
Canada, estimate	550
Yellowstone Park	200
In Captivity	**256**
Total	**1,091**

Hornaday, *The Extermination of the American Bison*, 1889

The first twenty cowboys he hired only succeeded in getting a few buffalo at a time to the railroad and loaded at Ravalli, Montana.

Cowboy artist Charlie Russell joined the Pablo crew for a time and described one of his buffalo roundups in a letter to a friend. He wrote:

"The first day they got 300 in the whings [wings] but they broke back an all the riders on earth couldent hold them. They only got in with about 120. I wish you could have seen them take the river. They hit the water on a ded run . . . We all went to bed that night sadisfide with 120 in the trap but woke up with one cow. The rest had climed the cliff an got away. The next day they onely got 6 an a snow storm struck us an the round-up was called off till next summer." As he often did, Russell illustrated his letter, with a sketch of the escapees taking the river.

Moving half-wild buffalo bulls proved almost impossible. David Dary describes the attempt to load ten full-grown bulls in boxcars, using three expert ropers on well-trained horses. Four of the bulls died from the furious exertion of their resistance during the day's heat. Three grew sullen, lay down before they reached the rail cars and refused to budge, regardless of how hard they were pulled, pushed and prodded. Of the ten bulls the cowboys succeeded in loading only three.

Pablo's last seven buffalo—perhaps the wildest of all—were hauled to the railroad one at a time in special high-sided wagons built to hold one buffalo each.

Pete Dupree ran his buffalo on the Great Sioux Reservation. For ten years his herd increased. Then

The artist Charlie Russell joined a buffalo roundup with the Pablo crew. In a letter to a friend, along with this sketch, he wrote, "I wish you could have seen them take the river. They hit the water on a ded run . . . an all the riders on earth couldent hold them." CM Russell. *The Buffalo Book*, David A Dary.

in 1898 Pete died. His sister's husband, administering the estate, found a willing buyer in James "Scotty" Philip, of Fort Pierre, who ran cattle with his wife Sarah "Sally" on private land and her allotment—as a Lakota-French woman from Cheyenne River.

Philip sent six cowboys to round up the Dupree herd and drive them the 100 miles to his pasture. His nephew George Philip, a budding lawyer, was pressed into service and later wrote about the difficult venture. A formidable task. George wrote that they finally brought to the Philip gate eighty-three half-wild buffalo, plus a number of cattalo. They'd had to let go the renegade bulls that escaped their several roundups. Some of these big old bulls that broke away were shot for their heads in the next few years by Scotty Philip and his sporting friends. By then, large buffalo heads were selling for $500 to $1,000 in New York markets.

Philip declared the cattalo worthless and quickly sold or butchered them, according to his biographer, Wayne C. Lee, in *Scotty Philip: The Man Who Saved the Buffalo*. Like the Duprees, the Philips had a mission. They intended to do what they could to save the buffalo from extinction.

"We must not let the buffalo die. My people might need them again," said Sally Philip. Perhaps she was thinking not only of Lakota needs for food, shelter and clothing, but also their close spiritual and emotional ties to the buffalo, still important today in their heritage.

A buffalo pasture

When the U.S. opened the Great Sioux Reservation lands in South Dakota for homesteading, Scotty Philip asked that 3,500 acres on the Missouri River bluffs north of Fort Pierre be set aside for grazing native buffalo. Congress agreed and located the reserve just north of Philip's own buffalo pasture, leasing it to him for $50 a year.

Philip had emigrated from the Scottish Highlands at age fifteen and came west in search of adventure. He tried his hand working as a ranch hand, cowboy and scout in the U.S. Army, gold miner in the Black Hills, and then went into cattle ranching. In 1879 he married Sally Larribee, a Lakota and French woman from Cheyenne River and moved his cattle onto the Great Sioux Reservation where she held grazing rights.

When the opportunity came to buy Pete Dupree's buffalo for $10,000, Sally urged him to buy. He agreed that helping to save the buffalo was a way he could support his Native friends, who often were not treated well.

On the Missouri River bluffs his buffalo became a well-known tourist attraction. Special excursion boats brought visitors upriver from Pierre to view the amazing buffalo ranging in the rugged badlands. One day a delegation of Mexican officials from Juarez came to see the buffalo. They laughed and declared the big bulls lazy and slow moving. Certainly unworthy

The Floyd Johnson herd grazes a leafy draw near Shadehill Buffalo Jump. Courtesy of Jim Strand.

of comparison with their fiery Mexican fighting bulls.

Scotty Philip and his Fort Pierre friends took offense and challenged a bull fight. This actually took place the following January in the bull-fighting ring in Juarez. Fortunately, Phillip's nephew George was called on to attend the two buffalo bulls shipped there and described the fight in delightful detail, when a blizzard emergency kept Scotty at home with his cattle. *(See Box: Mexican Bullfight.)*

Buffalo numbers continued to decline around the turn of the century. Yet, despite the many strikes against them, the hardy buffalo did survive, after all.

"The buffalo were saved because a handful of men captured a few wild buffalo and raised them in captivity during the 1880s and 1890s," writes David Dary.

Their rescuers were Indian and white. Both men and women had a hand in it, according to modern historians.

Five groups and families are especially honored as critical in saving the buffalo from extinction. They are the families of Pete Dupree and his herd purchaser Scotty Philip in South Dakota; Samuel Walking Coyote and his herd purchasers Charles Allard and Michel Pablo in western Montana; James McKay and neighbors in Manitoba, Canada, and the two white ranching families, the Charles Goodnights of Texas and Buffalo Jones of Kansas.

The first three of these had Native American roots and knew well the cultural importance of buffalo in the lives of their people. They all held a deep cultural stake in buffalo survival. Rather than butchering or selling the increase, they mostly grew their herds, multiplying and strengthening the numbers. Left alone, such herds usually increased at a fairly steady rate, doubling and redoubling every eight to ten years. They cherished the natural wild traits of the buffalo without trying to alter them. Cross-breeding, when it occurred was accidental, the result of cattle and buffalo sharing the same ranges.

The white ranching families, the Goodnights and Buffalo Jones, respected the natural world, cherished their buffalo and appreciated their own roles in preserving them. However, perhaps more than the others, both these non-Indian families hoped to reap economic benefits and engaged in much buying and selling of buffalo. Also, both experimented with cross-breeding in the hope of developing hardier, more productive beef animals. Today cross-breeding is discouraged and violates the Code of Ethics of both the National Bison Association and the Intertribal Buffalo Council.

Indubitably, other people raised buffalo for a time here and there. Yet these five family groups made special efforts to care for their herds and raised sustainable adult herds for many years.

Ken Zontek, buffalo historian,

An uneasy mother locates her wandering calf. Badlands Reflections Photography.

raises an interesting point. While conservation-minded people in the east put forth a valuable effort in founding wildlife parks and sanctuaries for long-term survival of the buffalo, they would have failed, he notes, had it not been for westerners who caught and saved calves. It's true. But for those rescuers caring for the small starving calves, the buffalo would not have been saved. Without them there'd be no buffalo left alive today.

They were westerners, tribal people, ranchers and buffalo hunters. To a greater or lesser extent their vision involved the survival of an endangered species. Their herds flourished and eventually became the foundation of all the buffalo herds now populating the United States and Canada.

While men received most of the credit from early historians for saving the buffalo, women were much involved, as well, and are celebrated today. Native American women went on all the big hunts and watched the great herds disappear. They despaired over the ruthless slaughter of commercial hunters with powerful, long-range rifles.

"Mary Ann Good Elk Woman Dupree and Sally Philip were unsung heroines in the saga, largely ignored by historians but credited by their families for their roles," writes Pat Springer in the *Rapid City Journal*. "Both women were Lakota, for whom the buffalo are sacred. And both, according to their descendants, helped persuade their husbands to rescue buffalo for their preservation."

Mary Ann Dupree "regarded the possible imminent disappearance of the buffalo as a major catastrophe," says Donovan Sprague, of his great-great grandmother. "She knew the sacredness of the buffalo—the depletion and the slaughter going on." Other descendants, cousins Jim Garrett and Joseph Dupris, affirm the leading role Mary Ann played in bringing back the buffalo. According to their oral traditions, hers was the primary influence in capturing and raising buffalo calves.

Jackie Means, of Black Hawk, S.D., recalls that her grandmother, Sally Philip "always bemoaned the loss of the buffalo." She wept over them until, according to family tradition, her husband Scotty said, "Well, we'll see if we can find some buffalo."

Mary Ann "Molly" Goodnight, wife of Charles Goodnight, persuaded her cattle rancher husband to rescue a few orphaned buffalo calves for her to raise, reported Susan Ricci, manager of the Buffalo Museum in Rapid City. "A great lover of animals, she was saddened by the senseless slaughter of the buffalo."

The men "may have been considered 'Buffalo Kings' by their fellow ranchers, but it was the wives who encouraged their decisions and should be remembered as the 'Buffalo Queens,'" says Ricci.

No doubt women—and children, too—were involved in the early feeding of orphaned calves and helped coax nurse cows to accept them.

Of the five groups, perhaps the Dupree and Philip families were most concerned from the beginning with saving the buffalo for posterity. They lived on what was then the Great Sioux Reservation in Dakota Territory—the location where the last free-ranging buffalo came in 1880 to make their last stand. They knew the prophesy of elders who said these last buffalo returned to fulfill a mission—to provide desperately needed food, clothing and shelter for their Lakota brothers and sisters before they disappeared forever.

Promoting national parks

In Washington, D.C., and New York, William Hornaday lectured and wrote impassioned articles on the need to set aside national reserves for buffalo and enact stronger game laws.

George Bird Grinnell and others joined the cause. Like fellow conservationists Hornaday and Theodore Roosevelt, Grinnell had hunted buffalo in the west.

He rode with General Custer in the Black Hills in 1874 and explored the Glacier Park area. As editor of *Forest and Stream*, Grinnell wrote often of the need for wildlife conservation in the American west, and was largely responsible for adding Glacier to the National Park System in 1910.

Even laws regulating hunting were often ignored, such as the Yellowstone Park Protection Act that forbade hunting in the Park. Grinnell accompanied the Yellowstone Park expedition and added his own scathing report on the widespread poaching there of buffalo, deer, elk and antelope hides.

Other laws sought to protect Indian reservations from encroachment by non-Indian hunters. But white hunters expected leniency in western courts, as they received when Native policemen with Indian Agent James McLaughlin caught five white hide hunters red-handed skinning buffalo on the Standing Rock reservation and sent them to Bismarck for trial. No judge or jury would convict them. In no uncertain terms, Hornaday expressed his anger and despair.

"We are weary of witnessing the greed, selfishness and cruelty of 'civilized' man toward the wild creatures of the earth. We are sick of tales of slaughter and pictures of carnage. It is time for sweeping reformation; and that is precisely what we now demand. … If the majority of the people of America feel that so long as there is any game alive there must be an annual two months or four months open season for its slaughter, then assuredly we soon will have a gameless continent."

Yet, the west teemed with wildlife and the risk seemed unlikely. Westerners generally opposed laws to restrict hunting, knowing that many desperate pioneers on the frontier survived by hunting and selling hides and meat. Congress shrugged the conservation concerns aside.

As for using public land for grazing buffalo, that was highly unlikely when the public clamored for more homestead land.

American Bison Society

When Theodore Roosevelt came to the North Dakota Badlands in 1883 to hunt big game and set up a ranch, he soon realized that the elk, bighorn sheep, and buffalo that he so admired would not survive relentless overhunting or the destruction of their ranges due to human civilization.

Roosevelt became increasingly convinced of the need to protect these magnificent animals and provide large, safe places for them to live. After he became president in 1901, Roosevelt used his authority for the purpose of conserving wilderness areas by setting aside forests, mountains, grasslands and more as public lands.

"The extermination of the buffalo has been a veritable tragedy of the animal world," declared President Theodore Roosevelt.

While Hornaday was giving a series of lectures about the devastation of the buffalo, an audience member asked, "Why not form a society dedicated to the permanent preservation of the buffalo?" Hornaday passed the suggestion on to the president.

In his message to Congress, Dec. 5, 1905, the "Conservation President" Theodore Roosevelt called for a buffalo refuge:

"The most characteristic animal of the western plains was the great shaggy-maned wild ox, the bison, commonly known as buffalo. Such a herd as that on the Flathead Reservation should not be allowed to go out of existence. Either on some reservation or some forest reserve or refuge, provision should be made for the preservation of such a herd."

At last—a president with a heart for conservation, who understood both buffalo and western ranching from his time as a rancher in western North Dakota. Three days later, on Dec 8th, the American Bison Society was born, electing William Hornaday president and Roosevelt as honorary president.

The Bison Society immediately set to work with Congress to establish fenced buffalo refuges on federal lands, stocking them with donated buffalo and buffalo bought with donated funds. Within six months Congress appropriated money to enclose 8,000 acres of the National Wichita

A calf calls for his mother. His cry has been described as "a low-pitched, pig-like grunt through the nose." Badlands Reflections Photography.

Forest Reserve in southwest Oklahoma with a high wire fence for a wildlife refuge and stocked it with fifteen buffalo donated from the New York Zoo.

Wind Cave in the Black Hills received fourteen buffalo by rail from the New York Zoological Society and along with six more from Yellowstone Park grew into a closed system of 350 animals with genetics that are still unique today.

The National Bison Range in western Montana's beautiful Flathead Valley delighted William Hornaday with its magnificent view of the snow-packed Mission mountains. At last his wildest dreams were coming true.

He helped raise $10,000 to buy thirty-four buffalo from the original Allard herd, owned by Alicia Conrad of Kalispell. She donated two more, the New Hampshire game preserve gave three and Charles Goodnight sent one buffalo from Texas to bring the total to forty head.

"It is beautiful and perfect beyond compare," Hornaday marveled. "As the crates were opened, the bison backed out of them, looked about for a moment, saw their Paradise Regained looming up … and climbed up into their new home . . . the richest and most beautiful grazing grounds ever trodden by bison hoofs."

Within ten years the Bison Society counted its successes and proclaimed the "future of the

Mexican Bullfight

One day a group of Mexican dignitaries from Juarez, visiting in Pierre, SD, came up the Missouri River on the tourist boat to have a look at Scotty Philip's famous buffalo herd. With great interest they eyed the shaggy beasts grazing up the draws and steep bluffs. As the tour boat came to a stop along the river's west bank, they pointed out to each other the big buffalo bulls and mocked their apparent lethargic demeanor.

Contrasting these with their own flashy fighting bulls, they boasted to the tour guide and other passengers, with a trifle too much exuberance, that their feisty Mexican bulls would make short work of these lazy, slow-moving buffalo bulls.

In the frontier town of Fort Pierre, miffed locals took offense. Scotty Philip's sporting friends made their own boasts and persuaded him to challenge the visitors to a contest. One thing led to another and the two factions agreed to meet that winter in the Juarez bull fighting ring. A bet was rumored at $10,000.

Scotty Philip and his crew selected two bulls—a mature eight-year old herd bull in his prime and an energetic four-year-old—and named them *Pierre* and *Pierre Junior*.

In early January 1907 the two bulls and three South Dakotan men shipped out in a railroad car bound for El Paso and Juarez, just across the Mexican border. The rail car was fitted with heavy planking and penned off for each bull.

At the last minute, a severe January blizzard cut short Scotty Philip's plans and he had to stay home with cattle emergencies. Instead, he again recruited his nephew George, to represent his interests in Mexico.

A lawyer just starting his law practice in Fort Pierre, George Philip learned the cowboy life as a young Scottish immigrant on his uncle's ranch. With him travelled two local experts, Bob Yokum, an enthusiastic promoter, and Eb Jones, cowman and buffalo handler.

With a large and enthusiastic bull-fighting crowd in the stands, the first Sunday in January opened the bull-fighting season with a parade of matadors, banderilleros and picadors dressed in red, blue and silver finery, dazzling with tinsel and sequins.

The main event featured what the Mexican audience fully expected to be a humiliation for the big, slow-moving buffalo. Pierre walked slowly into the ring, favoring his left hind leg, and stood quietly,

Pierre pivoted and met the red Mexican bull face on, cracking heads—and knocked him flat. He regarded the bulls with disinterest, then lay down—the mighty monarch of the plains and prairies. Badlands Reflections Photography.

perhaps stunned by the hot southern sunshine in the middle of winter.

The crowd taunted him and jeered loudly.

Seated in the governor's box as guests, Pierre's anxious South Dakota handlers murmured to each other their concerns. They worried that Pierre had ridden seven straight days cooped up in one end of a boxcar and now suddenly was prodded and pushed into the middle of a bull-fighting arena, in totally strange surroundings, filled with shouting people and odd smells. He was plunged into a hot climate, an abrupt change from the extreme cold that his heavy winter hair coat had prepared him for. On top of all this, he suffered a dislocated left fetlock, apparently from kicking the sides of the boxcar.

Cheering swelled from the stands as another gate opened and into the ring pranced a handsome red Mexican bull with sharp, treacherous horns, head up, two colorful darts flying from his withers. He stopped at a little distance and took the measure of his opponent, shaking his head fiercely and pawing the ground.

Pierre turned to confront him with massive head and shoulders, three-quartering his flank away. Seeking an easier target, the Mexican bull circled.

Suddenly he charged at full speed, intent on slashing the buffalo's flank with his long sharp horns, in what seemed certain to lead to a bloody goring.

Pierre stood still an instant and then in one smooth, rapid movement, pivoted his light hind quarters out of the way and met the bull face on, cracking heads.

The Mexican bull backed off in confusion, evidently surprised at how powerfully the huge, hard head whacked the center of his smaller head, while escaping the twist of his sharp, treacherous horns.

He maneuvered a better angle of attack. Again he charged. Again Pierre pivoted swiftly on his front legs, swinging his rear out of range—unlike the expected back-leg-pivot of fighting bulls in the ring. Again Pierre met the Mexican bull head on, this time with extra force that knocked the smaller fighter to his knees.

Not lacking in courage, the gutsy red bull charged a third time, against another powerful slash of Pierre's huge head and horns, which knocked him flat.

Pierre simply stood his ground. He met every charge but didn't follow up his advantage. After knocking the bull down, he ignored him, allowing him to rise and fight again.

The bull tried one last time and was again knocked flat, this time with an angry shake of Pierre's head. The courageous Mexican fighting bull had had enough. He circled the arena looking in vain for an escape gate.

The spectators roared their disappointment and disapproval.

The ring manager asked the South Dakotans if they'd be willing to let their buffalo fight another bull.

"The red bull is not feeling well today," he said. "Another will surely put up a better fight."

The three men agreed. They'd come a long way to see Pierre fight as they knew he could. A buffalo bull does not remain a top herd bull without fighting continual fierce battles.

A second Mexican bull entered the ring with fire and fury. He eyed the strange shaggy beast quartering his flank away from him and charged—only to smash unexpectedly into that massive, well-armed head. Three times Pierre knocked him flat. Twice he rose to attack again. The last time he ran for the gate and could not be persuaded to fight either buffalo or matador.

Another bull entered the ring, with the same results.

Three panicked fighting bulls now circled the ring looking for escape. Three bull fighters waved red capes and pricked their hides with silver swords, trying desperately to get them to fight. All the bulls refused.

Pierre regarded them with disinterest. He lay down, nonchalantly resting, chewing a cud, secure in the knowledge that, of course, he was the top bull.

At last, the crowd stood up and cheered him.

"Now I know this isn't very sporting, but the bulls have disappointed me." The ring master approached the visitors again. "I would like it if you'll agree that I may turn in one more bull."

"Turn in all the bulls you want, just make sure you give that buffalo room to turn around," said one of the men.

By the fourth fighting bull, Pierre was getting irritated. He rose to his feet and for the first time, pawed the dirt, warning the other bull away. He charged. A loud crash and the smaller Mexican bull flew backward and landed in a heap. He didn't try again, and Pierre disdained following up his victory.

The Mexican promoters called for a fight the next Sunday between Pierre Junior, the lively four-year-old, and a Matador with sword and cape in hand.

That day an exceptionally large and enthusiastic crowd came to watch the contest, advertised as four bull fights with matadors, followed by the buffalo and matador fight. All were sorely disappointed.

The first bull let into the ring was the same handsome red bull of Pierre's first fight from the Sunday before. Reputed to be one of the most splendid fighting bulls in the Juarez bull ring, the red bull shook his head, refused to fight the matador and ran for an escape opening. Upon coming into the ring, the next three bulls repeated that dismal performance.

Finally, an aggressive Pierre Junior charged into the ring looking for trouble. But the governor called off the match almost as it began, unwilling for their best fighters to suffer more humiliation. He promised the crowd to refund their tickets.

As it turned out Scotty Philip was right. The Mexican fighting bulls—although gallant, fiery, highly-trained and said to be the finest in Mexico—were no match for a buffalo herd bull.

Pierre Junior, his dignity intact, stood alone in the middle of the ring while the crowd cheered the magnificent stranger from South Dakota—mighty monarch of the plains and prairies.

Source: George Philip, "Buffaloes versus Mexican Bulls," SD Historical Review II (Jan 1937)

EPILOGUE: *In another version of this event that George Philip published in the SD Historical Collections, he added that one of the men heard from a woman who saw these two fights in Juarez. She told him that several Sundays later, after Pierre's leg had fully healed, he was advertised to fight again in Juarez. (Since they were not allowed to bring the bulls back into the U.S. after crossing into Mexico, the South Dakotans had sold the bulls for $200 to the ring master and a butcher.)*

They had built a pen of four by four timbers in the middle of the ring, with a chute leading into it, the woman said. Pierre was run down the chute, and a Mexican fighting bull followed. The bull could not escape and Pierre fought with him and killed him.

A second and third fighting bull followed and Pierre killed them both. A fourth bull was run in and when the buffalo bull killed him he shoved his slain opponent through the side of the pen. She said she heard that the big buffalo bull went on to fight in Chihuahua, Mexico City and Madrid. George Philip ended this story with the question, "Maybe the lady had the story straight. Who knows?"

species now seems assured."

Buffalo herds were thriving and multiplying in the Oklahoma Wichita herd, in Niobrara, Nebraska, and in South Dakota's Custer State Park. Even Yellowstone Park's "wild herd, once almost abandoned," was restored and growing in Montana and Wyoming.

President Theodore Roosevelt appointed Buffalo Jones, a friend from the National Bison Society as first game warden of Yellowstone Park.

The president expanded his conservation efforts, establishing numerous wildlife refuges teeming with buffalo and other wild animals and bird life. He created the present day Forest Service with 150 national forests and a Federal Bird Reserve of fifty-one refuges managed by the new Fish and Wildlife Service. He helped create twenty-three new national sites that became part of the National Park Service, established 230 million acres of public lands.

As this nation's greatest conservation president, President Theodore Roosevelt earned a place for himself on Mt. Rushmore, along with three of its greatest leaders, George Washington, Thomas Jefferson and Abraham Lincoln.

History rightly gives the Duprees, Philips, Walking Coyotes, and Pablo, Allard, McKay, Goodnight and Jones a great deal of credit for saving the buffalo. These are the families with boots on the ground who kept the species alive in buffalo pastures.

Also honored for the distinction of saving the buffalo are the visionary conservationists, William Hornaday, George Bird Grinnell and President Theodore Roosevelt, who ensured the preservation of buffalo in wildlife sanctuaries throughout the United States.

A Yellowstone Park herd travels from one grassy knoll to another as they graze. NPS.

Working buffalo at the Steve and Roxann McFarland ranch on a cold January morning. Family and buffalo-wise friends, everyone knows their job and executes it quietly without fanfare. Afterward the calves are sorted in the corral for sale. The cows head quickly back out to pasture. FM Berg.

11

Buffalo Ranching Across America

You will soon discover that most bison ranchers
choose to provide a home for these beautiful creatures
not for the allure of quick profits.
But simply because they love the animal
and the peace and tranquility that one enjoys
as they come to know the great American bison.
—Loren Smeester
Silver Bison Ranch, Baldwin, Wisconsin

Private ranchers have been important since the beginning in restoring buffalo to the North American ecosystem, and still play a key role today.

Many owners take it on in the spirit of adventure. Historians agree, you have to be a special person to raise buffalo—a person with a passion for it, in for the long haul; an open-minded person willing to learn something new.

"It started as a hobby," recalled Toots Marquis, a Gillette, Wyoming rancher. "(But) buffalo are like rabbits. If you're not careful, pretty soon

"Working buffalo is always an adventure," notes one veterinarian. Loading and trucking brings a few surprises. "Buffalo can bound six feet straight up when cornered. Or in a standing long jump he can clear fourteen feet," says a seasoned owner. Here, a buffalo, once successfully loaded, decides to leave the truck. Photo by Kim Sutton, *American Bison Assoc.*

you've got too many."

In 1922, Marquis' father-in-law bought two cows and a bull "just for fun" from Scotty Philip. The herd grew to 500 animals before they cut it back to seventy-five, a "nice hobby herd," Marquis said. "Buffalo do beautifully on what nature provides. They're a nice animal to have around. They take absolutely no care. They live and die right there. When we want some meat, we drive out into the pasture and shoot one."

About 400,000 buffalo live in North America today, most in private hands. In the U.S., 192,110 buffalo are spread over 4,500 privately owned ranches in herds averaging fifty or fewer. In public herds are 36,863 buffalo, including tribal herds. In Canada, private herds total 150,142 buffalo and public herds 12,449.

The buffalo industry has grown rapidly in recent years with strong markets, but it has a history of fluctuating dramatically due to climate and market conditions. In the drought-prone Great Plains, a year of low rainfall like 2017 quickly shrinks the size of herds. Market counts too—high prices mean quick sales.

In the U. S., the Upper Great Plains contain the heart of buffalo ranching, with South Dakotans raising herds totaling 40,000, nearly 10,000 more than the next three states, North Dakota, Montana and Nebraska. However, buffalo ranches can be found across the nation, from New York to Virginia to Wyoming.

Generations of wisdom: Low stress strategies

Steve and Roxann McFarland take pride in their fourth-generation herd, just across the South Dakota state line south of Hettinger, ND. Steve's great-grandfather Frank McFarland was known as a man who "liked to try something new," and started in 1955 with two buffalo cows and a bull. The herd, numbering sixty or seventy head, has flourished, and the family cattle and buffalo ranch has passed from Frank to his son Roy, to grandson Eugene, and now great-grandson Steve.

"Grandpa enjoyed taking care of them, watching them," says Verna McFarland, Steve's mother. "Every day they came in by the buildings to water. We kept them in with only a three-wire barbed wire fence. Usually no problems. We butchered our own meat and always ate buffalo."

The McFarlands have developed a low-stress approach to managing their herd, and have evolved their corral and practices based on experiences and knowledge passed from generation to generation.

Buffalo are different from cattle, and the techniques used to handle them have to be different as well. In a sense, as wild animals, buffalo are easier to raise than cattle because, as a native species of the Great Plains, their calving and behavior are adapted to the harsh conditions of the prairie. However, buffalo retain their wild traits. They are large, strong, and can be unpredictable. When approached or herded, they can panic easily. Ranchers and veterinarians have learned through difficult, even deadly experiences, that buffalo may die of heart attacks while being handled, or trample each other to death during the panic of being loaded and transported. As wild animals, buffalo are dangerous to people and other animals. Even the most careful of ranchers still risk harm to themselves and the herd when handling buffalo.

"It's always an adventure to work buffalo," says Dr. Don Safratowich, a Hettinger veterinarian who has helped ranchers care for their buffalo herds in North Dakota and South

---

The Bison Advantage in Ranching

- No barn (artificial shelter) needed. Outdoors, year-round, no matter the weather
- Efficient feed utilizers
- Long productive life
- Primary requirements: fresh water and adequate nutrition
- Calving rarely requires human intervention
- Superior hardiness results in disease resistance
- Thrive in many environments with no ill effects
- The meat they provide is low fat and high protein
- There is steady growth in consumer's demand for bison meat. The demand currently exceeds the supply
- Free enterprise market without excessive intervention

Minnesota Buffalo Assoc; USDA RMA. mnbison.org, www.rma.usda.gov

Dakota since 1967, including the McFarlands. "I enjoy them. Except when they pile up in the chute!"

Buffalo do not respond well to the "stampede method," herding techniques involving multiple people, horses, and vehicles creating a lot of noise and threat.

"We can then expect the whole process to be arduous for everyone involved," says Mark Kossler, manager of the Vermejo Park Ranch in New Mexico. "(But) if we have been successful in getting them into the corral without excessively pressuring them, then we have set the stage for them to work for us in a reasonable manner that helps everyone."

What buffalo experts and animal behavior specialists such as Colorado State University's Dr. Temple Grandin call the "low stress" method can be seen in use on the McFarland ranch. The method is supported by the ranch's curved corral, which has evolved over the years through experience and adaptation. The heavy bridge planks, splintered through the years by the powerful thrust of big bulls, repaired, are covered over and transitioned to curved alleyways and high-sided perforated metal panels with catwalks. When the McFarlands need to separate buffalo cows and fall calves, the animals being worked move slowly through successively smaller pens and alleyways, each one holding fewer until each cow is alone, but calm, and trapped in the alleyway next to the chute.

Other ranches use different materials, but the same approach, said Koosler. "Some use two electric wires for pasture separations with little or no problems. And some use minimal corrals made of wood, rubber belting, wildlife screening, or big

Working buffalo at the Stephens Creek facility in Yellowstone National Park. NPS

straw bales to routinely work their animals. As long as the animals are in a low-stress environment, they are unlikely to be looking for an escape."

Buffalo and tourism

In the early part of the last century, buffalo ranchers Martin and Leonida Collins found a way to help tourists enjoy buffalo close-up and personal. Living near the Black Hills and with a major tourist road cutting through their ranch, they built a small show pasture of strong steel mesh. Here they kept some of their gentler buffalo during the day. People enjoyed feeding them hay through the wire. Each evening Martin moved these peaceable buffalo into a rotation pasture on good grass, and each morning brought them back to the show pasture by the highway.

A rodeo rider and rodeo clown during the 1920s, Martin Collins rode his bucking buffalo bull "Buff" at rodeos. His interest in buffalo began at age six when his father took him by buggy to Ft. Pierre to see Scotty Philip's buffalo herd.

"I remember looking out from the house in the morning and seeing the big old bull on the hill. Something went off in my mind and I said, someday I'm going to have some buffalo," he said. The Collins placed a donation box by their tourist attraction and collected some money for expenses. But they said their greatest compensation was the pleasure of meeting and talking with people from all over the world.

"You'd be surprised how many people said, 'But I thought buffalo were extinct!'"

Relishing his role as host, Martin liked to stay home and talk to the several thousand visitors who came yearly from every

Cows and calves cross the highway. In forests they often prefer to move via paved roads. Vehicles give buffalo the right-of-way. NPS.

Small band of buffalo moves down a ridge in the badlands. Badlands Reflections Photography.

state and many foreign countries. Looking back in 1990, he said, "Just having the wonderful animals here to live and work with brings our nearly 90 years of life to a wonderful finish."

The Houck buffalo ranch near Ft. Pierre, South Dakota, provided roaming herds of buffalo and the picturesque setting for the movie *Dances with Wolves,* which won the Academy Award for Best Picture in 1990. Roy and Nellie Houck started the Triple U Buffalo Ranch with a small herd of twenty-three animals in 1959, near the pasture where Sally and Scotty Philips raised the survivors of the last great buffalo hunts.

"Buffalo always had an appeal for us and we had a longing for them," said Houck. What started as a hobby grew to a ranching enterprise of 4,500 head of buffalo grazing on 50,000 acres. The Triple U built a federally approved Grade A packing plant on the ranch, fitted with "the best sanitation equipment and huge freezers capable" to ensure the freshest, highest-quality product, said Houck.

Over the years that the Houcks were involved in buffalo ranching, they saw the market and demand for buffalo meat and products grow. Roy Houck—called the "Dean of the Bison Industry"—was instrumental in helping start the National Bison Association to assist producers with marketing. Roy died in 1992.

Roy and Nellie's daughter, Kaye Ingle, and her family took over operation of the Triple U Buffalo Ranch and over the years reduced the herd to 2,500 head of buffalo. In 2015 the family sold the Triple U, along with its buffalo and wild horses, to media mogul Ted Turner.

Turner founded Turner Broadcasting and the Cable News Network (CNN), and is now considered the second-largest private land owner in the U.S., with about two million acres. He owns fifteen ranches in seven states stocked with buffalo, and three in Argentina. The 3,000 buffalo purchased from the Triple U made Turner the world's number one buffalo owner, with 54,000 head. The Turner Ranches "strives for management that is both ecologically sensitive and commercially sustainable," according to its website.

There are a variety of views about how best to raise buffalo and how to bring their meat to market. For Dan O'Brien, the business of buffalo ranching is as much about restoring a threatened ecosystem, the Great Plains, as it is about supporting families or providing tourists with experiences or supplying meat.

From ranch to table: The buffalo meat market

A proud South Dakotan, Dan O'Brien, of the Broken Heart Ranch, started his herd by trading his work one fall at a large buffalo ranch where he helped with roundup for thirteen small rejected calves. He was looking for something more than a hobby.

"I was desperate to rediscover purpose in my life, and on that cold South Dakota day those thirteen imperiled packages of fur and sinew seemed kindred souls. I wanted us to move on to a better life, I wanted my ranch as balanced and healthy as it could be."

O'Brien explains in his book, *Buffalo for the Broken Heart,* how he found that sense of purpose and raised grass-fed buffalo in a time-honored, satisfying way.

Consumer demand for bison meat is high today. This is because buffalo meat appeals to consumers who are both health conscious and gourmet eaters. Growing numbers of people are discovering the direct connection between diet and health, and are actively seeking flavorful meats produced without growth hormones or antibiotics, reports the American Bison Association. "A growing legion of restaurants and gourmet chefs are adding a variety of recipes featuring all types of bison cuts, everything from brisket to short ribs,"

And just in case diners think eating buffalo might contribute to their depletion, a cosmopolitan eatery in San Francisco reassures them. A large plaque explains the bull issue:

"The meat is secured from slaughtering the excess bulls annually. As many male as female calves are born, but if the ratio of bulls is not cut to one for every ten adult cows, the males fight and gore one another so unmercifully that they neglect their job of fathering a progeny and the herd does not increase as it should."

Research by Dr. Marty Marchello at North Dakota State University shows that meat from buffalo is highly nutritious. It provides more protein, iron and other nutrients, with comparatively less fat, calories and cholesterol than most other meats.

When Glenn and Lorri Bayger moved from suburban Boston to raise buffalo in western New York State, they researched various markets and found great acceptance by selling bison meat to restaurants in Buffalo, New York and other towns.

The Silver Bison Ranch of Baldwin, Wisconsin, markets all natural meat products to restaurants in the Minneapolis-St. Paul area. "Our meat contains no steroids, growth hormones or antibiotics. All bison at the ranch are open range raised and are never exposed to a feed lot. They only eat the native grasses that grow here naturally at the ranch," says Loren Smeester in promotional material. "We never apply pesticides or herbicides to our pastures, which allows us to produce the most wholesome and healthy protein on the market today."

Even though Smeester's ranch aims to raise and supply metropolitan restaurants with hand-raised, nutritious meat, the diligence that goes into raising buffalo means that buffalo ranching has to also be a labor of love, says Smeester.

"You will soon discover that most bison ranchers choose to provide a home for these beautiful creatures not for the allure of quick profits," he says. "But simply because they love the animal and the peace and tranquility that one enjoys as they come to know the great American bison."

NUTRITIONAL COMPARISONS
Per 100 Gram (3.5 oz.) Serving – Cooked Meat – Updated January 2013

SPECIES	FAT g	PROTEIN g	CALORIES kcal	CHOLESTEROL mg	IRON mg	VITAMIN B-12 mcg
BISON	2.42	28.44	143	82	3.42	2.86
Beef (Choice)	18.54	27.21	283	87	2.72	2.50
Beef (Select)	8.09	29.89	201	86	2.99	2.64
Pork	9.21	27.51	201	84	1.0	0.68
Chicken (Skinless)	7.41	28.93	190	89	1.21	0.33
Sockeye Salmon	6.69	25.40	169	84	0.50	5.67

Bison, separable lean only, cooked, roasted. USDA NDB No. 17157
Beef, composite of trimmed retail cuts, separable lean only trimmed to 0" fat, choice, cooked USDA NDB No. 13362
Beef, composite of trimmed retail cuts, separable lean only trimmed to 0" fat, select, cooked USDA NDB No. 13366
Pork, fresh, composite of trimmed retail cuts (leg, loin and shoulder), separable lean only, cooked USDA NDB No. 10093
Chicken, broilers or fryers, meat only, roasted USDA NDB No. 05013
Salmon, sockeye, cooked, dry heat USDA NDB No. 15086

Original USDA research by Dr. Marty Marchello at North Dakota State University in 1996, updated in 2013.

Low Stress Buffalo Handling

The most important trait for the buffalo handler is calmness, the experts say. Establish yourself at the top of the pecking order in a calm and confident way. The goal is to develop a calm herd, with the animals content and unafraid.

Fearful buffalo cause great risk both to themselves and humans, warns Dr. Temple Grandin, Department of Animal Sciences at Colorado State University, a well-known expert on animal behavior. She's a scientist who understands autism, and applies some of the related philosophy in her work. As wild animals, she explains, buffalo are always on the alert for danger, and ready to respond with fight or flight. When alarmed, fear shoots through their system and they are instantly on trigger.

People who work with buffalo need to watch for signals of fear, she says. The first subtle signs are licking, blinking, huddling, raising the tail, milling in a circle, backing up and balking. As fear and panic increase, so do signs such as hard breathing, frothing at the mouth, vocalizing, bulging eyes, running, pushing, goring, attacking, sitting, jumping or trying to scramble free of the enclosure. The last stage of fear is immobility, lying down without responding to stimuli or prodding. Paying attention to these signals and responding appropriately teaches buffalo what behavior you want. They need the opportunity to willingly comply.

The key to helping buffalo understand this is skilled use of their comfort or flight zone, according to Mark Kossler, manager of the Vermejo Park Ranch, New Mexico, writing in the *Bison Produc-*

Owners round corral corners and build solid walls so buffalo don't spook at distractions, or attempt an escape back to the hills. Only one animal in the chute leading up to the headgate avoids pileups. Parks Canada.

ers' Handbook, published by the National Bison Association.

"The gentle dance of us applying pressure, the animal moving away from the pressure and us releasing the pressure, is the main method of getting our animals to move for us in a low stress manner," Kossler says. "This sets up a positive cause and effect relationship. That is, we get into their flight zone

Gates open and close with ropes and pulleys at Stephens Creek, Yellowstone Park. Handlers stay up on walkways and out of corrals as much as possible. NPS.

by putting pressure on them, and they, by moving away from us get released from that pressure."

The *flight zone* is how much personal space a buffalo needs. This is more space than for domestic animals, and may differ somewhat for each animal. When someone enters that personal space an alarm goes off in its brain. The optimal handler position is at the boundary of that zone. This allows him or her to manipulate the animal in a low stress manner.

Another sensitive place is the balance point at the shoulder. Movement behind the shoulder by the handler causes the animal to go forward. Ahead of that point and it typically moves back. In moving buffalo, handlers work with both the flight zone and the balance point.

What causes high stress, Kossler warns, is "putting pressure on them and never releasing it. Or worse, no matter what they do, continually increasing the pressure."

Too much pressure and the buffalo panics. If unable to flee, he will fight ferociously.

Low stress means handlers work quietly and smoothly. They've learned what not to do: avoid shouting, moving fast or erratically, rushing or trying to "force" the buffalo. Instead, they give the animal time to think things over, analyze and respond calmly.

Low stress handling also implies an appropriate set-up of corrals and chutes. Following Dr. Grandin's advice and research, owners round corral corners and build solid walls so buffalo don't spook at distractions, or attempt an escape back to the hills.

McFarland's corrals wrap around a machinery shed. The buffalo move in a circular direction from a large corral at the upper end, around through chutes and successively smaller corrals until they hold only one animal leading up to the headgate. FM Berg.

12

Homecoming on Tribal Lands

This is a historic moment for us,
They're bringing back the buffalo.
We're rebuilding our lives,
We're healing from historical trauma.
—Iris Grey Bull, Sioux tribal member
on releasing buffalo at Fort Peck

Standing Rock Sioux Reservation, which spans the North and South Dakota border, has a long history of raising buffalo. The first permanent tribal herd arrived in 1955—one bull and four cows, a gift from the Theodore Roosevelt National Park, according to Mike Faith, tribal chairman. Now they help other tribes through the Intertribal Buffalo Council.

Other buffalo came as donations from Wind Cave and Badlands National Parks in South Dakota, or with tribal funds and grants through the years. To improve genetic diversity, Faith says the tribe bought bulls from the Custer State Park buffalo sale. The tribal buffalo manager for nearly twenty years, Mike Faith is the great-great-grandson of Miles Crazy Walking, who as a young man was honored as leader of the scouts during

Buffalo bull travels across a large prairie dog town at Teddy Roosvelt Park. Badlands Reflections Photography.

the 1882 Hiddenwood Creek great hunt *(see Chapter 1)*.

Standing Rock limits its two buffalo herds to a total of about 350, recognizing the importance of not overgrazing the drought-prone plains. The north pasture borders Highway 1806 on the road to Bismarck, near the tribal casino. Here the terrain is mostly rolling, carpeted thickly with green grass, less dramatic than the rugged Porcupine Breaks pasture.

As happens off and on through an ordinary week, a knot of people gathers, watching the buffalo herd through the double-high woven wire fence. Smiling, murmuring softly—they might be familiar visitors from Standing Rock. Or a school tour from nearby Bullhead, Eagle Butte or Wakpala. Or tourists from Japan or Norway spilling from a charter bus. Or perhaps a visiting group of native people in traditional dress performing a buffalo ceremonial.

They've parked along the highway or on the side road.

"We'd like a drive-off, so people can stop more easily," explains LaDonna Brave Bull Allard, former director of tourism and historian for the Standing Rock Sioux Tribe.

Each year Standing Rock harvests fifteen to twenty-five young bulls for its own use, Faith explains. Processed in Mobridge under federal inspection, the meat is donated to the tribal diabetes program and other distribution programs. Some elderly persons receive a monthly portion. The tribe provides buffalo roasts and stew meat for celebrations, funerals and naming ceremonies. Faith hopes to get this meat into the school system of eight hundred students.

Throughout Indian country buffalo have been staging a homecoming.

Restoring the buffalo and life

"My grandma says, 'We don't go past the buffalo without acknowledging them,'" says Allard.

She waves toward a nearby herd of about forty buffalo cows and calves grazing peacefully through the middle of a prairie dog town in the tribe's rugged

As director of tourism, LaDonna Brave Bull Allard guided tours for visitors on Standing Rock history and culture for many years. L Allard.

Buffalo move through a prairie dog town in the Porcupine Breaks pasture, while the town dwellers yip indignantly. Having buffalo nearby is important to restoring the native culture, says LaDonna Allard.

Porcupine Breaks pasture. The magnificent buffalo cows, along with their new calves, yearlings and two-year-olds, ignore the indignant prairie dogs yipping at the edges. It's July and some of the massive, dark buffalo bodies are almost black, their shedding capes a faded golden tan.

"We wave. We say 'Hi,' We leave food for them."

Allard says having the buffalo on their two Standing Rock ranges is important to restoring the native culture of the people who live here. "Our tribe is the original 'Buffalo Nation—*Pte Oyate*.' Everything we do is related to the buffalo. In our ceremonies we use all parts of the buffalo. In the powwow we dance like the buffalo. How we raise our children. . ."

As she watches, younger bulls graze in small bachelor groups off at some distance—while an old lone bull rubs and itches his hide against the polished trunk of a box-elder tree, scraping off raggedy pieces of winter coat, his long beard brushing the ground.

Allard says people can learn much from the buffalo. Parenting skills for example. Allard tells the story of a Native woman who neglected her children and the tribal judge placed them in a foster home. He sentenced her to go each day for six months to watch the buffalo herd, write down what she saw, and report back.

In six months she returned to court.

"What did you learn?" the judge asked.

"I learned that buffalo mothers protect and praise, and constantly care for their children. They teach them and discipline them when they're naughty, but in a good way."

"Do you think you can do that?"

"Yes. I want my children back. I'll try to be a better mother. Like the buffalo."

Lessons learned from the buffalo, Allard explains, are valuing young and old, respecting both male and female, keeping physically active, drinking good water, eating healthy foods and caring for each other.

Mike Faith agrees that buffalo care for each other. They watch each other for warning signs. Faith recalls one morning when he saw

Standing Rock Sioux Tribe's north pasture extends from the casino on Highway 24 (ND 1806), down toward the Missouri River on the east. This part of the herd came recently from the Theodore Roosevelt park in North Dakota. FM Berg.

three cows acting strangely. One at a time they walked to the edge of a cutbank, looked down for awhile, then returned to grazing. But they stayed close and occasionally went back and looked over the bank again.

He drove around where he could see better. There, down below, two coyotes circled a young calf at some distance. The coyotes ran when they saw him. But he had no doubt if they came too close the buffalo cows would charge down and chase them away. The mother's two companions were helping her keep watch.

Intertribal Buffalo Council

Faith serves as vice-chairman of the Intertribal Buffalo Council, the organization of Indian tribes that is working to help each other obtain and care for their own buffalo herds.

Many plains tribes have a long history of raising buffalo. But it was never easy going it alone without guidelines or experience. Some succeeded, others not so well. Today, more than sixty tribes have joined the Intertribal Buffalo Council. Most own a buffalo herd, for a total of about 15,000 buffalo living in tribal herds across the United States. Many are plains tribes with a long history of dependence on buffalo for food, shelter and clothing. Others have no known history of hunting buffalo, but want the cultural experience.

"Having the buffalo back helps rejuvenate the culture," says Jim Stone, Rapid City, Executive Secretary of the Intertribal Buffalo Council and a Yankton Lakota. "In my tribe, like others, the buffalo was honored through ceremony and songs. There were buffalo hunts and prayers to give thanks to the buffalo."

The council has adopted the mission of "Restoring buffalo to Indian Country, to preserve our historical, cultural and traditional and spiritual relationship for future generations."

"We have many cultural connections to the buffalo," says Alvah Quinn, a Sisseton Wahpeton Oyate from South Dakota, former manager of the tribal buffalo program. "I grew up hearing about the buffalo, but we didn't have any around on the reservation." His tribe's last recorded buffalo hunt was in 1879.

Quinn remembers the night in September 1992 when he helped bring the first forty buffalo to his home reservation.

"I was really surprised that night. There were sixty tribal

members waiting in the cold and rain to welcome the buffalo back home. After a 112-year absence!"

They now own 360 buffalo—one of many success stories.

After more than two decades, Intertribal Council leaders are even more convinced of the value of these buffalo herds. Daily they are reminded that buffalo represent the spirit of native people and how their lives were once lived, free and in harmony with nature. They've seen how bringing buffalo back to tribal lands helps to heal the spirit of Indian people.

Today some tribes own very large buffalo herds, for commercial as well as cultural purposes. The Crow Tribe has 2,000 buffalo running free-range on their large, mountainous reservation spanning the state line between Billings, Montana, and Sheridan, Wyoming, according to Patrick Toomey, Tech Services Provider at the Intertribal Buffalo Council. At Pine Ridge, SD, the Oglala Sioux raise 1,100 including both tribal and college herds. Rosebud also raises 300 under a tribal umbrella,

Other tribes set goals for a small herd mostly for cultural and educational purposes, explains Mike Faith. They might slaughter only one or two buffalo a year for special celebrations and ceremonial use. It depends on land available, land uses on the reservation, tribal population and historic dependence on buffalo.

"Quality over quantity is what counts," says Faith. "Whether they want a small herd—twenty or thirty—or a larger commercial herd, we can give help and technical assistance."

No matter the numbers, Faith suggests it is important that new tribes take their buffalo venture

Onlookers cheered as thirty-four Yellowstone Park buffalo were coaxed off the trailer and went racing off onto the 1,000 acre pasture on the plains of the Fort Belknap Reservation in Montana in 2013. *Photo by Rion Sanders. Reprinted with permission from the Great Falls Tribune.*

Restoring the Buffalo

Early on a gorgeous July morning, sweet breezes waft across the flat between the higher bluffs and the badlands below, as Robert "Robbie" Magnan, director of the Fort Peck Fish and Wildlife Department, headed his pickup north into the quarantine pasture. I was privileged to ride along over the green hills that summer morning in 2014.

We were looking for the thirty-nine buffalo from Yellowstone Park that recently came to live in this generous pasture. It is large—about twenty square miles (equal to a rugged chunk of land four miles by five)—13,000 acres. So they have lots of room and might be anywhere—up on the grassy plateau or down one of many gravel draws.

Magnan says the buffalo often walk eight or more miles a day while grazing. They keep moving, so he never knows where to find them.

"I promised I'd look at them every day and that's what I do."

He chuckles and you know there's nothing he enjoys more than bouncing over the grassy flat, up and over the dam and out on a high point of land each morning to scan the badland draws below for the little Yellowstone Park herd.

He checks a well and progress on the new, higher and stronger quarantine fence being built within the quarantine pasture for later arrivals. A pasture within a pasture, for extra security.

Magnan is pleased with the new six-wire buffalo-tight wildlife fences—a smooth wire on top and bottom for deer to jump over and antelope to crawl under,

The Yellowstone Park herd at Fort Peck Assiniboine and Sioux reservation in northeastern Montana. Curious and friendly, several walk over to sniff the pickup. They grunt their greetings—a magical interchange. FM Berg.

with four taut barbed wires between.

"As long as they have grass like this, water and the minerals they need—and we test the soils for that—they'll stay in," he says. If not, they'll go looking for what's missing.

"We call them wide-ranging, not free-ranging like in Yellowstone. It's not realistic to think buffalo will ever be free-ranging without fencing. They will always be in a fence."

This lovely summer morning Magnan drives over two hours before finding the Yellowstone herd.

"Just one more place to look!"

Over the next hill, down a draw, and sure enough, there they are.

Magnificent, extra-large, extra-dark beauties, thirty-nine adults, with twelve calves, bunched together as they graze.

Curious and friendly, several walk over to surround the pickup, to sniff at us and grunt their greetings for a few minutes. It is a magical interchange.

Best of all, there's a new baby calf. It's already mid-summer and the older calves are turning dark, the crests of their heads nearly black between little nubs of black horns. But this baby, only one day old, is pure red-gold. He shines bright in the morning sun. In the distance, in another pasture, we glimpse a hundred or so of the Ft. Peck tribe's other herd filing down a long hill to water.

Magnan calls those *our business herd*. The Yellowstone Park buffalo are their *cultural herd*.

"To us these are extremely valuable, like registered cattle. They'll never be sold. We'll use them only for cultural purposes."

He tells the amazing story of this small priceless herd and the quarantine research that brought it here. The research, still ongoing, studies whether Yellowstone Park buffalo that test negative for brucellosis as calves can continue to live disease-free. The goal is to grow the herd and then, if still disease free, establish them in a wider area, such as on tribal lands.

As we watched the Yellowstone herd, the buffalo spread out a bit, grazing, while several calves took the opportunity to nurse. Then, still grazing, the herd came together in a small, compact band and moved up the green draw around a rocky point out of sight.

Magnan wants to increase this cultural herd enough to achieve a natural diversity with a self-sustaining genetic base. He has worked with the Fort Peck Fish and Wildlife for twenty years, sixteen of them with the tribal buffalo herd.

"From the beginning of time, the buffalo have taken care of Native Americans. Now they need our help. The money we generate from our business herd is to take care of our cultural herd. This is a way we could feed our people if the social programs were stopped," he explains.

One problem that concerns Robbie Magnan is that none of these buffalo grew up in a multi-generational herd, since they were separated from their mothers and quarantined together as calves. He wonders: how will they learn the wisdom of the herd? How will they understand the complexities of normal buffalo relationships?

So far, the quarantine is working. No brucellosis outbreaks outside the park.

Magnan and his staff have shown themselves capable. When it came time to relocate an additional 145 buffalo that had been held five years on Ted Turner's Green Ranch near Bozeman, and before that in Yellowstone Park quarantine. Montana authorities decided it was too soon to divide them among various entities, as planned, and instead trucked them to Fort Peck. His buffalo crew took over managing the two Yellowstone herds.

"I enjoy them," he says. "After sixteen years they are still teaching me."

When the new herd arrived from Yellowstone Park at the Ft. Peck pasture, it was already dark. As the trucks rolled across the bridge leading to the release site near Poplar, a group of Assiniboine people stood waiting, singing a welcome. It was an unforgettable moment for those on the bridge.

"We sang for them—a buffalo song," said Larry Wetsit, vice president of community services at Fort Peck Community College. "It's a special day. Our people have been waiting and praying about this."

During early reservation days hundreds of tribal members had starved, including his own ancestors, he said. "It was all about having no buffalo. That was the low part in our history, the lowest we could go. This is a road to recovery."

Larry Schweiger, president of the National Wildlife Federation, one of the agencies involved in the Interagency Bison Management Plan for dealing with Yellowstone Park brucellosis problems, was on hand for the release.

"We believe it's the right thing to do for wildlife. It's the right thing to do for the tribes. And ultimately the right thing to do for the landscape," he said.

"What this means to me is the return of prosperity to our people," said Wetsit. An Assiniboine, he has been the medicine lodge keeper for over twenty years, a ceremony he learned as a young man. "It's a celebration of our life with the buffalo. What we've always been told, always prayed about, is that the

The viewing stand in the Oneida tribal buffalo pasture brings children and adults into a closer relationship with their own buffalo herd. Courtesy Oneida Tribe.

buffalo represents prosperity. When times were good it was because our Creator gave us more buffalo."

Iris Grey Bull, a Sioux member—the Fort Peck reservation is home to both Assiniboine and Sioux tribes—spoke about their close ties to the buffalo.

"The waters of our reservation form the shapes of buffalo," she said. "One male is to the east and four females to the west. Now they're bringing back the buffalo. This is a historic moment for us. We're rebuilding our lives. We're healing from historical trauma."

"I watched the bison come out of the trailers," Schweiger recalled. "I was watching the faces of tribal elders and the women and children watching these big animals charge out of the trailers. I was so moved to see the reaction—a powerful thing to witness. After the animals were released the drummers sang a blessing. The snow was blowing, it was cold, it was dark, but there was a lot of warmth."

On August 22, 2013, the remaining thirty-four buffalo of the same pure Yellowstone Park strain as those at Fort Peck had been released on nearby Fort Belknap Reservation.

Montana's governor Brian Schweitzer called the event a historic opportunity to bring genetically pure buffalo to this special place on the planet.

"These are the bison that will be breeding stock to re-populate the entire western United States, in every place that people desire to have them," he said.

One hundred-fifty people gathered to welcome them with a pipe ceremony.

"It's a great day for Indians and Indian country," announced Mark Azure, who heads the Fort Belknap tribe's buffalo program, as the last two big bulls flipped up their tails and ran from the trailer to join the herd.

Mike Fox, tribal councilman, said the tribe's goal is to manage the special buffalo herd and use it as seed stock for other places wanting to reintroduce the Yellowstone strain.

"It's a homecoming for them," Fox said. "They took care of us and now it's time for us to take care of them."

Robert Magnan would like to develop a Yellowstone Park setting in which families can drive among the buffalo and enjoy watching them close up. Some tribes build viewing shelters or bring some of their gentler buffalo into pastures near town as a way to enhance spiritual and cultural connections with people of all ages.

South Dakota Lakota gather near the butchering facility in Yellowstone Park to honor the buffalo. NPS.

seriously. Hiring a knowledgeable buffalo manager is critical.

The Intertribal Council offers training and educational programs and coordinates transfer of buffalo. Experts are available to help tribal leaders work out management and marketing plans that fit their particular concerns and goals, if desired.

Success stories

The Eight Northern Pueblo tribes of New Mexico, like many other Native Ameri-cans, live on the land of their ancestors. Five maintain buffalo herds and cooperate to diversify bloodlines.

The Picurís herd began over a decade ago with one female and one bull. It has grown to eighty head, not including calves. The buffalo are pastured in a field close to the road, so visitors often stop. Tribal herd manager Danny Sam cautions them that it is not safe to walk among the buffalo.

Sam serves as secretary for the Intertribal Buffalo Council and has been involved with the program since the beginning. He has seen many changes. One he does not care for is that federal inspections, taken over from the state, require more paperwork, charge a fee and classify buffalo as an exotic species, rather than livestock.

"They're not an exotic species," Sam says. "They're native to this country."

In 1997, the Oneida Tribe of Wisconsin started their buffalo herd with thirteen heifers and a bull from Wind Cave National Park after Pat Cornelius saw the delighted response of native people on western reservations to the return of buffalo. Now Oneida herd manager and former board member of the Intertribal Bison Cooperative, Cornelius' conviction that her people would be heartened as well by a herd of their own came true when she saw the first fourteen buffalo arrive.

It was an awesome spiritual moment. "The earth shook!" when the animals jumped from trucks, she said.

By 2007, the Oneidas owned 120 cows and bulls, with forty-three calves. The presence of buffalo has made a big difference to them, Cornelius says, describing the many local people visiting daily in summer and winter from an especially-built viewing mound and shelter.

Alaska may not seem like a natural home for buffalo. But bones and petroglyphs prove the larger wood buffalo lived and were hunted there in ancient times.

Athabascan tribes began introducing plains buffalo at Stevens Village near Delta Junction, the first Alaskan group to join the restoration program. The new herd, includes thirty-

The Oneida Tribe in Wisconsin began their buffalo herd with thirteen heifers and one bull from Wind Cave National Park, after Pat Cornelius, herd manager, saw the delighted response of other tribes. "The earth shook!" she said, when their buffalo jumped off the trucks. Oneida Tribe.

eight buffalo, fourteen of them calves, obtained with help from the Intertribal Buffalo Council.

Rocky Afraid of Hawk, a Lakota Oyate elder and the Council's spiritual advisor, flew to Alaska from South Dakota for a welcoming ceremony. He told the Athabascan people that buffalo were placed on earth to teach people how to live.

"You can learn from them." he said.

Afraid of Hawk presented the village with a buffalo skull to use in ceremonials and prayers. To bless the event, he burned sagebrush in a metal can with coals from the fire.

Randy Mayo, first chief of the Stevens Village tribal council, carried the smoldering sage to guests so they could wave smoke over their faces. The village presented Afraid of Hawk with tobacco and salmon strips.

Traditional chief David Salmon, a Chalkyitsik elder, sat on a folding chair beside a wood fire, relating buffalo stories told by his grandfather. Beside him, Herb George, a Stevens Village tribal council member, stirred a bubbling soup made with buffalo meat. He said he was making soup the way his father taught him—like a traditional potlatch soup, but with buffalo bones instead of moose.

Mayo believes being around the buffalo can help people work through their problems.

He acknowledged that when the village voted to move forward with raising buffalo, he didn't know much about the animal that had provided food, clothing and shelter to his ancestors. He has learned a lot.

"Every time I come here it lifts me up," said Mayo. "Just observing them, you never get tired of it."

Stevens Village leaders encourage other villages to start their own buffalo herds. They report Fort Yukon and other Yukon Flat villages join them in a desire for some of the rare, larger wood buffalo native to the area.

A historic 2014 across-the-border treaty signed by U.S. Tribes and Canadian First Nations brings this possibility closer. Called the *Medicine Line Northern Tribes Buffalo Treaty*, the international agreement focuses on buffalo restoration on tribal lands of both countries.

The Intertribal Buffalo Council recognizes that even after more than a century of recovery, many Native Americans still feel an acute sense of loss over the destruction of the wild buffalo and all that represents in their lives.

"As we bring our buffalo herd back to health, we also bring our own people back to health, and that's what it's all about," said Fred DuBray, as a leading founder of the organization and its first president.

The Council leaders are committed to establishing buffalo herds on Indian lands in a way that promotes economic development, ecological restoration and spiritual revitalization. They suggest that for people who may be hurting, contemplating their own tribal buffalo can help them heal and bring a sense of wholeness and peace.

A holistic approach

Lisa Colome, Technical Service Provider for the Intertribal Buffalo Council in Rapid City, served as rangeland specialist, but like others who work there, she takes a holistic approach.

A Cherokee elder who came from Oklahoma for training told her of their first herd. "I can't tell you what it meant to us," he said. "I really believe with the return of the buffalo there'll be an awakening of our people."

A group of buffalo cools off in a stream in mid-summer. NPS.

Teaching young people about traditional relationships and spiritual connections to the buffalo is important to Colome.

"Native kids have a natural connection to the buffalo," she says, her dark eyes warming. "They're just naturally born with this awe. They are never disrespectful and show genuine caring. This is what tribes are seeking."

She enjoys bringing children to see the buffalo.

"Once I brought a group of sixth graders. They watched silently as the buffalo ran over the hill out of sight. I said, 'Just wait, I think they'll come back if we're quiet.'

"We peeked over the hill. The buffalo circled back and came within twenty-five feet. The kids had never been that close before."

It's easy to see that Colome is excited about her work, whether her day focuses on herd and forage health, or cultural and spiritual ties. Not always do tribal herds bring financial benefits, she knows—often quite the opposite. But always she sees cultural value.

"I love being a part of developing tactics, plans and solutions that ensure buffalo are here for generations to come," she says. "Return of the buffalo awakens the native spirit—it gives us hope of better lives."

Herdsmen play a special role. Caring for buffalo enhances feelings of self-worth and pride in the men and women who work with them, reports Art Schmidt, Flandreau Santee Sioux buffalo herd manager. He sees an amazing change in the attitudes of people he hires.

"Knowing they are taking care of that beautiful magnificent creature—it becomes part of who they are and gives them a sense of pride in their culture," Schmidt says. "They're not just going out and doing their job and collecting a paycheck and going home."

Schmidt suggests caring for buffalo is not just an eight-to-five job. The crew must be ready for emergencies—such as an escape in the middle of the night.

His tribe received several buffalo from the South Dakota Crow Creek Sioux. But one morning the newcomers were gone. When the herdsmen found them they were headed straight west down Highway 34 toward Ft. Thompson and the Crow Creek reservation.

Oneida boys and girls from a nearby school visit the working chutes during their buffalo roundup. Oneida Tribe.

The homesick buffalo were going home.

Alvah Quinn, with over twenty-seven years of buffalo experience, notes that herdsmen look forward to the annual roundup when the buffalo are pregnancy tested and tagged. He shared results of a roundup of the Sisseton Wahpeton herd of 434 buffalo.

"We worked the herd in March. Of 170 cows, 83 percent were pregnant which is up from the year before of 72.5 percent. Our oldest animal is an eighteen-year-old cow, one of the pregnant animals. This year the herd received new microchips in addition to their ear tags. The microchips are scanned during the roundup and tell the details on each animal.

"One of our grants was to do a DNA genotyping study. We found we had eight bison that exhibited less than a 100 percent bison blood. They will be culled for traditional ceremonies, powwows, the elderly program and Wellness Center."

Quinn's tribe is proud of providing replacement buffalo to other tribes. After roundup they shipped a breeding bull to the Ute Tribe in Colorado, three cows to the Winnebago Tribe in Nebraska and ten bull calves destined for Fort Hall, an Idaho tribe just getting started raising buffalo.

Dozens of people came to watch the Ho-Chunk roundup, bringing in buffalo and moving them through a series of pastures into the corrals. Some were tribal members—both young and old—who had never seen a buffalo up close before. Ho-Chunk is a

Wisconsin tribe with a healthy buffalo herd that started in 1997, after purchase of land with casino profits. Beginning with four animals, it grew to nearly 400 in a decade, now holds at about sixty.

This roundup began with herdsmen sprinkling a trail of what they call "candy corn." A mixture of molasses, corn and oats, it led the buffalo through gates from larger pastures into smaller ones closer to the corrals. Buffalo have a keen sense of smell and are attracted by the scent of molasses.

The Ho-Chunk people like to keep their buffalo a bit wild, in their natural state, so move them as little as possible. Their annual roundup for vaccinating and working the animals is staged in December to avoid stressing them in hot weather.

They use pickups and tractors to persuade the animals to move along, since their horses are not trained to chase buffalo. Four-wheelers are also considered too dangerous.

"In our traditional way of life, we hold the buffalo in high esteem," said Tribal Chief Clayton Winneshiek. "It is recognized as a spirit blessed by our creator and given to us to use."

Tribal leaders look forward to the return of 1,550 acres from the former Badger Army Ammunition plant near Baraboo, declared surplus by the Army after almost twenty-five years of inactivity. There the Ho-Chunk hope to eventually establish a large herd on the Baraboo land to produce more meat for their people, and possibly sell commercially outside the tribe.

Cherishing buffalo meat

"The meat that satisfies—has a ping to it."

This is how Lakota hunters from the Cheyenne River Sioux tribe described the taste of buffalo to the missionary Thomas Riggs on their last winter hunt in 1880-1881.

Others call it hearty, sweet and rich, tasty and tender and nearly fat-free. The opportunity to again eat buffalo meat is cherished by Native Americans.

"Eat the meat of the buffalo. It's healing. It keeps our people strong. It fills the soul as well as the body," say native elders.

Tribes with buffalo herds use much of their own buffalo meat within the community. Butchering and caring for the meat is regarded as an integral part of the circle of life, and as an important skill to teach children.

"We take our children to the kill," explains LaDonna Allard. The process is carried out with due ceremony, with prayer and thanksgiving, she says. "We thank the buffalo."

A high-powered rifle takes down the buffalo. It is then skinned and cut up in traditional ways, with all parts used in ceremonies—horns, skulls, bones and hides.

"Every part has a meaning. We use them all," Allard explains.

The Fort Peck tribes in Montana have built their own butchering facility, out near the corrals, for tribal members who want to purchase and slaughter their own buffalo from the business herd of about 200 head. Robert Magnan, Fort Peck Fish and Game Director, says he buys a buffalo himself each year and shares it with relatives, as do around three dozen other tribal members.

"We have all the equipment—saws, grinder—and they bring their own wrap. We teach them how to cut up the different parts—roast, steaks. Grind the tougher cuts and scraps for hamburger. [We teach] how to cook them."

But first, says Magnan, "We talk to the buffalo. Tell them we need meat to feed our families. Thank them for their willingness to take care of us."

For meat used in the tribes' federally subsidized programs they haul live animals to the nearby small town of Scobey, where they are processed in a USDA meat inspected plant. A buffalo carries less meat than a steer, he says, about 800 pounds on the carcass.

Fort Peck offers buffalo hunts, as many as forty or fifty a year from the business herd. In 2014 hunters paid $850 for a two-year-old buffalo, $1,200 for a dry cow, $1,500 for an ordinary bull, and up to $10,000 for a big bull with well-formed horns. Many are return hunters who come from Korea, Germany, Texas and other states throughout the U.S.

His staff instructs hunters to wait until they can shoot an animal off by itself—one of the five or six with blue ear tags, designated for hunting—and not to fire into the herd. Magnan insists the buffalo be put down quickly. He carries a rifle and finishes the job himself if the paying hunter only wounds it.

In many tribes, anyone putting on a community feed can request buffalo meat. Buffalo is served at graduations, namings and community celebrations, and has become an honored part of the healthy foods in diabetes programs.

Buffalo meat is low in fat and cholesterol and high in protein, highly absorbable iron and zinc, and is considered delicious and exceptionally healthy. When grass fed, it is even more nutrient-dense.

Diabetes is a serious concern in many Indian tribes. Tribal leaders attribute their higher risk to genetics and reservation living,

Many tribes offer buffalo hunts of carefully selected excess animals. NPS.

which often leads to sedentary life and diets high in sugar and fat—far from traditional active lifestyles with lean, high protein diets.

"Buffalo meat, grass-fed meat—this is something people with diabetes can eat that is good for them," Alvah Quinn explains in talks at schools. "We can offer 100 percent pure buffalo meat to our tribal members for nothing or almost nothing. With all the diabetes in Indian Country, eating right is important."

Buffalo hunting

Just outside the borders of Yellowstone Park, Native Americans are hunting buffalo again.

These are ancient buffalo hunting grounds for certain tribes from farther west: the Confederated Salish and Kootenai, the Nez Perce of Idaho, Shoshone-Bannock and Umatilla tribes. Because buffalo-hunting rights were specified in their treaty of 1855, these tribes have recently been granted special rights to hunt buffalo that migrate out of Yellowstone Park in winter.

For the hunters it's a healing kind of thing, giving them a renewed sense of pride, reports Tom McDonald of the Confederated tribes' natural resources office in Pendleton, Oregon. They can enjoy the beauty of a spectacular mountain hunt in the quiet of winter, watch buffalo sweep deep snow aside by swinging their heads, feed their families abundantly on buffalo meat and share with the community.

People love the taste of the meat and are willing to pay a premium, McDonald says. "Ninety-seven percent of the people who return to eating bison find it exceptional."

The Yellowstone buffalo hunting season starts in early November and runs through mid-March. The key is to be at the site where buffalo leave the park—in the valleys on its north and west borders— at the precise time they decide to come out.

Harsh winters and high populations bring buffalo and elk down in great numbers, invading cattle ranches, hay meadows and stacked hay supplies outside the park. In easy winters, not so many come down and it can be hard to find them.

In mid-February, 2014, three brothers, Brad, Kevin and Greg

Buffalo graze through the sagebrush. NPS.

Marengo of the Confederated Tribes set off for Yellowstone Park. All had buffalo tags. With a long drive and perhaps costly effort ahead, their trip reflects the investment of their ancestors—who spent months on buffalo hunting trips travelling east across the Continental Divide to the Yellowstone area from their Columbia River homelands.

"I think it's a pretty special thing, after so many years, to rekindle that tradition of travel to provide food for the long house," says Carl Scheeler, wildlife program manager for the Confederated Tribes' Department of Natural Resources in Pendleton, Oregon. He says many will be participating as families.

"You have to be ready to go at a moment's notice," Brad Marengo says. "Sometimes you have to take off work because you might not get another chance."

On the first day the three brothers failed to find any buffalo along the Park's northern boundary. A single bull came out the second day and crossed the Yellowstone River. Realizing his mistake, he plunged into the underbrush and escaped back inside.

No shooting inside the park, of course.

"He outfoxed us," says Kevin Marengo.

The third day the brothers made their way to Beattie Gulch. There, at last, five buffalo crossed the park border. They fired three times and three buffalo fell.

"If you shoot them right behind the ear, they just drop," advises Greg Marengo. "Don't shoot anywhere else because you don't want to just wound them. They'll head back inside the park."

Buffalo hunting often becomes a family event for tribal members, McDonald says. "It's a return to something that existed a long time ago for Native people. It's very rewarding."

If this hunting fails to sufficiently reduce the herds, some of the Yellowstone surplus is trucked to a nearby slaughter facility for tribal use.

In 2013, the Indian hunts killed 212 buffalo, according to Montana Fish, Wildlife and Parks. The 2015 target called for removal of 800 to 900 buffalo to bring the Yellowstone herds down from a total of 4,900 to the desired 3,000. This meant either more hunting or the federal government shipping more animals to slaughter, or both.

Almost everyone agrees that hunting is preferable. "Our goal is as much as possible to manage the population level through hunting as opposed to other means," says Pat Flowers, the Yellowstone region supervisor for Montana Fish, Wildlife and Parks.

"It's not sport hunting, it's a community event," Scheeler says. "I'm very much looking forward to it becoming a family tradition."

McDonald says the hunts are culturally and spiritually satisfying and have increased local pride and feelings of self-worth.

"Hunting bison again has rekindled songs, a sense of place," he says. "It's been amazing."

A herd of buffalo on the move. SD Tourism.

13

Herds in Public Places

*This scenery already rich pleasing and beautiful
Was still further heightened by immense herds of Buffaloe,
Deer Elk and Antelopes, which we saw in every direction
Feeding on the hills and plains.*
　　　　　　　　　—Meriwether Lewis
　　　　　　　　　　the Upper Missouri River, Sept. 17, 1804

Public parks are a vital component in the restoration of buffalo. About 34,000 buffalo are living in herds found on national, state, and provincial parks and refuges in the United States and Canada, as of 2016. Two-thirds of these live in publicly-owned herds in the United States, and one-third in Canada.*

Each September, Custer State Park near Custer, SD, hosts a fall roundup of the park's buffalo herd. Public herds, such as the one at Custer State Park, have contributed significantly to the restoration of the buffalo as a species in North America. Because of the decimation of the buffalo,

---

*This figure shows a drop in numbers for Canada due to drought and other factors, but will likely recover before long, says Dave Carter of the National Bison Assoc.

The Custer Park roundup. Horses are seldom used in today's roundups, as it's considered dangerous for both horse and rider. SD Tourism.

President Theodore Roosevelt took a special interest in establishing the national parks system and federally protected lands to save wildlife, and to preserve wilderness areas for them to live. States such as South Dakota followed suit, taking an active role in maintaining buffalo herds on state lands.

This writer attended the Custer roundup on a gorgeous Indian summer morning, with stray breezes sending the golden leaves dancing amongst the cottonwood trees along French Creek.

More than 14,000 spectators from neighboring ranches and faraway countries had gathered for the annual running of the herd. In anticipation of seeing 1,300 buffalo running across the prairie on their way to the corrals for working, hundreds have been waiting for hours, arriving early in the morning to ensure a front row spot. The sun glanced off thousands of cars parked discreetly far from the creek. Thankfully, no one accidentally tripped a car alarm or honked a horn. The crowd lining both sides of the creek, leaned against fences, sat on camp chairs, knelt in the grass, murmuring quietly while awaiting the buffalo.

Custer State Park's buffalo herd started with thirty-six buffalo from Scotty and Sally Philips. The Philips bought their buffalo from the Dupree family, who saved five calves during the last great tribal buffalo hunts in the 1880s.

Few among the large crowd realize that they are about to see buffalo whose ancestors were among the few remaining survivors of the massive, ancient herds that once ranged across North America in the tens of millions—the calves rescued by the Dupree family. While the buffalo were hunted nearly to extinction by the early 1900s, they avoided that fate through efforts of a few Native American and white ranchers who found and saved survivors.

Someone shouted: "Here they come!"

Excitement rippled through the crowd.

Suddenly the buffalo came running down a side draw into French Creek. The herd was guided at a distance on each side and from behind by park rangers in white Custer State Park pickup trucks. Colorful cowboys and cowgirls on horseback, riding for their own enjoyment, edged in behind the pickups at a cautious distance.

Dust flew in the air and the ground shook from the power of thousands of pounding hooves.

The herd passed by the tourists and other spectators on schedule, and thankfully, with no accidents, stumbles, or other potentially dangerous surprises.

Even though the buffalo in Custer State Park are more familiar with humans and their vehicles than other wild, free-ranging herds, when a big buffalo herd starts running there's always risk of a stampede. Buffalo stampede from fear of the huge animals charging behind them, writes Patricia Lee, of the University of Illinois, in *The Buffalo Producer's Guide,* published by the National Bison Association.

"It's a snowball effect. They dare not stop. They are afraid of the masses of thundering bodies coming behind them . . . of other, more dominant, horned, excited and very heavy bison at their heels," Lee writes. They know they could be gored or trampled to death if they stop, she says.

Over the decades, public and private buffalo roundups have had their pile-ups and fatalities. Those incidents are less common today now that most handlers understand buffalo require low-stress handling. While cattle are domesticated, and tolerate being driven in a herd, buffalo are not cattle. They remain, even after a century of being around humans, wild animals. They demand respect and need their space. It helps, too, that buffalo handlers exclude the older, more aggressive bulls from the roundups. Past experience has shown that mature bulls are dangerous, and it is disruptive to attempt to bring them in with the others.

All goes smoothly this time. These herdsmen, whether on horseback or in a pickup, know when to press the stragglers and when to hold back. Also, while these Custer Park buffalo are wild and free-roaming, they are less excitable than large herds on some other ranges. They live in daily contact with tourists and vehicles, explains Gary Brundige, head of Custer State Park resource management. More than 1.8 million visitors come through this park annually, most of them looking for buffalo and driving among them on the park's loop roads.

The first gate into the creek pasture is open and the cows head toward it.

A working event that welcomes visitors, the Custer State Roundup in September is well attended . FM Berg.

The second gate stands open to direct the buffalo across the paved highway. The lead cows know the routine, but don't go through the gate immediately. Rather, they circle into fence corners to check the dimensions of this smaller pasture, and test if there might be a weak spot in the fence. Some of the less curious spill onto fresh grass and spread out across the flat, grazing.

The park's herd managers roll their pickups to a stop and the riders hold back, allowing the animals time to explore and relax.

All this happens midway between the two crowds of spectators, clustered on their two hillsides. It's as though the lead cows know these visitors have come long distances, waited hours and will appreciate a bit of a show.

Finally, the buffalo head for the second gate. The older cows, some more than twenty years old, know just where to go as they've done this many times before. Some ranchers coax their buffalo through gates and into corrals with grain or range cake. However, no treats are needed here to lure them on, says Brundige, because this pasture system is carefully designed and tested over many years to bring the animals closer to the corrals by leading them from the wider range onto rich, ungrazed grass in progressively smaller pastures.

When they're good and ready, the lead buffalo cross the highway, run through the gate and on beyond the corrals to another fresh pasture, with the herd close behind. The park herd managers will hold the buffalo here to calm down and adjust to new surroundings for two or three days before working them in the chutes. Then seasoned handlers will cut out about 250 buffalo for the park's annual November sale.

Visitors to the park's annual buffalo roundup get to see a demonstration of what that fall work looks like. Already in the corrals stand a hundred head of buffalo to be worked that afternoon, brought in a few days earlier to give them time to adjust to their new surroundings and recover from the stress of being moved there by the crew.

Because the pens and chutes have high, solid walls that hide any glimpse of the open prairie and freedom, the buffalo grunt and grumble, but move calmly through these state-of-the-art corrals that significantly reduce the injuries or fatalities that can happen when agitated buffalo try to escape.

The pens are narrow enough

The chutes and working corrals at the Custer State Park roundup. FM Berg.

About half the crowd is routed to the south side and half to the north. Note the hundreds of vehicles parked higher on the hill opposite, with people seated on the slope just below. Visitors line the fence on this side. FM Berg.

that a solid, three-way folding gate mounted on the front of a tractor sweeps smoothly through each pen, emptying it in one pass, without risk to workers or animals. The Custer park crew call this gadget a "turkey catcher."

On their way to the headgate, the buffalo move through an intricate system of corrals, gates and single-animal alleyways. At the headgate, handlers and veterinarians monitor health, run tests, pregnancy check, vaccinate, brand and ear tag as needed.

At noon, hungry tourists enjoy an outdoor meal featuring tender, tasty buffalo meat, perfectly roasted and sliced on a bun. Seated at picnic tables they are surrounded by the golden grasses, dark pines, and infinite sapphire skies that make September in the Dakotas exquisite. The fall buffalo roundup at South Dakota's Custer State Park in the Black Hills is likely the largest and most celebrated event of its kind in the world.

Public herds in Dakota

By inviting tourists to the roundup, Custer State Park brings a bit of dramatic Old West staging to the event. The cowboys and cowgirls carrying flags are a nice touch, as are the riders on horseback. But they are seldom seen in today's buffalo roundups—too dangerous for horses and riders. The chutes and corrals are designed with utmost safety—for viewers, handlers, and buffalo.

Custer State Park has played a major role in helping save and return the buffalo to the plains and prairies. The park's annual roundup and sale has helped start dozens of park and ranch buffalo herds across North America, says Emilie Miller, Program Specialist, South Dakota State Parks. In over forty years, more than 17,000 buffalo have been sent to start new herds and replenish where needed.

While Custer State Park opens its fall roundup to the public as a special event, most other parks prefer to conduct their fall work without fanfare, allowing visitors only by special arrangement.

At the fall roundup in the nearby Badlands National Park, signs on the buffalo chutes bear the message: *Quiet Area*. Workers speak in hushed tones. Only a small group of high school students visit from nearby Kadoka, watching in silent awe from out of sight up on the catwalk.

"I'm very happy to let them do that" says Brian Kenner, the ranger in charge of the buffalo roundup and Chief of Science and Natural Resources at Badlands National Park, of the Custer roundup. "I know they've got it under control. But it looks like a lot of pressure on the guys responsible for it."

Robert Magnan, Director of Fish and Wildlife for the Sioux and Assiniboine tribes at Ft. Peck, Montana, concurs. Even though his crew might take several days to move their herd with pickups through successively smaller pastures, once in the corral they don't hold them long.

"We like to work them fast and get them back out on pasture," he says. "It's too stressful for them."

A helicopter may be needed to bring the buffalo out of rugged badland terrain. In the North Dakota Badlands of Theodore Roosevelt National Park near Medora, a helicopter guides 600 buffalo into the south unit working pens.

Up to 250 buffalo are cut from that herd to gift tribal herds in North and South Dakota, says wildlife biologist Blake McCann. Selected are breeding stocks of mixed age and gender and from different maternal groups, to bring a diverse mix into those donated herds. The partnership with the National Park Service requires

Buffalo Population 2016

	U.S.	Canada	Total
Bison on U.S. Ranches in 2012 (USDA Census)	162,110		
Bison on Canadian Ranches in 2011 (Census of Agric)		125,142	
Bison since last Census (NBA Estimate)	30,000	25,000	
Bison in Federal Herds (DOI 2014)	9,855		
Bison in State and other Public Herds (USFWS 2011)	9,008	1,949	
Additional animals in Public Herds since 2011 (Est.)	3,000	10,500	
Tribal Herds (Est.)	15,000	—	
Total Buffalo	**228,973**	**162,591**	**391,564**

Source: National Bison Association

Buffalo seek the warmth of geysers in wintertime in Yellowstone Park. NPS.

keep the South Unit herd at about 300 to 500, and fewer than 300 in the North Unit.

In the chutes, buffalo are checked by the same veterinarian for over forty years. William "Doc" Tidball, of Beach, tests each animal for brucellosis, an infectious disease that can sicken humans and cattle. Each animal is marked with a microchip and a metal ear tag. Once again, every buffalo is disease-free. Brucellosis has never been detected in Teddy Roosevelt Park.

the animals be kept alive and not butchered for at least a year.

Teddy Roosevelt Park, as it's known locally, is a closed buffalo population, he explains, and has been since the 1950s, without new animals being introduced, partly for disease prevention. These buffalo are very healthy, and while it may make biologic sense to broaden the genetic base, there are no plans for this. The target is to

Buffalo in Yellowstone Park

Some of the nation's largest public herds can be found in Montana. Yellowstone National

In some parks with insufficient winter grazing, buffalo are fed hay. NPS.

Park spans 3,500 square miles across Wyoming, Idaho and Montana. Home to the oldest and largest public buffalo herd in the United States it was established in 1872 as the first national park in the world. Target population is 3,000 buffalo, though it occasionally rises to over 5,000.

Often, the herds can be found grazing in Hayden Valley, an open meadowland that stretches seven miles from the highway into the park, which is ninety percent forest.

"These are the most important free-ranging herds in the nation," according to buffalo historian Tom McHugh, who worked there for three seasons on his doctoral studies of buffalo behavior and wrote *The Time of the Buffalo*.

Yellowstone Park buffalo are reputed to be wild and genetically pure and as such are highly cherished. Yet it could be argued otherwise.

Yellowstone is a place where wild buffalo lived for tens of thousands of years. At least sometimes they lived there, although mountains were not the natural, year-around home of plains bison. And at least some of the buffalo originated there but only about two dozen survived before the park was restocked with a mix from many sources.

Still, Yellowstone is unique because the park staff take a hands-off, wilderness approach to the buffalo. They manage the park as a natural system, so do not vaccinate

North American Buffalo 1888-2016

Year	Survey taken by	U.S.	Canada	Total
1888	London Field magazine (Miller Christy)			1,300
1889	Smithsonian (William T. Hornaday)	541	550	1,091
1895	Ernest Thompson Seton			800
1900	Boston Evening Transcript (Mark Sullivan)			1,024
1902	US Dept. of Interior (S.P. Langley)			1,394
1905	Smithsonian Institution (Frank Baker)			1,697
1910	American Bison Society (William P. Wharton)			2,108
1916	American Bison Society (Edmund Seymour)			5,592
1920	American Bison Society (Martin S. Garretson)			8,473
1926	American Bison Society (Martin S. Garretson)			16,417
1933	American Bison Society (Martin S. Garretson)			21,701
1951	Henry H. Collins, Jr.	9,252	13,902	23,154
1972	David A. Dary			30,100
1982	David A. Dary (Estimated)			83,000
1989	David A Dary (Estimated)	78,000	20,000	98,000
2010	National Bison Assoc. (Producers Handbook) [2]	225,000	200,000	425,000
2016	National Bison Assoc. (Dave Carter)	228,973	162,591	391,564

[1] Totals from 1888 through 1989 are from The Buffalo Book, by David A. Dary, 1989 edition, page 287.

[2] Totals for 2010 and 2016 were compiled by the National Bison Association using a combination of USDA Agricultural Census Data, Canadian Census data, U.S. Fish & Wildlife information, reports from the InterTribal Buffalo Council, and some educated guesses about the growth of herd sizes since the last official figures were reported.

or treat any of the animals, and large predators—wolves, grizzlies and mountain lions—hunt them.*

Another place of surprisingly pure and ancient genetics is the Wind Cave buffalo herd in the Black Hills, which originated mostly from the Bronx Zoo in New York in 1913. Genetic testing shows high levels of diversity, including ten genetic variations that experts haven't seen anywhere else, and no sign of cattle genes.

In 2017 their handlers transferred two new herds from Wind Cave to sanctuaries in Kansas and Arizona. This makes these herds scientifically interesting, and desirable as foundation animals for tribal herds.

A visitor views a bull bison from the safety of a vehicle along the Elk Island Parkway, Elk Island National Park. Parks Canada.

Canadian herds— a grand mix

Because of extreme hunting pressures only wood buffalo, about 500 of them, remained in northern Canada at Hornaday's census. The Northwest Mounted Police then took charge and the northern wood buffalo herd grew—to over 1,500 by 1922 when Wood Buffalo National Park was established, sprawling across northeastern Alberta and southern Northwest Territories.

Today the herd of 5,000 in Wood Buffalo Park is considered the largest free-roaming buffalo herd in the world. (Yellowstone Park currently has built up to 5,000 as well, but the target goal there remains at 3,000. Keeping too many buffalo promotes over-grazing, fewer calves born and buffalo leaving the park.

A small display herd of plains buffalo was started long ago in Banff National Park near the mountain resort of Banff and Lake Louise. Three buffalo came from Charles Goodnight's Texas herd in 1887, and thirteen were donated from the Bedson herd by Sir Donald A. Smith, originating with James McKay in Saskatchewan.

In 1912 Michel Pablo delivered the last of his 716 plains buffalo to Canada. Healthy and fertile, the Pablo buffalo became the foundation for most of Canada's plains buffalo

---

*Unfortunately, the buffalo in Yellowstone Park are highly infected with brucellosis. Research shows between 40 and 60 percent test positive for the disease, according to Montana Fish, Wildlife and Parks. *(continued on page 242)*

White Cloud Dynasty

Once in a great while, rare as it is, a ghostly little white newcomer is born into a buffalo herd. A form of albinism, this can occur in any living thing, animal or plant. From ancient times Native Americans honored white buffalo and white robes as sacred and carried out special ceremonies to celebrate them. Many Native people continue these traditions.

The best place in the world to see an authentic rare white buffalo is probably Jamestown, ND. The white buffalo Dakota Miracle grazes there at the edge of town with a brown herd in a hilly pasture between Interstate 94 and the World's Largest Buffalo monument. He is part of the White Cloud dynasty that began in 1996 when his mother White Cloud was born that July on the Shirek Buffalo Ranch not far from Jamestown. The owners offered to share their joy and excitement with visitors through a special lease agreement. When old enough, White Cloud joined the Jamestown herd and Indian elders welcomed her with drums and sage.

In 2007 White Cloud gave birth to Dakota Miracle after first raising three brown calves. Then in 2008, Dakota Legend, believed to be a granddaughter, was born to a brown mother there. White Cloud was a true certified albino with pink eyes and skin and not quite black horns. The others have blue or brown eyes and dark horns and hooves.

In a hilly buffalo pasture between I-94 and the city, the sharp-eyed tourist has often spotted one… two…and at one time, even *three* creamy-white buffalo of purest beauty, grazing there in a small herd of brown buffalo.

Dakota Miracle is the current star of the Jamestown buffalo herd, grazing along US Interstate 94 at the edge of town. He is the son of White Cloud. ND Tourism.

It has been a fitting location for them. Years ago Jamestown leaders erected a huge cement buffalo on the hill above town celebrating their heritage. Twenty-six feet high, this 'World's Largest Buffalo' honors the great herds that once grazed these rich grasslands and followed a major migration along the James River valley. A prime hunting location, the twice-yearly migration was well known to Native hunters.

A historic Frontier Town sprang up around the big monument. Then a buffalo herd found pasture there and the area was selected by the buffalo association for the National Buffalo Museum. The ND Buffalo Foundation, a local nonprofit, owns both the buffalo herd and museum. White Cloud died of old age in Nov. 2016. She is mounted and on display at the National Buffalo Museum in Jamestown.

The most celebrated and long-lived white buffalo known was Big Medicine. He was born in 1933 on the National Bison Range and lived there all his twenty-six years. His eyes were blue and a thick top-knot of brown hair grew on his head.

The buffalo expert, California biology professor Dale Lott was born on the range there in 1933, the same year as Big Medicine. He grew up among the buffalo at the National Bison Range in Montana, where his grandfather was the Range Superintendent and veterinarian. His father lived and worked there and married the boss's daughter. Later his parents bought his father's home ranch only three miles away, so all through his growing up years "the bison herds were visible as dark patches on distant hills," according to his book *American Bison.*

Called "Old Whitey," by park employees, Big Medicine spent much of his long life in an exhibition pasture with a few females, where he could be more easily seen by visitors. Out on the bigger range by age ten, he contended in battle with other big bulls for a time before returning to the smaller pasture. After his death he was mounted and exhibited at the Montana State Historical Society museum in Helena.

Miracle, was born in 1994 on the 45-acre farm owned by Dave and Valerie Heider, of Janesville, Wisconsin. She lived her entire life there and died at age ten. Miracle was a symbol of harmony to Native visitors, marking the rebirth of their culture and peace among all people. At one point, Miracle drew about 2,000 visitors per day.

Two more white calves were born on the Heider farm but did not survive. Another noted white calf, was Lightning Medicine Cloud, born May 11, 2011, on the Texas ranch of Arby Little Soldier. A Lakota who moved there from South Dakota and the great-great-great grandson of Sitting Bull, Little Soldier welcomed the calf with joy and organized a traditional Naming Ceremony for his first birthday. Sadly the little white calf died before that celebration.

Three hundred miles farther north of Jamestown in Canada, Blizzard, a white yearling buffalo bull arrived at the Winnipeg Assiniboine Zoo in a fierce snowstorm. Born in June 2004 in a U.S. herd, he was purchased by the Zoo Curator, Dr. Robert E. Wrigley, to honor the buffalo as Manitoba's Provincial emblem. The buffalo is celebrated there for the central role played in the livelihood and culture of local First Nations, Métis and European hunters and settlers.

Dr. Wrigley says Blizzard's first meeting with his Canadian herd mates caused great excitement. "I have never heard so much grunting and snorting, and witnessed such astonishing speed from these huge animals, as the herd charged back and forth across the field. Heads colliding and horns pounding into rib cages is not a reassuring sight or sound."

Finally, things settled down, and the dominant females accepted him. To the curator's surprise, groups of First Nations people soon arrived to honor the white buffalo. Touched to see their emotional reactions at being so close to their spiritual animal, he reported, "Blizzard always responds with interest and gentleness, taking bunches of grass from their hands with his long and soft tongue."

Custer, a seven-year-old white buffalo bull, came in a cattle trailer in June 2014 to the Briarwood Safari Ranch, owned by Ron and Deborah Nease, in Bybee, Tennessee. For years the Neases had looked for a white buffalo to add to their exotic collection of seventy species and 300 to 400 total animals.

"They're just a gorgeous animal," said Ron Nease. They found Custer on a North Dakota ranch whose owners prefer not to be named, he says.

"He was real wild when we got him," Nease said. Released from the trailer, Custer "took off like a streak" up a hill. At first he stood apart, but now he waits for the other buffalo and ambles up to a Briarwood wagon for food treats. Visitors drive their cars through or take a two-mile guided trip in open-sided wagons pulled by tractors to view Custer and other animals.

In Alaska a free-roaming herd was started with twenty buffalo shipped to Delta Junction in 1928 from Big Medicine's own herd at the National Bison Range. This was before Big Medicine was born, but some buffalo apparently carried the genetics for albinism that he did when born five years later.

The first Alaskan white calf was born in 1939 and another the next year. Seen together several times, both then disappeared. In 1949 another was killed by a truck on the road.

Twelve white buffalo calves were sighted in the next fifty years, some only briefly, some only by airplane, says David Dary. One had a brown top-knot on his head, as did Big Medicine. Living in wild herds in mountains, the white calves were difficult to keep track of. Reportedly, none survived to the age of three.

Alaskan wildlife officials say no white buffalo has been sighted since 1973 among the 500 plains buffalo living in the 90,000-acre Delta Bison Sanctuary. However, the genetics that can result in white hair still exist in the Delta bison herd.

"If both parents had the recessive gene there would be a twenty-five percent chance that their offspring would be white," says Bob Schmidt, of Alaska Fish and Game.

He notes that buffalo can be white without being albino, "There is a difference between an animal having white or light hair and albinism." There are many types of albinism, all of which involve lack of the pigment in varying degrees that gives color to the skin, hair and eyes. Unfortunately, albinism may be associated with eye problems and more susceptibility to sunburn and skin cancers.

Albinism is the complete absence of tissue pigment. Albino can just happen—it doesn't have to be genetic, says Schmidt. Buffalo with light or white hair have some pigment and some have been known to change color over time. He says "As a general rule, animals with light hair have low survival rates. Albino animals likely have an even higher mortality rate than white animals,"

Lott agrees, "White buffalo . . . don't seem to do well. Far from going forth and multiplying, they dwindle and disappear." He says white can be a good winter color for animals such as some rabbits that turn white in winter to blend with snowy background, thus making them safer from wolf attack. "But probably not for buffalo calves. . . .the answer probably lies in winter. A dark coat [which absorbs sunshine and heat] may be a lifesaver in winter. Bison seldom if ever die of heat, but they often die of cold… Bison evolved in really terrible winters; and even now, especially severe winters kill many of the old and the young."

White bison are considered sacred by many Native Americans. Historically many Indian tribes consider the white buffalo and a white buffalo robe to have special powers.

Whenever spotted in a wild herd, a white buffalo was the one most likely to be killed. It was said they were so highly desired that few lived more than a few years.

"Albino buffaloes were always so highly prized that not a single one, so far as I can learn, ever had the good fortune to attain adult size, their appearance being so striking, in contrast with the other members of the herd, as to draw upon them an unusual number of enemies, and cause their speedy destruction," William Hornaday reported from his investigations in 1887.

"From all accounts it appears that not over ten or eleven white buffaloes, or white buffalo skins, were ever seen by white men. Pied individuals [with various spotted patterns] were occasionally obtained, but they too were and are rare."

There may be a possible genetic connection between some of these known white buffalo, since the ranch where White Cloud was born has purchased buffalo from the home of Big Medicine, according to their local veterinarian Dr. Ken Throlson.

Steven Rinella cautions tourists that some so-called "sacred white buffalo . . . a fixture of Western tourist traps, may be the result of crossbreeding between buffalo and white breeds of cattle."

Wherever white buffalo appear, Native people come to welcome them. Elders ensure the proper ceremonials are followed in showing respect to this highly spiritual animal.

Ceremonies and blessings often involve a smoky smudge of lighted sweet grass and singing prayers to the beat of a drum. Visitors leave gifts of tobacco ties, colored scarves and dream-catchers. They regard a little white calf as good news, a sign of peace and harmony—and good times to come. They affirm the white buffalo symbolizes spiritual renewal and the hope of bringing people of all backgrounds closer together. Some also see the white buffalo as a manifestation of the White Buffalo Calf Maiden, long revered as a prophet.

The welcoming ceremonies were experiences he will never forget, says Dr. Wrigley. "I felt like I was stepping back into an ancient time to observe the most-sacred and private of ceremonies of a people little known to my culture."

He says this has been, "A wonderful experience interacting with numerous individuals from First Nations and Métis communities, and they have taught me so much about their traditional relationships with Nature and the spiritual world."

The most famous white buffalo, Big Medicine, was born in 1933 on the National Bison Range in Montana, with a brown top-knot between his horns. He lived to age 26. MHS.

White Cloud, Dakota Miracle and Dakota Legend, grandson of White Cloud. Summer months were very hard on White Cloud. As an albino, she could not regulate her body temperature as well in the heat. ND Tourism.

At Elk Island in Canada buffalo calves are lovingly referred to as "Little Reds" because of their reddish-orange color. NPS.

herds. Within ten years they had outgrown their Alberta ranges at Elk Island and Wainwright, and 6,673 head were transferred to the new Wood Buffalo National Park.

These came from Samuel Walking Coyote's Montana herd, to which had been added in 1893 twenty-six buffalo from the grand mix that was Buffalo Jones' herd—from Saskatchewan, Montana, Texas, Kansas and likely Alberta and Nebraska.

Valerius Geist, Canadian zoologist and University of Calgary professor, asserts that all plains buffalo other than the Yellowstone herd originated from eighty-eight bison, mainly calves captured between 1873 and 1889. All buffalo herds were quite thoroughly mixed by the turn of the century, except for Pete Dupree's South Dakota buffalo. When Pete died in 1898, his buffalo still ran half-wild on the Great Sioux Reservation.

For over 100 years Parks Canada has maintained herds at Elk Island National Park—plains bison beginning in 1907 and wood bison in 1967. A recent census counted 383 plains buffalo and 333 wood buffalo there. Each animal is disease-tested, vaccinated if needed, tagged and processed in alternate years, the plains buffalo one year in the corrals and chutes north of Hwy 16; the next year wood bison south of Hwy 16. State of the art handling facilities were planned with the help of Dr. Temple Grandin, Colorado State University expert on animal behavior, using her principles of low stress buffalo handling. Because of its long history of health records and quarantine policies, Elk Island has become a font for buffalo conservation programs around the world.

What's new?

What's new in Canada is the launching with much fanfare of sixteen young buffalo from Elk Creek Park into the backcountry of rugged Banff National Park where they'll live as a free-ranging wild herd. Children and adults are urged to follow this venture online and share interesting news from rangers as this progresses *(www.pc.gc.ca/en/pn-np/ab/banff/info/gestion-management/bison/blog).*

The plan is to hold the new herd on "summer vacation" in

Herds in Public Places 231

The wood bison handling facility at Elk Island features round corrals into which the buffalo are sorted. Then they move along the alleyway, around the swing gate tub, through single-animal chutes to the squeeze room in the very center where each is processed. Parks Canada.

a mountain enclosure at Banff for two calving seasons, while allowing them to return to winter in a more-protected Elk Island environment.

"In all the advice we've received from bison ranchers … and reintroduction experts, the single most important thing you can do to bond those animals to their new home is to have them calve successfully," says Karsten Heuer, spokesperson for Parks Canada.

Thus, ten healthy bison calves were born in Banff's remote backcountry between April 22 and the end of May 2017, bringing the herd number to twenty-six. These new arrivals represent the future of bison in the Banff park.

"In July, we moved them from their six-hectare winter pasture into a twelve-hectare summer pasture that includes tasty mountain grass (instead of dry hay), a clear river to drink from (instead of a trough), and hills to climb and explore.

It's a pretty big change for these animals. There are no steep hills or moving water in Elk Island National Park where they came from or in the winter pasture where

A wood buffalo rises from his dust bath roll and rubbing down in Wood Buffalo National Park. Parks Canada.

they've lived for the past five months. We got to see the herd cross a river for the first time in their lives!"

Heuer encourages young people to follow the herd from home and share photos on facebook, twitter and blogs.

A bright future

Public sanctuaries, Indian tribal lands and private ranches—both white and Indian—have all played an important part in restoring buffalo throughout North America. Today nearly 400,000 buffalo range across the face of North America, including some 228,973 in the United States and 162,591 head in Canada, as well as small herds in countries throughout the world. Not as many as the millions from their heyday—but still a substantial number. Nearly every year their population increases and we can feel quite confident they will not disappear again.

This is an incredible comeback for a species that hovered at the edge of extinction scarcely more than a century ago.

Americans love the buffalo. The vision of buffalo herds roaming the hills and valleys of the west stirs our souls. While buffalo won't take the place of cattle in feeding the world's hungry, they can enrich our lives on this earth in countless ways.

Granted, there are still problems. Opinions differ on what policies to pursue. Some yearn to keep buffalo wild and free of fences forever. Some would prefer them safe from disease and less dangerous. Others just want to enjoy them from a safe distance.

Bringing the buffalo back from the edge of extinction has not been easy. Buffalo are strong, hardy animals, well adapted to the grasses and climate of the plains. The industry has grown rapidly in recent years, although it has a history of fluctuating dramatically due to weather and market conditions.

Yet the vast free-range grasslands are now filled with cities, roads, farms and ranches. Roaming herds of buffalo tend to be destructive and dangerous, so every buffalo herd needs wise management. Extra numbers have to be culled. Herd sizes quickly become larger than the amount of land ranchers and policy makers have available to keep them healthy. Land, fencing and caring for the animals have costs.

Still, the future looks bright for the American buffalo.

Saving the buffalo is a noble venture. Amazingly, it was accomplished without plan or coordination. Those involved simply dug in and did what they could until the species seemed secure.

The buffalo is symbolic of our success in wildlife conservation. According to Valerius Geist, the Canadian expert, the buffalo shows that conservation does work. He concludes, "We have not done gloriously well conserving the bison, but the bison is still with us."

Yes. Fractious, feisty—and magnificent—the buffalo are still with us, as ever.

David A. Dary sums up the positives in *The Buffalo Book*, and offers his own parting shot. "The increasing buffalo population, the growing market for buffalo meat and related products and breeding stock, and the continued efforts of governments and private citizens to preserve the buffalo as part of our heritage are signs that suggest the buffalo's future is bright.

"But the ultimate decision as to the fate of the buffalo rests with the creature who nearly exterminated him and then paradoxically saved him—man."

At Elk Island a long health history is maintained for the separate herds of plains and wood buffalo. They are evaluated biennially, on alternate years. A dependable source for international sales. Parks Canada.

BUFFALO TIMELINE

43,000 to 9,000 years ago. Several large species of bison arrived in North America from Asia, crossing on the Bering Land Bridge in Alaska when seas were low. All but one species vanished around 9,000 years ago. Recent evidence suggests there may have been an earlier wave of bison that came 195,000 to 135,000 years ago.

Early 1800s . . An estimated 30 million buffalo ranged through North America, the majority in the great plains and central grasslands.

mid 1860s . . . Buffalo migrated west out of what is now North and South Dakota due to hunting pressure.

1865-1869 . . . Building the Union Pacific railroad increased hunting for 100 miles on either side of the tracks, splitting the buffalo into northern and southern herds.

by 1875 . . . . . The southern herd was annihilated by hide hunters.

1876 . . . . Lt. Col. George A. Custer and 225 men of 7th Cavalry were killed in the Battle of the Little Big Horn.

1880 . . . . Remnants of the northern herd migrated to Miles City, Montana. Half went north across the Yellowstone River and were soon killed. The other half, about 50,000, travelled east onto the Great Sioux Reservation.

1880-81 . . . . . Thomas Riggs, Congregational Missionary, joined a Cheyenne River hunting party in the Slim Buttes on their last winter hunt.

1881 or 1882 Pete Dupree came to the buffalo range on the South Grand River with a buckboard wagon, caught and raised 5 wild buffalo calves. Rescuers in four other areas of North America also saved and raised calves.

1882 . . . . In June, Indian Agent James McLaughlin came with a hunting party of 2,000 Sioux men, women and children from Ft. Yates. Near Hiddenwood Cliff they killed 5,000 buffalo in three days.

1883 . . . . In October 1883 the last 1,200 buffalo were killed by a hunting party of Sitting Bull and his band in the same general area.

1889 . . . . William Hornaday, sent by the Smithsonian to take a buffalo census, reported that only 1,091 buffalo remained alive.

1895 . . . . Ernest Thompson Seton surveyed buffalo numbers and reported the low point of 800 left alive.

from 1880 . . . During the homestead era, pioneers throughout the western plains gathered and sold buffalo bones. They also burned buffalo chips for fuel.

2016 . . . . Buffalo survey taken by the National Bison Association counted 391,564 buffalo in the United States and Canada, about 90 percent in privately owned herds.

SD Tourism.

Bibliography

Allard, LaDonna. *Personal communication.* June 2014, 2015, 2016.

Allen, William A. Adventures with Indians and Game or Twenty years in the Rocky Mountains, Chicago, 1903.

American Bison Society. *Annual Report,* 13 vols. New York, 1907-1931.

Animal Diversity Web. *American Bison.* Retrieved July 20, 2011.

Archambault, Dave, Ft. Yates, ND. *Personal communication,* 2014.

Audubon, John James, and the Rev. John Bachman. *The Quadrupeds of North America,* 2 vols. New York: V. G. Audubon; 1849, 1954.

Badhorse, Beverley. Cheyenne buffalo hat. *Personal Communication.*

Barsness, Larry. *Heads, Hides & Horns. The Complete Buffalo Book.* Fort Worth, 1985.

Beckwith, Martha W. Mythology of the Oglala Dakota. Journal of American Folk-Lore, 43:339-342, 1930.

Berg, Francie M. *Buffalo Trails in the Dakota Buttes: Self-Guided Tour.* Dakota Buttes Visitors Council: Hettinger, ND. 2017. *South Dakota: Land of Shining Gold.* Flying Diamond Books: Hettinger, ND. 1983. *North Dakota: Land of Changing Seasons.* Flying Diamond Books: Hettinger, ND. 1997, 1989. *The Last Great Buffalo Hunts: Traditional Hunts in 1880 to 1883 by Teton Lakota People.* ND: Dakota Buttes Visitors Council, Hettinger, ND. 1995.

Berg, Francie M. Brink, Anne Brink Krickel, Jeanie Brink Thiessen. *Montana Stirrups, Sage and Shenanigans: Western Ranch Life in a Forgotten Era.* Flying Diamond Books, Hettinger, ND. 2013.

Berger, Joel; Carol Cunningham. *Bison: Mating and conservation in small populations.* Columbia University Press. p. 162. June 1994.

BiblioBazaar, *Blackfeet Indian Stories,* 2007; ISBN 978-1-4346-0730-0; *The Cheyenne Indians, Vol. 2: War, Ceremonies, and Religion,* ISBN 978-0-8032-5772-6; Bison Books, 1972.

Billings Gazette, Brett French, See also National Park Service. Feb. 20, 2014. *Tribes return to hunt Yellowstone Park bison.* Jan 23, 2011. http://billingsgazette.com/news/state-and-regional/montana/yellowstone-plans-slaughter-of-to-bison/article_3842666e-ce32-5820-a49d-75ef0714fd07.html#ixzz2uZzkm5Em. Brett French. Feb 11, 2014. *Yellowstone treaty tribes get preference.* Jan. 23, 2011.

Bismarck Tribune, May 29, 1883. *Letter signed by 10 Mandan and Gros Ventre Chiefs,* Oct 6, 1882; May 29, 1883. *Yellowstone park contemplates killing 1,000 bison this winter.* Nov 19, 2015. *Donor aids effort to preserve white bison.* Dec 20, 2016. *Meyer ranch buffalo under quarantine in poison probe.* Jan 22, 2017. *Bison gores park visitor, campers come to rescue.* July 9, 2017.

Bison roundup to benefit tribes. Oct 17, 2017. *Park workers thin bison herd.* Oct 27, 2017. *Tribe, federal agencies work to expand buffalo herd.* Oct 29, 2017. *Selling Houck to Ted Turner.* 2017.

Boller, Henry A. *Among the Indians: Eight Years in the Far West, 1858-1866.* Philadelphia: TE Zell, 1868.

Bozeman Daily Chronicle, *Yellowstone planning for large bison slaughter.* Billings, MT (AP). Feb 11, 2014.

Branch, E. Douglas. *The Hunting of the Buffalo.* New York-London: D. Appleton and Co. 1929.

Brewerton, George D. *Overland with Kit Carson.* New York, 1930.

Brink, Jack W. *Imagining Head-Smashed-In: Aboriginal Buffalo Hunting on the Northern Plains.* Athabasca University Press, Edmonton AB Canada. 2008.

Brown, M.H. and W.R. Felton. *Before Barbed Wire: LA Huffman, Photographer on Horseback..* New York: Holt. 1956.

Brown, Barnum. *The Buffalo Drive.* Natural History, 32: 1932.

Brundige, *Pers Communication.* SD State Park, Custer. Sep 2014.

Buffalo Tracks. *Finally, Buffalo Return Home.* Injunction to stop move to Ft Belknap and Ft Peck lost, p22. Winter 2014.

Burdick, Usher L. *Tales from Buffalo Land: The Story of Fort Buford.* Cheltenham, Maryland, 1940.

Burlingame, Merrill G.: *The Buffalo in Trade and Commerce.* ND Historical Quarterly, Vol III, No.4 p262-91. July 1929.

Calvin Dupree. *The First Dupree into SD.* (Unpublished; Dupree Family File.) SD State Archives, SD State Archives Pierre, 61.

Camp Crook Centennial, 1884.

Carbyn LN, Trottier T. *Descriptions of Wolf Attacks on Bison Calves in Wood Buffalo National Park.* Arctic 41 (4): 297–302. doi:10.14430/arctic1736. 1988.

Carter, Dave. *Personal communication.* National Bison Assoc. Also NBA Personal communication; USDA statistics. Oct. 25, 2017.

Cartwright, David Wl, and Bailey, Mary F. *Natural History of Western Wild Animals and Guide for Hunters, Trappers and Sportsmen.* Toledo, 1875.

Catlin, George. *North American Indians.* Edited by P. Batthiessen. New York: Penguin. 1989. *Letters and notes on North American Indians.* Tosswill and Myers, London. New York: Putnam & Wiley, 1841.

Chittenden, Hiram M. *The History of the American Fur Trade of the Far West,* 3 vols. New York, 1902.

Cody, William F. *Life and Adventures of Buffalo Bill.* Chicago, 1917.

Cook, James H. *Fifty Years on the Old Frontier as Cowboy, Hunter, Guide, Scout and Ranchman.* New Haven, 1923.

Cook, John R. *The Border and the Buffalo.* Topeka, 1907.

Colome, Lisa. *Interview and Pers communication.* Technical Service Provider for the Intertribal Buffalo Council in Rapid City, SD. Jul 2014.

Cornelius, Patricia (Pat) A. *Pers. Correspondence.* Manager; Oneida Nation Farms and Agricultural Center. 920-833-7952, farm@oneidanation.org

Cote, Steve. *Stockmanship: a powerful tool for grazing lands management.* Butte Soil and Water Conservation Dist, Arco, ID, USDA Natural Resources Conservation Service, Boise, ID. 2004.

Custer, Gen. George Armstrong. *My Life on the Plains.* 1876. Reprint, University of Nebraska Press 1972.

Darkwell. www. darkwell.com/lor297.htm; http://www.ilhawaii.net/~stony/lore122.html

Dary, David A. *The Buffalo Book: The Full Saga of the American Animal.* 3, 4-19, 127-9, 133. Bull fight, 159. Chicago:Swallow Press. 1974. Avon Books, Hearst, 1975.

Davies, Henry E. Ten Days on the Plains. New York, 1871

Davis, Leslie B, John W. Fisher. *Pisskan: Interpreting First Peoples Bison Kills at Heritage Parks.* U of Utah Press, Salt Lake City: 2016.

Deland, Charles E. *Basil Clement (Claymore): The Mountain Trappers,* SD Historical Collections, 1940, Pierre.)20; 391, 393.

Densmore, Frances. *Teton Sioux Music; Song To Secure Buffalo in Time of Famine.* https://www.questia.com/read/77737640/teton-sioux-music In the Densmore book the Sioux words are also given as well as the musical score. https://www.questia.com/read/77737640/teton-sioux-music No. 44. *A Buffalo Said to Me.* Sung by Braye Buffalo. Smithsonian Institution, Bureau of American Ethnology, Bulletin 61, Government Printing Office, Washington DC 1918. Reprint NY: Da Capo Press. 1972.

Dickinson Press. Dickinson, ND. 701-225-8111, www.thedickinsonpress.com

Dobie, J. Frank. *Life and Literature of the Southwest.* Dallas, 1958.

Dodge, R.I. *The Plains of the Great West and Their Inhabitants.* [1877] Reprint. New York: Archer House. 1959.

Duncan, Bob. *Buffalo Country. New York, 1959.*

Dupree, Calvin. *The Call of the Prairie.* Eagle Butte News, January 29, 1981.

Duvall, Mary. *Buffalo beliefs and behaviors.* Buffalo! National Buffalo Association. 1987.

Elk Island Park buffalo. http://pc.gc.ca/en/pn-np/ab/elkisland/activ/activ19

Ellis, Richard, 1989:26, 28. Park Manager at Madison Jump Park, Bozeman, MT. from intro of Pisskan, pg 65.

Ellsworth, Lincoln. *The Last Wild Buffalo Hunt.* New York, 1916.

Ewers, John C. *The Blackfeet: Raiders on the Northwestern Plains.* Norman: U of Oklahoma Press, 1958.

Faith, Mike. *Personal communication,* 2015, 2016, 2017.

Fargo Forum. *Bison pushed as country's national mammal.* Josh Francis. Sep 15, 2015.

www.firstpeople.us/FP-Html-Legends/OriginoftheBuffalo-Cheyenne.html; Legends/ThePassingoftheBuffalo-Kiowa.html

Foster, J.E., D. Harrison and I.S. MacLaren, eds. *Buffalo.* Edmonton University of Alberta Pres. 1992.

Frison, George C. *Paleoindian Large Mammal Hunters on the Plains of North America.* Proceedings of Natl Academy of Sci of the U.S. 95: 14576-83. 1998. Frison, George C. *Prehistoric Hunter-Gatherers of the High Plains and Rockies, third edition.* See Kornfeld.

Froese, Duane, Mathias Stiller, Peter D. Heintzman, Alberto V. Reyes, et al. *Fossil and genomic evidence constrains the timing of bison arrival in North America.* Proceedings of the National Academy of Sciences of the USA. 114(13): 3457-3462, 2017. http://www.pnas.org/content/114/13/3457

Gard, Wayne. *The Great Buffalo Hunt.* New York: Alfred A. Knopf. Lincoln: U of Nebraska Press. 1959.

Garcia, Louis. Personal Communication and *The History and Culture of the Spirit Lake Dakota.* Tokio, ND. 2014.

Geist, Valerius. *Buffalo Nation: History and Legend of the North American Bison.* Voyageur Press; Stillwater, NM. 1996.

Gilbert, Col C.C. At Ft. Yates with the 17th Infantry, correspondence Indian Agent Joseph A. Stephan, Dickinson, 1881.

Gilfillan, Archer B. South Dakota Highway Magazine. Black Hills Chief, 1939-1940. This is the bluff that Gilfillan, the sheepherder philosopher, author of the classic book *Sheep*, described in 1939. For the SD Highway Magazine, as published in the Black Hills Chief, 1939-1940.

Goble, Paul. *Buffalo Woman.* Bradbury Press 1984.

Great Falls Tribune. Rion Sanders. *Thirty-four genetically pure bison released onto a 1,000-acre pasture on the Fort Belknap Reservation on Thursday.* http://indiancountrytodaymedianetwork.com/2013/08/23/bison-return-fort-belknap-after-century-151007. Aug 22, 2013.

Grinnell, George Bird. *Last Stand: the Battle to Save the Buffalo, and the Birth of the New West,* by Michael Punke. *The Cheyenne Indians: Their History and Ways of Life*, Vol 1 and Vol 2, Yale U Press 1923; Reprint 1972, Bison Book, U of Nebr Press, Lincoln. *The Fighting Cheyennes*, Charles Scribner's Sons, 1915; Reprint Norman: U Oklahoma Press, 1956, 1958.

The *Last of the Buffalo.* Scribner's Magazine, Vol XII, No 3. p 267-86. July-Dec. Charles Scribner's Sons New York, 1892. NY: Reprint American Environmental Studies, Arno Press, 1970. *When Buffalo Ran. The Last of the Buffalo* (American Environmental Studies), Ayer Co Pub, 1970. Yale U Press, 1920; Norman: Univ of Oklahoma Press, 1966; 2008.

Haley, James L. *The Buffalo War*. NY: Doubleday, 1976.

Hanson, Harold. Personal communication. Reeder, ND.

Harper's Weekly, *The Buffalo Hunt.* Vol XI, No 549. p426, 1867.

Harris, Adam Duncan. *George Catlin's American Buffalo.* Smithsonian American Art Museum, Washington, DC. 2013.

Head-Smashed-in Buffalo Jump. *Personal visit,* June 15-23, 2016.

Hoffbeck, Steven R. *Personal Communication.* Minot State U, ND. 2014.

Hornaday, William Temple. *The Extermination of the American Bison: With a sketch of its discovery and life history.* Report of the National Museum, 1887. Washington: Gov Printing Office: 1889. Reprinted from Annual Report of the Board of Regents of the Smithsonian Institution for the Year 1887, Part 2, pp. 369-548. Washington, DC: Government Printing Office, 1889. *Our Vanishing Wildlife: Its Extermination and Preservation.* NY Zoological Society 1913. Reprint Arno and NY Times, 1970.

Hunter, John D. Manners and Customs of Indian Tribes. Philadelphia, 1823.

Inman, Colonel Henry. *Buffalo Jones' Forty Years of Adventure,* compiled by Colonel Henry Inman, 1899. Compiled from CJ Jones' journals. 1899, publishers Crane & Co., Topeka, Kansas. Digitized by the Internet Archive in 2007. http://www.archive.org/details/buffalojonesfort00jonerich

Interagency Bison Management Plan for Yellowstone Park buffalo website. http://www.ibmp.info/

Indian Country Today, Media Network.com. *Genetically Pure Bison Returned to Fort Belknap After a Century Away.* indiancountrytodaymedianetwork.com/2013/08/23/bison-return-fort-belknap-after-century-151007. Aug 23, 2013. *Bison Return to Fort Peck: A Special Day, 200 Years.* Jack McNeel, http://www.lakotacountrytimes.com Mar 22, 2012.

InterTribal Buffalo Council. *Buffalo Tracks.* Vols Spring, Summer, Fall, Winter. itbcbuffalo.com

Johnsgard, Paul A. *Prairie Dog Empire: Saga of the Shortgrass Prairie.* Lincoln: University of Nebraska Press. 2005.

Kane, Paul. *Wandering of an Artist among the Indians of North America.* London: 1859.

Keating, William. *Describing a group of buffalo hunters encountered.* 1824.

Kern, Karen. *Personal Communication* 4-27-2016.

Kidder, John. *Montana Miracle: It saved the Buffalo.* Montana Magazine of Western History; Helena. Spring 1965.

Knoxville News Sentinel. *Rare white buffalo Custer takes stand at East Tennessee ranch.* Amy McRary, Jul 11, 2014.

Koehler, Justin. *Documentary: Buffalo King: The Man Who Saved the Buffalo.* Video. Editor, Aaron Pendergast. Nowlin Town Productions, 2013; Justin Koehler. South Dakota Public Broadcasting Documentary, 2013.

Kornfeld, Marcel, George C Frison; Mary Lou Larson. *Prehistoric Hunter-Gatherers of the High Plains and Rockies, third edition.* 1991 by Academic Press. Left Coast Press, Walnut Creek, CA. 2010.

Koucky, MD, Rudolph W. *The Buffalo Disaster of 1882.* North Dakota History, J of the Northern Plains, Vol 50, Winter 1983.

Krause, Herbert, and Gary Olson. *Custer's Prelude to Glory,* 1974. Brevet Press.

Kroeber, Alfred L. *Cheyenne Tales.* Journal of American Folk-Lore, 13 (25). 1900.

LaFlesche, Francis. *The Omaha Buffalo Medicine-Men.* Journal of American Folk-Lore, 3:1890.

Laidlaw, G.E. *Ojibwe Myths and Tales,* Wisconsin Archeologist 1[1]:28-38. Why the Buffalo has a Hump. http://www.mpm.edu/wirp/ICW-141.html#buffalo 1922.

Lame Deer, John (Fire) and Richard Erdoes. *Lame Deer Seeker of Visions.* New York: Simon and Schuster, 1972.

Larpenteur, Charles. *Forty Years a Fur Trader on the Upper Missouri: The Personal Narrative of Charles Larpenteur. 1833-1872.* A Bison Book, University of Nebraska Press: Lincoln, 1989.

Larson, Floyd. *The Role of the Bison in Maintaining the Short Grass Plains.* Ecology, 21 (2). 1940

Lee, Wayne C. *Scotty Philip: The Man Who Saved the Buffalo.* 157, 225, 233, 276-285. Caldwell, Idaho, Caxton 1975.

Lewis and Clark. *Original Journals of the Lewis and Clark Expedition, 1804-1806.* Vol 2 (of 7). 1904. Madison, Wisc. New York: Arno Press, New York Times, 1969.

Lott, Dale F. *American Bison: A Natural History.* Berkeley: U of California Press. 2002.

Lowie, Robert H. *Indians of the Plains.* McGraw-Hill, 1954. Reprinted American Museum of Natural History; American Museum Science Books, 1963. *The Crow Indians.* 1935. Reprinted NY: Holt, Rinehart and Winston, 1956. *Dance Associations of the Eastern Dakota*, American Museum Natural History, NY. 1913.

Magnan, Robert H. Fort Peck Sioux and Assiniboine Reservation. *Interview and Personal Communication* Sep 2015; Nov 2017.

Manske, Llewellyn L. *History and Land Use Practices in Western North Dakota*, Paper presented at the Leafy Spurge Strategic Planning Workshop, NDSU Dickinson Research Extension Center, Dickinson, ND. March 1994. *Prehistorical Conditions of Rangelands in the Northern Plains.* Range Management Report, March 2008. Personal communication July 15, 2015.

Marchello, Marty J. United States Department of Agriculture. *Nutrient Content of Bison Meat from Grass- and Grain-Finished Bulls. Nutrition Comparisons Chart: Cooked Meat.* Animal and Range Sciences Department, North Dakota State University, Fargo. USDA. Research by Dr. Marty Marchello at NDSU in 1996, updated in 2013.

Martin, Cy. *The Saga of the Buffalo.* New York, 1973.

Matheson, Jim. Asst Director. *Personal Communication.* Natl Bison Assoc, Colo, NBA. 2014, 2016.

Mayer, Frank H and Charles B Roth. *The Buffalo Harvest.* Denver: Sage Books; 1958.

McCracken, Harold. *The Charles M. Russell Book: The Life and Work of the Cowboy Artist.* Doubleday: Garden City, NY. 1957.

McFarland, Steve. *Personal Communication.* Jan 2015. 2016.

McFarland, Verna. *Personal Communication.* 2015.

McHugh, Tom. *The Time of the Buffalo.* New York: Alfred A. Knopf, 1972.

McLaughlin, James. *My Friend the Indian: The Great Buffalo Hunt at Standing Rock,* 1910, 1926. Houghton Mifflin Co., Boston and New York. Bison Book, University of Nebraska Press, Reprint 1989. *His Letters: Correspondence with Washington.* Federal Indian Service in Washington, D.C, with other Indian Agents, and other individuals. Collection of his papers: Dickinson State University, Dickinson ND. 1881-1890.

McLuhan, T.C. *Touch the Earth: A Self-Portrait of Indian Existence.* Chief Plenty Coups. Outerbridge & Lazard, 1971. Pocket Edition NY: Simon & Schuster, 1972.

Meagher, Mary. *Mammalian Species: Bison bison.* The American Society of Mammalogists. 266: 1–8; 16 June 1986. *Snow as a Factor Influencing Bison Distribution and Numbers in Pelican Valley, Yellowstone National Park.* Yellowstone National Park Report 9, 1971.

Medicine, Beatrice. *Learning to be an Anthropologist & Remaining 'Native.'* U of Illlinois Press: Chicago. 2001.

Medicine Rocks. *Personal visit.* Access information available from ND State Historical society.

Merritt, J. I. *The Last Buffalo Hunt & Other Stories.* South River Press, Pennington, NJ, 2012.

Miller, Emilie. *Personal communication.* SD State Parks. Aug. 14, 2014.

Minnesota Buffalo Assoc. *The Bison Advantage.* USDA RMA. mnbison.org

Missoulian, *Beyond black eye, bison hunt near Yellowstone benefits CSKT, other tribes.* Feb 21, 2014. *Beyond black eye, bison hunt near Yellowstone benefits CS KT, other tribes. CSKT truck 17 Yellowstone Park bison to Ronan for slaughter.* Tom McDonald: Nez Perce, Shoshone-Bannock and Umatilla. Feb 21, 2014. *Montana officials approve expanded bison hunt.* AP. Missoula MT; Feb14, 2014.

Badlands Reflections Photography

Moore, Ely. *A Buffalo Hunt with the Miamis* in 1854. Transactions of the Kansas State Historical Society, 10. 1908.

Montana Standard, Butte. *Bison transferred from Yellowstone Park to Fort Belknap Reservation.* August 24, 2013.

Montana The Magazine of Western History, Montana Historical Society, 225 N Roberts, Helena, MT. *Montana Miracle--It Saved the Buffalo,* Kidder, vol. 15, Spring 1965, pp. 52-67. *Blizzards and Buffalo: Hunt in the Winter of 1880,* by Wm. Wilson, vol. 19, Winter 1969, pp. 36-49. *The American Bison: The Annihilation and Preservation,* James A. Dolph and C. Ivar Dolph, Summer 1975. *Ghastly Harvest: Montana's Buffalo Bone Trade,* Barnett, vol. 25, Summer 1975, pp. 2-13.

National Bison Association. *The Bison Producers' Handbook: A complete guide to Production and Marketing.* Also *Bison World,* Published quarterly, Westminister, CO. National Bison Assoc. www.bisoncentral.com

National Buffalo Association. *Buffalo Producer's Guide to Management & Marketing.* Website: bisoncentral.com. Ft. Pierre, SD: Rapid City, SD: National Bison Association. 1990. *Buffalo! Buffalo Beliefs and Behaviors.* 1973-1989 volumes.

National Geographic. *American Bison.* Archived from the original on December 6, 2010.

National Park Service. *www.nps.gov*

Neihardt, John G. *Black Elk Speaks.* Lincoln NE: U of Nebraska Press, 1961.

Nelson, Bruce. *Land of the Dacotahs.* MN: University of Minnesota Press, 1946.

North Dakota Dept. Public Instruction. *The History and Culture of the Standing Rock Oyate.* Office of Indian Education, ND DPI. 1995.

O'Brien, Dan. *Buffalo for the Broken Heart: Restoring Life to a Black Hills Ranch.* NY: Random House, 2001.

Paine, Bayard H. Pioneers, *Indians and Buffaloes.* Curtis, Nebraska, 1935.

Parker, Ronald D. *Wild Buffaloes were practically extinct in Eastern SD.* Sioux Falls Argus, Oct 16, 1949. See also Stevenson, *Buffalo East of the Missouri,* SD collections 1X, 390-391. Philip, George. *James (Scotty) Philip 1858-1910.* South Dakota Historical Review, Vol.1, No.1, p1-48, South Dakota Historical Society, Pierre, SD, Jan. 1935. *South Dakota Buffaloes versus Mexican Bulls.* South Dakota Historical Review, Vol.II, No.2, p51-72. South Dakota Historical Society, Pierre, SD, Jan. 1937. *South Dakota Buffaloes Versus Mexican Bulls,* p409-430. South Dakota Historical Collections, Vol XX; Also Dupree saving calves, same volume 291-294. 1940.

Picha, Paul, chief archaeologist for the State Historical Society of North Dakota, Bismarck. The Archaeology & Historic Preservation Division of ND State Hist Society; state archaeologist. Pers. Communication, 2016 and Correspondence August 2017.

Plenty Coup, Chief. From his autobiography, first published as *American: The Life Story of a Great Indian: Plenty-coups, Chief of the Crows,* Frank Linderman. New York: John Day, 1930.

www.pyramidmesa.com/kiowa1.htm; http://www.firstpeople.us/FP.html

Raadin, Paull. *The Winnebago Tribe.* Annual Report of the Bureau of American Ethnology, 37, 1915-1916.

Ramsey, Douglas. *One to Remember: The Relentless Blizzard of March 1966.*

Ricci, Susan. *Buffalo Museum storyboard exhibits; personal visit and communication* with Susan Ricci, July 31, 2014.

Riggs, Thomas L. *Sunset to Sunset: A Lifetime with my Brothers, the Dakotas. The Last Buffalo Hunt.* As told to his niece Margaret Kellogg Howard, forward by eldest son Theodore Foster Riggs, MD. South Dakota Dept of History: Report and Historical Collection. Vol. XXIX. Compiled SD State Historical Society, Pierre, SD, 1958.

Rinella, Steven. *American Buffalo: In search of a lost icon.* New York: Spiegel & Grau. 2008.

Roberts, Monty. *The Man Who Listens to Horses: The Story of a Real-Life Horse Whisperer.* New York: Random House, 1996.

Robinson, Elwyn B. *History of North Dakota.* University of Nebraska Press, 1966.

Roe, Frank G. *The Indian and the Horse.* Norman. 1955.

Roosevelt, Theodore. *Hunting trips of a ranchman: Sketches of Sport on the Northern Cattle Plains,* GP Putnam's Sons, 1885, pg 277-287. Reprinted by Literature House, Gregg Press, Upper Saddle River, NJ. 1970. *Ranch Life in the Far West.* Century Magazine, 1888.Olynpic Valley CA: Outbooks,1978. Reprint 1981. *The Works of T Roosevelt, Memorial Edition, Hunting trips of a ranchman.* Vol 1, p22-249, 1923.

Roosevelt, Theodore, and Grinnell, George Bird, editors. *American Big-Game Hunting,* The Book of the Boone and Crockett Club. Forest and Stream Publishing Co 1893, NY. DeVinne Press, NY.

Ross, Alexcander. *The Red River Settlement: Its Rise, Progress and Present State.* London: Smith, Elder and Co. 1856.

Rush, WM. *Wild Animals of the Rockies.* New York, 1942.

Russell, Don. *The Lives and Legends of Buffalo Bill.* Norman: University of Oklahoma Press. 1960.

Russell, Charles M. *Good Medicine: The Illustrated Letters of Charles M Russell.* 138-39. Doubleday. 1966.

Sandoz, Mari. *The Buffalo Hunters: The Story of the Hide Men.* NY: Hastings House. 1954. Reprint U of Nebraska Press, Lincoln. 1978.

Schult, Milo J., Arnold O. Haugen. *Where Buffalo Roam.* Badlands Natural History Assoc.: Interior, SD. 1979.

Schmidt, Bob. Alaska Fish and Game, *Personal communication* 2015, 2016.

Seton, Ernest Thompson. *Life-Histories of Northern Animals, Vol 1 Grass-eaters, 1909.* https://archive.org/details/lifehistoriesofn-01seto, Naturalist to the Government of Manitoba. http://www.unz.org/Pub/SetonErnest-1909, 247-303. Charles Schribner. 1909.

Seton, ET. *Lives of Game Animals, Vol 3—Part II. Hoofed Animals.* 4 vols. New York Zoological Society. Doubleday, Doran. 1910. *The American Buffalo or Bison.* Scribner's Magazine, Oct 1906.

Shirek, Ken. *Personal Communication*, 2015, 2018.

Smet, Father Pierre Jean de. Life, *Letters and Travels, 1801-1873.* 4 vols, New York: Francis Harper, 1905.

Smith, Victor Grant. *The Champion Buffalo Hunter: The frontier memoirs of Yellowstone Vic Smith.* Edited by Jeanette Hortick Prodgers. Billings, MT: Falcon Publishing Co, Inc., 1997.

Smith, Winston O. *The Sharps Rifle: Its History, Development and Operation.* New York, 1943.

South Dakota Historical Collections. Vol. 37. p134. *Maps: Reduction of the Great Sioux Reservation,. Reservoir and Reservation: The Oahe Dam and the Cheyenne River Sioux.* Michael Lee Lawson. Compiled SD State Historical Society and the Board of Cultural Preservation. SD State Historical Society, Pierre, SD, 1974.

South Dakota State Historical Society. *Buffalo in South Dakota, Unit 3, Lesson 3: Preservation of the Buffalo.* The Weekly South Dakotan: South Dakota Treasure Chest for 4th-Grade History, www.sd4history.com. Identifies the South Grand River as the place where Pete Dupree caught his five calves. Also the south fork of Grand River is identified as the place where Pete caught his five calves by Wayne C. Lee in Scotty Philip, the Man Who Saved the Buffalo, p157 and p225. Caxton 1975.

Sprague, Donovin. *Ziebach County 1910-2010; Images of America.* Arcadia Publishing; Chicago. 2010

Springer, Patrick. Rapid City Journal; Oct. 12, 2009. Fargo Forum; Aug 18, 2008.

Stegner, W. Beyond the Hundredth Meridian: John Wesley Powell and the Second Opening of the West. Boston: Houghton Mifflin. 1954.

Stevenson, *Buffalo East of the Missouri,* SD collections 1X.

Stewart, Ken. *Personal Communication.* Jan 14. South Dakota State Archives. 2014, 2017.

Stone, Jim. *Personal communication.* Rapid City, Executive Secretary, Intertribal Buffalo Council. 2015, 2016.

Throlson, Dr. Ken. *Personal communication.* Oct 2016, Sept 2017.

Thwaites, Reuben Gold. *Early Western Travels.* 32 vols. Cleveland: AH Clark: 1904-1907.

Toom, Dennis L. and Cynthia Kordecki. *Shadehill Reservoir Project Area Cultural Resources Inveentory, Perkins Country, South Dakota, 1992 Field Season.* University of North Dakota, Dept of Anthropology, Hariman Research Center, Grand Forks. Contribution No 290. Work performed for US Bureau of Reclamation, Dakotas Area Office, Bismarck. Dec. 1994.

Traditional stories. http://www.firstpeople.us/FP-Html-Legends/OriginoftheBuffalo-Cheyenne.html; Legends/ThePassingoftheBuffalo-Kiowa.html; http://darkwell.com/lor297.htm; http://www.ilhawaii.net/~stony/lore122.html; http://www.firstpeople.us/FP-Html-Legends/TheHunterAndTheBuffalo-Unknown.html; http://www.pyramidmesa.com/kiowa1.htm; http://www.firstpeople.us/FP-Html

Ulm Pishkun State Park. Personal visit. June 15-23, 2016.

US Department of Agriculture Veterinary Services, Animal and Plant Health Inspection Service, Veterinary Services. *National Brucellosis Surveillance Strategy.* For more information about brucellosis in Yellowstone bison, contact APHIS Legislative and Public Affairs (202-720-2511), Forest Service Public Affairs (202-205-1760), the National Park Service Office of Public Affairs (202-482-6843), Montana Department of Livestock, Helena (406-4444-9431).

Vasey, George. *The Natural History of Bulls, Bisons and Buffaloes*, London, 1851.

VegLahn, Nancy. *The Buffalo King: The Story of Scotty Philip.* Scribner, 1971.

Vestal, Stanley. *Queen of the Cowtowns: Dodge City.* New York, 1952.

Vore Buffalo Jump. *Personal visit and interviews.* 2016.

Waggoner, Josephine, Bettelyoun; Susan Bordeaux. *With My Own Eyes: A Lakota Woman tells her People's History.* Edited by Emily Levine, Lincoln: U of Nebraska Press, 1998.

Waggoner, Josephine. *Witness: A Hunkpapha Historian's Strong-Heart Song of the Lakotas.* Edited by Emily Levine, Lincoln: U of Nebraska Press, 2013.

Washington Star, Wash DC, Mar 10, 1888.

Webb, Walter P. *The Great Plains.* New York, Boston: Ginn and Co. 1931. *Buffalo Land.* Philadelphia: Hubbard Brothers, 1872.

Welch, A.B. Colonel. *Oral Histories of the Sioux, Mandan, Arikara and Hidatsa Tribes from 1920's.* Source: Online www.Welchdakotapapers.com. Oral history of the Dakota Tribes 1800s-1945: As Told to Colonel A.B. Welch the first White man adopted by the Sioux Nation, posted June 20, 2013, most posted 2012-13.

Willard, Jim, *James 'Scotty' Philip saved the buffalo.* Reporter Herald, Loveland, CO. www.rma.usda.gov July 31, 2014.

Wishek, Nina Farley. *Along the Trails of Yesterday.* Ashley Tribune; McIntosh County. 1941. Berg, Francie M. *North Dakota; Land of Changing Seasons*, Flying Diamond Books: Hettinger, ND. 1997, 1989.

Wood County Reporter, Grand Rapids, WI, Oct 16, 1884.

Yellowstone Journal, Miles City, MT, Jan 17, 1880.

Zontek, Ken. *Buffalo Nation: American Indian Efforts to Restore the Bison.* Lincoln: University of Nebraska Press, 37-38, 42-43, 47, 51, 55. 2007. *Hunt, Capture, Raise, Increase: the People Who Saved the Bison.* Digitalcommons.unl.edu/greatplainsquarterly/1009. Great Plains Quarterly. 1009. University of Nebraska-Lincoln: U of Idaho 1995.

Low-stress Buffalo Handling

Bud Williams Schools. www.stockmanship.com ; Excellent videos on Low-Stress Handling. No longer provide workshops.

Cote, Steve. *Stockmanship: A Powerful Tool for Grazing Lands*

Management. Natural Resources Conservation Service; Arco, Idaho. USDA. 2004.

Grandin, Temple. *The Calming of American Bison (Bison bison) During Routine Handling*. www.grandin.com, Temple Grandin, PhD, Department of Animal Sciences, Colorado State University, Ft Collins. With Jennifer L. Lanier; Dept of Animal Sciences Colorado State University Ft. Collins, CO 80523.

InterTribal Buffalo Council, Resources; for more information, 605-394-9730. Website. itbcbuffalo.com

Kossler, Mark. *Low Stress Bison Handling*. Bison Producers' Handbook, National Bison Association. 2010.

National Bison Association. Contact NBA for references and recommendations for members who are using Low Stress Livestock methods on their ranches. bisoncentral.com

Brucellosis
(continued from page 225)

Unfortunately, the buffalo in Yellowstone Park are highly infected with brucellosis. Research shows between 40 and 60 percent test positive for the disease, according to Montana Fish, Wildlife and Parks.

The wild elk that join them on winter bed grounds and then trek in and out of the park, are similarly infected. Brucellosis—also called bangs and, in humans, undulant fever—is an Old World disease causing abortions among cattle. It spreads through birth secretions during calving.

Except for states bordering Yellowstone, the United States has been brucellosis free for many years. The devastating disease was wiped out at great expense, hardship and heartache to livestock owners between 1940 and the 1980s, when federal and state agencies destroyed infected cattle and buffalo herds. Strict eradication efforts continued to reduce the disease from 124,00 infected herds in 1956, to 700 in 1992, to only six by 2000.

Current vaccines are not totally effective in cattle and less so in buffalo. Needed is a more effective vaccine, and perhaps a way of administering it remotely.

Ranchers bordering the Park watch uneasily. They pay a price for living there. Many have lived on their land four or five generations. They love their land. They cherish their livestock and their homes, communities and nearby ranching towns. They are good stewards of the land.

However, they fear brucellosis that can condemn their cattle herds or throw them into long-term quarantine. Repeatedly they test and vaccinate, but still find themselves at a disadvantage. It's a festering sore for them. They know how quickly their state's hard-fought brucellosis-free certification can be lost in condemning a single herd.

"A major issue, of course, is brucellosis," says Connie Townsend, former director of Montana Beef Council who ranches with her husband Herb, their adult children and grandchildren near White Sulfur Springs, Montana. "Boundaries are nonexistent for the buffalo supposedly confined in Yellowstone National Park. A concentrated management effort has been less than successful."

The Interagency Bison Management Plan brings together affected agencies to deal with the Yellowstone Park problems. Among other changes, the interagency group is trying to maintain the population near its new target of 3,000 buffalo. With the smaller number the herd is less likely to overgraze or leave the park.

Photo Credits

**LaDonna Brave Bull Allard,
Fort Yates, ND:**
(pg 78) Standing Rock tribal herd near Ft. Yates, ND; **(pg 119)** Buffalo robe painted with buffalo hunt images; **(pg 120)** Beaded moccasins, belts and hatbands; **(pg 126)** Painted buffalo skull with feathers; **(pg 200)** LaDonna Brave Bull Allard talks with visitors; **(pg 201)** Tribal herd grazes through prairie dog town.

Amon Carter Museum of American Art, (Emily Olson)
Forth Worth, TX:
Cover *The Buffalo Hunt No 39*, 1919, Charles M Russell, (1864-1926), Oil on canvas. 1961.146; **(8)** *Indians Sighting Buffalo*, 1896, Charles M Russell (1864-1926). Transparent and opaque watercolor over graphite on paper, 1961.166; **(10)** *The Buffalo Hunt No 39*, 1919, Charles M Russell, (1864-1926), Oil on canvas. 1961.146; **(19)** *The Medicine Man*, 1908, Charles M Russell (1864-1926). Oil on canvas. 1961.171; **(24)** *Indian Women Moving*, 1898, Charles M Russell (1864-1926). Oil on canvas. 1972.46.8; **(34)** Buffalo Hunt [No. 15], 1896, Charles M Russell (1864-1926). Transparent and opaque watercolor and graphite on paper. 1961.153; **(37)** *The Buffalo Hunt*, 1907, Charles M Russell (1864-1926). Trichromatic halftone. P1976.48.930; **(38)** *Curing Buffalo Hides Cheyenne Village*, 1880, Unknown. P1976-24-663 6x6-400; **(41)** *Lost in a Snowstorm – We Are Friends*, 1888, Charles M Russell (1864-1926). Oil on canvas. 1961.144; **(48)** *The Silk Robe*, 1890, Charles M Russell (1864-1926). Oil on canvas. 1961.135; **(58)** *Indian Scouting Party*, 1900. Charles M Russell (1864-1926). Transparent and opaque watercolor over graphite. 1961.169; **(122)** *Buffalo Dance*, ca. 1844, George Catlin. TToned lithograph with applied watercolor. 1972.46.8; **(127)** *The Picture Robe*, 1899, Charles M Russell (1864-1926). Ink and graphite on paper. 1961.143; **(143)** *Buffalo Hunt Surround*, between 1875 and 1878, after George Caitlin (1796-1872). Lithograph with applied watercolor. 2004.18.9; **(147)** *Watching for the Smoke Signal*, between 1875 and 1878, Charles M Russell (1864-1926). Transparent and opaque watercolor over graphite on paper. 1961.172; **(149)** *Buffalo Hunt, Under the White Wolf Skin*, 1907, after George Caitlin (1796-1872). Lithograph with applied watercolor. 2004.18.13; **(156)** *Buffalo Hunt [No. 15]*, 1896, Charles M Russell (1864-1926). Transparent and opaque watercolor and graphite on paper. 1961.153; **(158)** *Early Day White Buffalo Hunters*, ca 1922, Charles M Russell (1864-1926). Ink, opaque watercolor, and graphite on paper mounted on cardboard. 1961.323; **(165)** *Buffalo Hunt*, ca. 1838-1842, Alfred Jacob Miller (1810-1874). Oil on wood panel. 2003.10; **(Back Cover)** *The Silk Robe*, 1890, Charles M Russell (1864-1926). Oil on canvas. 1961.135.

Badlands Reflections Photography, (Rolan and Lisa Honeyman)
Dickinson, ND:
(Front End Sheet) *King of the Plateau*; **(2)** *A New Crop of Calves*, Custer State Park, SD; **(12)***Lone Calf*; **(13)** *Good Grazing*; **(20)** *Two Bulls;* **(26)** *Winter Endurance;* **(32)** *Easy Winter;* **(36)** *Summer Range;* **(44)** *River Crossing;* **(56)** *Thirst Quenching;* **(63)** *Splendid Bull;* **(64)** *On the Move;* **(76)** *At The Top Of The Hill;* **(78)** *Bull and Cow;* **(79)** *Yearling;* **(81)** *Brand New;* **(90)** *The Herd;* **(92)** *A Family;* **(94)** *Surveying the Competition;* **(96)** *Youthful Games;* **(98)** *Playful Calf Sequence 1;* **(99)** *Playful Calf Sequence 2;* **(100)** *Rest For Mom;* **(102)** *Courting;* **(104)** *Dust Bath;* **(105)** *Preening;* **(106)** *Winter Range;* **(108)** *Full Speed;* **(109)** *Fine Specimen;* **(112)** *In His Prime;* **(121)** *Hop Lope;* **(154)** *Ready for the Challenger;* **(166)** *Red Dogs of Spring;* **(169)** *Young Friends;* **(178)** *Watchful Mother;* **(181)** *Summer Sunbathing;* **(182)** *Watching You;* **(192)** *Walking the Ridge;* **(198)** *Prairie Pals;* **(238)** ; **(Back End Sheet)** *Valley Herd;* **(Back Cover)** *Regal Bull.*

SD Game, Fish & Parks.

Francie M. Berg
Hettinger, ND:
(132) First Peoples Buffalo Jump, west of Great Falls, Montana; **(133)** Drive lanes mapped on signage at Head-Smashed-In; **(134)** A rock cluster cairn marks location for drive line; **(137)** Drive line above First Peoples Buffalo Jump; **(139)** South Grand River, possible site of calf rescue; **(140)** Possible dry gulch trap above South Grand; **(164)** Buffalo bones broken by Native hunters to remove marrow; **(186)** Working buffalo in chutes at McFarlands' ranch; **(197)** McFarlands' corrals; **(202)** Standing Rock's north buffalo pasture; **(204)** Yellowstone Park herd at Fort Peck reservation; **(219)** Custer State Park Roundup; **(220)** Working corrals at Custer State Park; **(221)** Buffalo move toward the working corrals in Custer State Park Roundup.

Valerius Geist
Alberni, British Columbia, Canada:
Buffalo Nation: History and Legend of the North American Bison. Voyageur Press, Inc., St Paul, MN.
(72) Receipt from B. M. Hicks for buffalo bones, 1894; **(86)** Prehistoric bison, Valerius Geist; **(95)** *Buffalo and wolf pack*, George Caitlin; **(138)** *Hunting Bison in Snow*, George Caitlin.

Head-Smashed-In Buffalo Jump World Heritage Site:
(James Martin) **Alberta, Canada:**
(128) Head-Smashed-In buffalo jump colored drawing; **(130)** Buffalo jump sketch; **(134)** Making drive lines; **(141)** A narrow ravine trap.

William Temple Hornaday:
The Extermination of the American Bison: With a sketch of its discovery and life history. Report of the National Museum, 1887. Washington: Gov Printing Office: 1889.
(59) *The Still Hunt* sketch by JH Moser; **(80)** Development of The Horns; **(145)** The impound; **(173)** Hornaday's famous six-buffalo masterpiece in huge glass case set a new standard for Smithsonian Museum taxidermy in 1888.

Library of Congress, Washington, D.C.
(16) *Indians killing buffalos.* 3b23277u; **(67)** *The far west – shooting buffalo on the line of the Kansas Pacific Railroad.* Digital ID cph 3c33890.

Montana Historical Society: (Kendra Newhall)
(30) *Untitled (Indian on Horseback)*, ca. 1895, Charles M. Russell. Pen and ink.1980.60.01c; **(52)** *Indian Hunters' Return*, 1900, Charles M. Russell. Oil on canvas. X1954.02.01; **(117)** *Untitled (Indian Talking to Beaver and Coyote)*, Charles M. Russell. Print from "How the Buffalo Lost His Crown," by John H. Beacom and published by Forest and Stream publishing Co., 1894. Gift of Mark H. Brown. 1980 60 01b-; **(118)** *Inside the Lodge*, 1893, Charles M. Russell. Watercolor. Gift of Maude and Florence Fortune. X1954.01.02; **(153)** *The Scouting Party*, c. 1891, Charles M. Russell. Oil on canvas. 1981.64.01; **(155)** *Untitled (Mounted Warrior)*, 1898, Charles M. Russell. Watercolor. 2006.38.23; **(161)** *Canadian Cree Trapper*, 1905, Edgar S. Paxson. Watercolor. X1971.27.01; **(163)** *Red River half-breed camp and carts*, No date, photographer unidentified. 950-581; **(229)** *Big Medicine on the range at Moiese, Montana*, photographer unidentified. Pac 77-64 1.

National Park Service:
(22) Wind Cave Park; **(28)** Bison in snow, SGC, 1965; **(31)** Bison herd in snow on a dark winter day, Photographer unknown, 1972; **(35)** Bison drive in snow at Upper Nez Perce Creek, Mary Meagher, 1966; **(39)** Bison on ice after breaking through, Richard Lake, 1969; **(55)** Bison in Upper Geyser Basin, 1978, Frank Balthis; **(62)** Theodore Roosevelt as a Badlands hunter; **(66)** Bison cows & calves, Ed Austin/Herb Jones, 1978; **(70)** Photograph of bison hide coat, Buffalo Bill Historical Center, Cody, Wyoming; **(71)** Photograph of bison hides, JR Douglass, 1874; **(73)** Illustration of bison bone pickers, Martin S Garretson, 1913; **(74)** Skull pile at Michigan Carbon Works, 1880; **(74)** Photograph of bison bones, 1885, Buell; **(75)** Photo of pioneer woman with bison chips, Kansas State Historical Society; **(81)** Bison in snow at Oxbow Creek, Tom McHugh; **(82)** Bison & elk herds in winter in Lamar Valley, January 1996, Jim Peaco; **(83)** Bison with face covered with snow, R Robinson; **(84)** Bison at Gardner River & Lava Creek confluence, April 6, 2004, Jim Peaco; **(99)** Bison cows & calves, May 1991, Jim Peaco; **(101)** Bull bison fighting, Wind Cave National Park; **(103)** Bison at Fountain Flats, 1977, J Schmidt; **(107)** Bison & coyote; Ron Shade, 1979; **(125)** Bison skull, 1969, JR Douglass; **(168)** Bison herd, 1974, Harlan Kredit;

South Dakota Tourism.

(170) Bison in Hayden Valley, 1969, Mary Meagher; **(185)** Bison in meadow, 1970, John Good; **(190)** Stephens Creek bison pen, April 2004, Monty Simenson, Brian Helms, Ben Cunningham; Jim Peaco; **(191)** Bison at Fountain Paint Pots road, 1977, Frank Balthis; **(197)** Bison in pen at Stephens Creek, March 2003, Jim Peaco; **(207)** In honor of slain bison...Lakota Sioux spiritual leaders at Stephen's Creek bison capture facility, March 6, 1997, Jim Peaco; **(210)** Bison crossing Firehole River, 1971, Canter; **(213)** Bison in Upper Geyser Basin, 1977, J Schmidt; **(214)** Bison herd in Hayden Valley, 1977, J Schmidt; **(222)** Bison in snowstorm, 1977, J Schmidt; **(223)** Bison in winter at Old Faithful, 1970, Richard Lake; **(230)** Bison calf & cow - Little America Flats, May 2005, Jim Peaco.

North Dakota Historical Society: (John Hallberg)
(17) Hiddenwood Custer camp; **(160)** Red River cart.

North Dakota Tourism: (Cassie Theuer)
(116) White Cloud; **(226)** Dakota Miracle, son of White Cloud; **(229)** White Cloud, Dakota Miracle, son of White Cloud, and Dakota Legend, grandson of White Cloud.

Oneida Tribe, Oneida, Wisconsin:
(206) Viewing stand in the Oneida Tribe buffalo pasture; **(208)** Young buffalo calves playing; **(211)** Oneida youth watch tribal buffalo being worked.

Parks Canada: (Eric Magnan)
(87) Plains buffalo versus wood buffalo; **(196)** Working buffalo at Elk Island National Park facility; **(225)** Tourist viewing buffalo from the safety of vehicle; **(231)** Buffalo working facility at Elk Island National Park; **(231)** Wood buffalo at Elk Island National Park; **(233)** Plains Bison, Riding Mountain National Park, Eric Le Bel, photographer.

South Dakota Game, Fish & Parks: (Chris Hull)
(47) Some of South Dakota's wild horse herd race across the prairie in the Wild Horse Sanctuary at Hot Springs, SD; **(89)** Custer State Park buffalo herd in the Black Hills; **(104)** Lone buffalo face; **(115)** Custer State Park buffalo herd resting on hillside; **(150)** Some of the South Dakota's wild horse herd in the Wild Horse Sanctuary, Hot Springs, SD; **(242)** Buffalo in Custer State Park, Custer, SD; **(243)** Buffalo resting on a hill in Custer State Park.

South Dakota Tourism: (Chad Coppess)
(1) Buffalo bull in the fall colors in South Dakota's Custer State Park; **(4)** Lone buffalo bull on a ridge in South Dakota's Custer State Park; **(21)** Custer State Park buffalo herd graze and rest as they cross the landscape of the park; **(42)** A small herd of buffalo graze on fall grasses in South Dakota's Custer State Park; **(216)** Buffalo on the run during the Custer State Park annual roundup; **(218)** Cowboys and horses are part of the traditional Custer State Park annual roundup; **(234)** Buffalo on the run during the Custer State Park annual roundup; **(235)** Buffalo grazing on frosted grass on a cool, crisp morning in South Dakota's Custer State Park; **(243)** A small herd of buffalo graze on fall grasses in South Dakota's Custer State Park; **(244)** Calling all neighbors.

Jim Strand
Shadehill, SD:
(110) View scenic prairie; **(176)** Distant herd, bushes, draw.

Swallow Press, Chicago, IL:
The Buffalo Book: The Full Saga of the American Animal, David A Dary, Chicago. 1974, Avon Books, 1975.
(72) Buffalo skull sketch by OH Bacher; **(175)** Pablo roundup sketch by Charlie Russell; **(215)** Buffalo sketch by Charlie Russell; **(242)** Buffalo sniffing skull by Frederick Remington.

The Charles Russell Book: The Life and Work of the Cowboy Artist by Harold McCracken.
(14) *The Buffalo Hunt*; **(40)** *Tracks in the Snow*; **(46)** *Watchers of the Plains*; **(159)** *There's Only One Hold Shorter.*

Other:
45. Woolaroc Museum, *Visions of Yesteryear*, William R. Leigh, Bartlesville, OK. (Linda Stone)
51. Breakup of the Great Sioux Reservation. *The Indian frontier of the American West, 1846-1890*. Utley, Robert. University of New Mexico Press, Albuquerque, 1984.
60. After the Chase-North Montana-1882, LA Huffman.
61. CivilWarTalk.com, Image of Sitting Bull and Buffalo Bill was taken in Montreal, Canada in 1885.
68. Buffalo Hunt Decline, LA Hufmann.
114. Photo courtesy of Nicole Haase, New Leipzig, ND.
131. Chart courtesy of Intertribal Buffalo Council.
135. Shayne Tolman, *Imagining Head-Smashed-In: Aboriginal Buffalo Hunting on the Northern Plains* by Jack W. Brink. Athabasca Univ Press, Edmonton, AB Canada, 2008.
136. Photo of buffalo jump area taken from north side of Shadehill Reservoir at Ketterling's Point. Photo by Vince Gunn, Shadehill, SD.
173. Hornaday's mounted buffalo on display at Fort Benton, MT. Montana Agricultural Center and Museum, Fort Benton, MT.
188. Cover photo of buffalo jumping out of loading chute. Kim Sutton, photographer, Agar, SD. National Buffalo Association, *Buffalo!*, Volume 15, Number 6, November-December 1987
203. Thirty-four Yellowstone Park buffalo were coaxed off the trailer and went racing off onto the 1,000 acre pasture on the plains of the Fort Belknap Reservation in Montana in 2013 Photo by Rion Sanders. Reprinted with permission from the *Great Falls Tribune*.

Welcome to **Hettinger, ND**
Rural City of Progress and Innovation

An aerial view of Hettinger and Mirror Lake.

Nestled among the buttes, the city of Hettinger is the heart of a community that stretches for many miles in every direction to serve humanity in a multitude of ways. A small town in a rural area that can boast of one of the top 20 medical centers in the nation for rural healthcare, covering 20,000 square miles. Also located here is a North Dakota State University livestock research center nationally known for its sheep research, and a new veterinary clinic that has won national honors.

As a member of ND Governor Burgum's Main Street Initiative, Hettinger aims to build on three pillars of economic success: a skilled workforce; smart, efficient infrastructure; and healthy, vibrant communities. The community ascribes to the North Dakota values of respect for the past, gratitude for the present and inspiration for the future.

Hettinger is known for giving generously to a worthy cause, whether it's a family that lost everything in a home fire, or a piece of expensive new equipment for the medical clinic. The list is long of essential services provided by volunteers.

It's a caring town that doesn't neglect the finer points of planting trees and colorful hanging flower baskets on Main Street. There's a hundred-year history of providing a mostly-free three-day 4th of July celebration to ranching families who leave the hay fields to enjoy a parade, free barbeque, afternoon of visiting in Mirror Lake park, a talent show, free ice cream and, after dark, fireworks over the lake.

Special areas that make this a great city and community

- **West River Regional Medical Center.** Nationally recognized leader in rural health care . . . named one of TOP 20 Critical Access rural hospitals in nation . . . 8 clinics . . . 17 physicians and 8 visiting specialists . . . Western Horizons Living Centers . . . Ambulance covers 2,500 square miles through a vast network of volunteer first responders . . . Cardiac rehab . . . MRI technology . . . Diabetes education . . . West River Eye Clinic . . . Wellness & Fitness center . . . Residency program . . . Locally owned

- **West River Veterinary Clinic.** State-of-the-art clinic built in 2016 . . . Won national awards for design and innovation . . . Staffed by 5 veterinarians, 15 vet techs, technicians and assistants . . . Treatment radius 75 miles . . . Quality and compassionate service focuses on family and community

- **Hettinger Research Extension Center.** Began in 1909 with gift of 160 acres from interested citizens . . . Research on sheep, beef cattle, agronomy and wildlife

- **Agriculture.** Farm and Ranch based goods and services

- **Industries.** Killdeer Mountain Manufacturing produces electronic gear for aerospace . . . Honey companies help make North and South Dakota number one and two

- **County Seat.** Shared road maintenance and law enforcement between city and county . . . FSA, NRCS, VA . . . Social services and public health

- **Town Beautification.** Trees and hanging flower baskets on Main Street . . . Developed new Centennial Park with buffalo statue, picnic area shaded by large 100-year-old cottonwood tree . . . 5 city parks

- **Lifestyle.** Small town values . . . West River hospitality . . . Rural community . . . Population 1,300 . . . Safe, family centered lifestyle . . . Excellent school system . . . Low unemployment . . . Airport . . . AM and FM radio stations . . . Newspaper . . . Community-owned theatre, indoor pool, library, concert series

- **Outdoor activity.** Walking trail around Mirror Lake . . . 9-hole grass green golf course and Country Club . . . Upland and big game hunting . . . Hiking, camping, wildlife photography . . . State and forest service lands provide recreation . . . Large lakes through area, North Lemmon, Shadehill and Bowman Haley offer outstanding fishing, boating, water skiing

- **History.** Scene of last great buffalo hunts . . . Self-guided buffalo tour in area . . . Yellowstone Trail built by volunteers, began near here in 1912 with 3 of 13 original directors from Hettinger . . . first auto highway across upper tier of states . . . Hettinger began in 1907 when the Milwaukee railroad came . . . Buffalo history taught in area schools . . . Dakota Buttes Museum highlights pioneering, ranching, homesteading, town life . . . Historic tours

- **Churches.** Seven churches serve the community

- **Main Event.** July 4th 3-day celebration with mostly-free events . . . Draws crowds from all areas for parade, free noon meal . . . Rodeo . . . Street Fest . . . City-wide Rummage Sale . . . Chamber Pitchfork Fondue . . . Wakeup Santa Parade & Fireworks . . . Memorial Day . . . Adams County Fair . . . Weekly Burgers & Brats in summer

> *" Anybody looking for a place to live with affordable housing, four seasons, practically zero crime rate, non-congestion, wide-open spaces, clean air, abundant wildlife, quality health care and friendly and helpful people, I would definitely recommend relocating to Hettinger, North Dakota. "*
>
> —Dan Wilson
> moved from Fresno, Calif.

Living, working, playing, building and coming together for the good of the whole. Fresh air . . . sunshine . . . super sunsets . . . and a warm and safe, friendly welcome awaits you in Hettinger. Come and join us.

Acknowledgements

WE ARE GRATEFUL FOR THE HELP of the many persons who assisted in telling the remarkable buffalo story. Our deep appreciation goes to the Forest Service personnel at the Grand River National Grasslands, Director Alex Michalek, Paul Drayton, Mary Haase, in Lemmon, GIS Coordinator Phil Sjursen in Bismarck, and Otto Schwarz, Hettinger, for Grasslands guidance; Standing Rock Tourism Director LaDonna Brave Bull Allard and Mike Faith, Tribal Chairman and former Buffalo Herd Manager, Ft. Yates, ND; Intertribal Buffalo Council Executive Secretary Jim Stone, Technical Service Provider Lisa Calome, North Dakota Indian Affairs Executive Director Scott J. Davis, Ft. Peck Fish and Wildlife Director Robert Magnan, and Buffalo Museum Curator Susan Ricci; National Bison Association Director Dave Carter and Jim Matheson; North Dakota Tourism Director Sara Otte Coleman, Information Specialist Scooter Pursley, Global Marketing Manager Fred Walker, Program Specialist Tammy Backhaus, and South Dakota Tourism Director Jim Hagen; North Dakota Historical Society Chief Archeologist Paul Picha and Archives Reference Services Head Jim Davis; Dickinson State University library staff; NDSU Research Extension Center Director Kris Ringwall and Range Specialist Llewellyn Manske in Dickinson; Buffalo ranchers Steve and Roxann McFarland, Verna McFarland and Jim Strand, Hettinger, and Ken Shirek, Michigan, ND; Custer State Park Resource Manager Gary Brundige, Montana Beef Council Director Connie Townsend, Bob Schmidt, Alaska Fish and Game, Louie Garcia, Cankdeska Ckana College, Ft Totten, SD State Archivist Ken Stewart, Pierre, Buffalo Nation: History and Legend of the North American Bison author Valerius Geist, New Rockford veterinarian Ken Throlson, DVM, and to Duane Wamre, Donor and Caretaker of Hiddenwood Hunt Historic Site.

We are pleased that our area schools, Hettinger Principal Darin Seamands, and other educators and leaders throughout the buffalo trails area will be teaching local buffalo history, and we thank them for this. We also deeply appreciate the museums, institutions and individuals who have shared their photos and artwork—listed on page 243.

Finally a warm "Thank You" to our Dakota Buttes Visitors Council and Buffalo Trails Tour team, Cindy Ham, Steve and Jackie Hedstrom, Earleen Friez, Mark Baker, Carole Rosencrans, Ronda Fink, Connie Schwarz, Jim Goplin, Rochelle Shirek, Loren Luckow,. Thomas Jacobson, MD, Kortney Kindsfater, Ted Uecker, Rick Berg, Mike Berg and Vince Gunn, Shadehill; to Orby Reyzon Reyes for video development; Wendy Anderson Berg for Facebook and Social Media development; Linda Johnson, Sturgis, for arranging the Custer State Roundup visit; to Kendra Rosencrans, Kirkland, WA, for editorial help; and to Ronda Turbiville Fink for her dedication, talent and passion in designing and producing the two buffalo books. To my family for their continued help and support.

The only Place these Events all come Together

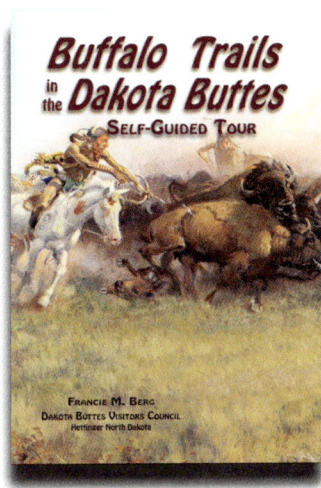

Learn the Rest of the Story

Buffalo Trails in the Dakota Buttes takes you to 10 buffalo-related sites within a relatively small area of rugged buttes and badlands. With a tour book in hand, complete with maps and narrative of what happened at each site, visitors can follow the yellow signs at their leisure. Included are two of the last great buffalo hunts and the valley of the last stand—the final harvest of 1,200 buffalo by Sitting Bull and his band in October 1883.

Then, just before the last wild herds disappeared forever, one Native American family came to the South Grand River to save buffalo calves. Pete Dupree and his brothers rescued 5 calves and became internationally famous. Also on the tour are a full-size mounted buffalo, an authentic buffalo jump, and perhaps a live buffalo herd. Plan a day or two and time for hiking and picnicking in forest service lands. For more information, see ndTourism.com/BuffaloTrails and hettingernd.com/buffalotrails

Print Book, softcover . . . $14.95
eBook. $9.99

Buffalo Heartbeats Across the Plains tells the incredible story of the last great buffalo hunts and the bottleneck of near extinction. It's a moving tale of tragedy, devastation and hard-fought recovery. The pages come alive with fascinating detail on the buffalo's origins and habits, stories of maternal dominance, the tenderness of 'noble fathers' saving newborn calves from wolves, and a herd bull's challenge to a feisty Mexican fighting bull.

Here are hunting tales of ancient foot surrounds, buffalo jumps, and the dangerous sport of running buffalo on horseback. It is truly an American story and an Indian story. With a wealth of history, stories and events, you'll learn even more about the majestic beast so closely entwined with the American experience, both Native and non-Native.

Along with *Buffalo Trails*, this companion book completes the package brought together by Hettinger's Dakota Buttes Visitors Council. Both books richly illustrated in full color.

Print Book, hardcover $34.95
eBook. $19.99

Print and e-Books are available from local businesses and Dakota Buttes Visitors Council at hettingernd.com/buffalotrails

About the Author

Francie M. Berg is a teacher, historian and author of seventeen books, with homestead and ranching roots in the Old West. Her earlier book *Buffalo Trails in the Dakota Buttes* provides a self-guided tour of ten historic and contemporary buffalo sites in western North and South Dakota. This new book *Buffalo Heartbeats Across the Plains* is written as a companion book and tells the rest of the buffalo story. Both books are published by the Hettinger Dakota Buttes Visitors Council, a volunteer group to which Francie has belonged since it began some forty years ago.

Born on the family homestead in the Missouri River Breaks, Francie grew up on a Montana ranch near Miles City and now lives in Hettinger, North Dakota, at the heart of the fascinating buffalo heritage of which she writes. She lives within a few miles of her grandparents' Shadehill, South Dakota homestead, established near the foot of an authentic buffalo jump prior to the creation of Shadehill Reservoir.

A graduate of Montana State University in Bozeman, Francie Berg is a licensed nutritionist and has a masters degree in family and anthropology from the University of Minnesota.

Her books on western history include *North Dakota Land of Changing Seasons, South Dakota Land of Shining Gold, Wyoming Land of Echoing Canyons, Ethnic Heritage in North Dakota, The Last Great Buffalo Hunts: Traditional Hunts in 1880-1883 by Teton Lakota* and *Montana Stirrups, Sage and Shenannigans*. See www.montanastirrupsandsage.com

Through her educational work with health, nutrition and wellness, Francie has presented seminars at national and international conferences, and been a guest on national television, including Oprah, Lezza and Inside Edition. She has four children and nine grandchildren.

INDEX

7th Cavalry, 17, 28, 235

A

Afraid of Hawk, Rocky, 209
Albinism, 226, 226
Allard, Charles, 174, 177, 185
Allard, LaDonna Brave Bull, 200-202, 212
American Bison Society, 180-181
Artwork, 125-126
Athabascan tribes, 209
Azure, Mark, 207

B

Badlands National Park, 198, 222
Banff National Park, 225, 231-232
Battle of the Little Bighorn, 43-44
Bears Arm, 157
Behavior, 92-111
   attacks on humans, 107-108
   dominance, 100-101
   jumping high, 83-83, 188
   protective nature, 82, 92-96
   social structure, 205
   wallowing, 104-106
Belcourt, Rev., 71-72
Bibliography, 236
Big Foot, Chief, 29
Big Medicine, 226-229
Bison bison athabascae, 86
Bison bison bison, 86
Bison latifrons, 85-86
Bison priscus, 86
Bison, see buffalo
Black Hills Agreement of 1876, 51
Blackfeet tribe, 170
Blizzard, 227
Boarding school, 44
Bones, 73-74, 135, 234

Box canyon traps, 140-143
Breaking up Great Sioux Reservation, 51, 54
Brink, Jack W., 132, 149
Bronx Zoo, 225
Brucellosis, 205-206, 225, 240
Brundige, Gary, 219-220
Buffalo care for each other, 202
Buffalo hunting
   accidents, 156
   ceremonial, 14-16
   current hunting, 213-215
   dogs in deep snow, 148
   illegal, 49
   impounding, 144-147
   jump, 128-130, 132-140, 188
   making a calf, 148
   methods after horses, 128, 150-165
   methods before horses, 128-149
   sand trap, 142
   scouts, 153
   surround, 143
   running the buffalo, 151-165
   traps, 140-143
   Yellowstone Park, 214-215
Buffalo hunts, 1880-1883, 6-7, 10-72, 234
Buffalo lore, 113-127
Buffalo ownership
   private, 186-197, 234
   public, 188, 216-233
   tribal, 198-215
Buffalo population, 88-91, 103, 168, 174, 188-189, 222, 224, 232, 234
Buffalo teach child care, 201
Bunn, RM, 68
Butchering, 212-213

C

Cairns, 133-134, 137
Callihoo, Victoria Belcourt, 161
Calves
   birth, 97-100
   playful, 98-100, 169
   rescuing, 169-171, 177
Canadian herds, 225, 230-232
Catlin, George, 102, 109, 122, 157, 166
Cave of origin, 114-115
Chalkyitsik tribe, 209
Cherokee tribe, 210
Cheyenne River Lakota, 13, 26-41, 212
Cheyenne River Reservation, 51
Chips, 74-75, 234
Cokantanka, 38-39
Collins, Martin and Leonida, 191
Colome, Lisa, 210-211
Columbus, Christopher, horses, 152
Confederated tribes, 214-215
Conrad, Alicia, 181
Cornelius, Pat, 208-209
Coronado, Francisco V. de, 96
Corral system, Elk Island, 190-191, 231
Corrals, Custer park, 221
Crazy Walking, Miles, 15, 25, 200
Crossbreeding, 86, 88, 178
Crow Creek Sioux, 211
Crow Tribe, 203
Custer State Park, 181, 198, 217-222
   roundup, 218-222
Custer, Lt. Col George A., 17, 28, 30, 180, 227, 234

D

Dakota Legend, 226
Dakota Miracle, 226
Dances with Wolves, 194
Dances, 122-123
Dary, David A, 169-170, 175, 177, 232-233
   buffalo population, 224
Delta Junction, 228
Densmore, Frances, 123-124
Description, 77-111
   agility, 83-84
   hair, 78-79
   hearing, 80
   horns, 79-80
   shedding, 104-107
   smell, sense of, 80
   stamina, 81-82, 85
   vision, 81
   weight, 79, 86-87
Disease theory, 68-69
Division of meat, 36
Dodge, Col., 110-110
Drive lines, 133-134, 137
Dry gulch trap, 142
DuBray, Fred, 210
Dupree family, 28, 185, 218
Dupree, Pete, 41, 171-172, 175-177, 179, 185, 230, 234
Dupris, Fred, 28, 29, 40, 171
Dupris, Mary Ann Good Elk Woman, 28, 29, 41, 171, 179

E

Eagle Man, 20, 22
Ecoffey, Dr. Trudy, 108
Elk Island National Park, 225, 231-233

F

Faith, Mike, 79, 103, 198, 200, 202, 207-208
First Nations, 210
First Peoples Buffalo Jump, 133, 135
Flandreau Santee Sioux, 211
Flathead tribe, 170
Flowers, Pat, 215
Fool Bear, 156-157
Fort Keogh, 172
Fort Peck, 213
Fox, Mike, 207
French Creek, 218
Frison, George C., 132-133
Froese, Duane, 85

G

Garcia, Louis, 144
Geist, Valerius, 85, 174, 230, 232
Genetic testing, 211, 224-225
George, Herb, 209
Glacier Park, 180
Goodnight, Charles, 171, 177-179, 181, 185, 225
Goodnight, Molly, 179
Grandin, Dr. Temple, 190, 196-197, 230
Grass, John, 148
Great Sioux Reservation, 13, 50-51, 175, 179, 230
   breakup of, 51, 54
Grey Bull, Iris, 198, 206
Grinnell, George Bird, 124, 144, 153, 156, 159, 180, 185

H

Handling facility, 190-191, 231
Head-Smashed-In Buffalo Jump, 132-135
Heider, Dave and Valerie, 227
Hettinger, 246
Heuer, Karston, 231-232
Hiddenwood Cliff, 12, 17-
Hiddenwood Creek, 11, 18
Hiddenwood hunt, 6-7, 10-25, 46, 152, 200, 234
Hind, Professor, 147
Ho-Chunk Tribe, 212
Honored by Indian, 113-127, 200-207
Hornaday buffalo count, 168, 174, 234
Hornaday, William, 7, 54-55, 58-61, 68-70, 77-80, 84-85, 88, 102, 104-106, 144-146, 152, 155, 158, 168-169, 172-174, 179-181, 185, 224, 229, 234
Horses
   arrived in America, 152
   culture, 152
   for buffalo hunting, 155
   taken from Indian owners, 44-45, 47
Houck, Roy and Nellie, 194
Huffman, LA, 60, 68
Humpback, 117-118
Hunting buffalo, *see Buffalo hunting*

I

Ice ages, 85
Impounding, 144-146
Indian Tribal herds, 198-215
Interagency Bison Management Plan, 240
Intertribal Bison Cooperative, 208
Intertribal Buffalo Council, 108, 178, 202-203, 208-210

J

Jaw, Charlie, 126
Jones, C.J. "Buffalo," 171, 174, 177-178, 185, 230
Jones, Eb, 182-184

K

Kane, Paul, 148, 151, 161-165
Kenner, Brian, 222
Kiowa
　storytelling, 127
　tribe, 127
Kootenai, 214
Kornfeld, Marcel, George Frison, Mary Lou Larson, 132
Kossler, Mark, 190-191, 196
Koucky, Dr. Rudolph, 69

L

Lakota Oyate, 209
Lame Deer, John (Fire), 113, 127
Laramie Treaty of 1868, 51
Last stand of buffalo, 13, 43-55
Lee, Patricia, 219
Lewis and Clark expedition, 88, 126, 156
Lightning Medicine Cloud, 227
Little Soldier, Arby, 227
Long Soldier, 15
Lott, Dale F., 82, 89-92, 227-228
Low stress handling, 189-190, 196-197
Lowie, Robert H., 123

M

Magnan, Robert, 204-207, 212-213, 222
Manske, Llewellyn, 85, 90
Marchello, Dr. Marty, 195
Marengo, Brad, 215
Marengo, Greg, 215
Marengo, Kevin, 215
Marquis, Toots, 188
Maternal herd, 96-98, 166
Mayo, Randy, 209-210
McDonald, Tom, 214-215
McFarland buffalo ranch, 189-191, 197
McFarland, Roxann, 185
McFarland, Steve, 185
McFarland, Verna, 189
McHugh, Thomas, 78-79, 96, 100-101, 225
McKay, James "Tonka Jim," 170-171, 177, 185
McLaughlin, James, 6, 11, 16, 14-25, 44, 47-49, 54-55, 125, 180, 234
Means, Jackie, 179
Meat, 212-214
Medicine bags, 124-125
Medicine Rocks, 126
Métis, 159-165, 229
　hunts, 159-161, 170
　rules for hunt, 162
Mexican bull fight, 176, 182-184
Migration, 108-111
Miller, Emilie, 222
Miracle, 227
Montana Beef Council, 240
Mt. Rushmore, 185

N

National Bison Association, 178, 234
National Bison Range, 181, 229
National Buffalo Museum, 226
National Parks, 179-185
National Wildlife Federation, 206
Nease, Ron and Deborah, 227
New York Zoo, 181
Nez Perce, 214
Northern Cheyenne, 125
Northern herd, 5, 234

O

O'Brien, Dan, 194
Oglala Sioux, 208
Oneida tribe, 207-209

P

Pablo, Michel, 174-175, 177, 185, 230
Pemmican, 163-164
Petroglyphs, 126-127
Philip, George, 176-177, 182-185
Philip, Sarah "Sally," 175-176, 179, 194, 218
Philip, James "Scotty," 123, 176-177, 179, 182-184, 185, 191, 194, 218
Photo Credits, 243
Picurís tribe, 208
Plains buffalo, 85-87
Plains vs. wood buffalo, 87
Plenty Coups, Chief, 43
Porcupine Breaks, 200
Prehistoric buffalo, 85-86
Protective nature, bulls, 82, 92-96
Public herds, 216-233
Pueblo, Northern, 208

Q

Quinn, Alvah, 203, 211

R

Railroad, Union Pacific, 234
Ranching, 186-197
　advantage, 189
Range, historic, 89-91
Red Horse, 15
Red River carts, 71-72, 160-161
Relationship with American Indians, 113-127, 200-207
Rescuing calves, 169-172
Reservation boundaries, 51, 54
Reservation division, 51
Ricci, Susan, 179
Riding down the bushes, 15
Riggs, Thomas, 6, 28-41, 125, 171-172, 234
Rinella, Steven, 81, 83, 229

Roan Bear, see Clarence Ward
Roosevelt, Theodore, 62-63, 84, 174, 180-181, 185, 218
Rosebud tribe, 208
Round-up, 174-175, 212, 217-223
Running Antelope, 11, 14
Russell, Charles M., 175; Illustrations, cover, 9-11, 14, 19, 24, 30, 34, 37, 40, 46, 48, 52-53, 58, 117-118, 127, 147, 153, 155-156, 158-159, 175, 180
Rutting season, 101-104

S
Safratowich, Dr. Don, 190
Salmon, David, 209
Sam, Danny, 208
Sand trap, 142
Saving the buffalo, 166-181, 185
Scheeler, Carl, 215
Schmidt, Art, 211
Schmidt, Bob, 228
Schweiger, Larry, 206
Schweitzer, Brian, 206
Scouts, 153
Seton, Ernest Thompson, 83, 89-90, 96, 103, 107, 109-110, 168-169, 234
Shadehill Buffalo Jump, 136-137
Shedding, 104-107
Shirek Buffalo Ranch, 226
Shoshone-Bannock, 214
Sisseton Wahpeton, 211
Sitting Bull hunt, 13, 25, 46, 48, 54-55, 227, 234
Skull, 5, 124, 126
Skunk, Peter, 22
Slim Buttes hunt, 26-41, 46, 125, 234
Smeester, Loren, 187, 195
Smith, Donald A, 225
Smith, Vic, 54-55

Smithsonian buffalo hunt, 172-174
Smithsonian museum, 7, 172-174
Songs to bring buffalo, 123-124
South Grand River, 234
Southern herd, 13, 60, 234
Sprague, Donovan, 179
Springer, Pat, 179
Stamina, 81-82, 85
Standing Rock Sioux Reservation, 51, 198, 200
Stevens Village, 209-210
Stone, Jim, 203
Storytelling, 113, 118-122
Strong Left Hand, 159
Surround, 143
Survivors, 56-75
Sutton, Kim, 188

T
Theodore Roosevelt National Park, 198, 222-223
Tidball, Dr. William, 223
Timeline, 234
Toomey, Patrick, 203
Tourism, 191
Townsend, Connie, 240
Traps, 140-143
Tribal herds, 198-215
Triple U, 194
Turkey catcher, 221
Turner, Ted, 194

U
Umatilla, 214
Union Pacific Railroad, 234
Uses of buffalo, 130-131
Ute Tribe, 211-212

V
Vore Buffalo Jump, 137

W
Waggoner, Josephine, 45, 49, 130, 144
Walking Coyote, Samuel, 169-170, 174, 177, 185, 230
Ward, Clarence (Roan Bear), 28, 29, 40
Weasel Tail, 143-144
Welch, AB, 148, 156
Wetsit, Larry, 206
White Buffalo dynasty, 226-229
White Buffalo Woman, 26, 116, 229
White hide hunters, 234
Wind Cave National Park, 181, 198, 208, 225
Winnebago Tribe, 212
Winneshiek, Clayton, 212
Winter Hunt, in Slim Buttes, 26-41, 46, 152
Wolf Necklace, 21
Wolves, 107
Wood Buffalo National Park, 225, 230-231
Wood buffalo, 85-87, 231
Working buffalo, 189-190, 197
World's Largest Buffalo, 226
Wrigley, Dr. Robert E., 227, 229

Y
Yellowstone Park, 180-181, 185, 190, 197; brucellosis, 225, 240, genetics, 224-225; population, 103, 169, 215, 224; hunting 214-215; restoring buffalo, 204-207
Yellowstone River, 215
Yokum, Bob, 182-184

Z
Zontak, Ken, 170, 179

Buffalo Trails in the Dakota Buttes

REVIEWS

WHAT A SPLENDID PROJECT!
—Valerius Geist, author of
*Buffalo Nation: History and Legend
of the North American Bison*

PEOPLE FROM ALL OVER THE WORLD are fascinated by the American West. We think this is going to be a great fit . . . a great tie-in.
—Sara Otte Coleman
North Dakota Tourism Director

FROM HISTORICAL DETAILS OF Native Americans' final great wild buffalo hunts to talks of the animal's rescue from near extinction, a new self-guided tour across 10 sites in the western Dakotas tells the story of the last stand of the American Bison, the National Mammal.
—*TRAVEL*, South Africa

THE 80-PAGE GUIDE TITLED *Buffalo Trails in the Dakota Buttes* and its companion book *Buffalo Heartbeats Across the Plains* are filled with stories that bring the events to life. They tell the little-known story of the last buffalo hunts—traditional Indian hunts rather than a slaughter by white hide hunters.

Just before the last wild herds disappeared, one Native American family came to the South Grand River determined to save buffalo calves. The likely place is identified where Pete Dupree and his brothers came by team and buckboard wagon.
—Linda Sailer
The Dickinson Press

AT THE CENTER OF THESE EVENTS are previously untold stories and authentic, unspoiled places to witness where they took place ... These are well-documented traditional Native American hunts that somehow

fell through the cracks of US history. Often showcased is the shameful history of the buffalo's final days as a wasteful slaughter by white hide hunters. That happened, of course, but it is not the whole story. Instead, it is a heroic saga befitting the noble beasts themselves.
—*Adams County Record*

THE BUFFALO IS AMERICA'S STORY. But the final chapter belongs to Hettinger, a small town in southwestern North Dakota. For several key years in the 1880s the area was ground zero for the very last of the wild and noble buffalo. For people willing to leave the asphalt and launch themselves into empty reaches of prairie that were once part of the Great Sioux Nation, the story unfolds in the scenery, in the imagination and in the history.

The handbook with detailed driving directions, encourages history-seekers to venture out on a bumpy two-track trail in government-owned pasture—taking care not to get high-centered in the ruts—then crawl under a barbed wire fence. One stands, brushing off dusty knees to look, and there below is a lazy curve of the South Grand River, bordered by old gnarly cottonwood trees.

The buffalo trail will be a draw for tourists from afar.
—Lauren Donovan
Bismarck Tribune

Spring Gathering, Badlands Reflections Photography